Seduce Me At Sunrise

"Has plenty to keep readers turning the pages: wit, suspense, secrets to learn, and, of course, lots of love and passion."
                                                        —*The Monitor*

"Each member of the family is a delight to meet, and the depths of emotions and love they have for each other are shown magnificently . . . a spectacular story that continues the saga of the Hathaway family."
                                                        —*Romance Reviews*

"Lushly sexy and thoroughly romantic . . . superbly crafted characters and an intriguing plot blend together brilliantly in this splendid romance."   —*Booklist*

Mine Till Midnight

"Vintage Kleypas . . . An unforgettable story peopled with remarkable characters and a depth of emotion that will leave you breathless with the wonderment of knowing what falling in love is really like."
                                                        —*Romantic Times BOOKreviews*

"Kleypas's effortless style makes for another sexy exploration of 19th-century passion and peccadilloes, riveting from start to finish."   —*Publishers Weekly*

"Will steal the hearts of readers."
                        —*Post and Courier* (Charleston, South Carolina)

MORE...

Love in the Afternoon

LISA KLEYPAS

St. Martin's Paperbacks

This is a work of fiction. All of the characters, organizations, and events portrayed in this novel are either products of the author's imagination or are used fictitiously.

LOVE IN THE AFTERNOON

Copyright © 2010 by Lisa Kleypas.
Excerpt from *Christmas Eve at Friday Harbor* copyright © 2010 by Lisa Kleypas.

Sketch of dog by Hillary James

For information address St. Martin's Press, 175 Fifth Avenue, New York, NY 10010.

ISBN: 978-0-312-60539-1

Printed in the United States of America

St. Martin's Paperbacks edition / July 2010

St. Martin's Paperbacks are published by St. Martin's Press, 175 Fifth Avenue, New York, NY 10010.

10 9 8 7 6 5 4 3 2 1

To my brilliant and utterly fabulous friend Eloisa. If I may paraphrase E.B. White: "It is not often that someone comes along who is a true friend and a good writer. Eloisa is both."

Love always,

L.K.

Prologue

Captain Christopher Phelan
1st Battalion Rifle Brigade
Cape Mapan
Crimea

June 1855

Dearest Christopher,

I can't write to you again.

I'm not who you think I am.

I didn't mean to send love letters, but that is what they became. On their way to you, my words turned into heartbeats on the page.

Come back, please come home and find me.

—[unsigned]

Chapter One

Hampshire, England
Eight months earlier

It all began with a letter.

To be precise, it was the mention of the dog.

"What about the dog?" Beatrix Hathaway asked. "Whose dog?"

Her friend Prudence, the reigning beauty of Hampshire County, looked up from the letter that had been sent by her suitor, Captain Christopher Phelan.

Although it wasn't proper for a gentleman to correspond with an unmarried girl, they had arranged to send letters back and forth with Phelan's sister-in-law as a go-between.

Prudence sent her a mock frown. "Really, Bea, you're displaying far more concern over a dog than you ever have for Captain Phelan."

"Captain Phelan has no need of my concern," Beatrix said pragmatically. "He has the concern of every marriageable miss in Hampshire. Besides, he chose to go to war, and I'm sure he's having a lovely time strutting about in his smart uniform."

"It's not at all smart," came Prudence's glum reply. "In fact, his new regiment has *dreadful* uniforms— very plain, dark green with black facings, and no gold braiding or lace at all. And when I asked why, Captain Phelan said it was to help the Rifles stay concealed, which makes no sense, as everyone knows that a British soldier is far too brave and proud to conceal himself during battle. But Christopher—that is, Captain Phelan—said it had something to do with . . . oh, he used some French word . . ."

"Camouflage?" Beatrix asked, intrigued.

"Yes, how did you know?"

"Many animals have ways of camouflaging themselves to keep from being seen. Chameleons, for example. Or the way an owl's feathering is mottled to help it blend with the bark of its tree. That way—"

"Heavens, Beatrix, do *not* start another lecture on animals."

"I'll stop if you tell me about the dog."

Prudence handed her the letter. "Read it for yourself."

"But Pru," Beatrix protested as the small, neat pages were pushed into her hands. "Captain Phelan may have written something personal."

"I should be so fortunate! It's utterly gloomy. Nothing but battles and bad news."

Although Christopher Phelan was the last man Beatrix would ever want to defend, she couldn't help pointing out, "He is away fighting in the Crimea, Pru. I'm not sure there are many pleasant things to write about in wartime."

"Well, I have no interest in foreign countries, and I've never pretended to."

A reluctant grin spread across Beatrix's face. "Pru, are you certain that you want to be an officer's wife?"

"Well, *of course* . . . most commissioned soldiers never go to war. They're very fashionable men-about-town, and if they agree to go on half pay, they have hardly any duties and they don't have to spend any time at all with the regiment. And that was the case with Captain Phelan, until he was alerted for foreign service." Prudence shrugged. "I suppose wars are always inconveniently timed. Thank heavens Captain Phelan will return to Hampshire soon."

"Will he? How do you know?"

"My parents say the war will be over by Christmas."

"I've heard that as well. However, one wonders if we aren't severely underestimating the Russians' abilities, and overestimating our own."

"How unpatriotic," Prudence exclaimed, a teasing light in her eyes.

"Patriotism has nothing to do with the fact that the War Office, in its enthusiasm, didn't do nearly enough planning before it launched thirty thousand men to the Crimea. We have neither adequate knowledge of the place, nor any sound strategy for its capture."

"How do you know so much about it?"

"From the *Times*. It's reported on every day. Don't you read the papers?"

"Not the political section. My parents say it's ill-bred for a young lady to take an interest in such things."

"My family discusses politics every night at dinner, and my sisters and I all take part." Beatrix paused deliberately before adding with an impish grin, "We even have *opinions*."

Prudence's eyes widened. "My goodness. Well, I shouldn't be surprised. Everyone knows your family is . . . different."

"Different" was a far kinder adjective than was often used to describe the Hathaway family. The Hathaways were comprised of five siblings, the oldest of which was Leo, followed by Amelia, Winnifred, Poppy, and Beatrix. After the death of their parents, the Hathaways had gone through an astonishing change of fortune. Although they were common born, they were distantly related to an aristocratic branch of the family. Through a series of unexpected events, Leo had inherited a viscountcy for which he and his sisters hadn't been remotely prepared. They had moved from their small village of Primrose Place to the Ramsay estate in the southern county of Hampshire.

After six years the Hathaways had managed to learn just enough to accommodate themselves in good society. However, none of them had learned to think like the nobility, nor had they acquired aristocratic values or mannerisms. They had wealth, but that was not nearly as important as breeding and connections. And whereas a family in similar circumstances would have endeavored to improve their situations by marrying their social betters, the Hathaways had so far chosen to marry for love.

As for Beatrix, there was doubt as to whether she would marry at all. She was only half civilized, spending most of her time out-of-doors, riding or rambling through the woodlands, marsh, and meadows of Hampshire. Beatrix preferred the company of animals to people, collecting injured and orphaned creatures and rehabilitating them. The creatures that couldn't survive on their own in the wild were kept as pets, and Beatrix occupied herself with caring for them. Out-of-doors, she was happy and fulfilled. Indoors, life was not nearly so perfect.

More and more frequently, Beatrix had become aware of a chafing sense of dissatisfaction. Of yearning. The problem was that Beatrix had never met a man who was right for her. Certainly none of the pale, overbred specimens of the London drawing rooms she had frequented. And although the more robust men in the country were appealing, none of them had the unnameable *something* Beatrix longed for. She dreamed of a man whose force of will matched her own. She wanted to be passionately loved . . . challenged . . . overtaken.

Beatrix glanced at the folded letter in her hands.

It wasn't that she disliked Christopher Phelan as much as she recognized that he was inimical to everything she was. Sophisticated and born to privilege, he was able to move with ease in the civilized environment that was so alien to her. He was the second son of a well-to-do local family, his maternal grandfather an earl, his father's family distinguished by a significant shipping fortune.

Although the Phelans were not in line for a title, the oldest son, John, would inherit the Riverton estate in Warwickshire upon the earl's death. John was a sober and thoughtful man, devoted to his wife, Audrey.

But the younger brother, Christopher, was another sort of man entirely. As often happened with second sons, Christopher had purchased an army commission at the age of twenty-two. He had gone in as a cornet, a perfect occupation for such a splendid-looking fellow, since his chief responsibility was to carry the cavalry colors during parades and drills. He was also a great favorite among the ladies of London, where he constantly went without proper leave, spending his time dancing, drinking, gaming, purchasing fine clothes, and indulging in scandalous love affairs.

Beatrix had met Christopher Phelan on two occasions, the first at a local dance, where she had judged him to be the most arrogant man in Hampshire. The next time she had met him was at a picnic, where she had revised her opinion: he was the most arrogant man in the entire world.

"That Hathaway girl is a peculiar creature," Beatrix had overhead him say to a companion.

"I find her charming and original," his companion

had protested. "And she can talk horses better than any woman I've ever met."

"Naturally," came Phelan's dry rejoinder. "She's more suited to the stables than the drawing room."

From then on, Beatrix had avoided him whenever possible. Not that she minded the implied comparison to a horse, since horses were lovely animals with generous and noble spirits. And she knew that although she wasn't a great beauty, she had her own charms. More than one man had commented favorably on her dark brown hair and blue eyes.

These moderate attractions, however, were nothing compared to Christopher Phelan's golden splendor. He was as fair as Lancelot. Gabriel. Perhaps Lucifer, if one believed that he had once been the most beautiful angel in heaven. Phelan was tall and silver eyed, his hair the color of dark winter wheat touched by the sun. His form was strong and soldierly, the shoulders straight and strong, the hips slim. Even as he moved with indolent grace, there was something undeniably potent about him, something selfishly predatory.

Recently Phelan had been one of the select few to be culled from various regiments to become part of the Rifle Brigade. The "Rifles," as they were called, were an unusual brand of soldier, trained to use their own initiative. They were encouraged to take up positions forward of their own front lines and pick off officers and horses that were usually beyond target range. Because of his singular marksmanship skills, Phelan had been promoted to a captaincy in the Rifle Brigade.

It had amused Beatrix to reflect that the honor probably hadn't pleased Phelan at all. Especially since he'd been obliged to trade his beautiful Hussars uniform, with its black coat and abundant gold braiding, for a plain dark green one.

"You're welcome to read it," Prudence said as she sat at her dressing table. "I must repair my coiffure before we go on our walk."

"Your hair looks lovely," Beatrix protested, unable to see any flaw in the elaborately pinned twist of blond braids. "And we're only walking to the village. None of the townspeople will know or care if your coiffure isn't perfect."

"*I'll* know. Besides, one never knows whom one might encounter."

Accustomed as she was to her friend's ceaseless preening, Beatrix grinned and shook her head. "All right. If you're certain you don't mind my looking at Captain Phelan's letter, I'll just read the part about the dog."

"You'll fall asleep long before you get to the dog," Prudence said, expertly inserting a hairpin into a twisted braid.

Beatrix looked down at the scrawled lines. The words looked cramped, tight coils of letters ready to spring from the page.

Dear Prudence,

I'm sitting in this dusty tent, trying to think of something eloquent to write. I'm at wit's end. You deserve beautiful words, but all I have left are these: I think of you constantly. I think of this letter in your hand and the scent of perfume on your wrist. I want silence and clear air, and a bed with a soft white pillow . . .

Beatrix felt her eyebrows lifting, and a quick rise of heat beneath the high collar of her dress. She paused and glanced at Prudence. "You find this boring?" she asked mildly, while her blush spread like spilled wine on linen.

"The beginning is the only good part," Prudence said. "Go on."

> . . . Two days ago in our march down the coast to Sebastopol, we fought the Russians at the Alma River. I'm told it was a victory for our side. It doesn't feel like one. We've lost at least two thirds of our regiment's officers, and a quarter of the noncommissioned men. Yesterday we dug graves. They call the final tally of dead and wounded the "butcher's bill." Three hundred and sixty British dead so far, and more as soldiers succumb to their wounds.
>
> One of the fallen, Captain Brighton, brought a rough terrier named Albert, who is undoubtedly the most badly behaved canine in existence. After Brighton was lowered into the ground, the dog sat by his grave and whined for hours, and tried to bite anyone who came near. I made the mistake of offering him a portion of a biscuit, and now the benighted creature follows me everywhere. At this moment he is sitting in my tent, staring at me with half-crazed eyes. The whining rarely stops. Whenever I get near, he tries to sink his teeth into my arm. I want to shoot him, but I'm too tired of killing.

Families are grieving for the lives I've taken. Sons, brothers, fathers. I've earned a place in hell for the things I've done, and the war's barely started. I'm changing, and not for the better. The man you knew is gone for good, and I fear you may not like his replacement nearly so well.

The smell of death, Pru . . . it's everywhere.

The battlefield is strewn with pieces of bodies, clothes, soles of boots. Imagine an explosion that could tear the soles from your shoes. They say that after a battle, wildlflowers are more abundant the next season—the ground is so churned and torn, it gives the new seeds room to take root. I want to grieve, but there is no place for it. No time. I have to put the feelings away somewhere.

Is there still some peaceful place in the world? Please write to me. Tell me about some bit of needlework you're working on, or your favorite song. Is it raining in Stony Cross? Have the leaves begun to change color?

Yours,

Christopher Phelan

By the time Beatrix had finished the letter, she was aware of a peculiar feeling, a sense of surprised compassion pressing against the walls of her heart.

It didn't seem possible that such a letter could have come from the arrogant Christopher Phelan. It wasn't at all what she had expected. There was a vulnerability, a quiet need, that had touched her.

"You must write to him, Pru," she said, closing the letter with far more care than she had previously handled it.

"I'll do no such thing. That would only encourage more complaining. I'll be silent, and perhaps that will spur him to write something more cheerful next time."

Beatrix frowned. "As you know, I have no great liking for Captain Phelan, but this letter . . . he deserves your sympathy, Pru. Just write him a few lines. A few words of comfort. It would take no time at all. And about the dog, I have some advice—"

"I am not writing anything about the dratted dog." Prudence gave an impatient sigh. "You write to him."

"*Me?* He doesn't want to hear from me. He thinks I'm peculiar."

"I can't imagine why. Just because you brought Medusa to the picnic . . ."

"She's a very well behaved hedgehog," Beatrix said defensively.

"The gentleman whose hand was pierced didn't seem to think so."

"That was only because he tried to handle her incorrectly. When you pick up a hedgehog—"

"No, there's no use telling me, since I'm never going to handle one. As for Captain Phelan . . . if you feel that strongly about it, write a response and sign my name."

"Won't he recognize that the handwriting is different?"

"No, because I haven't written to him yet."

"But he's not my suitor," Beatrix protested. "I don't know anything about him."

"You know as much as I do, actually. You're acquainted with his family, and you're very close to his sister-in-law. And I wouldn't say that Captain Phelan is my suitor, either. At least not my only one. I certainly won't promise to marry him until he comes back from the war with all his limbs intact. I don't want a husband I would have to push around in an invalid's chair for the rest of my life."

"Pru, you have the depth of a puddle."

Prudence grinned. "At least I'm honest."

Beatrix gave her a dubious glance. "You're actually delegating the writing of a love letter to one of your friends?"

Prudence waved her hand in a dismissive gesture. "Not a love letter. There was nothing of love in his letter to me. Just write something cheerful and encouraging."

Beatrix fumbled for the pocket of her walking dress, and tucked the letter inside. Inwardly she argued with herself, reflecting that it never ended well when one did something morally questionable for the right reasons. On the other hand . . . she couldn't rid herself of the image her mind had conjured, of an exhausted soldier scribbling a hasty letter in the privacy of his tent, his hands blistered from digging the graves of his comrades. And a ragged dog whining in the corner.

She felt entirely inadequate to the task of writing to him. And she suspected that Prudence did as well.

She tried to imagine what it was like for Christopher, leaving his elegant life behind, finding himself in a world where his survival was threatened day by day. Minute by minute. It was impossible to picture a spoiled, beautiful man like Christopher Phelan contending with danger and hardship. Hunger. Loneliness.

Beatrix stared at her friend pensively, their gazes meeting in the looking glass. "What *is* your favorite song, Pru?"

"I don't have one, actually. Tell him yours."

"Should we discuss this with Audrey?" Beatrix asked, referring to Phelan's sister-in-law.

"Certainly not. Audrey has a problem with honesty. She wouldn't send the letter if she knew I hadn't written it."

Beatrix made a sound that could have either been a laugh or a groan. "I wouldn't call that a *problem* with honesty. Oh, Pru, please change your mind and write to him. It would be so much easier."

But Prudence, when pressed to do something, usually turned intransigent, and this situation was no exception. "Easier for everyone but me," she said tartly. "I'm sure I don't know how to reply to such a letter. He's probably even forgotten that he's written it." Returning her attention to the looking glass, she applied a touch of rose-petal salve to her lips.

How lovely Prudence was, with her heart-shaped face, her brows thin and delicately arched over round green eyes. But how very little of a person the looking glass reflected. It was impossible to guess what Prudence truly felt for Christopher Phelan. Only one thing was certain: it was better to answer, no matter how ineptly, than to withhold a reply. Because sometimes silence could wound someone nearly as badly as a bullet.

In the privacy of her room at Ramsay House, Beatrix sat at her desk and dipped a pen nib into a well of dark blue ink. A three-legged gray cat named Lucky lounged at the corner of the desk, watching her alertly. Beatrix's pet hedgehog, Medusa, occupied the other side of the desk. Lucky, being an innately sensible creature, never bothered the bristly little hedgehog.

After consulting the letter from Phelan, Beatrix wrote:

Captain Christopher Phelan
1st Battalion Rifle Brigade
2nd Division Camp, Crimea

17 October 1854

Pausing, Beatrix reached out to stroke Lucky's remaining front paw with a gentle fingertip. "How would Pru start a letter?" she wondered aloud. "Would she call him darling? Dearest?" She wrinkled her nose at the idea.

The writing of letters was hardly Beatrix's forte. Although she came from a highly articulate family, she had always valued instinct and action more than words. In fact, she could learn far more about a person during a short walk outdoors than she could by sitting and conversing for hours.

After pondering various things one might write to a complete stranger while masquerading as someone else, Beatrix finally gave up. "Hang it, I'll just write as I please. He'll probably be too battle weary to notice that the letter doesn't sound like Pru."

Lucky settled her chin beside her paw and half closed her eyes. A purring sigh escaped her.

Beatrix began to write.

Dear Christopher,

I have been reading the reports about the
battle of the Alma. According to the account
by Mr. Russell of the Times, *you and two*

others of the Rifle Brigade went ahead of the
Coldstream Guards, and shot several enemy
officers, thereby disordering their columns.
Mr. Russell also remarked in admiration
that the Rifles never retreated or even
bobbed their heads when the bullets came
flying.

While I share his esteem, dear sir, I wish to
advise that in my opinion it would not
detract from your bravery to bob your head
when being shot at. Duck, dodge, sidestep,
or preferably hide behind a rock. I promise I
won't think the less of you!

Is Albert still with you? Still biting? According
to my friend Beatrix (she who brings hedgehogs
to picnics), the dog is overstimulated and
afraid. As dogs are wolves at heart and
require a leader, you must establish dominance
over him. Whenever he tries to bite you, take
his entire muzzle in your hand, apply light
pressure, and tell him "no" in a firm voice.

My favorite song is "Over the Hills and Far
Away." It rained in Hampshire yesterday, a
soft autumn storm that brought down hardly
any leaves. The dahlias are no longer in
stem, and frost has withered the chrysanthe-
mums, but the air smells divine, like old
leaves and wet bark, and ripe apples. Have
you ever noticed that each month has its
own smell? May and October are the
nicest-smelling months, in my opinion.

You ask if there is a peaceful place in the world, and I regret to say that it is not Stony Cross. Recently Mr. Mawdsley's donkey escaped from his stall, raced down the road, and somehow found his way into an enclosed pasture. Mr. Caird's prized mare was innocently grazing when the ill-bred seducer had his way with her. Now it appears the mare has conceived, and a feud is raging between Caird, who demands financial compensation, and Mawdsley, who insists that had the pasture fencing been in better repair, the clandestine meeting would never have occurred. Worse still, it has been suggested that the mare is a shameless lightskirt and did not try nearly hard enough to preserve her virtue.

Do you really think you've earned a place in hell? . . . I don't believe in hell, at least not in the afterlife. I think hell is brought about by man right here on earth.

You say the gentleman I knew has been replaced. How I wish I could offer better comfort than to say that no matter how you have changed, you will be welcomed when you return. Do what you must. If it helps you to endure, put the feelings away for now, and lock the door. Perhaps someday we'll air them out together.

Sincerely,

Prudence

Beatrix had never intentionally deceived anyone. She would have felt infinitely more comfortable writing to Phelan as herself. But she still remembered the disparaging remarks that he had once made about her. He would not want a letter from that "peculiar Beatrix Hathaway." He had asked for a letter from the beautiful golden-haired Prudence Mercer. And wasn't a letter written under false pretenses better than nothing at all? A man in Christopher's situation needed all the words of encouragement one could offer.

He needed to know that someone cared.

And for some reason, after having read his letter, Beatrix found that she did indeed care.

Chapter Two

The harvest moon brought dry, clear weather, and the Ramsay tenants and workers reaped the most abundant yields in memory. Like everyone else on the estate, Beatrix was occupied with the harvest and the local festival that followed. A massive al fresco dinner and dance was held on the grounds of Ramsay House for more than a thousand guests, including tenants, servants, and townspeople.

To Beatrix's disappointment, Audrey Phelan had not been able to attend the festivities, as her husband John had developed a persistent cough. She had stayed home to care for him. "The doctor has left us with some medicine that has already helped John to great effect," Audrey had written, "but he warned that uninterrupted bed rest is important for a complete recovery."

Near the end of November, Beatrix walked to the Phelans' house, taking a direct route through woodlands populated with gnarled oak and wide-gesturing beeches. The dark-branched trees seemed to have been dipped in crushed sugar. As the sun cracked through the veneer of clouds, it struck brilliant glints on the frost. The soles of Beatrix's sturdy shoes bit through the frozen mush of dried leaves and moss.

She approached the Phelan house, formerly a royal hunting lodge, a large ivy-covered home set among ten forested acres. Reaching a charming paved path, Beatrix skirted the side of the house and headed toward the front.

"Beatrix."

Hearing a quiet voice, she turned to behold Audrey Phelan sitting alone on a stone bench.

"Oh, hello," Beatrix said cheerfully. "I hadn't seen you in days, so I thought I would . . ." Her voice faded as she took a closer look at her friend.

Audrey was wearing a simple day gown, the gray fabric blending into the woods behind her. She had been so silent and still that Beatrix hadn't even noticed her.

They had been friends for three years, ever since Audrey had married John and moved to Stony Cross. There was a certain kind of friend one only visited when one had no problems—that was Prudence. But there was another kind of friend one went to in times of trouble or need—that was Audrey.

Beatrix frowned as she saw that Audrey's complexion was bleached of its usual healthy color, and her eyes and nose were red and sore-looking.

Beatrix frowned in concern. "You're not wearing a cloak or shawl."

"I'm fine," Audrey murmured, even though her shoulders were trembling. She shook her head and made a staying gesture as Beatrix took off her heavy wool cloak and went to drape it over Audrey's slender form. "No, Bea, don't—"

"I'm warm from the exertion of the walk," Beatrix insisted. She sat beside her friend on the icy stone bench. A wordless moment passed, while Audrey's throat worked visibly. Something was seriously wrong. Beatrix waited with forced patience, her heartbeat in her throat. "Audrey," she finally asked, "has something happened to Captain Phelan?"

Audrey responded with a blank stare, as if she were trying to decipher a foreign language. "Captain Phelan," she repeated quietly, and gave a little shake of her head. "No, as far as we know, Christopher is well. In fact, a packet of letters arrived from him yesterday. One of them is for Prudence."

Beatrix was nearly overcome with relief. "I'll take it to her, if you like," she volunteered, trying to sound diffident.

"Yes. That would be helpful." Audrey's pale fingers twisted in her lap, knotting and unknotting.

Slowly Beatrix reached out and put her hand over Audrey's. "Your husband's cough is worse?"

"The doctor left earlier." Taking a deep breath, Audrey said dazedly, "John has consumption."

Beatrix's hand tightened.

They were both silent, while a chilling wind crackled the trees.

The enormity of the unfairness was difficult to grasp. John Phelan was a decent man, always the first to call on someone when he had heard they needed help. He had paid for a cottager's wife to have medical treatment that the couple couldn't afford, and had made the piano in his home available for local children to take lessons, and invested in the rebuilding of the Stony Cross pie shop when it had nearly burned to the ground. And he did it all with great discretion, seeming almost embarrassed to be caught in a good deed. Why did someone like John have to be stricken?

"It's not a death sentence," Beatrix eventually said. "Some people survive it."

"One in five," Audrey agreed dully.

"Your husband is young and strong. And *someone* has to be the one out of the five. It will be John."

Audrey managed a nod but didn't reply.

They both knew that consumption was a particularly virulent disease, devastating the lungs, causing drastic loss of weight and fatigue. Worst of all was the consumptive cough, turning ever more persistent and bloody, until the lungs were finally too full for the sufferer to breathe any longer.

"My brother-in-law Cam is very knowledgeable about herbs and medicines," Beatrix volunteered. "His grandmother was a healer in his tribe."

"A Gypsy cure?" Audrey asked in a doubtful tone.

"You must try anything and everything," Beatrix insisted. "Including Gypsy cures. The Rom live in nature, and they know all about its power to heal. I'll ask Cam to make up a tonic that will help Mr. Phelan's lungs, and—"

"John probably won't take it," Audrey said. "And his mother would object. The Phelans are very conventional people. If it doesn't come from a vial in a doctor's case, or the apothecary's shop, they won't approve."

"I'm going to bring something from Cam all the same."

Audrey leaned her head to the side until it rested briefly on Beatrix's shoulder. "You're a good friend, Bea. I'm going to need you in the coming months."

"You have me." Beatrix said simply.

Another breeze whipped around them, biting through Beatrix's sleeves. Audrey shook herself from her dazed misery and stood, handing back the cloak. "Let's go into the house, and I'll find that letter for Pru."

The interior of the house was cozy and warm, the rooms wide with low timbered ceilings, thick-paned windows admitting the winter-colored light. It seemed every hearth in the house had been lit, heat rolling gently through the tidy rooms. Everything in the Phelan house was muted and tasteful, with stately furniture that had reached a comfortably venerable age.

A subdued-looking housemaid came to take Beatrix's cloak.

"Where is your mother-in-law?" Beatrix asked, following Audrey to the staircase.

"She went to rest in her room. The news is especially difficult for her." A fragile pause. "John has always been her favorite."

Beatrix was well aware of that, as was most of Stony Cross. Mrs. Phelan adored both her sons, the only children she had left after two of her other children, also sons, had died in their infancies, and a daughter who had been stillborn. But it was John in whom Mrs. Phelan had invested all her pride and ambition. Unfortunately no woman would ever have been good enough for John in his mother's eyes. Audrey had endured a great deal of criticism during the three years of her marriage, especially in her failure to conceive children.

Beatrix and Audrey ascended the staircase, past rows of family portraits in heavy gold frames. Most of the subjects were Beauchamps, the aristocratic side of the family. One couldn't help but notice that throughout the generations represented, the Beauchamps were an extraordinarily handsome people, with narrow noses and brilliant eyes and thick flowing hair.

As they reached the top of the stairs, a series of muffled coughs came from a room at the end of the hallway. Beatrix winced at the raw sound.

"Bea, would you mind waiting for a moment?" Audrey asked anxiously. "I must go to John—it's time for his medicine."

"Yes, of course."

"Christopher's room—the one he stays in when he visits—is right there. I put the letter on the dresser."

"I'll fetch it."

Audrey went to her husband, while Beatrix cautiously entered Christopher's room, first peering around the doorjamb.

The room was dim. Beatrix went to open one of the heavy curtains, letting daylight slide across the carpeted floor in a brilliant rectangle. The letter was on the dresser. Beatrix picked it up eagerly, her fingers itching to break the seal.

However, she admonished herself, it was addressed to Prudence.

With an impatient sigh, she slipped the unopened letter into the pocket of her walking dress. Lingering at the dresser, she surveyed the articles arranged neatly on a wooden tray.

A small silver-handled shaving brush . . . a folding-blade razor . . . an empty soap dish . . . a lidded porcelain box with a silver top. Unable to resist, Beatrix lifted the top and looked inside. She found three pairs of cuff links, two in silver, one in gold, a watch chain, and a brass button. Replacing the lid, Beatrix picked up the shaving brush and experimentally touched her cheek with it. The bristles were silky and soft. With the movement of the soft fibers, a pleasant scent was released from the brush. A spicy hint of shaving soap.

Holding the brush closer to her nose, Beatrix drew in the scent . . . masculine richness . . . cedar, lavender, bay leaves. She imagined Christopher spreading lather over his face, stretching his mouth to one side, all the masculine contortions she had seen her father and brother perform in the act of removing bristle from their faces.

"Beatrix?"

Guiltily she set aside the brush and went out into the hallway. "I found the letter," she said. "I opened the curtains—I'll pull them back together, and—"

"Oh, don't worry about that, let the light in. I abhor dark rooms." Audrey gave her a strained smile. "John took his medicine," she said. "It makes him sleepy. While he rests, I'm going downstairs to talk with Cook. John thinks he might be able to eat some white pudding."

They proceeded down the stairs together.

"Thank you for taking the letter to Prudence," Audrey said.

"It's very kind of you to facilitate a correspondence between them."

"Oh, it's no bother. It's for Christopher's sake that I agreed. I will admit to being surprised that Prudence took the time to write to Christopher."

"Why do you say that?"

"I don't think she gives a fig about him. I warned Christopher about her before he left, actually. But he was so taken with her looks and her high spirits that he managed to convince himself there was something genuine between them."

"I thought you liked Prudence."

"I do. Or at least . . . I'm trying to. Because of you." Audrey smiled wryly at Beatrix's expression. "I've resolved to be more like you, Bea."

"Like *me*? Oh, I wouldn't do that. Haven't you noticed how odd I am?"

Audrey's smile broadened into a grin, and for a moment she looked like the carefree young woman she had been before John's illness. "You accept people for what they are. I think you regard them as you do your creatures—you're patient, and you observe their habits and wants, and you don't judge them."

"I judged your brother-in-law severely," Beatrix pointed out, feeling guilty.

"More people should be severe on Christopher," Audrey said, her smile lingering. "It might improve his character."

The unopened letter in Beatrix's pocket was nothing less than a torment. She hurried back home, saddled a horse, and rode to Mercer House, an elaborately designed house with turrets, intricately turned porch posts, and stained-glass windows.

Having just arisen after attending a dance that lasted until three o'clock in the morning, Prudence received Beatrix in a velvet dressing gown trimmed with spills of white lace. "Oh, Bea, you should have gone to the dance last night! There were so many handsome young gentlemen there, including a cavalry detachment that is being sent to the Crimea in two days, and they looked so splendid in their uniforms—"

"I've just been to see Audrey," Beatrix said breathlessly, entering the private upstairs parlor and closing the door. "Poor Mr. Phelan isn't well, and—well, I'll tell you about that in a minute, but—here's a letter from Captain Phelan!"

Prudence smiled and took the letter. "Thank you, Bea. Now, about the officers I met last night . . . there was a dark-haired lieutenant who asked me to dance, and he—"

"Aren't you going to open it?" Beatrix asked, watching in dismay as Prudence laid the letter on a side table.

Prudence gave her a quizzical smile. "My, you're impatient today. You want me to open it this very moment?"

"*Yes.*" Beatrix promptly sat in a chair upholstered with flower-printed fabric.

"But I want to tell you about the lieutenant."

"I don't give a monkey about the lieutenant, I want to hear about Captain Phelan."

Prudence gave a low chuckle. "I haven't seen you this excited since you stole that fox that Lord Campdon imported from France last year."

"I didn't steal him, I rescued him. Importing a fox for a hunt . . . I call that very unsporting." Beatrix gestured to the letter. "Open it!"

Prudence broke the seal, skimmed the letter, and shook her head in amused disbelief. "Now he's writing about mules." She rolled her eyes and gave Beatrix the letter.

Miss Prudence Mercer
Stony Cross
Hampshire, England

    7 November 1854

    Dear Prudence,

    Regardless of the reports that describe
    the British soldier as unflinching, I
    assure you that when riflemen are under
    fire, we most certainly duck, bob, and
    run for cover. Per your advice, I have
    added a sidestep and a dodge to my
    repertoire, with excellent results. To my
    mind, the old fable has been disproved:
    there are times in life when one definitely
    wants to be the hare, not the tortoise.

    We fought at the southern port of
    Balaklava on the twenty-fourth of

October. Light Brigade was ordered to
charge directly into a battery of Russian guns for no comprehensible reason.
Five cavalry regiments were mowed
down without support. Two hundred
men and nearly four hundred horses
lost in twenty minutes. More fighting on
the fifth of November, at Inkerman.

We went to rescue soldiers stranded on
the field before the Russians could reach
them. Albert went out with me under a
storm of shot and shell, and helped to
identify the wounded so we could carry
them out of range of the guns. My
closest friend in the regiment was
killed.

Please thank your friend Beatrix for her
advice about Albert. His biting is less
frequent, and he never goes for me,
although he's taken a few nips at visitors
to the tent.

May and October, the best-smelling
months? I'll make a case for December:
evergreen, frost, wood smoke, cinnamon.
As for your favorite song . . . were you
aware that "Over the Hills and Far
Away" is the official music of the Rifle
Brigade?

It seems nearly everyone here has fallen
prey to some kind of illness except for

me. I've had no symptoms of cholera nor
any of the other diseases that have
swept through both divisions. I feel
I should at least feign some kind of
digestive problem for the sake of
decency.

Regarding the donkey feud: while I
have sympathy for Caird and his mare
of easy virtue, I feel compelled to point
out that the birth of a mule is not at all
a bad outcome. Mules are more sure-
footed than horses, generally healthier,
and best of all, they have very expressive ears. And they're not unduly
stubborn, as long they're managed well.
If you wonder at my apparent fondness
for mules, I should probably explain
that as a boy, I had a pet mule named
Hector, after the mule mentioned in the
Iliad.

I wouldn't presume to ask you to wait
for me, Pru, but I will ask that you
write to me again. I've read your last
letter more times than I can count.
Somehow you're more real to me now,
two thousand miles away, than you ever
were before.

Ever yours,
Christopher

P.S. Sketch of Albert included

Albert

As Beatrix read, she was alternately concerned, moved, and charmed out of her stockings. "Let me reply to him and sign your name," she begged. "One more letter. *Please*, Pru. I'll show it to you before I send it."

Prudence burst out laughing. "Honestly, this is the silliest thing I've ever . . . Oh, very well, write to him again if it amuses you."

For the next half hour Beatrix took part in a meaningless conversation about the dance, the guests who had attended, and the latest gossip from London. She slipped the letter from Christopher Phelan into her pocket . . . and froze as she felt an unfamiliar object. A metallic handle . . . and the silk bristle of a shaving brush. Blanching, she realized that she had unintentionally taken the shaving brush from Christopher's dresser.

Her problem was back.

Somehow Beatrix managed to keep smiling and chat-

ting calmly with Prudence, while inside she was filled
with turmoil.

Every now and then when Beatrix was nervous or
worried, she pocketed some small object from a shop
or residence. She had done it ever since her parents had
died. Sometimes she wasn't at all aware she had taken
something, whereas at other times the compulsion was
so irresistible that she began to perspire and tremble
until she finally gave in.

Stealing the objects was never any trouble at all. It
was only returning them that presented difficulties.
Beatrix and her family had always managed to restore
the objects to their proper places. But it had, on occasion, required extreme measures—paying calls at im-
proper times of the day, or inventing wild excuses to
roam through someone's house—that had only forti-
fied the Hathaways' reputation for eccentricity.

Thankfully, it wouldn't be that difficult to put back
the shaving brush. She could do it the next time she
visited Audrey.

"I suppose I ought to dress now," Prudence finally
said.

Beatrix took the cue without hesitation. "Certainly.
It's time for me to go home and attend to some chores."
She smiled and added lightly, "Including writing an-
other letter."

"Don't put anything peculiar in it," Prudence said.
"I have a reputation, you know."

Chapter Three

Captain Christopher Phelan
1st Battalian Rifle Brigade
Home Ridge Camp
Inkerman, Crimea

3 December 1854

Dear Christopher,

This morning I read that more than two thousand of our men were killed in a recent battle. One Rifle officer was said to have been bayoneted. It wasn't you, was it? Are you injured? I'm so afraid for you. And I'm so sorry that your friend was killed.

We are decorating for the holidays, hanging holly and mistletoe. I am enclosing a Christmas card done by a local artist. Note the tassel and string at the bottom—when you pull it, the merrymaking gentlemen on the

left will quaff their goblets of wine.
("Quaff" is such an odd word, isn't it?—
but it's one of my favorites.)

I love the old familiar carols. I love the
sameness of every Christmas. I love eating
the plum pudding even though I don't really
like plum pudding. There is comfort in
ritual, isn't there?

Albert looks like a lovely dog, perhaps not
outwardly a gentleman, but inside a loyal
and soulful fellow.

I worry that something's happened to you. I
hope you are safe. I light a candle for you on
the tree every night.

Answer me as soon as you're able.

Sincerely,
Prudence

P.S. I share your affection for mules. Very
unpretentious creatures who never boast
of their ancestry. One wishes certain
people would be a bit more mulish in that
regard.

Miss Prudence Mercer
Stony Cross
Hampshire

1 February 1854

Dear Pru,

I'm afraid I was indeed the bayoneted one. How did you guess? It happened as we were climbing a hill to overtake a battery of Russian guns. It was a minor shoulder wound, certainly not worth reporting.

There was a storm on the fourteenth of November that wrecked the camps and sank French and British ships in the harbor. More loss of life, and unfortunately most of the winter supplies and equipment are gone. I believe this is what is known as "rough campaigning." I'm hungry. Last night I dreamed of food. Ordinarily I dream of you, but last night I'm sorry to say that you were eclipsed by lamb with mint sauce.

It is bitterly cold. I am now sleeping with Albert. We're a pair of surly bedfellows, but we're both willing to endure it in the effort to keep from freezing to death. Albert has become indispensable to the company—he carries messages under fire and runs much faster than a man can. He's also an excellent sentry and scout.

Here are a few things I've learned from Albert—

1. Any food is fair game until it is actually swallowed by someone else.
2. Take a nap whenever you can.
3. Don't bark unless it's important.
4. Chasing one's tail is sometimes unavoidable.

I hope your Christmas was splendid. Thank you for the card—it reached me on the twenty-fourth of December, and it was passed all around my company, most of them never having seen a Christmas card before. Before it was finally handed back to me, the card-board gentlemen attached to the tassel had done a great deal of quaffing.

I also like the word "quaff." As a matter of fact, I've always liked unusual words. Here's one for you: "soleate," which refers to the shodding of a horse. Or "nidifice," a nest. Has Mr. Caird's mare given birth yet? Perhaps I'll ask my brother to make an offer. One never knows when one might need a good mule.

Dear Christopher,

It feels far too prosaic to send a letter by post. I wish I could find a more interesting way . . . I would tie a little scroll to a bird's leg, or send you a message in a bottle. However, in the interest of

*efficiency, I'll have to make do with the
Royal Mails.*

*I have just read in the Times that you have
been involved in yet more heroics. Why must
you take such risks? The ordinary duty of a
soldier is dangerous enough. Have a care for
your safety, Christopher—for my sake if not
your own. My request is entirely selfish . . . I
could not bear for your letters to stop coming.*

I'm so far away, Pru. I'm standing
outside my own life and looking in.
Amid all this brutality, I have discovered the simple pleasures of petting a
dog, reading a letter, and staring at the
night sky. Tonight I almost thought I
saw the ancient constellation named
Argo . . . after the ship that Jason and
his crew sailed in their quest to find the
golden fleece. You're not supposed to be
able to see Argo unless you're in Australia, but still, I was almost certain I
had a glimpse of it.

I beg you to forget what I wrote before:
I do want you to wait for me. Don't
marry anyone before I come home.

Wait for me.

Dear Christopher,

*This is the perfume of March: rain, loam,
feathers, mint. Every morning and afternoon*

I drink fresh mint tea sweetened with honey.
I've done a great deal of walking lately. I
seem to think better outdoors.

Last night was remarkably clear. I looked up
at the sky to find the Argo. I'm terrible at
constellations. I can never make out any of
them except for Orion and his belt. But the
longer I stared, the more the sky seemed like
an ocean, and then I saw an entire fleet of
ships made of stars. A flotilla was anchored
at the moon, while others were casting off. I
imagined we were on one of those ships,
sailing on moonlight.

In truth, I find the ocean unnerving. Too
vast. I much prefer the forests around Stony
Cross. They're always fascinating, and full
of commonplace miracles . . . spiderwebs
glittering with rain, new trees growing from
the trunks of fallen oaks. I wish you could
see them with me. And together we would
listen to the wind rushing through the leaves
overhead, a lovely swooshy melody . . . tree
music!

As I sit here writing to you, I have propped
my stocking feet much too close to the hearth.
I've actually singed my stockings on occasion, and once I had to stomp out my feet
when they started smoking. Even after that,
I still can't seem to rid myself of the habit.
There, now you could pick me out of a
crowd blindfolded. Simply follow the scent of
scorched stockings.

*Enclosed is a robin's feather that I found
during my walk this morning. It's for luck.
Keep it in your pocket.*

*Just now I had the oddest feeling while
writing this letter, as if you were standing in
the room with me. As if my pen had become
a magic wand, and I had conjured you right
here. If I wish hard enough . . .*

Dearest Prudence,

I have the robin's feather in my pocket.
How did you know I needed a token to
carry into battle? For the past two
weeks I've been in a rifle pit, sniping
back and forth with the Russians.
It's no longer a cavalry war, it's all
engineers and artillery. Albert stayed
in the trench with me, only going out
to carry messages up and down the
line.

During the lulls, I try to imagine being
in some other place. I imagine you with
your feet propped near the hearth, and
your breath sweet with mint tea. I
imagine walking through the Stony
Cross forests with you. I would love to
see some commonplace miracles, but I
don't think I could find them without
you. I need your help, Pru. I think you
might be my only chance of becoming
part of the world again.

I feel as if I have more memories of you than I actually do. I was with you on only a handful of occasions. A dance. A conversation. A kiss. I wish I could relive those moments. I would appreciate them more. I would appreciate everything more. Last night I dreamed of you again. I couldn't see your face, but I felt you near me. You were whispering to me.

The last time I held you, I didn't know who you truly were. Or who I was, for that matter. We never looked beneath the surface. Perhaps it's better we didn't—I don't think I could have left you, had I felt for you then what I do now.

I'll tell you what I'm fighting for. Not for England, nor her allies, nor any patriotic cause. It's all come down to the hope of being with you.

Dear Christopher,

You've made me realize that words are the most important things in the world. And never so much as now. The moment Audrey gave me your last letter, my heart started beating faster, and I had to run to my secret house to read it in private.

I haven't yet told you . . . last spring on one of my rambles, I found the oddest structure

*in the forest, a lone tower of brick and
stonework, all covered with ivy and moss. It
was on a distant portion of the Stony Cross
estate that belongs to Lord Westcliff. Later
when I asked Lady Westcliff about it, she
said that keeping a secret house was a local
custom in medieval times. The lord of the
manor might have used it as a place to keep
his mistress. Once a Westcliff ancestor
actually hid there from his own bloodthirsty
retainers. Lady Westcliff said I could visit
the secret house whenever I wanted, since it
has long been abandoned. I go there often.
It's my hiding place, my sanctuary . . . and
now that you know about it, it's yours as
well.*

*I've just lit a candle and set it in a window.
A very tiny lodestar, for you to follow home.*

Dearest Prudence,

Amid all the noise and men and madness, I try to think of you in your secret
house . . . my princess in a tower. And
my lodestar in the window.

The things one has to do in war . . . I
thought it would all become easier as
time went on. And I'm sorry to say I
was right. I fear for my soul. The things
I have done, Pru. The things I have yet
to do. If I don't expect God to forgive
me, how can I ask you to?

Dear Christopher,

Love forgives all things. You don't even need to ask.

Ever since you wrote to me about the Argos, I've been reading about stars. We've loads of books about them, as the subject was of particular interest to my father. Aristotle taught that stars are made of a different matter than the four earthly elements—a quintessence—that also happens to be what the human psyche is made of. Which is why man's spirit corresponds to the stars. Perhaps that's not a very scientific view, but I do like the idea that there's a little starlight in each of us.

I carry thoughts of you like my own personal constellation. How far away you are, dearest friend, but no farther than those fixed stars in my soul.

Dear Pru,

We're settling in for a long siege. It's uncertain as to when I'll have the chance to write again. This is not my last letter, only the last for a while. Do not doubt that I am coming back to you someday.

Until I can hold you in my arms, these worn and ramshackle words are the

only way to reach you. What a poor
translation of love they are. Words
could never do justice to you, or capture
what you mean to me.

Still . . . I love you. I swear by the
starlight . . . I will not leave this earth
until you hear those words from me.

Sitting on a massive fallen oak deep in the forest,
Beatrix looked up from the letter. She didn't realize she
was crying until she felt the stroke of a breeze against
her wet cheeks. The muscles of her face ached as she
tried to compose herself.

He had written to her on the thirtieth of June, without knowing she had written to him on the same day.
One couldn't help but take that as a sign.

She hadn't experienced such a depth of bitter loss, of
agonized longing, since her parents had died. It was a
different kind of grief, of course, but it carried the same
flavor of hopeless need.

What have I done?

She, who had always gone through life with unsparing
honesty, had carried out an unforgivable deception. And
the truth would only make matters worse. If Christopher
Phelan ever discovered that she had written to him under
false pretenses, he would despise her. And if he never
found out, Beatrix would always be "the girl who belonged in the stables." Nothing more.

"Do not doubt that I am coming back to you . . ."

Those words had been meant for Beatrix, no matter
that it had been addressed to Prudence.

"I love you," she whispered, and her tears spilled
faster.

How had these feelings crept up on her? Good God,

she could hardly remember what Christopher Phelan looked like, and yet her heart was breaking over him. Worst of all, it was entirely likely that Christopher's declarations had been inspired by the hardships of wartime. This Christopher she knew from the letters . . . the man she loved . . . might vanish once he returned home.

Nothing good would come of this situation. She had to put a stop to it. She could not pretend to be Prudence any longer. It wasn't fair to any of them, especially Christopher.

Beatrix walked home slowly. As she entered Ramsay House, she encountered Amelia, who was taking her young son Rye outside.

"There you are," Amelia exclaimed. "Would you like to go out to the stable with us? Rye is going to ride his pony."

"No, thank you." Beatrix's smile felt as if it had been tacked on with pins. Every member of her family was quick to include her in their lives. They were all extraordinarily generous in that regard. And yet she sensed herself being cast, incrementally and inexorably, as the spinster aunt.

She felt eccentric and alone. A misfit, like the animals she kept.

Her mind made a disjointed leap, summoning recollections of the men she had met during dances and dinners and soirees. She had never lacked for male attention. Perhaps she should encourage one of them, just pick a likely candidate for attachment and be done with it. Perhaps having her own life was worth being married to a man she didn't love.

But that would be another form of misery.

Her fingers slipped into the pocket of her dress to touch the letter from Christopher Phelan. The feel of the parchment, which he had folded, caused her stomach to tighten with a hot, pleasurable pang.

"You've been very quiet of late," Amelia said, her blue eyes searching. "You look as though you've been crying. Is something troubling you, dear?"

Beatrix shrugged uneasily. "I suppose I'm melancholy because of Mr. Phelan's illness. According to Audrey, he has taken a turn for the worse."

"Oh . . ." Amelia's expression was soft with concern. "I wish there were something we could do. If I fill a basket with plum brandy and blancmange, will you take it to them?"

"Of course. I'll go later this afternoon."

Retreating to the privacy of her room, Beatrix sat at her desk and took out the letter. She would write to Christopher one last time, something impersonal, a gentle withdrawal. Better that than to continue deceiving him.

Carefully she uncapped the inkwell and dipped her pen, and began to write.

> *Dear Christopher,*
>
> *As much as I esteem you, dear friend, it would be unwise for either of us to be precipitate while you are still away. You have my earnest wishes for your well-being and safety. However, I think it best that any mention of more personal feelings between us should be delayed until you return. In fact, it is probably best that we end our correspondence . . .*

With each sentence, it became more difficult to make her fingers work properly. The pen trembled in her fierce grip, and she felt her tears well again. *"Rubbish,"* she said.

It literally hurt to write such lies. Her throat had gone nearly too tight to breathe.

She decided that before she could finish it, she would write the truth, the letter she longed to send to him, and then destroy it.

Breathing with effort, Beatrix snatched another piece of paper and hastily wrote a few lines, only for her eyes, hoping it would ease the intense pain that had clamped around her heart.

> *Dearest Christopher,*
>
> *I can't write to you again.*
>
> *I'm not who you think I am.*
>
> *I didn't mean to send love letters, but that is what they became. On their way to you, my words turned into heartbeats on the page.*
>
> *Come back, please come home and find me.*

Beatrix's eyes blurred. Setting the page aside, she returned to her original letter and finished it, expressing her wishes and prayers for his safe return.

As for the love letter, she crumpled it and shoved it into the drawer. Later she would burn it in her own private ceremony, and watch every heartfelt word burn to ashes.

Chapter Four

Later in the afternoon, Beatrix walked to the Phelan home. She carried a substantial basket weighted with the brandy and blancmange, a round of mild white cheese, and a small "homely cake," dry and bare of icing, only slightly sweet. Whether or not the Phelans needed such items didn't matter nearly so much as the gesture itself.

Amelia had urged Beatrix to ride to the Phelan home in a carriage or cart, as the basket was a bit unwieldy. However, Beatrix wanted the exertion of walking, hoping it would help to calm her troubled spirits. She set her feet to a steady rhythm, and drew the early-summer air into her lungs. *This is the smell of June,* she wanted to write to Christopher . . . *honeysuckle, green hay, wet linen hung out to dry . . .*

By the time she reached her destination, both her arms ached from having held the basket for so long.

The house, dressed in thick ivy, resembled a man huddling in his overcoat. Beatrix felt prickles of apprehension as she went to the front door and knocked. She was ushered inside by a solemn-faced butler who relieved her of the basket and showed her to the front receiving room.

The house seemed overheated, especially after her walk. Beatrix felt a bloom of perspiration emerge beneath the layers of her walking dress and inside her sturdy ankle boots.

Audrey entered the room, thin and untidy, her hair half up, half down. She was wearing an apron with dark ruddy blotches on it.

Bloodstains.

As Audrey met Beatrix's concerned gaze, she attempted a wan smile. "As you see, I'm not prepared to receive anyone. But you're one of the few people I don't have to maintain appearances for." Realizing that she was still wearing the apron, she untied it and rolled it into a little bundle. "Thank you for the basket. I told the butler to pour a glass of the plum brandy and give it to Mrs. Phelan. She's taken to her bed."

"Is she ill?" Beatrix asked as Audrey sat beside her.

Audrey shook her head in answer. "Only distraught."

"And . . . your husband?"

"He's dying," Audrey said flatly. "He doesn't have long. A matter of days, the doctor says."

Beatrix began to reach for her, wishing to gather her in as she might one of her wounded creatures.

Audrey flinched and raised her hands defensively. "No, don't. I can't be touched. I'll break into pieces. I have to be strong for John. Let's talk quickly. I have only a few minutes."

Immediately Beatrix folded her hands in her lap. "Let me do something," she said, her voice low. "Let me sit with him while you rest. At least for an hour."

Audrey managed a faint smile. "Thank you, dear. But I can't let anyone else sit with him. It has to be me."

"Then shall I go to his mother?"

Audrey rubbed her eyes. "You're very kind to offer. I don't think she wants companionship, however." She sighed. "Were it left to her, she would rather die along with John than go on without him."

"But she still has another son."

"She has no affection for Christopher. It was all for John."

As Beatrix tried to absorb that, the tall case clock ticked as if in disapproval, its pendulum swinging like the negative shake of a head. "That can't be true," she finally said.

"Certainly it can," Audrey said, with a faint, rueful smile. "Some people have an infinite supply of love to give. Like your family. But for others it's a limited resource. Mrs. Phelan's love is all poured out. She had just enough for her husband and John." Audrey lifted her shoulders in an exhausted shrug. "It's of no importance whether she loves Christopher or not. Nothing seems important at the moment."

Beatrix reached into her pocket and withdrew the letter. "I have this for him," she said. "For Captain Phelan From Pru."

Audrey took it with an unreadable expression. "Thank you. I'll send it along with a letter about John's condition. He'll want to know. Poor Christopher . . . so far away."

Beatrix wondered if perhaps she should take the letter back. It would be the worst possible time to distance herself from Christopher. On the other hand, perhaps it would be the best time. One small injury inflicted simultaneously with a far greater one.

Audrey watched the play of emotion on her face. "Are you ever going to tell him?" she asked gently.

Beatrix blinked. "Tell him what?"

That earned an exasperated little huff. "I'm not a half-wit, Bea. Prudence is in London at this very moment, attending balls and soirees and all those silly.

trivial events of the season. She couldn't have written that letter."

Beatrix felt herself turn scarlet, then bone-white. "She gave it to me before she left."

"Because of her devotion to Christopher?" Audrey's lips twisted. "The last time I saw her, she didn't even remember to ask after him. And why is it that you're always the one delivering and fetching letters?" She gave Beatrix a fond but chiding glance. "From what Christopher has written in his letters to me and John, it's obvious he's quite taken with Prudence. Because of what *she* has written to him. And if I end up with that ninnyhead as a sister-in-law, Bea, it will be your fault."

Seeing the quiver of Beatrix's chin and the glitter in her eyes, Audrey took her hand and pressed it. "Knowing you, I've no doubt your intentions were good. But I rather doubt the results will be." She sighed. "I have to go back to John."

As Beatrix went with Audrey to the entrance hall, she was overwhelmed by the knowledge that her friend would soon have to endure the death of her husband.

"Audrey," she said unsteadily, "I wish I could bear this for you."

Audrey stared at her for a long moment, her face flushing with emotion. "That, Beatrix, is what makes you a true friend."

Two days later the Hathaways received word that John Phelan had passed away in the night. Filled with compassion, the Hathaways considered how best they could help the bereaved women. Ordinarily it would have fallen to Leo, the lord of the manor, to call on the Phelans and offer his services. However, Leo was in London, as Parliament was still in session. Currently a political debate was raging over the incompetence and indifference that had resulted in the Crimean troops being so appallingly ill supported and badly supplied.

It was decided that Merripen, Win's husband, would go to the Phelan home on behalf of the family. No one had any expectation that he would be received, since the mourners would undoubtedly be too grief-stricken to speak with anyone. However, Merripen would deliver a letter to offer any manner of assistance that might be needed.

"Merripen," Beatrix asked before he left, "would you convey my affection to Audrey, and ask if I might help with any of the funeral arrangements? Or ask if perhaps she wants someone to sit with her."

"Of course," Merripen replied, his dark eyes filled with warmth. Having been raised with the Hathaways since boyhood, Merripen was very much like a brother to all of them. "Why don't you write a note to her? I'll give it to the servants."

"I'll only be a minute." Beatrix dashed toward the stairs, pulling up great handfuls of her skirts to keep from tripping as she hurried to her room.

She went to her desk and pulled out her writing papers and pens, and reached for the top of the inkwell. Her hand froze in midair as she saw the half-crumpled letter in the drawer.

It was the polite, distancing letter she had written to Christopher Phelan.

It had never been sent.

Beatrix went cold all over, her knees threatening to give out from beneath her. "Oh, God," she whispered, sitting on the nearby chair with such force that it wobbled dangerously.

She must have given Audrey the wrong letter. The unsigned one that had started with "I can't write to you again. I'm not who you think I am . . ."

Beatrix's heart pounded, straining with the force of panic. She tried to calm her buzzing thoughts enough to think. Had the letter been posted yet? Perhaps there was still time to retrieve it. She would ask Audrey . . . but no, that would be the height of selfishness and inconsideration. Audrey's husband had just died. She did not deserve to be bothered with trivialities at such a time.

It was too late. Beatrix would have to let it be, and let Christopher Phelan make what he would of the odd note.

"Come back, please come home and find me . . ."

Groaning, Beatrix leaned forward and rested her head on the table. Perspiration caused her forehead to stick to the polished wood. She was aware of Lucky leaping up to the table and nuzzling her hair and purring.

Please, dear God, she thought desperately, *don't let Christopher reply. Let it all be finished. Never let him find out it was me.*

Chapter Five

Scutari, Crimea

"It occurs to me," Christopher said conversationally as he lifted a cup of broth to a wounded man's lips, "that a hospital may be the worst possible place for a man to try to get well."

The young soldier he was feeding—no more than nineteen or twenty years of age—made a slight sound of amusement as he drank.

Christopher had been brought to the barracks hospital in Scutari three days earlier. He had been wounded during an assault on the Redan during the endless siege on Sebastopol. One moment he'd been accompanying a group of sappers as they carried a ladder toward a Russian bunker, and the next there was an explosion and the sensations of being struck simultaneously in the side and right leg.

The converted barracks were crowded with casualties, rats, and vermin. The only source of water was a fountain at which orderlies queued up to catch a fetid trickle in their pails. As the water was unfit for drinking, it was used for washing and soaking off bandages.

Christopher had bribed the orderlies to bring him a cup of strong spirits. He had sluiced the alcohol over his wounds in the hopes that it would keep them from suppurating. The first time he'd done it, the burst of raw fire had caused him to faint and topple from the bed to the floor, a spectacle that had caused no end of hilarity from the other patients in the ward. Christopher had good-naturedly endured their teasing afterward, knowing that a moment of levity was sorely needed in this squalid place.

The shrapnel had been removed from his side and leg, but the injuries weren't healing properly. This morning he had discovered that the skin around them was red and tight. The prospect of falling seriously ill in this place was frightening.

Yesterday, despite the outraged protests of the soldiers in the long row of beds, the orderlies had begun to sew a man into his own bloodstained blanket, and take him to the communal burial pit before he had quite finished dying. In response to the patients' angry cries, the orderlies replied that the man was insensible, and was only minutes away from death, and the bed was desperately needed. All of which was true. However, as one of the few men able to leave his bed, Christopher had interceded, telling them he would wait with the man on the floor until he had breathed his last. For an hour he had sat on the hard stone, brushing away insects, letting the man's head rest on his uninjured leg.

"You think you did any good for him?" one of the orderlies asked sardonically, when the poor fellow had finally passed away, and Christopher had allowed them to take him.

"Not for him," Christopher said, his voice low. "But perhaps for them." He had nodded in the direction of the rows of ragged cots, where the patients lay and watched. It was important for them to believe that if or when their time came, they would be treated with at least a flicker of humanity.

The young soldier in the bed next to Christopher's was unable to do much of anything for himself, as he had lost an entire arm, and a hand off the other one. Since there were no nurses to spare, Christopher had undertaken to feed him. Wincing and flinching as he knelt by the cot, he lifted the man's head and helped him to drink from the cup of broth.

"Captain Phelan," came the crisp voice of one of the Sisters of Charity. With her stern demeanor and forbidding expression, the nun was so intimidating that some of the soldiers had suggested—out of her hearing, of course—that if she were dispatched to fight the Russians, the war would be won in a matter of hours.

Her bristly gray brows rose as she saw Christopher beside the patient's cot. "Making trouble again?" she asked. "You will return to your own bed, Captain. And do not leave it again . . . unless your intention is to make yourself so ill that we'll be forced to keep you here indefinitely."

Obediently Christopher lurched back into his cot.

She came to him and laid a cool hand on his brow.

"Fever," he heard her announce. "Do not move from this bed, or I'll have you tied to it, Captain." Her hand was withdrawn, and something was placed on his chest.

Slitting his eyes open, Christopher saw that she had given him a packet of letters.

Prudence.

He seized it eagerly, fumbling in his eagerness to break the seal.

There were two letters in the packet.

He waited until the sister had left before he opened the one from Prudence. The sight of her handwriting engulfed him with emotion. He wanted her, needed her, with an intensity he couldn't contain.

Somehow, half a world away, he had fallen in love with her. It didn't matter that he hardly knew her. What little he knew of her, he loved.

Christopher read the few spare lines.

The words seemed to rearrange themselves like a child's alphabet game. He puzzled over them until they became coherent.

"... *I'm not who you think I am ... please come home and find me ...*"

His lips formed her name soundlessly. He put his hand over his chest, trapping the letter against his rough heartbeat.

What had happened to Prudence?

The strange, impulsive note aroused a tumult in him.

"I'm not who you think I am," he found himself repeating inaudibly.

No, of course she was not. Neither was he. He was not this broken, feverish creature on a hospital cot, and she was not the vapid flirt everyone had taken her to be. Through their letters, they had found the promise of more in each other.

"... *please come home and find me ...*"

His hands felt swollen and tight as he fumbled with the other letter, from Audrey. The fever was making him clumsy. His head had begun to ache ... vicious throbbing ... he had to read the words in between the pulses of pain.

Dear Christopher,

There is no way for me to express this gently. John's condition has worsened. He is facing

the prospect of death with the same patience
and grace that he has shown during his life.
By the time this letter reaches you, there is
no doubt that he will be gone . . .

Christopher's mind closed against the rest of it. Later there would be time to read more. Time to grieve.

John wasn't supposed to be ill. He was supposed to stay safe in Stony Cross and father children with Audrey. He was supposed to be there when Christopher came back home.

Christopher managed to huddle on his side. He tugged the blanket high enough to create a shelter for himself. Around him, the other soldiers continued to pass the time . . . talking, playing cards when possible. Mercifully, deliberately, they paid him no attention, allowing him the privacy he needed.

Chapter Six

There had been no correspondence from Christopher Phelan in the ten months after Beatrix had last written to him. He had exchanged letters with Audrey, but in her grief over John's death, Audrey found it difficult to talk to anyone, even Beatrix.

Christopher had been wounded, Audrey relayed, but he had recovered in the hospital and returned to battle. Hunting constantly for any mention of Christopher in the newspapers, Beatrix found innumerable accounts of his bravery. During the months-long siege of Sebastopol, he had become the most decorated soldier of the artillery. Not only had Christopher been awarded the order of the Bath, and the Crimea campaign medal with clasps for Alma, Inkerman, Balaklava, and Sebastopol, he had also been made a knight of the Legion of Honor by the French, and had received the *Medjidie* from the Turks.

To Beatrix's regret, her friendship with Prudence had cooled, starting with the day when Beatrix had told her that she could no longer write to Christopher.

"But why?" Prudence had protested. "I thought you enjoyed corresponding with him."

"I don't enjoy it any longer," Beatrix had replied in a suffocated voice.

Her friend had given her an incredulous glance. "I can scarcely believe that you would abandon him like this. What is he to think when the letters stop coming?"

The question made Beatrix's stomach feel heavy with guilt and wanting. She hardly trusted herself to speak. "I can't continue to write to him without telling him the truth. It's becoming too personal. I . . . feelings are involved. Do you understand what I'm trying to say?"

"All I understand is that you're being selfish. You've made it so that I can't send a letter to him, because he would notice the difference between your penmanship and mine. The least you could do is keep him on the string for me until he returns."

"Why do you want him?" Beatrix had asked with a frown. She didn't like the phrase "keep him on the string" . . . as if Christopher were a dead fish. One among many. "You have many suitors."

"Yes, but Captain Phelan has become a war hero. He may even be invited to dine with the queen upon his return. And now that his brother is dead, he will inherit the Riverton estate. All that makes him nearly as good a catch as a peer."

Although Beatrix had once been amused by Prudence's shallowness, she now felt a stab of annoyance. Christopher deserved much more than to be valued for such superficial things.

"Has it occurred to you that he'll be altered as a result of the war?" she asked quietly.

"Well, he may yet be wounded, but I certainly hope not."

"I meant altered in character."

"Because he's been in battle?" Prudence shrugged. "I suppose that has had an effect on him."

"Have you followed any of the reports about him?"

"I've been very occupied," Prudence said defensively.

"Captain Phelan won the *Medjidie* medal by saving a wounded Turkish officer. A few weeks later, Captain Phelan crawled to a magazine that had just been shelled, with ten French soldiers killed and five guns disabled. He took possession of the remaining gun and held the position alone, against the enemy, for eight hours. On another occasion—"

"I don't need to hear about all that," Prudence protested. "What is your point, Bea?"

"That he may come back as a different man. And if you care for him at all, you should try to understand what he has gone through." She gave Prudence a packet of letters tied with a narrow blue ribbon. "To start with, you should read these. I should have copied the letters that I wrote to him, so you could read them as well. But I'm afraid I didn't think of it."

Prudence had accepted them reluctantly. "Very well, I'll read them. But I'm certain that Christopher won't want to talk about letters when he returns—he'll have me right there with him."

"You should try to know him better," Beatrix said. "I think you want him for the wrong reasons . . . when there are so many right reasons. He's earned it. Not because of his bravery in battle and all those shiny medals . . . in fact, that's the least part of what he is." Falling silent for a moment, Beatrix had reflected ruefully that from then on she really should avoid people and go back to spending her time with animals. "Captain Phelan wrote that when you and he knew each other, neither of you looked beneath the surface."

"The surface of what?"

Beatrix gave her a bleak look, reflecting that for

Prudence, the only thing beneath the surface was more surface. "He said you might be his only chance of belonging to the world again."

Prudence had stared at her strangely. "Perhaps it's better after all that you stop writing to him. You seem rather fixed on him. I hope you have no thought that Christopher would ever . . ." She paused delicately. "Never mind."

"I know what you were going to say," Beatrix had said in a matter-of-fact manner. "Of course I have no illusions about that. I haven't forgotten that he once compared me to a horse."

"He did not compare you to a horse," Prudence said. "He merely said you belonged in the stables. However, he is a sophisticated man, and he would never be happy with a girl who spends most of her time with animals."

"I much prefer the company of animals to that of any person I know," Beatrix shot back. Instantly she regretted the tactless statement, especially as she saw that Prudence had taken it as a personal affront. "I'm sorry. I didn't mean—"

"Perhaps you had better leave, then, and go to your pets," Prudence had said in a frosty tone. "You'll be happier conversing with someone who can't talk back to you."

Chastened and vexed, Beatrix had left Mercer House. But not before Prudence had said, "For all our sakes, Bea, you must promise me never to tell Captain Phelan that you wrote the letters. There would be no point to it. Even if you told him, he wouldn't want you. It would only be an embarrassment, and a source of resentment. A man like that would never forgive such a deception."

Ever since that day, Beatrix and Prudence had not seen each other except in passing. And no further letters were written.

It tormented Beatrix, wondering how Christopher was, if Albert was with him, if his wounds had healed properly . . . but it was no longer her right to ask questions of him.

It never had been.

To the jubilation of all England, Sebastopol fell in September 1855, and peace negotiations began in February of the next year. Beatrix's brother-in-law Cam remarked that even though Britain had won, war was always a pyrrhic victory, as one could never put a price on each life that had been damaged or lost. It was a Romany sentiment that Beatrix agreed with. All totaled, more than one hundred and fifty thousand of the allied soldiers had died of battle wounds or disease, as well as over one hundred thousand Russians.

When the long-awaited order was given for the regiments to return home, Audrey and Mrs. Phelan learned that Christopher's Rifle Brigade would arrive in Dover in mid-April, and proceed to London. The Rifles' arrival was keenly anticipated, as Christopher was considered a national hero. His picture had been cut out of newspapers and posted in shop windows, and the accounts of his bravery were repeated in taverns and coffeehouses. Long testimonial rolls were written by villages and counties to be presented to him, and no fewer than three ceremonial swords, engraved with his name and set with jewels, had been struck by politicians eager to reward him for service.

However, on the day the Rifles landed at Dover, Christopher was mysteriously absent from the festivities. The crowds at the quay cheered the Rifle Brigade and demanded the appearance of its famed sharpshooter, but it seemed that Christopher had chosen to avoid the cheering crowds, the ceremonies and banquets . . . he

even failed to appear at the celebration dinner hosted by
the queen and her consort.

"What do you suppose has happened to Captain
Phelan?" Beatrix's older sister Amelia asked, after he
had gone missing for three days. "From what I remember of the man, he was a social fellow who would have
adored being the center of so much attention."

"He's gaining even more attention by his absence,"
Cam pointed out.

"He doesn't want attention," Beatrix couldn't resist
saying. "He's run to ground."

Cam lifted a dark brow, looking amused. "Like a
fox?" he asked.

"Yes. Foxes are wily. Even when they seem to head
directly away from their goal, they always turn and
make it good at the last." Beatrix hesitated, her gaze
distant as she stared through the nearby window, at the
forest shadowed by a harsh and backward spring . . .
too much easterly wind, too much rain. "Captain Phelan
wants to come home. But he'll stay aground until the
hounds stop drawing for him."

She was quiet and contemplative after that, while
Cam and Amelia continued to talk. It was only her
imagination . . . but she had the curious feeling that
Christopher Phelan was somewhere close by.

"Beatrix." Amelia stood beside her at the window,
laying a gentle arm across her shoulders. "Are you feeling melancholy, dear? Perhaps you should have gone
to London for the season as your friend Prudence did.
You could stay with Leo and Catherine, or with Poppy
and Harry at the hotel—"

"I have no interest whatsoever in taking part in the
season," Beatrix said. "I've done it four times, and that
was three times too many."

"But you were very sought after. The gentlemen

adored you. And perhaps there will be someone new there."

Beatrix lifted her gaze heavenward. "There's never anyone new in London society."

"True," Amelia said after a moment's thought. "Still, I think you would better off in town than staying here in the country. It's too quiet for you here."

A small, dark-haired boy charged into the room on a stick horse, letting out a warlike cry as he brandished a sword. It was Rye, Cam and Amelia's four-and-a-half-year-old son. As the boy sped by, the end of the stick horse accidentally knocked against a floor lamp with a blue glass shade. Cam dove reflexively and caught the lamp before it smashed against the floor.

Turning around, Rye beheld his father on the floor and leaped on him, giggling.

Cam wrestled with his son, pausing briefly to inform his wife, "It's not that quiet here."

"I miss Jàdo," Rye complained, referring to his cousin and favorite playmate. "When is he coming back?"

Merripen, Amelia's sister Win, and their young son Jason, nicknamed Jàdo, had left a month earlier for Ireland to visit the estate that Merripen would someday inherit. As his grandfather was ailing, Merripen had agreed to stay for an indeterminate time to become familiar with the estate and its tenants.

"Not for a while," Cam informed him regretfully. "Perhaps not until Christmas."

"That's too long," Rye said with a wistful sigh.

"You have other cousins, darling," Amelia pointed out.

"They're all in London."

"Edward and Emmaline will be here in the summer. And in the meantime, you have your little brother."

"But Alex is hardly any fun," Rye said. "He can't talk or throw a ball. And he leaks."

"At both ends," Cam added, his amber eyes sparkling as he looked up at his wife.

Amelia tried, without success, to stifle a laugh. "He won't leak forever."

Straddling his father's chest, Rye glanced at Beatrix. "Will you play with me, Aunt?"

"Certainly. Marbles? Jackstraws?"

"War," the boy said with relish. "I'll be the cavalry and you be the Russians, and I'll chase you around the hedgerow."

"Couldn't we reenact the Treaty of Paris instead?"

"You *can't* do a treaty before you have the war," Rye protested. "There would be nothing to talk about."

Beatrix grinned at her sister. "Very logical."

Rye jumped up to grab Beatrix's hand, and he began to drag her outside. "Come, Auntie," he coaxed. "I promise I won't whack you with my sword like the last time."

"Don't go into the woods, Rye," Cam called after them. "One of the tenants said a stray dog came out of the hazel copse this morning and nearly attacked him. He thought the creature might be mad."

Beatrix stopped and looked back at Cam. "What kind of dog?"

"A mongrel with a rough coat like a terrier's. The tenant claims the dog stole one of his hens."

"Don't worry, Papa," Rye said confidently. "I'll be safe with Beatrix. All animals love her, even the mad ones."

Chapter Seven

After an hour of romping along the hedgerow and through the orchard, Beatrix took Rye back to the house for his afternoon lessons.

"I don't like lessons," Rye said, heaving a sigh as they approached the French doors at the side of the house. "I'd much rather play."

"Yes, but you must learn your maths."

"I don't need to, really. I already know how to count to a hundred. And I'm sure I'll never need more than a hundred of anything."

Beatrix grinned. "Practice your letters, then. And you'll be able to read lots of adventure stories."

"But if I spend my time *reading* about adventures," Rye said, "I won't actually be *having* them."

Beatrix shook her head and laughed. "I should know better than to debate with you, Rye. You're as clever as a cart full of monkeys."

The child scampered up the stairs and turned to look back at her. "Aren't you coming in, Auntie?"

"Not yet," she said absently, her gaze drawn to the forest beyond Ramsay House. "I think I'll go for a walk."

"Shall I come with you?"

"Thank you, Rye, but at the moment I need a solitary walk."

"You're going to look for the dog," he said wisely.

Beatrix smiled. "I might."

Rye regarded her speculatively. "Auntie?"

"Yes?"

"Are you ever going to marry?"

"I hope so, Rye. But I have to find the right gentleman first."

"If no one else will marry you, I will when I'm grown up. But only if I'm taller, because I wouldn't want to look up at you."

"Thank you," she said gravely, suppressing a smile as she turned and strode toward the forest.

It was a walk she had taken hundreds of times before. The scenery was familiar, shadows broken by sunlight that came in shards through the tree limbs. Bark was frosted with pale green moss, except for the dark erosions where wood had turned into dust. The woodland floor was soft with mud, overlaid by papery leaves, ferns, and hazel catkins. The sounds were familiar, birdsong and swishing leaves, and the rustlings of a million small creatures.

For all her acquaintance with these woods, however, Beatrix was aware of a new feeling. A sense that she should be cautious. The air was charged with the promise of . . . something. As she went farther, the feeling intensified. Her heart behaved strangely, a wild pulse awakening in her wrists and throat and even in her knees.

There was movement ahead, a shape sliding low through the trees and rippling the bracken. It was not a human shape.

Picking up a fallen branch, Beatrix deftly snapped it to the length of a walking stick.

The creature went still, and silence descended over the forest.

"Come here," Beatrix called out.

A dog came bounding toward her, crashing through brush and leaves. He gave the distinctive bay of a terrier. Halting a few yards away from her, the dog snarled and bared long white teeth.

Beatrix held still and studied him calmly. He was lean, his wiry fur stripped short except for comical whisks of it on his face and ears and near his eyes. Such expressive bright eyes, round as shillings.

There was no mistaking that distinctive face. She had seen it before.

"Albert?" she said in wonder.

The dog's ears twitched at the name. Crouching, he growled in his throat, a sound of angry confusion.

"He brought you back with him," Beatrix said, dropping the stick. Her eyes prickled with the beginnings of tears, even as she let out a little laugh. "I'm so glad you made it through the war safely. Come, Albert, let's be friends." She stayed unmoving and let the dog approach her cautiously. He sniffed at her skirts, circling slowly. In a moment she felt his cold wet nose nudge the side of her hand. She didn't move to pet him, only allowed him to become familiar with her scent. When she saw the change in his face, the jaw muscles relaxing and his mouth hanging open, she spoke firmly. "Sit, Albert."

His bottom dropped to the ground. A whine whistled from his throat. Beatrix reached out to stroke his head and scratch behind his ears. Albert panted eagerly, his eyes half closed in enjoyment.

"So you've run off from him, have you?" Beatrix asked, smoothing the wiry ruff on his head. "Naughty boy. I suppose you've had a fine old time chasing rabbits and squirrels. And there's a damaging rumor about a missing chicken. You had better stay out of poultry yards, or it won't go well for you in Stony Cross. Shall I take you home, boy? He's probably looking for you. He—"

She stopped at the sound of something . . . someone . . . moving through the thicket. Albert turned his head and let out a happy bark, bounding toward the approaching figure.

Beatrix was slow to lift her head. She struggled to moderate her breathing, and tried to calm the frantic stutters of her heart. She was aware of the dog bounding joyfully back to her, tongue dangling. He glanced back at his master as if to convey *Look what I found!*

Letting out a slow breath, Beatrix looked up at the man who had stopped approximately three yards away.

Christopher.

It seemed the entire world stopped.

Beatrix tried to compare the man standing before her with the cavalier rake he had once been. But it seemed impossible that he could be the same person. No longer a god descending from Olympus . . . now a warrior hardened by bitter experience.

His complexion was a deep mixture of gold and copper, as if he had been slowly steeped in sun. The dark wheaten locks of his hair had been cut in efficiently short layers. His face was impassive, but something volatile was contained in the stillness.

How bleak he looked. How alone.

She wanted to run to him. She wanted to touch him. The effort of standing motionless caused her muscles to tremble in protest.

She heard herself speak in a voice that wasn't quite steady. "Welcome home, Captain Phelan."

He was silent, staring at her without apparent recognition. Dear Lord, those eyes . . . frost and fire, his gaze burning through her awareness.

"I'm Beatrix Hathaway," she managed to say. "My family—"

"I remember you."

The rough velvet of his voice was a pleasure-stroke against her ears. Fascinated, bewildered, Beatrix stared at his guarded face.

To Christopher Phelan, she was a stranger. But the memories of his letters were between them, even if he wasn't aware of it.

Her hand moved gently over Albert's rough fur. "You were absent in London," she said. "There was a great deal of hullabaloo on your behalf."

"I wasn't ready for it."

So much was expressed in that spare handful of words. Of course he wasn't ready. The contrast would be too jarring, the blood-soaked brutality of war followed by a fanfare of parades and trumpets and flower petals. "I can't imagine any sane man would be," she said. "It's quite an uproar. Your picture is in all the shop windows. And they're naming things after you."

"Things," he repeated cautiously.

"There's a Phelan hat."

His brows lowered. "No there isn't."

"Oh, yes there is. Rounded at the top. Narrow-brimmed. Sold in shades of gray or black. They have one featured at the milliner's in Stony Cross."

Scowling, Christopher muttered something beneath his breath.

Beatrix played gently with Albert's ears. "I . . . heard about Albert, from Prudence. How lovely that you brought him back with you."

"It was a mistake," he said flatly. "He's behaved like

a mad creature ever since we landed at Dover. So far he's tried to bite two people, including one of my servants. He won't stop barking. I had to shut him in a garden shed last night, and he escaped."

"He's fearful," Beatrix said. "He thinks if he acts that way, no one will harm him." Eagerly the dog stood on his hind legs and set his front paws on her. Beatrix bumped a knee gently against his chest.

"Here," Christopher said, in a tone of such quiet menace that it sent a chill down Beatrix's spine. The dog slunk to him, tail between his legs. Christopher took a coiled leather leash from his coat pocket and looped it around the dog's neck. He glanced at Beatrix, his gaze traveling from the two smears of mud on her skirts to the gentle curves of her breasts. "My apologies," he said brusquely.

"No harm done. I don't mind. But he should be taught not to jump on people."

"He's only been with soldiers. He knows nothing of polite company."

"He can learn. I'm sure he'll be a fine dog once he becomes used to his new surroundings." Beatrix paused before offering, "I could work with him the next time I visit Audrey. I'm very good with dogs."

Christopher gave her a brooding glance. "I'd forgotten you were friends with my sister-in-law."

"Yes." Beatrix hesitated. "I should have said earlier that I'm very sorry for the loss of your—"

His hand lifted in a staying gesture. As he brought it to his side, his fingers curled into a tight fist.

Beatrix understood. The pain of his brother's death was still too acute. It was territory he couldn't yet traverse. "You haven't been able to grieve yet, have you?" she asked gently. "I suppose his death wasn't entirely real to you, until you came back to Stony Cross."

Christopher gave her a warning glance.

Beatrix had seen that look from captured animals, the helpless animosity toward anyone who approached. She had learned to respect such a glance, understanding that wild creatures were at their most dangerous when they had the fewest defenses. She returned her attention to the dog, smoothing his fur repeatedly.

"How is Prudence?" she heard him ask. It hurt to hear the note of wary longing in his voice.

"Quite well, I believe. She's in London for the season." Beatrix hesitated before adding carefully, "We are still friends, but perhaps not as fond of each other as we once were."

"Why?"

His gaze was alert now. Clearly any mention of Prudence earned his close attention.

Because of you, Beatrix thought, and managed a faint, wry smile. "It seems we have different interests." *I'm interested in you, and she's interested in your inheritance.*

"You're hardly cut from the same cloth."

Hearing the sardonic note in his voice, Beatrix tilted her head and regarded him curiously. "I don't take your meaning."

He hesitated. "I only meant that Miss Mercer is conventional. And you're . . . not." His tone was seasoned with the merest hint of condescension . . . but there was no mistaking it.

Abruptly all the feelings of compassion and tenderness disappeared as Beatrix realized that Christopher Phelan had not changed in one regard: he still didn't like her.

"I would never want to be a conventional person," she said. "They're usually dull and superficial."

It seemed he took that as a slight against Prudence.

"As compared to people who bring garden pests to picnics? No one could accuse you of being dull, Miss Hathaway."

Beatrix felt the blood drain from her face. He had insulted her. The realization made her numb.

"You may insult me," she said, half amazed that she could still speak. "But leave my hedgehog alone."

Whirling around, she walked away from him in long, digging strides. Albert whimpered and began to follow, which forced Christopher to call him back.

Beatrix didn't glance over her shoulder, only plowed forward. Bad enough to love a man who didn't love her. But it was exponentially worse to love a man who actively disliked her.

Ridiculously, she wished she could write to *her* Christopher about the stranger she had just met.

He was so contemptuous, she would write. *He dismissed me as someone who didn't deserve a modicum of respect. Clearly he thinks I'm wild and more than a little mad. And the worst part is that he's probably right.*

It crossed her mind that this was why she preferred the company of animals to people. Animals weren't deceitful. They didn't give one conflicting impressions of who they were. And one was never tempted to hope that an animal might change its nature.

Christopher walked back home with Albert padding calmly beside him. For some reason the dog seemed improved after meeting Beatrix Hathaway. As Christopher gave him a damning glance, Albert looked up at him with a toothy grin, his tongue lolling.

"Idiot," Christopher muttered, although he wasn't certain if the word was directed at his dog or himself.

He felt troubled and guilty. He knew he'd behaved

like an ass to Beatrix Hathaway. She had tried to be friendly, and he had been cold and condescending.

He hadn't meant to be offensive. It was just that he was nearly mad with longing for Prudence, for the sweet, artless voice that had saved his sanity. Every word of every letter she'd sent him still resonated through his soul.

"I've done a great deal of walking lately. I seem to think better outdoors . . ."

And when Christopher had set out to find Albert, and found himself walking through the forest, a mad idea had taken hold of him . . . that *she* was nearby, and fate would bring them together that quickly, that simply.

But instead of finding the woman he had dreamed of, craved, needed for so long, he had found Beatrix Hathaway.

It wasn't that he disliked her. Beatrix was an odd creature, but fairly engaging, and far more attractive than he had remembered. In fact, she had become a beauty in his absence, her gangly coltish shape now curved and graceful . . .

Christopher shook his head impatiently, trying to redirect his thoughts. But the image of Beatrix Hathaway remained. A lovely oval face, a gently erotic mouth, and haunting blue eyes, a blue so rich and deep it seemed to contain hints of purple. And that silky dark hair, pinned up haphazardly, with teasing locks slipping free.

Christ, it had been too long since he'd had a woman. He was randy as the devil, and lonely, and filled with equal measures of grief and anger. He had so many unfulfilled needs, and he didn't begin to know how to address any of them. But finding Prudence seemed like a good start.

He would rest here for a few days. When he felt

more like his former self, he would go to Prudence in
London. At the moment, however, it was fairly clear
that his old way with words had left him. And Christopher knew that whereas he had once been relaxed and
charming, he was now guarded and wooden.

Part of the problem was that he wasn't sleeping well.
Any slight noise, a creak of the house settling, a rap of
a branch against the window, woke him to full heart-
pounding readiness. And it happened in the daylight
hours as well. Yesterday Audrey had dropped a book
from a stack she was carrying, and Christopher had
nearly jumped out of his shoes. He had instinctively
reached for a weapon before recalling in the next instant that he no longer carried a gun. His rifle had become as familiar as one of his own limbs . . . he often
felt it as a phantom presence.

Christopher's steps slowed. He stopped to crouch
beside Albert, looking into that shaggy fur-whisked
face. "Hard to leave the war behind, isn't it?" he murmured, petting the dog with affectionate roughness.
Albert panted and lunged against him, and tried to lick
his face. "Poor fellow, you have no idea what's going
on, do you? For all you know, shells may start exploding overhead at any moment."

Albert flopped to his back and arched up his tummy,
begging for a scratch. Christopher obliged him, and
stood. "Let's go back," he said. "I'll let you inside the
house again—but God help you if you bite anyone."

Unfortunately, as soon as they went into the ivy-covered
mansion, Albert erupted in the same hostility he had
shown before. Grimly Christopher dragged him to the
parlor, where his mother and Audrey were having tea.

Albert barked at the women. He barked at a terrified

housemaid. He barked at a fly on the wall. He barked at the teapot.

"*Quiet,*" Christopher said through gritted teeth, pulling the crazed canine to the settee. He tied one end of the leash to a leg of the settee. "*Sit,* Albert. Down."

Warily the dog settled on the floor and growled in his throat.

Audrey pasted a false smile on her face and inquired in a parody of teatime manners, "Shall I pour?"

"Thank you," Christopher said in a dry tone, and went to join them at the tea table.

His mother's face pleated, accordionlike, and her voice emerged in a strained tone. "It's leaving mud on the carpet. *Must* you inflict that creature on us, Christopher?"

"Yes, I must. He has to become accustomed to staying in the house."

"*I* won't become accustomed to it," his mother retorted. "I understand that the dog assisted you during the war. But surely you have no need of it now."

"Sugar? Milk?" Audrey asked, her soft brown eyes now unsmiling as she gazed from Christopher to his mother.

"Only sugar." Christopher watched as she stirred a lump of sugar into tea with a little spoon. He took the cup and concentrated on the steaming liquid, while he struggled with a rush of untoward rage. This, too, was a new problem, these surges of feeling that were entirely out of proportion to the circumstances.

When Christopher had calmed himself sufficiently to speak, he said, "Albert did more than assist me. When I spent days at a time in a muddy trench, he kept watch over me so that I could sleep without fear of being taken by surprise. He took messages up and down the lines, so that we didn't make mistakes in carrying out orders. He alerted us when he sensed the enemy approaching, long before our eyes or ears could have detected anyone." Christopher paused as he glanced into his mother's taut, unhappy face. "I owe him my life, and my loyalty. And unsightly and ill mannered though he is, I happen to love him." He slitted a glance at Albert.

Albert's tail thumped the floor enthusiastically.

Audrey looked dubious. His mother looked angry.

Christopher drank his tea in the ensuing silence. It tore at his heart to see the changes in both women. They were both thin and pale. His mother's hair had gone white. No doubt John's prolonged illness had taken a toll on them before his death, and nearly a year of mourning had finished the job.

Not for the first time, Christopher thought it a shame that the rules of mourning imposed such solitude on people, when it probably would have benefited them to have company and pleasant distractions.

Setting down her half-finished cup of tea, his mother pushed back from the table. Christopher rose to help her with the chair.

"I can't enjoy my tea with that beast staring at me," she said. "At any moment, it could leap forward and rip my throat out."

"His leash is tied to the furniture, Mother," Audrey pointed out.

"That doesn't matter. It's a savage creature, and I detest it." She swept out of the room, her head high with indignation.

Freed of the necessity for good manners, Audrey rested an elbow on the table and leaned her hand on her chin. "Your uncle and aunt have invited her to stay with them in Hertfordshire," she said. "I've encouraged her to accept their offer. She needs a change of view."

"The house is too dark," Christopher said. "Why are all the shutters closed and the curtains drawn?"

"The light hurts her eyes."

"The devil it does." Christopher stared at her with a slight frown. "She should go," he said. "She's been holed up in this morgue for far too long. And so have you."

Audrey sighed. "It's almost been a year. Soon I'll be out of full mourning and I can go into half-mourning."

"What is half-mourning, exactly?" Christopher asked, having only a vague notion of such female-oriented rituals.

"It means I can stop wearing veils" Audrey said without enthusiasm. "I can wear gray and lavender dresses, and ornaments without shine. And I may attend a few limited social events, as long as I don't actually appear to be enjoying myself."

Christopher snorted derisively. "Who invents these rules?"

"I don't know. But heaven help us, we must follow them or face the wrath of society." Audrey paused. "Your mother says she won't go into half-mourning. She intends to wear black for the rest of her life."

Christopher nodded, unsurprised. His mother's devotion had only been strengthened by death. "It's clear that every time she looks at me," he said, "she thinks I should have been the son she lost."

Audrey opened her mouth to argue, then closed it. "It was hardly your fault that you came back alive," she said eventually. "I'm glad you're here. And I believe that somewhere in her heart, your mother is glad as well. But she's become slightly unbalanced during the past year. I don't think she's always entirely aware of what she says or does. I believe some time away from Hampshire will do her good." She paused. "I'm going to leave, too, Christopher. I want to see my family in London. And it wouldn't be appropriate for the two of us to stay here unchaperoned."

"I'll escort you to London in a few days, if you like. I had already planned to go there to see Prudence Mercer."

Audrey frowned. "Oh."

Christopher gave her a questioning glance. "I gather your opinion of her has not changed."

"Oh, it has. It's worsened."

He couldn't help but feel defensive on Prudence's behalf. "Why?"

"For the past two years, Prudence has earned a reputation as a shameless flirt. Her ambition to marry a wealthy man, preferably a peer, is known to everyone. I hope you have no illusions that she pined for you in your absence."

"I would hardly expect her to don sackcloth while I was gone."

"Good, because she didn't. In fact, from all appearances you slipped from her mind completely." Audrey paused before adding bitterly, "However, soon after John passed away and you became the new heir to Riverton, Prudence evinced a great deal of renewed interest in you."

Christopher showed no expression as he puzzled over this unwelcome information. It sounded nothing like the woman who had corresponded with him. Clearly Prudence was the victim of vicious rumors—and in light of her beauty and charm, that was entirely expected.

However, he had no desire to start an argument with his sister-in-law. Hoping to distract her from the volatile subject of Prudence Mercer, he said, "I happened to meet one of your friends today, when I chanced upon her during a walk."

"Who?"

"Miss Hathaway."

"Beatrix?" Audrey looked at him attentively. "I hope you were polite to her."

"Not especially," he admitted.

"What did you say to her?"

He scowled into his teacup. "I insulted her hedge-hog," he muttered.

Audrey looked exasperated. "Oh, good God." She began to stir her tea so vigorously that the spoon threatened to crack the porcelain cup. "And to think you were once renowned for your silver tongue. What perverse instinct drives you to repeatedly offend one of the nicest women I've ever known?"

"I haven't *repeatedly* offended her, I just did it today."

Her mouth twisted in derision. "How conveniently short your memory is. All of Stony Cross knows that you once said she belonged in the stables."

"I would never have said that to a woman, no matter how damned eccentric she was. *Is*."

"Beatrix overheard you telling it to one of your friends, at the harvest dance held at Stony Cross Manor."

"And she told everyone?"

"No, she made the mistake of confiding in Prudence, who told everyone. Prudence is an incurable gossip."

"Obviously you have no liking for Prudence," he began, "but if you—"

"I've tried my best to like her. I thought if one peeled away the layers of artifice, one would find the real Prudence beneath. But there's nothing beneath. And I doubt there ever will be."

"And you find Beatrix Hathaway superior to her?"

"In every regard, except perhaps beauty."

"There you have it wrong," he informed her. "Miss Hathaway *is* a beauty."

Audrey's brows lifted. "Do you think so?" she asked idly, lifting the teacup to her lips.

"It's obvious. Regardless of what I think of her character, Miss Hathaway is an exceptionally attractive woman."

"Oh, I don't know . . ." Audrey devoted careful attention to her tea, adding a tiny lump of sugar. "She's rather tall."

"She has the ideal height and form."

"And brown hair is so common . . ."

"It's not the usual shade of brown, it's as dark as sable. And those eyes . . ."

"Blue," Audrey said with a dismissive wave.

"The deepest, purest blue I've ever seen. No artist could capture—" Christopher broke off abruptly. "Never mind. I'm straying from the point."

"What *is* your point?" Audrey asked sweetly.

"That it is of no significance to me whether Miss Hathaway is a beauty or not. She's peculiar, and so is her family, and I have no interest in any of them. By the same token, I don't give a damn if Prudence Mercer is beautiful—I'm interested in the workings of her mind. Her lovely, original, absolutely compelling mind."

"I see. Beatrix's mind is peculiar, and Prudence's is original and compelling."

"Just so."

Audrey shook her head slowly. "There is something I want to tell you. But it's going to become more obvious over time. And you wouldn't believe it if I told you, or at least you wouldn't want to believe it. This is one of those things that must be discovered for oneself."

"Audrey, what the devil are you talking about?"

Folding her narrow arms across her chest, his sister-in-law contemplated him sternly. And yet a strange little smile kept tugging at the corners of her lips. "If you are at all a gentleman," she finally said, "you will call on Beatrix tomorrow and apologize for hurting her feelings. Go during one of your walks with Albert—she'll be glad to see *him*, if not you."

Chapter Eight

Christopher walked to Ramsay House the next afternoon. Not because he actually wanted to. However, he had no plans for the day, and unless he wanted to contend with his mother's unforgiving stares, or worse, Audrey's quiet stoicism, he had to go somewhere. The stillness of the rooms, the memories tucked in every nook and shadow, were more than he could face.

He had yet to ask Audrey what it had been like for John the last few days of his life . . . what his last words had been.

Beatrix Hathaway had been right when she'd guessed that John's death hadn't been real to him until he'd come home.

As they went through the forest, Albert bounded this way and that, foraging through the bracken. Christopher felt morose and restless as he anticipated his welcome—or lack thereof—when he arrived at Ramsay House. No doubt Beatrix had told her family about his ungentlemanly behavior. They would be angry with him, rightfully so. It was common knowledge that the Hathaway family was a close-knit, clannish group, fiercely protective of each other. And they had to be,

with a pair of Romany brothers-in-law, not to mention
their own lack of blood and breeding.

It was only the peerage title, held by Leo, Lord
Ramsay, that afforded the family any social foothold
whatsoever. Fortunately for them, they were received
by Lord Westcliff, one of the most powerful and re-
spected peers of the realm. That connection gave them
entrée into circles that otherwise would have excluded
them. However, what annoyed the local gentry was
that the Hathaways didn't seem to care one way or the
other.

As he approached Ramsay House, Christopher wondered what the devil he was doing, calling on the
Hathaways unannounced. It probably wasn't a proper
visiting day, and certainly not an appropriate time. But
he rather doubted they would notice.

The Ramsay estate was small but productive, with
three thousand acres of arable land and two hundred
prosperous tenant farms. In addition, the estate possessed a large forest that yielded a lucrative annual
timber yield. The charming and distinctive roofline of
the manor home came into view, a central medieval
dormer sided by rows of high peaked gables, Jacobean
pierced crestings and strap work, and a tidy square
Georgian addition to the left. The effect of mixed ar-
chitectural features wasn't all that unusual. Many older
homes featured additions in a variety of styles. But
since this was the Hathaway family, it only seemed to
underscore their strangeness.

Christopher put Albert on a leash and proceeded
to the entrance of the house with a little stab of dread.

If he were fortunate, no one would be available to
receive him.

After tying Albert's leash to a slender porch column,
Christopher knocked at the door and waited tensely.

He reared back as the portal was flung open by a frantic-faced housekeeper.

"I beg your pardon, sir, we're in the middle of—" She paused at the sound of porcelain crashing from somewhere inside the house. "Oh, merciful Lord," she moaned, and gestured to the front parlor. "Wait there if you please, and—"

"I've got her," a masculine voice called. And then, "Damn it, no I don't. She's heading for the stairs."

"Do *not* let her come upstairs!" a woman screamed. A baby was crying in strident gusts. "Oh, that dratted creature has woken the baby. Where are the housemaids?"

"Hiding, I expect."

Christopher hesitated in the entryway, blinking as he heard a bleating noise. He asked the housekeeper blankly, "Are they keeping farm animals in here?"

"No, of course not," she said hastily, trying to push him into the parlor. "That's . . . a baby crying. Yes. A baby."

"It doesn't sound like one," he said.

Christopher heard Albert barking from the porch. A three-legged cat came streaking through the hallway, followed by a bristling hedgehog that scuttled a great deal faster than one might have expected. The housekeeper hastened after them.

"Pandora, come back here!" came a new voice— Beatrix Hathaway's voice—and Christopher's senses sparked in recognition. He twitched uneasily at the commotion, his reflexes urging him to take some kind of action, although he wasn't yet certain what the bloody hell was going on.

A large white goat came leaping and capering and twisting through the hallway.

And then Beatrix Hathaway appeared, tearing around the corner. She skidded to a halt. "You might have tried to stop her," she exclaimed. As she glanced up at Christopher, a scowl flitted across her face. "Oh. It's you."

"Miss Hathaway—" he began.

"Hold this."

Something warm and wriggling was thrust into his grasp, and Beatrix dashed off to pursue the goat.

Dumbfounded, Christopher glanced at the creature in his hands. A baby goat, cream colored, with a brown head. He fumbled to keep from dropping the creature as he glanced at Beatrix's retreating form and realized she was wearing breeches and boots.

Christopher had seen women in every imaginable state of dress or undress. But he had never seen one wearing the clothes of a stablehand.

"I must be having a dream," he told the squirming kid absently. "A very odd dream about Beatrix Hathaway and goats . . ."

"I have her!" the masculine voice called out. "Beatrix, I told you the pen needed to be made taller."

"She didn't leap over it," came Beatrix's protest, "she ate *through* it."

"Who let her into the house?"

"No one. She butted one of the side doors open."

An inaudible conversation followed.

As Christopher waited, a dark-haired boy of approximately four or five years of age made a breathless entrance through the front door. He was carrying a wooden sword and had tied a handkerchief around his head, which gave him the appearance of a miniature pirate. "Did they catch the goat?" he asked Christopher without preamble.

"I believe so."

"Oh, thunderbolts. I missed all the fun." The boy sighed. He looked up at Christopher. "Who are you?"

"Captain Phelan."

The child's gaze sharpened with interest. "Where's your uniform?"

"I don't wear it now that the war is over."

"Did you come to see my father?"

"No, I . . . came to call on Miss Hathaway."

"Are you one of her suitors?"

Christopher gave a decisive shake of his head.

"You might be one," the boy said wisely, "and just not know it yet."

Christopher felt a smile—his first genuine smile in a long time—pulling at his lips. "Does Miss Hathaway have many suitors?"

"Oh, yes. But none of them want to marry her."

"Why is that, do you imagine?"

"They don't want to get shot," the child said, shrugging.

"Pardon?" Christopher's brows lifted.

"Before you marry, you have to get shot by an arrow and fall in love," the boy explained. He paused thoughtfully. "But I don't think the rest of it hurts as much as the beginning."

Christopher couldn't prevent a grin. At that moment, Beatrix returned to the hallway, dragging the nanny goat on a rope lead.

Beatrix looked at Christopher with an arrested expression.

His smile faded, and he found himself staring into her blue-on-blue eyes. They were astonishingly direct and lucid . . . the eyes of a vagabond angel. One had the sense that no matter what she beheld of the sinful world, she would never be jaded. She reminded him that the things he had seen and done could not be polished away like tarnish from silver.

Gradually her gaze lowered from his. "Rye," she said, handing the lead to the boy. "Take Pandora to the barn, will you? And the baby goat as well." Reaching out, she took the kid from Christopher's arms. The touch of her hands against his shirtfront elicited an unnerving response, a pleasurable heaviness in his groin.

"Yes, Auntie." The boy left through the front door, somehow managing to retain possession of the goats and the wooden sword.

Christopher stood facing Beatrix, trying not to gape. And failing utterly. She might as well have been standing there in her undergarments. In fact, that would have been preferable, because at least it wouldn't have seemed so singularly erotic. He could see the feminine outline of her hips and thighs clad in the masculine garments. And she didn't seem at all self-conscious. Confound her, what kind of woman was she?

He struggled with his reaction to her, a mixture of annoyance, fascination, and arousal. With her hair threatening to tumble from its pins, and her cheeks flushed from exertion, she was the epitome of glowing female health.

"Why are you here?" she asked.

"I came to apologize," he said. "I was . . . discourteous yesterday."

"No, you were rude."

"You're right. I'm truly sorry." At her lack of response, Christopher fumbled for words. He, who had once spoken to women so glibly. "I've been too long in rough company. Since I left the Crimea, I find myself reacting irritably without cause. I . . . words are too important for me to be so careless with them."

Perhaps it was his imagination, but he thought her face softened a little.

"You don't have to be sorry for disliking me," she said. "Only for being discourteous."

"Rude," Christopher corrected. "And I don't."

"You don't what?" she asked with a frown.

"Dislike you. That is . . . I don't know you well enough to either like or dislike you."

"I'm fairly certain, Captain," she said, "that the more you discover about me, the more you will dislike me. Therefore, let's cut to the chase and acknowledge that we don't like each other. Then we won't have to bother with the in-between part."

She was so bloody frank and practical about the whole thing that Christopher couldn't help but be amused. "I'm afraid I can't oblige you."

"Why not?"

"Because when you said that just now, I found myself starting to like you."

"You'll recover," she said.

Her decisive tone made him want to smile. "It's getting worse, actually," he told her. "Now I'm absolutely convinced that I like you."

Beatrix gave him a patently skeptical stare. "What about my hedgehog? Do you like her, too?"

Christopher considered that. "Affection for rodents can't be rushed."

"Medusa isn't a rodent. She's an erinaceid."

"Why did you bring her to the picnic?" Christopher couldn't resist asking.

"Because I thought her company would be preferable to that of the people I would meet there." A faint smile played at the corners of her lips. "And I was right." She paused. "We're about to have tea," she said. "Will you join us?"

Christopher began to shake his head before she had even finished. They would ask questions, and he would have to come up with careful answers, and the thought of a prolonged conversation was wearying and anxiety provoking. "Thank you, but no. I—"

"It's a condition of my forgiveness," Beatrix said. Those dark blue eyes, lit with a provocative glint, stared directly into his.

Surprised and diverted, Christopher wondered how an unworldly young woman in her early twenties had the gall to give him orders.

However, it was turning out to be a strangely entertaining afternoon. Why not stay? He wasn't expected anywhere. And no matter how it turned out, it would be preferable to going back to those somber dark rooms at home. "In that case—" He broke off, startled, as Beatrix leaned toward him.

"Oh, bother." She was looking closely at the lapels of his tweed sack coat. "You're covered with goat hair." She began to brush at his lapels vigorously.

It took Christopher a full five seconds to remember how to breathe. "Miss Hathaway—" In her efforts to whisk away the scattering of stray goat hairs, she was standing much too close. He wanted her even closer. What would it feel like to wrap his arms around her, and press his cheek into that mass of shiny dark hair?

"Don't move," Beatrix said, continuing to bat at the front of his coat. "I've almost brushed it off."

"No, I don't . . . that's not . . ." Christopher's control broke. He snatched her slender wrists with his hands, holding them suspended. God, the feel of her . . . the smooth skin . . . the exquisite throb of her veins against his fingertips. A subtle tremor ran through her. He wanted to follow it with his hands, smooth his palms over the supple curves of her. He wanted to wrap her around him, her legs, her arms, her hair.

But despite her undeniable attractions, he would

never pursue a woman like Beatrix Hathaway, even if he weren't already in love with Prudence. What he truly wanted, needed, was a return to normalcy. To the kind of life that would restore him to peace.

Slowly Beatrix pulled her arms free of his manacling fingers. She stared at him, her gaze wary and intent.

They both started at the sound of approaching footsteps.

"Good afternoon," came a pleasant feminine voice.

It was the oldest Hathaway sister, Amelia. She was shorter and more voluptuous than her younger sister. There was a warm maternal air about her, as if she were prepared to ladle out sympathy and comfort at a moment's notice.

"Mrs. Rohan," Christopher murmured, and bowed.

"Sir," she replied with a questioning lilt. Although they had met before, she clearly didn't recognize him.

"This is Captain Phelan, Amelia," Beatrix said.

The blue eyes widened. "What a lovely surprise," she exclaimed, giving Christopher her hand.

"Captain Phelan and I dislike each other," Beatrix told her. "In fact, we're sworn enemies."

Christopher glanced at her quickly. "When did we become sworn enemies?"

Ignoring him, Beatrix said to her sister, "Regardless, he's staying for tea."

"Wonderful," Amelia said equably. "Why are you enemies, dear?"

"I met him yesterday while I was out walking," Beatrix explained. "And he called Medusa a 'garden pest,' and faulted me for bringing her to a picnic."

Amelia smiled at Christopher. "Medusa has been called many worse things around here, including 'diseased pincushion,' and 'perambulating cactus.'"

"I've never understood," Beatrix said, "why people have such unreasonable dislike of hedgehogs."

"They dig up the garden," Amelia said, "and they're not what one would call cuddlesome. Captain Phelan has a point, dear—you might have brought your cat to the picnic instead."

"Don't be silly. Cats don't like picnics nearly as much as hedgehogs."

The conversation proceeded at such quicksilver speed that there was little opportunity for Christopher to break in. Somehow he managed to find an opening. "I apologized to Miss Hathaway for my remarks," he told Amelia uncomfortably.

This earned an approving glance. "Delightful. A man who's not afraid to apologize. But really, apologies are wasted on our family—we're usually pleased by the things we should be offended by, and vice versa. Come in, Captain, you're among friends."

Christopher found himself being ushered into a bright, cheery house, with abundant windows and piles of books everywhere.

"Beatrix," Amelia said over her shoulder as they proceeded through the hallway. "Perhaps you should reconsider your attire. Poor Captain Phelan may find it somewhat shocking."

"But he's already seen me like this," came Beatrix's voice from behind Christopher, "and I've already shocked him. What is the point in changing clothes? Captain, would you feel more comfortable if I took my breeches off?"

"No," he said hastily.

"Good, I'll keep them on. Really, I don't see why women shouldn't dress like this all the time. One can walk freely and even leap. How is one to chase after a goat in skirts?"

"It's something the dressmakers should consider," Amelia said. "Although my concern is more in the direction of chasing after children, not goats."

They entered a room lined with a semicircular row of tall windows overlooking a spring garden. It was a comfortable room, with overstuffed furniture and embroidered pillows. A housemaid was busy setting out china plates on a tea table. Christopher couldn't help contrasting this cozy scene with yesterday's stilted teatime in the Phelans' immaculate formal parlor.

"Please set another place, Tillie," Amelia said. "We have a guest."

"Yes, mum." The housemaid looked distinctly worried. "Is the goat gone?"

"Entirely gone," came the soothing reply. "You may bring out the tea tray when it's ready." Amelia sent a mock frown to Christopher. "That goat has been nothing but trouble. And the dratted creature isn't even picturesque. Goats resemble nothing so much as badly dressed sheep."

"That's quite unfair," Beatrix said. "Goats have far more character and intelligence than sheep, who are nothing but followers. I've met far too many in London."

"Sheep?" Christopher asked blankly.

"My sister is speaking figuratively, Captain Phelan," Amelia said.

"Well, I have met some actual sheep in London," Beatrix said. "But yes, I was mainly referring to people. They all tell you the same gossip, which is tedious. They adhere to the current fashions and the popular opinions, no matter how silly. And one never improves in their company. One starts falling in line and baaing."

A quiet laugh came from the doorway as Cam Rohan entered the room. "Obviously Hathaways are not sheep. Because I've tried to herd the lot of you for years, without any success."

From what Christopher remembered of Rohan, he had worked at a London gaming club for a time, and then had made a fortune in manufacturing investments. Although his devotion to his wife and family was well-known in Stony Cross, Rohan was hardly the image of a staid and respectable patriarch. With his longish dark hair, exotic amber eyes, and the diamond stud flashing in his ear, his Romany heritage was obvious.

Approaching Christopher, Rohan exchanged a bow and surveyed him with a friendly gaze. "Captain Phelan. It is good to see you. We were hoping for your safe return."

"Thank you. I hope my presence is not an imposition."

"Not in the least. With Lord Ramsay and his wife still in London, and my brother Merripen and his wife visiting Ireland, it's been far too peaceful here of late." Rohan paused, a glitter of amusement entering his eyes. "Fugitive goats notwithstanding."

The ladies were seated, and finger bowls and napkins were brought out, followed by a sumptuously laden tea tray. As Amelia poured, Christopher noticed that she had added a few crushed green leaves to Beatrix's cup.

Seeing his interest, Amelia said, "My sister prefers her tea flavored with mint. Would you like some as well, Captain?"

"No, thank you, I . . ." Christopher's voice faded as he watched her stir a spoonful of honey into the cup.

"Every morning and afternoon I drink fresh mint tea sweetened with honey . . ."

The reminder of Prudence awakened the familiar

yearning, and Christopher steeled himself against it. He forced himself to focus solely on this situation, these people.

In the ensuing pause, he heard the sound of Albert barking outside. With despairing impatience, Christopher wondered if the blasted dog was ever going to be quiet.

"He wants to protect you," Beatrix said. "He's wondering where I've taken you."

Christopher let out a taut sigh. "Perhaps I shouldn't stay. He'll bark for hours."

"Nonsense. Albert must learn to adapt to your plans. I'll bring him inside."

Her authoritative manner rankled Christopher, no matter that she was right. "He might damage something," he said, rising to his feet.

"He can't do any worse than the goat," Beatrix replied, standing to face him.

Politely Rohan stood as well, watching the two of them.

"Miss Hathaway—" Christopher continued to object, but he fell silent, blinking, as she reached out and touched his chest. Her fingertips rested over his heart for the space of one heartbeat.

"Let me try," she said gently.

Christopher fell back a step, his breath catching. His body responded to her touch with disconcerting swiftness. A lady never put her hand to any area of a man's torso unless the circumstances were so extreme that . . . well, he couldn't even imagine what would justify it. Perhaps if his waistcoat was on fire, and she was trying to put it out. Other than that, he couldn't think of any defensible reason.

And yet if he were to point out the breach of etiquette, the act of correcting a lady was just as graceless. Troubled and aroused, Christopher gave her a single nod.

The men resumed their seats after Beatrix had left the room.

"Forgive us, Captain Phelan," Amelia murmured. "I can see that my sister startled you. Really, we've tried to learn better manners, but we're Philistines, all of us. And while Beatrix is out of hearing, I would like to assure you that she doesn't usually dress so outlandishly. However, every now and then she goes on an undertaking that makes long skirts inadvisable. Replacing a bird in a nest, for example, or training a horse, and so forth."

"A more conventional solution," Christopher said carefully, "would be to forbid the activity that necessitated the wearing of men's garments."

Rohan grinned. "One of my private rules for dealing with Hathaways," he said, "is never to forbid them anything. Because that guarantees they'll keep doing it."

"Heavens, we're not as bad as all that," Amelia protested.

Rohan gave his wife a speaking glance, his smile lingering. "Hathaways require freedom," he told Christopher, "Beatrix in particular. An ordinary life—being contained in parlors and drawing rooms—would be a prison for her. She relates to the world in a far more vital and natural way than any *gadji* I've ever known." Seeing Christopher's incomprehension, he added, "That's the word the Rom uses for females of your kind."

"And because of Beatrix," Amelia said, "we possess a menagerie of creatures no one else wants: a goat with an undershot jaw, a three-legged cat, a portly hedgehog, a mule with an unbalanced build, and so forth."

"A mule?" Christopher stared at her intently, but

before he could ask about it, Beatrix returned with Albert on the leash.

Christopher stood and moved to take the dog, but Beatrix shook her head. "Thank you, Captain, but I have him in hand."

Albert wagged his tail wildly at the sight of Christopher and lunged toward him with a bark.

"No," Beatrix scolded, pulling him back and putting her hand briefly to his muzzle. "Your master is safe. No need to make a fuss. Come." Reaching for a pillow from a low-backed settee, she placed it in the corner.

Christopher watched as she led the dog to the pillow and removed the leash. Albert whimpered and refused to lie down, but he remained obediently in the corner. "Stay," she told him.

To Christopher's amazement, Albert didn't move. A dog who thought nothing of running through gunfire was completely cowed by Beatrix Hathaway.

"I think he'll behave," Beatrix said, returning to the table. "But it would be best if we paid him no attention." She sat, placed a napkin in her lap, and reached for her teacup. She smiled as she saw Christopher's expression. "Be at ease, Captain," she said gently. "The more relaxed you are, the calmer he will be."

In the hour that followed, Christopher drank cups of hot sugared tea and let the gently animated conversation flow around him. Slowly, a string of tight, cold knots inside his chest began to loosen. A plate filled with sandwiches and tarts was set before him. Occasionally he glanced at Albert, who had settled in the corner, his chin on his paws.

The Hathaways were new in Christopher's experience. They were intelligent, amusing, their conversation veering and dashing in unexpected directions. And it was clear to him that the sisters were too clever for polite society. The one subject they didn't tread upon was the Crimea, for which Christopher was grateful. They seemed to understand that the topic of war was the last thing he wanted to discuss. For that reason among others, he liked them.

But Beatrix was a problem.

Christopher didn't know what to make of her. He was mystified and annoyed by the familiar way she spoke to him. And the sight of her in those breeches, her legs crossed like a man's, was unsettling. She was strange. Subversive and half tame.

When the tea was concluded, Christopher thanked them for the agreeable afternoon.

"You will call again soon, I hope," Amelia said.

"Yes," Christopher said, not meaning it. He was fairly certain that the Hathaways, although enjoyable, were best taken in small, infrequent doses.

"I'll walk with you to the edge of the forest," Beatrix announced, going to collect Albert.

Christopher suppressed a twinge of exasperation. "That won't be necessary, Miss Hathaway."

"Oh, I know it's not," she said. "But I want to."

Christopher's jaw tightened. He reached for Albert's leash.

"I have him," Beatrix said, retaining the leash.

Conscious of Rohan's amused regard, Christopher bit back a retort, and followed Beatrix from the house.

Amelia went to the parlor windows and watched the two distant figures proceed through the orchard toward the forest. The apple trees, frosted with light green buds and white blossoms, soon conspired to hide the pair from view.

She puzzled over the way Beatrix had behaved with the stern-faced soldier, pecking and chirping at him, almost as if she were trying to remind him of something he'd forgotten.

Cam joined her at the window, standing behind her. She leaned back against him, taking comfort in her husband's steady, strong presence. One of his hands glided along her front. She shivered in pleasure at the casual sensuality of his touch.

"Poor man," Amelia murmured, thinking of Phelan's haunting eyes. "I didn't recognize him at first. I wonder if he knows how much he has changed?"

Cam's lips played lightly at her temple as he replied. "I suspect he is realizing it now that he's home."

"He was very charming before. Now he seems so austere. And the way he stares sometimes, as if he's looking right through one . . ."

"He's spent two years burying his friends," Cam replied quietly. "And he's taken part in the kind of close combat that makes a man as hard as nails." He paused reflectively. "Some of it you can't leave behind. The faces of the men you kill stay with you forever."

Knowing that he was remembering a particular episode of his own past, Amelia turned and hugged herself close to him.

"The Rom don't believe in war," Cam said against her hair. "Conflict, arguing, fighting, yes. But not in taking the life of a man with whom one has no personal grievance. Which is one of many reasons why I would not make a good soldier."

"But for those same reasons, you make a *very* good husband."

Cam's arms tightened around her, and he whispered something in Romany. Although she didn't understand the words, the rough-soft sound of them caused her nerves to tingle.

Amelia nestled closer. With her cheek against his chest, she reflected aloud, "It's obvious that Beatrix is fascinated by Captain Phelan."

"She's always been drawn to wounded creatures."

"The wounded ones are often the most dangerous."

His hand moved in a soothing stroke along her spine. "We'll keep a close watch on her, *monisha*."

Beatrix kept pace easily with Christopher as they headed toward the forest. It nagged at him to have someone else holding Albert's leash. Beatrix's assertiveness was like a pebble lodged in the toe of his shoe. And yet when she was near, it was impossible to feel detached from his surroundings. She had a knack of keeping him anchored in the present.

He couldn't stop watching how her legs and hips moved in those breeches. What was her family thinking, to allow her to dress this way? Even in private it was unacceptable. A humorless smile curved his lips as he reflected that he had at least one thing in common with Beatrix Hathaway—neither of them was in step with the rest of the world.

The difference was that he wanted to be.

It had been so easy for him, before the war. He had always known the right thing to do or say. Now the prospect of reentering polite society seemed rather like playing a game in which he had forgotten the rules.

"Will you sell your army commission soon?" Beatrix asked.

Christopher nodded. "I'm leaving for London in a few days to make the arrangements."

"Oh." Beatrix's tone was noticeably subdued as she said, "I suppose you'll call on Prudence."

Christopher made a noncommittal sound. Inside his

coat pocket rested the small, tattered note he carried with him always.

> *I'm not who you think I am . . .*
> *Come back, please come home and find me.*

Yes. He would find her, and discover why she had written those haunting words. And then he would marry her.

"Now that your brother is gone," Beatrix said, "you'll have to learn how to manage the Riverton estate."

"Among other things," he said curtly.

"Riverton encompasses a large part of the forest of Arden."

"I was aware of that," Christopher said gently.

She didn't seem to notice the touch of sarcasm. "Some estate owners are overcutting, to supply the local manufacturing businesses. I hope you won't do that."

Christopher remained silent, hoping that would quell further conversation.

"Do you *want* to inherit Riverton?" Beatrix surprised him by asking.

"It doesn't matter whether I want it or not. I'm next in line, and I'll do what is required."

"But it does matter," Beatrix said. "That's why I asked."

Losing his patience, Christopher said, "The answer is no, I don't want it. It was always supposed to be for John. I feel like a bloody impostor trying to assume his place."

With anyone else, the burst of vehemence would have put an end to the questioning. But Beatrix persisted. "What would you have done if he was still alive? You would still sell your commission, wouldn't you?"

"Yes. I've had enough of the army."

"And then? What would you do?"

"I don't know."

"What are your aptitudes? Your talents?"

Their footsteps slowed as they reached the woods. His talents . . . he could hold his liquor, beat a man at billiards or cards, seduce a woman. He was a crack shot and an excellent rider.

Then Christopher thought of the thing in his life he had most been lauded for, and showered with praise and medals.

"I have one talent," he said, taking Albert's leash from Beatrix's hand. He looked down into her round eyes. "I'm good at killing."

Without another word, he left her standing at the edge of the forest.

Chapter Nine

In the week after Christopher had returned to Hampshire, the discord between him and his mother became so pronounced that they found it difficult to occupy the same room for more than a few minutes at a time. Poor Audrey did her best to serve as peacemaker, without much success.

Mrs. Phelan had fallen into a habit of relentless complaining. She couldn't go through a room without tossing out nagging comments like a flower girl flinging handfuls of petals at a wedding. Her nerves were acutely sensitive, obliging her to lie quietly in a dark room in the middle of the day, every day. A collection of aches and pains kept her from supervising the household, and as a result, nothing was ever done to her satisfaction.

During Mrs. Phelan's daily resting period, she reacted to the rattling of plates in the kitchen as if she had been stabbed with invisible knives. The murmur of voices or the thud of feet on the upper floors were agony to her nerves. The entire household had to tread upon eggs for fear of disturbing her.

"I've seen men who had just lost arms or legs and complained far less than my mother," Christopher told Audrey, who had grinned ruefully.

Sobering, Audrey said, "Lately she has become fixed in her mourning rituals ... almost as if her grieving will keep John with her in some way. I'm glad your uncle is coming for her tomorrow. The pattern of her days needs to be broken."

At least four mornings a week, Mrs. Phelan went to the family burial plot at the graveyard of the Stony Cross church, and spent an hour at John's grave. Since she did not want to go unaccompanied, she usually asked Audrey to go with her. However, yesterday Mrs. Phelan had insisted that Christopher escort her. He had waited for an hour in grim-faced silence while she knelt by John's headstone and let a few tears fall.

After she had finally indicated that she wished to rise, and Christopher had gone to help her to her feet, she had wanted him to kneel and pray as she had.

He hadn't been able to do it, not even to please her.

"I'll mourn in my own way," Christopher had told her. "At a time of my choosing, not yours."

"It's not decent," Mrs. Phelan said heatedly, "this lack of respect for him. Your brother deserves to be mourned, or at least be given a show of it, by the man who has profited so greatly by his death."

Christopher had stared at her in disbelief. "I have *profited*?" he had repeated in a low voice. "You know I never gave a damn about inheriting Riverton. I would give everything I have, if it would bring him back. If I could have sacrificed my life to save his, I would have."

"How I wish that had been possible," she had said acidly, and they had ridden back to the house in silence.

And all the while, Christopher had wondered how many hours she had sat at John's grave and wished that one son were in the place of the other.

John had been the perfect son, responsible and reliable. Christopher, however, had been the wilder, rougher son, sensual and reckless and careless. Like his father, William. Every time William had been caught up in some kind of scandal in London, often involving some other man's wife, Mrs. Phelan had been cold and distant to Christopher, as if he had been the designated proxy of her unfaithful husband. When William Phelan died as a result of being thrown by a horse, it had been whispered in London that the only surprise was that he had not been shot by some outraged husband or father of one of the women he had debauched.

Christopher had been twelve at the time. In his father's absence, he had gradually inhabited the role of wild-living rake. It seemed to have been expected of him. The truth was that he had reveled in the pleasures of the city, no matter that such enjoyments were fleeting and hollow. Being an army officer had been the perfect employment for him . . . he had found it enjoyable in every regard. Until, Christopher reflected with a grim, private smile, he'd actually been called to go to war.

Christopher had been far more effective in combat than he or anyone else had ever expected. And the more successful he'd become at bringing death to others, the more dead he had felt inside.

But there was Prudence. That was the only decent part of him left, the part that loved her. The thought of going to her filled him with agitation.

He still found it difficult to sleep, often waking up bolt upright in the middle of a nightmare. And there were moments in the day when he twitched at a sudden noise and found himself fumbling for a rifle that wasn't there. But he was certain all of that would improve in time.

It had to.

Chapter Ten

Obviously there was no reason to hope for anything, where Christopher Phelan was concerned. Beatrix kept reminding herself of that fact. He wanted Prudence. Beautiful, golden-haired, conventional Prudence.

It was the first time in Beatrix's life that she had wanted to be someone other than who she really was.

"I think you might be my only chance of becoming part of the world again . . ."

Perhaps Prudence, after all, was best suited to help Christopher. She was at ease with society in a way that Beatrix could never be. Very well. If that was best for him, Beatrix could not find it in her heart to blame him for that. The man had endured enough pain and hardship—Beatrix did not want to cause any further difficulties for him.

Except . . . she couldn't stop thinking about him. It was like an illness. It was impossible for her to carry on as usual. She was constantly on the verge of tears. She felt feverish and fatigued and bereft of appetite. In fact, she had become so morose that Amelia had insisted on brewing a pot of sorrel tonic for her.

"You're not yourself," Amelia had said. "You're usually so cheerful."

"Why should I be cheerful if there's no reason for it?" Beatrix had asked sullenly.

"Is there a reason to be miserable?"

Beatrix had longed to confide in her sister, but she had kept silent. There was nothing Amelia could do about the situation. Besides, telling a hundred people, a thousand, wouldn't have made her feel any better. She was pining for a man she could never have, and she didn't want to be told how ridiculous it was. She didn't even want to stop pining. The desperate strength of her wanting was her one frail link with Christopher.

She was so obsessed with him that she had actually considered going to London for the rest of the season. She would be able to visit Audrey, and she would also be able to see Christopher. Except that she would also be forced to see him with Prudence . . . dancing, flirting, courting . . . and Beatrix was quite certain that she couldn't bear that.

No, she would stay in Hampshire where she belonged.

Audrey had said that was a wise decision.

"He has changed, Bea, and not for the better. When Christopher first returned from the Crimea, I was so tempted to tell him the truth about the letters. That you were the one who had written to him, and not Prudence. But now I'm glad I didn't. I wouldn't want to encourage an attachment between you and Christopher. He's not himself. He drinks more than he should. He's easily startled. Sometimes he'll hear or see something that isn't there. And I know he's not sleeping—I often hear him wandering through the house at night. But when I try to talk to him, he brushes my questions away as if I'm being silly. And sometimes a simple

question—anything to do with the war, especially—
sends him into a rage that he has difficulty controlling.
I wonder . . ."

"What?" Beatrix whispered, wrenched with concern.

Audrey had looked at her directly. "I wonder if Prudence can manage him. He's so determined to have
her . . . but he's not the man he was. And Prudence
won't have the sense to realize it. I even wonder if he'll
be a danger to her."

Pondering Audrey's ominous words, Beatrix walked
to the Phelans' house with a mission in mind. Although
there was nothing she could do for Christopher, there
was a great deal she could do for Albert. An aggressive
dog was likely to do harm to others, and he would
be deprived of necessary love and attention. Dogs were
inherently sociable animals, and therefore Albert *must*
be taught how to get on with other creatures.

The Phelan housekeeper, Mrs. Clocker, greeted her
at the door and said that Audrey was not at home, but
was soon expected to return from a visit to the village.
"Will you want to wait for her, Miss Hathaway?"

"As a matter of fact, I would like to speak to Captain
Phelan on a particular business." Beatrix smiled faintly
at the housekeeper's questioning gaze. "I want to offer to
look after Albert while Captain Phelan is in London."

The housekeeper's eyes widened. "The master had
planned to leave the creature here, and have the servants look after it." Leaning close, she whispered, "He
is a hound of Hades, miss. The devil himself wouldn't
have such a dog."

Beatrix smiled sympathetically. "I hope that I may
influence him for the better. If Captain Phelan allows, I
will take Albert with me today, and relieve you of the
burden of managing him."

Mrs. Clocker looked positively exuberant. "Oh, that

is *very* kind of you, Miss Hathaway! I will inform Captain Phelan immediately." She hurried off as if she feared Beatrix might leave.

When Christopher's tall form entered the front receiving room, Beatrix was instantly covered with a full-bodied flush. *Stop this at once, Beatrix Hathaway,* she told herself sternly. *If you insist on being idiotic, you will have to go home and drink an entire bottle of sorrel tonic.*

"Miss Hathaway," Christopher said, bowing with meticulous politeness.

The dark smudges of sleeplessness beneath his eyes made him even more appealing, if that was possible, lending a human texture to the hard contours of his face.

Beatrix managed to pull up a casual smile. "Good morning, Captain Phelan."

"It's afternoon."

"Oh, is it?" She glanced over his shoulder at the mantel clock. Half-past twelve. "Good afternoon, then."

One of his brows lifted. "Is there something I may do for you?"

"The reverse, I hope. I would like to keep Albert with me at Ramsay House while you are away to London."

His eyes narrowed. "Why?"

"I want very much to help him adjust to his new life. Albert would receive the best of care, and I would work with him, train him . . ." Her voice faded as she saw his forbidding expression. It had not occurred to her that he might refuse her offer.

"Thank you, Miss Hathaway. But I think it in his best interests to remain here with the servants."

"You . . . you doubt I could help him?" Beatrix managed to ask.

"The dog is excitable. He has need of absolute peace

and quiet. I mean no offense in saying that the atmosphere at Ramsay House is too tumultuous for him."

Her brows rushed downward. "I beg your pardon, Captain, but you are entirely wrong. That is precisely the kind of environment Albert needs. You see, from a dog's perspective—"

"I don't need your advice."

"Yes you do," Beatrix said impulsively. "How can you be so certain that you're right? You could at least spare a moment to listen—I daresay I know more about dogs than you."

Christopher skewered her with the hard stare of a man who was not accustomed to having his decisions questioned. "No doubt you do. But I know more about this one."

"Yes, but—"

"It's time for you to leave, Miss Hathaway."

Beatrix was filled with a surge of bitter disappointment. "What do you think your servants will do with him in your absence?" she demanded, and rushed on before he could reply. "They'll keep him shut away in a shed, or locked in a room, because they're frightened of him, and that will make Albert even more of a danger. He's angry and anxious and lonely. He doesn't know what's expected of him. He needs constant attention and care, and I'm the only person who has the time and the willingness to provide those things."

"That dog has been my companion for two years," Christopher snapped. "The last thing I would subject him to is that bedlam of a household. He doesn't need chaos. He doesn't need noise and confusion—"

He was interrupted by an explosion of wild barking, accompanied by an earsplitting metallic crash. Albert had come racing through the entrance hall and had crossed paths with a housemaid bearing a tray of polished silver flatware.

Beatrix caught a glimpse of forks and spoons scattering to the doorway, just before she was thrown bodily to the receiving room floor. The impact robbed her of breath.

Stunned, she found herself pinned to the carpet and covered by a heavy masculine weight.

Dazedly she tried to take in the situation. Christopher had jumped on her. His arms were around her head . . . he had instinctively moved to shelter her with his own body. They lay together in a confusion of limbs and disheveled garments and panting breaths.

Lifting his head, Christopher cast a wary glance at their surroundings. For a moment, the blank ferocity of his face frightened Beatrix. *This,* she realized, was how he had looked in battle. This was what his enemies had seen as he had cut them down.

Albert rushed toward them, baying furiously.

"No," Beatrix said in a low tone, extending her arm to point at him. "Down."

The dog's barking flattened into a growl, and he slowly lowered to the floor. His gaze didn't move from his master.

Beatrix turned her attention back to Christopher. He was gasping and swallowing, struggling to regain his wits. "Christopher," she said carefully, but he didn't seem to hear. At this moment, no words would reach him.

She slid her arms around him, one at his shoulders, the other at his waist. He was a large man, superbly fit, his powerful body trembling. A feeling of searing tenderness swept through her, and she let her fingers stroke the rigid nape of his neck.

Albert whined softly, watching the two of them.

Beyond Christopher's shoulder, Beatrix glimpsed the housemaid standing uncertainly at the doorway, stray forks clutched in her hand.

Although Beatrix didn't give a fig about appearances or scandal, she cared very much about shielding Christopher during a vulnerable moment. He would not want anyone to see him when he was not fully in command of himself.

"Leave us," she said quietly.

"Yes, miss." Gratefully the maid fled, closing the door behind her.

Beatrix returned her attention to Christopher, who didn't seem to have noticed the exchange. Carefully she drew his head down and turned her cheek against his glinting amber hair. And she waited, letting him feel the even rhythm of her breathing.

The scent of him was clean, summery, like hot sun and saffron. Her eyes closed as she felt his body press along hers with intriguing firmness, his knees digging into the billowing mass of her skirts.

A minute passed, and another. For the rest of her life she would remember lying alone with him in a bright square of sunlight from the window . . . the delicious weight of him, the intimate heat of his breath collecting against her neck. She would have lived in that moment forever, if it were possible. *I love you,* she thought. *I am madly, desperately, permanently in love with you.*

His head lifted, and he looked down at her with bewildered gray eyes. "Beatrix." His ragged whisper thrilled along her nerves. His hands cradled her head, long fingers weaving gently through her tumbled dark locks. "Have I hurt you?"

Beatrix's stomach went tight. She shook her head, unable to speak. Oh, the way he was looking at her, *really* looking at her . . . this was the Christopher of her dreams. This was the man who had written to her. He was so caring, and real, and dazzling, that she wanted to weep.

"I thought . . ." Christopher broke off and drew his thumb over the hot surface of her cheek.

"I know," she whispered, her nerves sparking at his touch.

"I didn't mean to do that."

"I know."

His gaze went to her parted lips, lingering until she felt it like a caress. Her heart labored to supply blood to her nerveless limbs. Every breath caused her body to lift up against his, a teasing friction of firm flesh and clean, warm linen.

Beatrix was transfixed by the subtle changes in his face, the heightening color, the silver brightness of his eyes. Possibilities entered the quietness, like sun breaking through forest canopy.

She wondered if he were going to kiss her.

And a single word flashed through her mind.

Please.

Chapter Eleven

Christopher tensed against the shaking in his muscles. His heartbeat roared in his ears. He struggled to comprehend how he had so utterly lost control of the situation. A noise had startled him, and he had reacted without thinking. He had been aware of nothing until he had found himself lying over Beatrix, trying to protect her, trying to protect them both . . . and when the ferocious heartbeat had faded from his ears, he was suffused with the hideous awareness of what he had done.

Knocking a defenseless woman to the ground. Leaping on her like a madman. *Christ*. He felt disoriented, and more than a little crazed. He might have injured her.

He had to help her up, offer an apology. Instead he watched as his exploring fingertips went to her throat, stroking a tiny pulse. Holy hell, what was he doing?

It had been a long time since a woman had held him. It felt so good that he couldn't make himself release her just yet. Her body cradled his with supple feminine strength. Those slim, gentle fingers continued to stroke the back of his neck. He had never seen such blue eyes, clear and dark like Bristol blue glass.

Christopher tried to remember the reasons why he shouldn't want her. He even tried to summon thoughts of Prudence, but it was impossible. He closed his eyes and felt her breath striking his chin. He felt her everywhere, with his entire body, her scent in his nose and throat, her warmth sinking into him.

It seemed as if all the months and years of need had distilled to this one moment, this slender form tucked beneath his. He was actually afraid of what he might do to her. He knew he should roll away, put distance between them, but all he could do was gather in the sensations of her, the enticing rise and fall of her breasts, the feel of her legs splayed beneath the layers of her skirts. The stroke of her fingers on his nape raised chills of pleasure, and at the same time turned his flesh hot with need.

Desperately he groped for her hands and pinned them over her head.

Better.

And worse.

Her gaze provoked him, invited him closer. He could feel the force of will in her, radiant as heat, and everything in him responded to it. Fascinated, he watched a blush spread over her skin. He wanted to follow the spreading color with his fingers and mouth.

Instead he shook his head to clear it. "I'm sorry," he said, and took a rough breath. "I'm sorry," he repeated. A humorless laugh scraped in his throat. "I'm always apologizing to you."

Her wrists relaxed in his hold. "This wasn't your fault."

Christopher wondered how the hell she could appear

so composed. Aside from the stain of color in her cheeks, she showed no sign of unease. He had a quick, annoying sense of being managed. "I threw you to the floor."

"Not intentionally."

Her efforts to make him feel better were having the opposite effect. "Intentions don't matter when you've been knocked over by someone twice your size."

"Intentions always matter," Beatrix said. "And I'm used to being knocked over."

He let go of her hands. "This happens to you often?" he asked sardonically.

"Oh, yes. Dogs, children . . . everyone leaps on me."

Christopher could well understand that. Leaping on her was the most pleasurable thing he'd done in years. "Being neither a dog nor a child," he said, "I have no excuse."

"The maid dropped a tray. Your reaction was perfectly understandable."

"Was it?" Christopher asked bitterly, rolling off her. "I'll be damned if I understand it."

"Of course it was," Beatrix said as he helped her up from the floor. "For a long time you've been conditioned to dive for cover every time a shell or canister exploded, or a bullet was fired. Just because you've come back home doesn't mean that such reflexes can be easily discarded."

Christopher couldn't help wondering . . . Would Prudence have forgiven him so quickly, or reacted with such self-possession?

His face darkened as a new thought occurred to him. Did he have any right to go to Prudence, when his behavior was so unpredictable? He couldn't put her at risk. He had to gain control over himself. But how? His reflexes were too strong, too fast.

At Christopher's prolonged silence, Beatrix went to

Albert and bent to pet him. The dog rolled on his back, offering his tummy.

Christopher straightened his clothes and shoved his hands into his trouser pockets.

"Will you reconsider your decision?" Beatrix asked. "About letting me take Albert?"

"No," Christopher said brusquely.

"No?" she repeated, as if his refusal were inconceivable.

Christopher scowled. "You needn't worry about him. I've left the servants specific instructions. He will be well cared for."

Beatrix's face was taut with indignation. "I'm sure you believe so."

Nettled, he snapped, "I wish I took the same enjoyment in hearing your opinions that you take in airing them, Miss Hathaway."

"I stand by my opinions when I know I'm right, Captain Phelan. Whereas you stand by yours merely because you're stubborn."

Christopher gave her a stony stare. "I will escort you out."

"Don't bother. I know the way." She strode to the threshold, her back very straight.

Albert began to follow, until Christopher commanded him to come back.

Pausing at the threshold, Beatrix turned to give Christopher an oddly intent stare. "Please convey my fondness to Audrey. You both have my hopes for a pleasant journey to London." She hesitated. "If you wouldn't mind, please relay my good wishes to Prudence when you see her, and give her a message."

"What is it?"

"Tell her," Beatrix said quietly, "that I won't break my promise."

"What promise is that?"

"She'll understand."

Precisely three days after Christopher and Audrey had left for London, Beatrix went to the Phelans' house to ask after Albert. As she had expected, the dog had set the household into chaos, having barked and howled incessantly, ripped carpeting and upholstery to shreds, and bitten a footman's hand.

"And in addition," the housekeeper, Mrs. Clocker, told Beatrix, "he won't eat. One can already see his ribs. And the master will be furious if we let anything happen to him. Oh, this is the most trying dog, the most detestable creature I've ever encountered."

A housemaid who was busy polishing the banister couldn't seem to resist commenting, "He scares me witless. I can't sleep at night, because he howls fit to wake the dead."

The housekeeper looked aggrieved. "So he does. However, the master said we mustn't let anyone take Albert. And as much as I long to be rid of the vicious beast, I fear the master's displeasure even more."

"I can help him," Beatrix said softly. "I know I can."

"The master or the dog?" Mrs. Clocker asked, as if she couldn't help herself. Her tone was wry and despairing.

"I can start with the dog," Beatrix said in a low undertone.

They exchanged a glance.

"I wish you could be given the chance," Mrs. Clocker murmured. "This household doesn't seem like a place where anyone could get better. It feels like a place where things wane and are extinguished."

This, more than anything, spurred Beatrix into a decision. "Mrs. Clocker, I would never ask you to disobey Captain Phelan's instructions. However . . . if I were to *overhear* you telling one of the housemaids where Albert is being kept at the moment, that's hardly your fault, is it? And if Albert manages to escape and run off . . . and if some unknown person were to take Albert in and care for him but did not tell you about it immediately, you could not be blamed, could you?"

Mrs. Clocker beamed at her. "You are devious, Miss Hathaway."

Beatrix smiled. "Yes, I know."

The housekeeper turned to the housemaid. "Nellie," she said clearly and distinctly. "I want to remind you that we're keeping Albert in the little blue shed next to the kitchen garden.

"Yes, mum." The housemaid didn't even glance at Beatrix. "And I should remind *you,* mum, that his leash is on the half-moon table in the entrance hall."

"Very good, Nellie. Perhaps you should run and tell the other servants and the gardener not to notice if anyone goes out to visit the blue shed."

"Yes, mum."

As the housemaid hurried away, Mrs. Clocker gave Beatrix a grateful glance. "I've heard that you work miracles with animals, Miss Hathaway. And that's indeed what it will take, to tame that flea-ridden fiend."

"I offer no miracles," Beatrix said with a smile. "Merely persistence."

"God bless you, miss. He's a savage creature. If dog is man's best friend, I worry for Captain Phelan."

"So do I," Beatrix said sincerely.

In a few minutes she had found the blue shed.

The shed, built to contain light gardening implements, shuddered as the creature inside lunged against the wall. A fury of barking erupted as Beatrix drew closer. Although Beatrix had no doubt of her ability to handle him, his ferocious baying, which sounded almost unearthly, was enough to give her pause.

"Albert?"

The barking became more passionate, with cries and whimpers breaking in.

Slowly Beatrix lowered to the ground and sat with her back against the shed. "Calm yourself, Albert," she said. "I'll let you out as soon as you're quiet."

The terrier growled and pawed at the door.

Having consulted several books on the subject of dogs, one on rough terriers in particular, Beatrix was fairly certain that training Albert with techniques involving dominance or punishment would not be at all effective. In fact, they would probably make his behavior worse. Terriers, the book had said, frequently tried to outsmart humans. The only method left was to reward his good behavior with praise and food and kindness.

"Of course you're unhappy, poor boy. He's gone away, and your place is by his side. But I've come to collect you, and while he's gone, we'll work on your manners. Perhaps we can't turn you into a perfect lapdog . . . but I'll help you learn to get on with others." She paused before adding with a reflective grin, "Of course, I can't manage to behave properly in polite society. I've always thought there's a fair amount of dishonesty involved in politeness. There, you're quiet now." She stood and pulled at the latch. "Here is your first rule, Albert: it's very rude to maul people."

Albert burst out and jumped on her. Had she not been holding on to the support of the shed's frame, she would have been knocked over. Whining and wagging his tail, Albert stood on his hind legs and dove his face against her. He was rawboned and ragged, and distinctly malodorous.

"My good boy," Beatrix said, petting and scratching

his coarse fur. She tried to slip the leash around his neck, but was prevented as he wriggled to his back, his quivering legs stuck straight into the air. Laughing, she obliged him with a tummy rub. "Come home with me, Albert. I think you'll do very well with the Hathaways—or at least you will after I've given you a bath."

Chapter Twelve

Christopher delivered Audrey safely to London, where her family, the Kelseys, had welcomed her eagerly. The large Kelsey brood was overjoyed to have their sister with them. For reasons no one had quite understood, Audrey had refused to allow any of her relations to come stay with her in Hampshire after John's death. She had insisted on grieving with Mrs. Phelan unaccompanied by anyone else.

"Your mother was the only one who felt John's loss as keenly as I did," Audrey had explained to Christopher during the carriage drive to London. "There was a kind of relief in that. Any of my family would have tried to make me feel better, and surrounded me with love and comfort, which would have kept me from grieving properly. The whole thing would have been drawn out. No, it was the right thing to live in grief for as long as I needed. Now it's time to recover."

"You're very good at organizing your feelings, aren't you?" Christopher had asked dryly.

"I suppose I am. I wish I could organize yours. At present they seem to resemble an overturned drawer of neckcloths."

"Not neckcloths," he said. "Flatware, with sharp edges."

Audrey had smiled. "I pity those who find themselves in the way of your feelings." Pausing, she had studied Christopher with fond concern. "How difficult it is to look at you," she commented, startling him. "It's the resemblance you bear to John. You're more handsome than he was, of course, but I preferred his face. A wonderful everyday face—I never tired of it. Yours is a bit too intimidating for my taste. You resemble an aristocrat far more than John did, you know."

Christopher's gaze darkened as he thought of some of the men he'd fought with, who'd been fortunate to survive their wounds, but had suffered some manner of disfigurement. They had wondered how they would be received upon their return home, if wives or sweethearts would turn away in horror from their ruined appearances. "It doesn't matter what someone looks like," he said. "All that matters is what he is."

"I'm so very glad to hear you say that."

Christopher gave her a speculative glance. "What are you leading to?"

"Nothing. Except . . . I want to ask you something. If another woman—say, Beatrix Hathaway—and Prudence Mercer were to exchange appearances, and all that you esteemed in Prudence was transferred to Beatrix . . . would you want Beatrix?"

"Good God, no."

"Why not?" she asked indignantly.

"Because I know Beatrix Hathaway, and she's nothing like Pru."

"You do not know Beatrix. You haven't spent nearly enough time with her."

"I know that she's unruly, opinionated, and far more cheerful than any reasoning person should be. She wears breeches, climbs trees, and roams wherever she pleases without a chaperone. I also know that she has overrun Ramsay House with squirrels, hedgehogs, and goats, and the man unlucky enough to marry her will be driven to financial ruin from the veterinary bills. Would you care to contradict any of those points?"

Audrey folded her arms and gave him a sour look. "Yes. She doesn't have a squirrel."

Reaching inside his coat, Christopher pulled out the letter from Pru, the one he carried with him always. It had become a talisman, a symbol of what he had fought for. A reason for living. He looked down at the bit of folded paper, not even needing to open it. The words had been seared into his heart.

"Please come home and find me . . ."

In the past he had wondered if he were incapable of love. None of his love affairs had ever lasted more than a matter of months, and although they had blazed on a physical level, they had never transcended that. Ultimately no particular woman had ever seemed all that different from the rest.

Until those letters. The sentences had looped around him with a spirit so artless and adorable, he had loved it, loved her, immediately.

His thumb moved over the parchment as if it were sensitive living skin. "Mark my words, Audrey—I'm going to marry the woman who wrote this letter."

"I am marking your words," she assured him. "We'll see if you live up to them."

The London season would last until August, when Parliament ended and the aristocracy would retire to their country estates. There they would hunt, shoot, and indulge in Friday-to-Monday amusements. While in town, Christopher would sell his army commission and meet with his grandfather to discuss his new responsibilities as the heir of Riverton. He would also renew acquaintances with old friends and spend time with some men from his regiment.

And most importantly, he would find Prudence.

Christopher was uncertain how to approach her, after the way she had broken off their correspondence.

It was his fault. He had declared himself too early. He had been too impetuous.

No doubt Prudence had been wise to break off their communications. She was a gently bred young woman. Serious courtship had to be approached with patience and moderation.

If that was what Prudence wanted of him, she would have it.

He arranged for a suite of rooms at the Rutledge, an elegant hotel favored by European royalty, American entrepreneurs, and British aristocrats who did not maintain town residences. The Rutledge was unparalleled in comfort and luxury, and was arguably worth the exorbitant price of lodging there. As Christopher checked into the hotel and conversed with the concierge, he remarked on a portrait that hung over the marble mantel in the lobby. The subject was a singularly beautiful woman with mahogany-colored hair and striking blue eyes.

"That is a portrait of Mrs. Rutledge, sir," the concierge said with a touch of fond pride. "A beauty, is she not? A better, kinder lady could not be found anywhere."

Christopher regarded the portrait with casual interest. He recalled that Amelia Hathaway had said one of her sisters had married Harry Rutledge, the owner of the hotel. "Then Mrs. Rutledge is one of the Hathaway sisters of Hampshire?"

"Just so, sir."

That had brought a quizzical smile to Christopher's
lips. Harry Rutledge, being a wealthy and well-connected
man, could have had any woman he wanted. What madness had inspired him to marry into such a family? It
was the eyes, Christopher decided, looking closer, un-
willingly fascinated. Hathaway blue, heavily lashed.
Exactly like Beatrix's.

The day after Christopher took up residence in the
Rutledge, invitations flooded in. Balls, soirees, dinners,
musical evenings . . . even a summons to dine at Buck-
ingham Palace, where the composer Johann Strauss and
his orchestra would play.

After a few inquiries, Christopher accepted an invitation to a private ball that, it was confirmed, Miss Prudence Mercer and her mother had consented to attend.
The ball was held at a Mayfair mansion, built on a grand
scale in the Italianate style, with an extensive outer fore-
court and a central balconied hall that rose three full
stories. Populated by aristocrats, foreign diplomats, and
celebrated artists in various fields, the ball was a glittering display of wealth and social prominence.

The crowded atmosphere engendered a feeling of
vague panic in Christopher's chest. Battening down
the anxiety, he went to exchange pleasantries with the
hosts. Although he would have preferred to wear civilian attire, he was obliged to wear his dress uniform of
rifle green and black, with epaulettes of worsted crescents at the shoulders. As his commission had not yet
been sold, it would have caused much comment and
disapproval had he not worn the uniform. Worse, he
was also obliged to wear all the medals that had been
bestowed on him—to leave one off would have been in
bad form. The medals had been intended as badges of
honor. To Christopher, they represented events he longed
to forget.

There were other officers in their various uniforms, scarlet or black trimmed with gold. The attention they garnered, especially from women, only increased Christopher's unease.

He searched for Prudence, but she wasn't in the parlor or drawing room. Minute after painstaking minute he made his way through the crowd, stopping frequently as he was recognized by an acquaintance and forced to make conversation.

Where the devil was Prudence?

"... *you could pick me out of a crowd blindfolded. Simply follow the scent of scorched stockings.*"

The thought brought a faint smile to his lips.

Restless and full of wanting, he went into the ballroom. His heartbeat had lodged in the base of his throat.

His breath fractured as he saw her.

Prudence was even more beautiful than he had remembered. She wore a pink gown with lace-trimmed ruffles, her hands tucked into little white gloves. Having just concluded a dance, she stood chatting with an admirer, her expression serene.

Christopher felt as if he had traveled a million miles to reach her. The extent of his own need stunned him. The sight of her, along with the luminous echo of her words, gave him a sense of something he had not felt for a long time.

Hope.

As Christopher reached her, Prudence turned and looked up at him. Her clear green eyes widened, and she laughed with incredulous delight. "My dear Captain Phelan." She extended her gloved hand, and he bent over it and closed his eyes briefly. Her hand in his.

How long he had waited for this moment. How he had dreamed of it.

"As dashing as ever." Prudence smiled at him.

"More so, actually. How does it feel to have so many medals pinned to one's chest?"

"Heavy," he said, and she laughed.

"I had despaired of ever seeing you . . ."

Thinking at first that she was referring to the Crimea, Christopher felt a thrill of heat.

But she continued, ". . . since you've been unforgivably elusive upon returning to England." She curved her lips in a provocative smile. "But of course you knew that would only make you more sought after."

"Believe me," he said, "it is not my wish to be sought after."

"You are, however. Every host and hostess in London would love to claim you as a guest." A delicate giggle escaped her. "And every girl wants to marry you."

He wanted to hold her. He wanted to bury his face in her hair. "I may not be fit to marry."

"*La,* of course you are. You're a national hero *and* the heir to Riverton. A man can scarcely be more fit than that."

Christopher stared into her beautiful, fine-featured face, at the gleam of her pearly teeth. She was talking to him as she always had, flirtatious, light, teasing.

"The inheritance of Riverton is hardly a foregone conclusion," he told her. "My grandfather could leave it to one of my cousins."

"After the way you distinguished yourself in the Crimea? I doubt that." She smiled at him. "What moved you to finally make your appearance in society?"

He replied in a low voice. "I followed my lodestar."

"Your . . ." Prudence hesitated and smiled. "Oh, yes. I remember."

But something about that hesitation bothered him.

The hot, joyous urgency began to fade.

No doubt it was unreasonable of him to expect

Prudence to remember everything. Christopher had read her letters a thousand times, until every word had been permanently engraved on his soul. But he could hardly expect that she would have done the same. Her life had gone on much the same. His had changed in every regard.

"Do you still like to dance, Captain?" she asked, her long lashes sweeping over vivid green eyes.

"With you as a partner, yes." He proffered his arm, and she took it without hesitation.

They danced. The woman he loved was in his arms.

It should have been the finest night of his life. But in a matter of minutes he began to realize that the long-awaited relief was no more substantial than a bridge made of smoke.

Something was wrong.

Something wasn't real.

Chapter Thirteen

In the weeks that followed, Christopher frequently re-called what Audrey had said about Prudence, that there was nothing beneath the layers of artifice. But there had to be. He hadn't imagined those letters. *Someone* had written them.

He had asked Prudence early on about the last letter she had written ... *"I'm not who you think I am"* ... about what she had meant, and why she had stopped corresponding with him.

Prudence had turned red and looked awkward, so different from her usual fetching blushes. It was the first sign of real emotion he had seen in her. "I ... I suppose I wrote that because ... I was embarrassed, you see."

"Why?" Christopher had asked tenderly, drawing her farther into the shadowed corner of a balcony ter-race. He had touched her upper arms with his gloved hands, exerting the faintest of pressures to bring her closer. "I adored the things you wrote." Longing pressed against his heart and made his pulse unsteady. "When you stopped ... I would have gone mad, except ... you asked me to come find you."

"Oh, yes, so I did. I suppose . . . I was alarmed by how I had behaved, writing such silly things . . ."

He eased her closer, every movement careful, as if she were infinitely fragile. His mouth pressed against the thin, delicate skin of her temple. "Pru . . . I dreamed of holding you like this . . . all those nights . . ."

Her arms slid around his neck, and her head tipped back naturally. He kissed her, his mouth gentle and searching. She responded at once, her lips parting softly. It was a lovely kiss. But it did nothing to satisfy him, nothing to ease the angry ache of need. It seemed that his dreams of kissing Prudence had somehow eclipsed reality.

Dreams had a way of doing that.

Prudence turned her face aside with a discomfited laugh. "You're very eager."

"Forgive me." Christopher released her at once. She stayed close to him, the floral scent of her perfume thickening the air around them. He kept his hands on her, his palms curving around her shoulders. He kept expecting to feel something . . . but the region around his heart was locked in ice.

Somehow he had thought . . . but that was unreasonable. No woman on earth could have fulfilled such expectations.

For the duration of the season, Christopher sought out Prudence, meeting her at dances and dinners, taking her and Mrs. Mercer on carriage drives, scenic walks, and to art and museum exhibits.

There was little that Christopher could fault in Prudence. She was beautiful and charming. She didn't ask uncomfortable questions. In fact, she rarely asked personal questions of him at all. She evinced no interest in the war or the battles he had fought, only in his medals.

He wondered if she thought of them as anything more than shiny decorations.

They had the same bland and pleasant conversations, spiced with gossip, that Christopher had had a thousand times before, with other women, during other seasons in London. And that had always been enough for him.

He wished to hell it were enough now.

He had thought . . . hoped . . . that Prudence cared for him in some way. But there was no sign of that now, no tenderness, no trace of the woman who had written *"I carry thoughts of you like my own personal constellation . . ."*

And he loved her so desperately, the Prudence of the letters. Where was she? Why was she hiding from him?

His dreams led him into dark forests, where he searched through bramble and bracken, pushing through the narrow spaces between the trees as he followed the pale form of a woman. She was always just ahead of him, always out of reach. He woke gasping and enraged, his hands clutching on emptiness.

During the days, Christopher kept his business appointments and social engagements. So many tiny, overstuffed, overdecorated rooms. So much pointless conversation. So many events of no consequence. He could not fathom that he had once enjoyed it all. And he was appalled to find himself remembering moments in the Crimea with something like nostalgia, actually yearning for the brief times when he had felt fully alive.

Even with the enemy in battle he had felt some form of connection, in their efforts to understand and reach and kill each other. But with these patricians trussed in elegant clothes and brittle sophistication, he no longer felt kinship or liking. He knew himself to be different. And he knew they sensed it as well.

Christopher comprehended just how desperate he was for something or someone familiar, when the prospect of visiting his grandfather was actually appealing.

Lord Annandale had always been a stern and intimidating grandparent, never one to spare his withering comments. None of Annandale's grandchildren, including the cousin who would someday inherit the earldom, had ever pleased the demanding old bastard. Except for John, of course. Christopher had deliberately gone the other way.

Christopher approached his grandfather with a mixture of dread and reluctant compassion, knowing that the old man must have been devastated by John's death.

Upon arriving at Annandale's luxuriously appointed London house, Christopher was shown to the library, where a fire had been lit in the hearth despite the fact that it was the height of summer.

"Good God, Grandfather," he said, nearly recoiling at the blast of heat as he entered the library. "You'll have us braised like a pair of game hens." Striding to the window, he flung it open and drew in a breath of outside air. "You could easily heat yourself with a walk out-of-doors."

His grandfather scowled at him from a chair beside the hearth. "The doctor has advised against outside air. I would advise you to negotiate your inheritance before you try to finish me off."

"There's nothing to negotiate. Leave me whatever you wish—or nothing, if it pleases you."

"Manipulative as always," Annandale muttered. "You assume I'll do the reverse of whatever you say."

Christopher smiled and shrugged out of his coat. He tossed it to a nearby chair as he approached his grandfather. He went to shake his hand, enclosing the frail and cold fingers in his own warm grasp. "Hello, sir. You're looking well."

"I am not well," Annandale retorted. "I'm old. Navigating life with this body is like trying to sail a shipwreck."

Taking the other chair, Christopher studied his grandfather. There was a new delicacy about Annandale, his skin like swaths of crumpled silk laid over an iron frame. The eyes, however, were the same, bright and piercing. And his brows, in defiance of the snowy whiteness of his hair, were the same thick black as ever.

"I've missed you," Christopher commented in a tone of mild surprise. "Though I can't decide why. It must be the glare—it brings me back to my childhood."

"You were ever a hellion," Annandale informed him, "and selfish to the bone. When I read Russell's reports of your battlefield heroics, I was certain they had mistaken you for someone else."

Christopher grinned. "If I was heroic, it was purely accidental. I was only trying to save my own skin."

A rumble of amusement came from the old man's throat before he could prevent it. His brows lowered again. "You conducted yourself with honor, it seems. There is talk of a knighthood being bestowed on you. To that end, you might try being receptive to the queen's invitations. Your refusal to stay in London upon your return from the Crimea was not well regarded."

Christopher gave him a baleful glance. "I don't want to entertain people like some trained monkey. I'm no different from thousands of other men who did what they were supposed to do."

"Such modesty is new for you," his grandfather observed idly. "Is it genuine, or merely for my benefit?"

Remaining morosely silent, Christopher tugged irritably at his cravat, untied and unwound it, and let it

hang on either side of his neck. When that didn't serve
to cool him, he went to the open window.

He looked down at the street. It was crowded and
quarrelsome—people lived out in public in the warmer
months—sitting or standing in doorways, eating,
drinking, and talking while vehicles and hooves stirred
up hot fetid dust. Christopher's attention was caught by
a dog that sat in the back of a little cart as his master
guided a swaybacked pony along the thoroughfare.
Thinking of Albert, he was wrenched with remorse.
He wished he had brought the dog to London. But no,
the hubbub and the confinement would have driven
poor Albert mad. He was better off in the country.

He dragged his attention back to his grandfather,
realizing that he was saying something.

". . . have reconsidered the question of your inheritance. I had originally set aside very little for you. The
lion's share was, of course, for your brother. If there
was ever a man who deserved Riverton more than John
Phelan, I have not met him."

"Agreed," Christopher said quietly.

"But now he is gone with no heir, which leaves only
you. And though your character has shown signs of
improvement, I'm not convinced that you're worthy of
Riverton."

"Neither am I." Christopher paused. "I want nothing
that you had originally intended for John."

"I will tell you what you will have, regardless of
what you want." Annandale's tone was firm, but not
unkind. "You have responsibilities, my boy, and they
are not to be dismissed or evaded. But before I lay out
your course, I want to ask something."

Christopher regarded him without expression. "Yes,
sir."

"Why did you fight as you did? Why did you risk

death so often? Did you do it for the good of the country?"

Christopher snorted in disgust. "The war wasn't for the good of the country. It was for the benefit of private mercantile interests, and fueled by the conceit of politicians."

"You fought for the glory and the medals, then?"

"Hardly."

"Then why?"

Silently Christopher sorted through possible answers. Finding the truth, he examined it with weary resignation before he spoke. "Everything I did was for my men. For the noncommissioned ones who had joined the army to avoid starvation or the workhouse. And for the junior officers who were experienced and long-serving but hadn't the means to buy a commission. I had the command only because I'd had money to purchase it, not for any reason of merit. Absurd. And the men in my company, the poor bastards, were supposed to follow me, whether I proved to be incompetent, an imbecile, or a coward. They had no choice but to depend on me. And therefore I had no choice but to try and be the leader they needed. I tried to keep them alive." He hesitated. "I failed far too often. And now I would love for someone to tell me how to live with their deaths on my conscience." Focusing blindly on a distant patch of carpeting, he heard himself say, "I don't want Riverton. I've had enough of being given things I don't deserve."

Annandale looked at him in a way he never had before, speculative and almost kind. "That is why you will have it. I won't pare a shilling or a single inch of land from what I would have given John. I am willing to gamble that you will care for your tenants and workingmen out of the same sense of responsibility you felt for your men." He paused. "Perhaps you and Riverton will be good for each other. It was to be John's burden. Now it is yours."

As a slow, hot August settled over London, the coagulating stench began to drive the town dwellers to the sweeter air of the country. Christopher was more than ready to return to Hampshire. It was becoming apparent that London had done him no good.

Nearly every day was fraught with images that leaped at him from nowhere, startlements, difficulty in concentrating. Nightmares and sweats when he slept, melancholy when he awakened. He heard the sound of guns and shells when there were none, felt his heartbeat begin to hammer or his hands tremble for no reason. It was impossible to lower his guard, regardless of the circumstances. He had visited old friends in his regiment, but when he had tentatively asked if they were suffering from the same mysterious ailments, he was met with determined silence. It was not to be discussed. It was to be managed alone, and privately, in any manner that worked.

The only thing that helped was strong spirits. Christopher dosed himself until the warm, blurring comfort of alcohol quieted his seething brain. And he tried to measure its effects so that he could be sober when he had to. Concealing the encroaching madness as well as he could, he wondered when or how or if he was going to get better.

As for Prudence . . . she was a dream he had to let go of. A ruined illusion. Part of him died a little more each time he saw her. She felt no real love for him, that was clear. Nothing like what she had written. Perhaps in an effort to entertain him, she had culled parts of novels or plays, and copied them into the letters. He had believed in an illusion.

He knew that Prudence and her parents hoped he would offer for her, now that the season was drawing to a close. Her mother, in particular, had been hinting heavily about marriage, a dowry, promises of beautiful children and domestic tranquility. He was in no condition, however, to be a fit husband for anyone.

With mingled dread and relief, Christopher went to the Mercers' London residence to make his farewells. When he asked for permission to speak privately with Prudence, her mother left them in the parlor for a few minutes with the door left conspicuously open.

"But . . . but . . ." Prudence said in dismay when he told her he was leaving town, "you won't go without first talking to my father, will you?"

"Talk to him about what?" Christopher asked, although he knew.

"I should think you'd want to ask for his permission to court me formally," Prudence said, looking indignant.

He met her green eyes directly. "At the moment, I'm not at liberty to do that."

"Not at liberty?" Prudence jumped up, obliging him to stand, and gave him a glance of baffled fury. "Of course you are. There is no other woman, is there?"

"No."

"Your business affairs are settled, and your inheritance is in order?"

"Yes."

"Then there is no reason to wait. You've certainly given every impression that you care for me. Especially when you first returned—you told me so many times how you had longed to see me, how much I had meant to you . . . Why have your passions cooled?"

"I expected—hoped—that you would be more like you were in the letters." Christopher paused, staring at her closely. "I've often wondered . . . did someone help you to write them?"

Although Prudence had the face of an angel, the fury in her eyes was the exact opposite of heavenly serenity. "Oh! Why are you always asking me about those stupid letters? They were only words. Words mean nothing!"

"You've made me realize that words are the most important things in the world . . ."

"Nothing," Christopher repeated, staring at her.

"Yes." Prudence looked slightly mollified as she saw that she had gained his entire attention. "I'm here, Christopher. I'm real. You don't need silly old letters now. You have *me*."

"What about when you wrote to me about the quintessence?" he asked. "Did that mean nothing?"

"The—" Prudence stared at him, flushing. "I can't recall what I meant by that."

"The fifth element, according to Aristotle," he prompted gently.

Her color drained, leaving her bone-white. She looked like a guilty child caught in an act of mischief. "What has that to do with anything?" she cried, taking refuge in anger. "I want to talk about something real. Who cares about Aristotle?"

"I do like the idea that there's a little starlight in each of us . . ."

She had never written those words.

For a moment Christopher couldn't react. One thought followed another, each connecting briefly like the hands of men in a torch race. Some entirely different woman had written to him . . . with Prudence's consent . . . he had been deceived . . . Audrey must have known . . . he had been made to care . . . and then the letters had stopped. *Why?*

"I'm not who you think I am . . ."

Christopher felt his throat and chest tightening, heard a rasp of something that sounded like a wondering laugh.

Prudence laughed as well, the sound edged with relief. She had no idea in hell what had caused his bitter amusement.

Had they wanted to make a fool of him? Had it been intended as revenge for some past slight? By God, he would find who had done it, and why.

He had loved and been betrayed by someone whose name he didn't know. He loved her still—that was the unforgivable part. And she would pay, whoever she was.

It felt good to have a purpose again, to hunt someone for the purpose of inflicting damage. It felt familiar. It was who he was.

His smile, thin as a knife edge, cut through the cold fury.

Prudence gazed at him uncertainly. "Christopher?" she faltered. "What are you thinking?"

He went to her and took her shoulders in his hands, thinking briefly of how easy it would be to slide his hands up to her neck and throttle her. He shaped his mouth into a charming smile. "Only that you're right," he said. "Words aren't important. This is what's important." He kissed her slowly, expertly, until he felt her slender body relax against his. Prudence made a little sound of pleasure, her arms linking around his neck. "Before I leave for Hampshire," Christopher murmured against her blushing cheek, "I'll ask your father for formal permission to court you. Does that please you?"

"Oh, yes," Prudence cried, her face radiant. "Oh, Christopher . . . do I have your heart?"

"You have my heart," Christopher said tonelessly,

holding her close, while his cold gaze fastened on a distant point outside the window.

Except that he had no heart left to give.

"Where is she?" were Christopher's first words to Audrey, the moment he had reached her parents' home in Kensington. He had gone to her immediately after leaving Prudence. "*Who* is she?"

His sister-in-law seemed unimpressed by his fury. "Please do not scowl at me. What are you talking about?"

"Did Prudence put the letters directly into your hand, or did someone else give them to you?"

"Oh." Audrey looked serene. Sitting on the parlor settee, she took up a small needlework hoop and examined a patch of embroidery. "So you've finally realized that Prudence didn't write them. What gave her away?"

"The fact that she knew the contents of my letters, but nothing of the ones *she* sent." Christopher stood over her, glowering. "It was one of her friends, wasn't it? Tell me which one."

"I can confirm nothing."

"Was Beatrix Hathaway part of it?"

Audrey rolled her eyes. "Why would Beatrix want to take part in something like this?"

"Revenge. Because I once said that she belonged in the stables."

"You denied having said that."

"*You* said that I said it! Set that hoop down, or I swear I'll wrap it around your throat. Understand something, Audrey: I am scarred from neck to foot. I have been shot, stabbed, bayoneted, struck by shrapnel, and treated by doctors so drunk they could barely stay on their feet." A savage pause. "And none of that hurt like this."

"I'm sorry," Audrey said in a subdued tone. "I would

never have agreed to any scheme that I thought would cause you unhappiness. It began as an act of kindness. At least that's what I believe."

Kindness? Christopher was revolted by the idea that he had been viewed as the object of pity. "Why in God's name did you help someone to deceive me?"

"I was barely aware of it," she flared. "I was half dead from caring for John—I wasn't eating or sleeping—and I was exhausted. I didn't think much about it at all, other than to decide that it would do no harm for someone to write to you."

"It did, damn you!"

"You wanted to believe it was Prudence," she accused. "Otherwise it would have been obvious that she wasn't the author of the letters."

"I was in the middle of a bloody *war.* I didn't have time to examine participles and prepositions while hauling my arse in and out of trenches—"

He was interrupted by a voice from the doorway. "Audrey." It was one of her tall, strapping brothers, Gavin. He leaned negligently against the frame, giving Christopher a warning stare. "One can't help hearing the pair of you quarreling all through the house. Do you need help?"

"No, thank you," Audrey said firmly. "I can manage this on my own, Gavin."

Her brother smiled faintly. "Actually, I was asking Phelan."

"He doesn't need help, either," Audrey said with great dignity. "Please allow us a few minutes alone, Gavin. We have something important to settle."

"Very well. But I won't go far."

Sighing, Audrey looked after her overprotective brother and returned her attention to Christopher.

He gave her a hard stare. "I want a name."

"Only if you swear that you will not hurt this woman."

"I swear it."

"Swear it on John's grave," she insisted.

A long silence passed.

"I knew it," Audrey said grimly. "If you can't be trusted not to hurt her, I certainly can't tell you who she is."

"Is she married?" A hoarse note had entered his voice.

"No."

"Is she in Hampshire?"

Audrey hesitated before giving him a wary nod.

"Tell her that I'll find her," he said. "And she'll regret it when I do."

In the tense silence, he went to the threshold and glanced over his shoulder. "In the meantime, you can be the first to congratulate me," he said. "Prudence and I are nearly betrothed."

Audrey looked ashen. "Christopher . . . what kind of game are you playing?"

"You'll find out," came his cold reply. "You and your mysterious friend should enjoy it—you both seem to like games."

Chapter Fourteen

"What the devil are you eating?" Leo, Lord Ramsay, stood in the family parlor at Ramsay House, viewing his dark-haired twins, Edward and Emmaline, who were playing on the carpeted floor.

His wife, Catherine, who was helping the babies to build block towers, looked up with a smile. "They're eating biscuits."

"These?" Leo glanced at a bowl of little brown biscuits that had been placed on a table. "They look revoltingly similar to the ones Beatrix has been feeding the dog."

"That's because they are."

"They're . . . Good God, Cat! What can you be thinking?" Lowering to his haunches, Leo tried to pry a sodden biscuit away from Edward.

Leo's efforts were met with an indignant squall.

"Mine!" Edward cried, clutching the biscuit more tightly.

"Let him have it," Catherine protested. "The twins are teething, and the biscuits are very hard. There's nothing harmful in them."

"How do you know that?"

"Beatrix made them."

"Beatrix doesn't cook. To my knowledge, she can barely butter her bread."

"I don't cook for people," Beatrix said cheerfully, coming into the parlor with Albert padding after her. "But I do for dogs."

"Naturally." Leo took one of the brown lumps from the bowl, examining it closely. "Would you care to reveal the ingredients of these disgusting objects?"

"Oats, honey, eggs . . . they're very nourishing."

As if to underscore the point, Catherine's pet ferret, Dodger, streaked up to Leo, took the biscuit from him, and slithered beneath a nearby chair.

Catherine laughed low in her throat as she saw Leo's expression. "They're made of the same stuff as teething biscuits, my lord."

"Very well," Leo said darkly. "But if the twins start barking and burying their toys, I'll know whom to blame." He lowered to the floor beside his daughter.

Emmaline gave him a wet grin and pushed her own sodden biscuit toward his mouth. "Here, Papa."

"No, thank you, darling." Becoming aware of Albert nosing at his shoulder, Leo turned to pet him. "Is this a dog or a street broom?"

"It's Albert," Beatrix replied.

The dog promptly collapsed to his side, tail thumping the floor repeatedly.

Beatrix smiled. Three months earlier, such a scene would have been unimaginable. Albert would have been so hostile and fearful that she wouldn't have dared to expose him to children.

But with patience, love, and discipline—not to mention a great deal of help from Rye—Albert had become a different dog altogether. Gradually he had become accustomed to the constant activity in the household, including the presence of other animals. Now he greeted newness with curiosity rather than fear and aggression.

Albert had also gained some much-needed weight, looking sleek and healthy. Beatrix had painstakingly groomed him, stripping and trimming his fur regularly, but leaving the adorable whisks that gave his face a whimsical expression. When Beatrix walked Albert to the village, children gathered around him, and he submitted happily to their petting. He loved to play and fetch. He stole shoes and tried to bury them when no one was looking. He was, in short, a thoroughly normal dog.

Although Beatrix was still pining after Christopher, still in despair over him, she had discovered that the best remedy for heartache was trying to make herself useful to others. There were always people in need of assistance, including the tenants and cottagers who resided on the Ramsay lands. And with her sister Win away in Ireland, and Amelia busy with the household, Beatrix was the only sister left who had the time and means for charitable work. She took food to the sick and poor in the village, read to an elderly woman with failing eyesight, and became involved with the causes of the local church. Beatrix found that such work was its own reward. She was far less likely to fall into melancholy when she was busy.

Now, watching Albert with Leo, Beatrix wondered how Christopher would react when he saw the changes in his dog.

"Is he a new member of the family?" Leo asked.

"No, merely a guest," Beatrix replied. "He belongs to Captain Phelan."

"We saw Phelan on a few occasions during the season," Leo remarked. A smile touched his lips. "I told him that if he insists on winning at cards every time we play, I would have to avoid him in the future."

"How was Captain Phelan when you saw him?" Beatrix asked, striving to sound diffident. "Did he seem well? Was he in good spirits?"

Catherine answered thoughtfully. "He looked to be in good health, and he was certainly very charming. He was often seen in the company of Prudence Mercer."

Beatrix felt a sickening pang of jealousy. She averted her face. "How nice," she said in a muffled voice. "I'm sure they make a handsome pair."

"There is a rumor of a betrothal," Catherine added. She sent a teasing smile to her husband. "Perhaps Captain Phelan will finally succumb to the love of a good woman."

"He's certainly succumbed to enough of the other kind," Leo replied, in a holier-than-thou tone that made her erupt in laughter.

"Pot, may I introduce you to kettle?" Catherine accused, her eyes twinkling.

"That was all in the past," Leo informed her.

"Are wicked women more entertaining?" Beatrix asked him.

"No, darling. But one needs them for contrast."

Beatrix was subdued for the rest of the evening, inwardly miserable at the thought of Christopher and Prudence together. Betrothed. Married. Sharing the same name.

Sharing the same bed.

She had never experienced jealousy before now, and it was agonizing. It was like a slow death by poison. Prudence had spent the summer being courted by a handsome and heroic soldier, whereas Beatrix had spent the summer with his dog.

And soon he would come to retrieve Albert, and she wouldn't even have his dog.

Immediately upon his return to Stony Cross, Christopher learned that Beatrix Hathaway had stolen Albert. The servants didn't even have the decency to look apologetic about it, offering some preposterous story about the dog having run off, and Beatrix having insisted on taking him in.

Although he was weary from the twelve-hour journey from London, and he was starved and travel dusty and in an unbelievably foul temper, Christopher found himself riding to Ramsay House. It was time to put a stop to Beatrix's meddling once and for all.

Dark was lowering by the time he reached Ramsay House, shadows creeping from the woodlands until the trees resembled curtains drawn back to present a view of the house. The last vestiges of light imparted a ruddy glow to the brick and glittered on the multipaned windows. With its charming irregular roofline and sprouting chimneys, the house seemed to have grown from the fertile Hampshire land as if it were part of the forest, a living thing that had sent down roots and was reaching toward the sky.

There was an orderly bustle of outside staff, footmen and gardeners and stablemen, retiring to the indoors after the day's labors. Animals were being led to the barn, horses to the stables. Christopher paused on the drive for a short, staying moment, assessing the situation. He felt apart from the scene, an intruder.

Determined to make the visit short and efficient, Christopher rode to the entrance, allowed a footman to take the reins, and strode to the front door.

The housekeeper came to greet him, and he asked to see Beatrix.

"The family is having dinner, sir—" the housekeeper began.

"I don't care. Either bring Miss Hathaway to me, or I'll find her myself." He had already resolved that the Hathaway household would do nothing to distract or divert him. No doubt after a summer spent with his cantankerous dog, they would hand Albert over without a qualm. As for Beatrix—he only hoped she would try to stop him, so that he could make a few things clear to her.

"Would you care to wait in the front parlor, sir?"

Christopher shook his head wordlessly.

Looking perturbed, the housekeeper left him in the entrance hall.

In no time at all, Beatrix appeared. She was wearing a white dress made of thin, flowing layers, the bodice wrapped intricately over the curves of her breasts. The translucence of her chest and upper arms gave her the look of emerging from the white silk.

For a woman who had stolen his dog, she was remarkably composed.

"Captain Phelan." She stopped before him with a graceful curtsy.

Christopher stared at her in fascination, trying to retain his righteous anger, but it was slipping away like sand through his fingers. "Where are your breeches?" he found himself asking in a husky voice.

Beatrix smiled. "I thought you might come to fetch Albert soon, and I didn't want to offend you by wearing masculine attire."

"If you were all that concerned about giving offense, you would have thought twice before abducting my dog."

"I didn't abduct him. He went with me willingly."

"I seem to recall telling you to stay away from him."

"Yes, I know." Her tone was contrite. "But Albert preferred to stay here for the summer. He has done very well with us, by the way." She paused, looking him over. "How are you?"

"I'm exhausted," Christopher said curtly. "I've just arrived from London."

"Poor man. You must be famished. Come have dinner."

"Thank you, but no. All I want is to collect my dog and go home." *And drink myself into a stupor.* "Where is Albert?"

"He'll be here momentarily. I asked our housekeeper to fetch him."

Christopher blinked. "She's not afraid of him?"

"Of Albert? Heavens, no, everyone adores him."

The concept of someone, *anyone,* adoring his belligerent pet was difficult to grasp. Having expected to receive an inventory of all the damage Albert had caused, Christopher gave her a blank look.

And then the housekeeper returned with an obedient and well-groomed dog trotting by her side.

"Albert?" Christopher said.

The dog looked at him, ears twitching. His whiskered face changed, eyes brightening with excitement. Without hesitating, Albert launched forward with a happy yelp. Christopher knelt on the floor, gathering up an armful of joyfully wriggling canine. Albert strained to lick him, and whimpered and dove against him repeatedly.

Christopher was overwhelmed by feelings of kinship and relief. Gripping the warm, compact body close, Christopher murmured his name and petted him roughly, and Albert whined and trembled.

"I missed you, Albert. Good boy. There's my boy." Unable to help himself, Christopher pressed his face against the rough fur. He was undone by guilt, humbled by the fact that even though he had abandoned Albert for the summer, the dog showed nothing but eager welcome. "I was away too long," Christopher murmured, looking into the soulful brown eyes. "I won't leave you again." He dragged his gaze up to Beatrix's. "It was a mistake to leave him," he said gruffly.

She was smiling at him. "Albert won't hold it against you. To err is human, to forgive, canine."

To his disbelief, Christopher felt an answering smile tug at the corners of his lips. He continued to pet the dog, who was fit and sleek. "You've taken good care of him."

"He's much better behaved than before," she said. "You can take him anywhere now."

Rising to his feet, Christopher looked down at her. "Why did you do it?" he asked softly.

"He's very much worth saving. Anyone could see that."

The awareness between them became unbearably acute. Christopher's heart worked in hard, uneven beats. How pretty she was in the white dress. She radiated a healthy female physicality that was very different from the fashionable frailty of London women. He wondered what it would be like to bed her, if she would be as direct in her passions as she was in everything else.

"Stay for dinner," she urged.

He shook his head. "I must go."

"Have you eaten already?"

"No. But I'll find something in the larder at home."

Albert sat and watched them attentively.

"You need a proper meal after traveling so far."

"Miss Hathaway—" But his breath was clipped as Beatrix took his arm with both hands, one at his wrist, one at his elbow. She gave a gentle tug. He felt it all the way to his groin, his body responding actively to her touch. Annoyed and aroused, he looked down into her dark blue eyes.

"I don't want to talk to anyone," he told her.

"Of course you don't. That's perfectly all right." Another small, entreating tug. "Come."

And somehow Christopher found himself going with Beatrix, through the entrance hall and along a hallway lined with pictures. Albert padded after them without a sound.

Beatrix released his arm as they entered a dining room filled with abundant candlelight. The table was laden with silver and crystal, and a great quantity of food. He recognized Leo, Lord Ramsay, and his wife, and Rohan and Amelia. The dark-haired boy, Rye, was also at the table. Pausing at the threshold, Christopher bowed and said uncomfortably, "Forgive me. I merely came to—"

"I've invited Captain Phelan to join us," Beatrix announced. "He doesn't want to talk. Do not ask him direct questions unless absolutely necessary."

The rest of the family received this unorthodox pronouncement without turning a hair. A footman was dispatched to set a place for him.

"Come in, Phelan," Leo said easily. "We love silent guests—it allows us to talk all the more. By all means, sit and say nothing."

"But if you can manage it," Catherine added with a smile, "try to look impressed by our wit and intelligence."

"I will attempt to add to the conversation," Christopher ventured, "if I can think of anything relevant."

"That never stops the rest of us," Cam remarked.

Christopher took an empty chair beside Rye. A liberally filled plate and a glass of wine were set before him. It wasn't until he began to eat that he realized how famished he was. While he devoured the excellent fare—baked sole, potatoes, smoked oysters wrapped in crisp bacon—the family talked of politics and estate business, and mulled over happenings in Stony Cross.

Rye behaved like a miniature adult. He listened respectfully to the conversation, occasionally asking questions that were readily answered by the others. To Christopher's knowledge, it was highly uncommon to allow a child to sit at the dinner table. Most upper-class families followed the custom of having children eat alone in the nursery.

"Do you always take dinner with the rest of the family?" Christopher asked him sotto voce.

"Most of the time," Rye whispered back. "They don't mind as long as you don't talk with food in your mouth or play with the potatoes."

"I'll try not," Christopher assured him gravely.

"And you mustn't feed Albert from the table, even when he begs. Aunt Beatrix says only plain food is good for him."

Christopher glanced at his dog, who was reclining placidly in the corner.

"Captain Phelan," Amelia asked, noticing the direction of his gaze, "what do you think of the change in Albert?"

"Nearly inconceivable," Christopher replied. "I had wondered if it would be possible to bring him from the battlefield to a peaceful life here." He looked at Beatrix, adding gravely, "I am in your debt."

Beatrix colored and smiled down at her plate. "Not at all."

"My sister has always had a remarkable ability with animals," Amelia said. "I've always wondered what would happen if Beatrix took it in her head to reform a man."

Leo grinned. "I propose we find a really revolting, amoral wastrel, and give him to Beatrix. She would set him to rights within a fortnight."

"I have no wish to reform bipeds," Beatrix said. "Four legs are the absolute minimum. Besides, Cam has forbidden me to put any more creatures in the barn."

"With the size of that barn?" Leo asked. "Don't say we've run out of room?"

"One has to draw the line somewhere," Cam said. "And I had to after the mule."

Christopher looked at Beatrix alertly. "You have a mule?"

"No," she said at once. Perhaps it was merely a trick of the light, but the color seemed to leave her face. "It's nothing. That is, yes, I have a mule. But I don't like to discuss him."

"I like to discuss him," Rye volunteered innocently. "Hector is a very nice mule, but he has a weak back and he's sickle-hocked. No one wanted him after he was born, so Aunt Beatrix went to Mr. Caird and said—"

"His name is Hector?" Christopher asked, his gaze locked on Beatrix.

She didn't answer.

A strange, severe sensation took over Christopher's body. He felt every hair lift, felt every distinct pulse of blood in his veins. "Did his sire belong to Mr. Mawdsley?" he asked.

"How did you know?" came Rye's voice.

Christopher's reply was very soft. "Someone wrote to me about it."

Lifting a glass of wine to his lips, Christopher tore his gaze from Beatrix's carefully blank face.

He did not look at her for the rest of the meal.

He couldn't, or he would lose all self-control.

Beatrix was nearly suffocated by the weight of her own worry during the rest of dinner. She had never regretted anything in her life as much as having urged Christopher to stay. What had he made of the news that she had acquired Mr. Caird's mule and given him the same name as the pet mule of his boyhood? He would want an explanation. She would have to pass it off as some bit of information that Prudence had relayed. *I suppose the name stuck in my head when Pru mentioned it,* she would say casually. *And it is a nice name for a mule. I hope you don't mind.*

Yes. That would work, as long as she seemed nonchalant about the whole matter.

Except that it was difficult to appear nonchalant when one was filled with panic.

Mercifully, Christopher had seemed to lose interest in the subject. In fact, he didn't so much as glance at her, but instead launched into a conversation with Leo and Cam about mutual acquaintances in London. He was relaxed and smiling, even laughing outright at some quip of Leo's.

Beatrix's anxiety faded as it became apparent that the subject of Hector was all but forgotten.

She stole surreptitious glances at Christopher, as she had been doing all evening, mesmerized by the sight of him. He was tawny and sun glazed, the candlelight finding threads of gold in his hair. The yellow glow struck sparkling glints in the new growth of bristle on his face. She was fascinated by the raw, restless masculinity beneath his quietness. She wanted to revel in him as one might dash out-of-doors in a storm, letting the elements have their way. Most of all she longed to talk with him . . . to pry each other open with words, share every thought and secret.

"My sincere thanks for your hospitality," Christopher finally said at the conclusion of the meal. "It was much needed."

"You must return soon," Cam said, "especially to view the timber yard in operation. We have installed some innovations that you may want to use at Riverton someday."

"Thank you. I would like to see them." Christopher looked directly at Beatrix. "Before I depart, Miss Hathaway, I wonder if you would introduce me to this notorious mule of yours?" His manner was relaxed . . . but his eyes were those of a predator.

Beatrix's mouth went dry. There would be no escaping him. That much was clear. He wanted answers. He would have them either now or later.

"Now?" she asked wanly. "Tonight?"

"If you don't mind," he said in a far too pleasant tone. "The barn is but a short walk from the house, is it not?"

"Yes," Beatrix said, rising from her chair. The men at the table stood obligingly. "Excuse us, please. I won't be long."

"May I go with you?" Rye asked eagerly.

"No, darling," Amelia said, "it's time for your bath."

"But why must I wash if I can't see any dirt?"

"Those of us who have a difficult time with godliness," Amelia replied with a grin, "must settle for cleanliness."

The family maintained a light conversation until Rye had gone upstairs, and Beatrix and Captain Phelan had left the house with Albert following them.

After a universal silence, Leo was the first to speak. "Did anyone else notice—"

"Yes," Catherine said. "What do you make of it?"

"I haven't decided yet." Leo frowned and took a sip of port. "He's not someone I would pair Bea with."

"Whom would you pair her with?"

"Hanged if I know," Leo said. "Someone with similar interests. The local veterinarian, perhaps?"

"He's eighty-three years old and deaf," Catherine said.

"They would never argue," Leo pointed out.

Amelia smiled and stirred her tea slowly. "Much as I hate to admit it, I agree with Leo. Not about the veterinarian, but . . . Beatrix with a soldier? That doesn't seem a likely match."

"Phelan did resign his commission," Cam said. "He's no longer a soldier."

"And if he inherits Riverton," Amelia mused, "Beatrix would have all that forest to roam . . ."

"I see a likeness between them," Catherine said reflectively.

Leo arched a brow. "How are they alike, pray tell? She likes animals, and he likes to shoot things."

"Beatrix puts a distance between herself and the rest of the world. She's very engaging, but also quite private in nature. I see the same qualities in Captain Phelan."

"Yes," Amelia said. "You're absolutely right, Catherine. Put that way, the match does seem more appropriate."

"I still have reservations," Leo said.

"You always do," Amelia replied. "If you'll recall, you objected to Cam in the beginning, but now you've accepted him."

"That's because the more brothers-in-law I acquire," Leo said, "the better Cam looks by comparison."

Chapter Fifteen

No words were exchanged as Beatrix and Christopher proceeded to the stable. The cloud-hazed moon was low in the sky, insubstantial as a smoke ring in the blackness.

Beatrix was absurdly aware of the sound of her breathing, of her shoes biting into the graveled ground, of the vital male presence beside her.

A stable boy nodded a greeting as they went into the warm, shadowy interior of the stables. Having become accustomed to Beatrix's frequent comings and goings, the stablehands had learned to let her do as she pleased.

The pungent smell of the stables—hay, horses, feed, manure—combined in a familiar and reassuring fragrance. Silently she led Christopher farther into the building, past Thoroughbreds, a cart horse, a matched carriage pair. The animals whickered and turned their heads as they passed.

Beatrix stopped at the mule's stall. "This is Hector," she said.

The small mule came forward to greet them. Despite his flaws, or perhaps because of them, he was an

endearing creature. His conformation was terrible, one
ear was crooked, and he wore a jaunty and perpetually
cheerful expression.

Christopher reached out to pet Hector, who nuzzled
against his hand. His gentleness with the animal was
reassuring. Perhaps, Beatrix thought hopefully, he wasn't
as angry as she had feared.

Taking a deep breath, she said, "The reason that I
named him Hector—"

"No." Christopher moved with startling swiftness,
trapping her against the post of the stall. His voice
was low and rough. "Let's start with this: did you help
Prudence to write those letters?"

Beatrix's eyes widened as she looked into his shadowed face. Her blood surged, a flush rising to the surface of her skin. "No," she managed to say, "I didn't
help her."

"Then who did?"

"No one helped her."

It was the truth. It just wasn't the entire truth.

"You know something," he insisted. "And you're going to tell me what it is."

She could feel his fury. The air was charged with it.
Her heart thrummed like a bird's. And she struggled to
contain a swell of emotion that was almost more than
she could bear.

"Let me go," she said with exceptional calm. "You're
doing neither of us any good with this behavior."

His eyes narrowed dangerously. "Don't use your
bloody dog-training voice on me."

"That wasn't my dog-training voice. And if you're
so intent on getting at the truth, why aren't you asking
Prudence?"

"I have asked her. She lied. As you are lying now."

"You've always wanted Prudence," Beatrix burst

out. "Now you can have her. Why should a handful of letters matter?"

"Because I was deceived. And I want to know how and why."

"Pride," Beatrix said bitterly. "That's all this is to you . . . your pride was hurt."

One of his hands sank into her hair, gripping in a gentle but inexorable hold. A gasp slipped from her throat as he pulled her head back.

"Don't try to divert the conversation. You know something you're not telling me." His free hand came to the exposed line of her throat. For a heart-stopping moment she thought he might choke her. Instead he caressed her gently, his thumb moving in a subtle swirl in the hollow at the base. The intensity of her own reaction astonished her.

Beatrix's eyes half closed. "Stop," she said faintly.

Taking her responsive shiver as a sign of distaste or fear, Christopher lowered his head until his breath fanned her cheek. "Not until I have the truth."

Never. If she told him, he would hate her for the way she had deceived and abandoned him. Some mistakes could not be forgiven.

"Go to hell," Beatrix said unsteadily. She had never used such a phrase in her life.

"I am in hell." His body corralled hers, his legs intruding amid the folds of her skirts.

Drowning in guilt and fear and desire, she tried to push his caressing hand away from her throat. His fingers delved into her hair with a grip just short of painful. His mouth was close to hers. He was surrounding her, all the strength and force and maleness of him, and she closed her eyes as her senses went quiet and dark in helpless waiting. "I'll make you tell me," she heard him mutter.

And then he was kissing her.

Somehow, Beatrix thought hazily, Christopher seemed to be under the impression she would find his kisses so objectionable that she would confess anything to make him desist. She couldn't think how he had come by such a notion. In fact, she couldn't really think at all.

His mouth moved over hers in supple, intimate angles, until he found some perfect alignment that made her weak all over. She reached around his neck to keep from dropping bonelessly to the floor. Gathering her closer into the hard support of his body, he explored her slowly, the tip of his tongue stroking, tasting.

Her body listed more heavily against his as her limbs became weighted with pleasure. She sensed the moment when his anger was eclipsed by passion, desire changing to white-hot need. Her fingers sank into his beautiful hair, the shorn locks heavy and vibrant, his scalp hot against her palms. With each inhalation, she drew in more of his fragrance, the trace of sandalwood on warm male skin.

His mouth slid from hers and dragged roughly along her throat, crossing sensitive places that made her writhe. Blindly turning her face, she rubbed her lips against his ear. He drew in a sharp breath and jerked his head back. His hand came to her jaw, clamping firmly.

"Tell me what you know," he said, his breath searing her lips. "Or I'll do worse than this. I'll take you here and now. Is that what you want?"

As a matter of fact . . .

However, recalling that this was supposed to be a punishment, a coercion, Beatrix managed a languid, "No. Stop." His mouth ravished hers again. She sighed and melted against him.

He kissed her harder, pressing her back against the slatted side of the stall, his hands roaming indecently.

Her body was laced and compressed and concealed in layers of feminine attire, frustrating his attempts to caress her.

His garments, however, presented far fewer obstacles. She slid her arms inside his coat, fumbling to touch him, tugging ardently at his waistcoat and shirt. Reaching beneath the straps of his trouser braces, she managed to pull part of his shirt free of the trousers, the fabric warm from his body.

They both gasped as her cool fingers touched the burning skin of his back. Fascinated, Beatrix explored the curvature of deep intrinsic muscles, the tight mesh of sinew and bone, the astonishing strength contained just beneath the surface. She found the texture of scars, vestiges of pain and survival. After stroking a healed-over line, she covered it tenderly with her palm.

A shudder racked his frame. Christopher groaned and crushed his mouth over hers, urging her body against his, until together they found an erotic pattern, a cadence. Instinctively Beatrix tried to draw him inside herself, pulling at his lips and tongue with her own.

Christopher broke the kiss abruptly, panting. Cradling her head in his hands, he pressed his forehead against hers.

"Is it you?" he asked hoarsely. "Is it?"

Beatrix felt tears slip from beneath her lashes, no matter how she tried to blink them back. Her heart was ablaze. It seemed that her entire life had led to this man, this moment of unexpressed love.

But she was too frightened of his scorn, and too ashamed of her own actions, to answer.

Christopher's fingertips found the tear marks on her damp skin. His mouth grazed her trembling lips, lingering at one soft corner, sliding up to the verge of a salt-flavored cheek.

Releasing her, he stepped back and stared at her with baffled anger. The desire exerted such force between them that Beatrix dazedly wondered how he could maintain even that small distance.

A shaken breath escaped him. He straightened his clothes, moving with undue care, as if he were intoxicated.

"Damn you." His voice was low and strained. He strode out of the stables.

Albert, who had been sitting by a stall, began to trot after him. Upon noticing that Beatrix wasn't going with them, the terrier dashed over to her and whimpered.

Beatrix bent to pet him. "Go on, boy," she whispered. Hesitating only a moment, Albert ran after his master.

And Beatrix watched them both with despair.

Two days later, a ball was given at Stony Cross Manor, the manorial residence of Lord and Lady Westcliff. It would have been difficult to find a more beautiful setting than the ancient dwelling built of honey-colored stone, surrounded by extensive gardens. The whole of it was situated on a bluff overlooking the Itchen River. As neighbors and friends of Lord and Lady Westcliff, the Hathaways were all invited. Cam in particular was a valued and frequent companion of the earl's, the two having been closely acquainted for many years.

Although Beatrix had been a guest at Stony Cross Manor on many previous occasions, she was still struck by the beauty of the home, especially the lavish interior. The ballroom was beyond compare, with intricately parqueted floors and a double row of chandeliers, two of the long walls fitted with semicircular niches containing velvet upholstered benches.

After partaking of refreshments at the long buffet tables, Beatrix entered the ballroom with Amelia and

Catherine. The scene was profligate with color, ladies
dressed in lavish ball gowns, the men clad in the formal ensemble of black and white. The sparkle of the
crystal chandeliers was very nearly matched by the
bountiful displays of jewels on feminine wrists, necks,
and ears.

The host of the evening, Lord Westcliff, approached
to exchange pleasantries with Beatrix, Amelia, and
Catherine. Beatrix had always liked the earl, a courteous and honorable man whose friendship had benefited
the Hathaways on countless occasions. With his rugged
features, coal-black hair, and dark eyes, he was striking rather than handsome. He wore an aura of power
comfortably and without fanfare. Westcliff asked Catherine to dance with him, a mark of favor that was
hardly lost on the other guests, and she complied with
a smile.

"How kind he is," Amelia said to Beatrix as they
watched the earl lead Catherine into the midst of the
whirling couples. "I've noticed that he always makes a
point of being obliging and gracious to the Hathaways.
That way, no one would dare cut or snub us."

"I think he likes unconventional people. He's not
nearly as staid as one might assume."

"Lady Westcliff has certainly said as much," Amelia
replied, smiling.

A rejoinder faded on Beatrix's lips as she caught
sight of a perfectly matched couple on the other side of
the room. Christopher Phelan was talking with Prudence Mercer. The scheme of formal black and white
was becoming to any man. On someone like Christopher, it was literally breathtaking. He wore the clothes
with natural ease, his posture relaxed but straight, his
shoulders broad. The crisp white of his starched cravat

provided a striking contrast to his tawny skin, while the light of chandeliers glittered over his golden-bronze hair.

Following her gaze, Amelia lifted her brows. "What an attractive man," she said. Her attention returned to Beatrix. "You like him, don't you?"

Before Beatrix could help herself, she sent her sister a pained glance. Letting her gaze drop to the floor, she said, "There have been a dozen times in the past when I should have liked a particular gentleman. When it would have been convenient, and appropriate, and easy. But no, I had to wait for someone special. Someone who would make my heart feel as if it's been trampled by elephants, thrown into the Amazon, and eaten by piranhas."

Amelia smiled at her compassionately. Her gloved hand slipped over Beatrix's. "Darling Bea. Would it console you to hear that such feelings of infatuation are perfectly ordinary?"

Beatrix turned her palm upward, returning the clasp of her sister's hand. Since their mother had died when Bea was twelve, Amelia had been a source of endless love and patience. "Is it infatuation?" she heard herself asking softly. "Because it feels much worse than that. Like a fatal disease."

"I don't know, dear. It's difficult to tell the difference between love and infatuation. Time will reveal it, eventually." Amelia paused. "He is attracted to you," she said. "We all noticed the other night. Why don't you encourage him, dear?"

Beatrix felt her throat tighten. "I can't."

"Why not?"

"I can't explain," Beatrix said miserably, "except to say that I've deceived him."

Amelia glanced at her in surprise. "That doesn't sound like you. You're the least deceptive person I've ever known."

"I didn't mean to do it. And he doesn't know that it was me. But I think he suspects."

"Oh." Amelia frowned as she absorbed the perplexing statement. "Well. This does seem to be a muddle. Perhaps you should confide in him. His reaction may surprise you. What is it that Mother used to say whenever we pushed her to the limits of her patience? . . . 'Love forgives all things.' Do you remember?"

"Of course," Beatrix said. She had written that exact phrase to Christopher in one of her letters. Her throat went very tight. "Amelia, I can't discuss this now. Or I'll start weeping and throw myself to the floor."

"Heavens, don't do that. Someone might trip over you."

Further conversation was forestalled as a gentleman came to ask Beatrix to dance. Although Beatrix hardly felt like dancing at the moment, it was the worst possible manners to refuse such an invitation at a private ball. Unless one had a plausible and obvious excuse, such as a broken leg, one danced.

And in truth, it was no hardship to partner this gentleman, Mr. Theo Chickering. He was an attractive and amiable young man, whom Beatrix had met during her last season in London.

"Would you do me the honor, Miss Hathaway?"

Beatrix smiled at him. "It would be my pleasure, Mr. Chickering." Letting go of her sister's hand, she went with him.

"You look lovely tonight, Miss Hathaway."

"Thank you, kind sir." Beatrix had worn her best gown, made of shimmering aniline violet. The bodice was scooped low, revealing a generous expanse of fair skin. Her hair had been curled and swept up with a multitude of pearl-tipped pins—other than that, she wore no adornment.

Feeling the hairs on her nape prickle with awareness, Beatrix sent a quick glance around the room. Her gaze was immediately caught by a pair of cool gray eyes. Christopher was staring at her, unsmiling.

Chickering gracefully pulled her into the waltz. Following the completion of one turn, Beatrix glanced over her shoulder, but Christopher was no longer staring at her.

In fact, he didn't glance at her even once after that.

Beatrix forced herself to laugh and dance with Chickering, while privately reflecting that there was nothing so trying as pretending you were happy when you weren't. Discreetly she watched Christopher, who was inundated with women who wanted to flirt with him and men who wanted to hear war stories. Everyone, it seemed, wanted to associate with the man whom many were calling England's most celebrated war hero. Christopher bore it all with equanimity, looking composed and courteous, occasionally flashing a charming smile.

"It's hard for a fellow to challenge *that*," Chickering told Beatrix dryly, nodding in Christopher's direction. "Fame, great wealth, and a full head of hair. And one can't even despise him, because he singlehandedly won the war."

Beatrix laughed and gave him a mock-pitying glance. "You're no less impressive than Captain Phelan, Mr. Chickering."

"By what measure? I wasn't in the military, and I have neither fame nor great wealth."

"But you do have a full head of hair," Beatrix pointed out.

Chickering grinned. "Dance with me again, and you can view my abundant tresses at your leisure."

"Thank you, but I've already danced with you twice, and any more would be scandalous."

"You have broken my heart," he informed her, and she laughed.

"There are many delightful ladies here who would be happy to mend it," she said. "Please go and favor them—a gentleman who dances as well as you should not be monopolized."

As Chickering left her reluctantly, Beatrix heard a familiar voice behind her.

"Beatrix."

Although she wanted to cringe, she squared her shoulders and turned to face her former friend. "Hello, Prudence," she said. "How are you?"

Prudence was sumptuously attired in an ivory gown, the skirts a massive froth of blond lace caught up at intervals with pink silk rosebuds. "I am very well, thank you. What a fashionable dress . . . you look very grown-up tonight, Bea."

Beatrix smiled wryly at this bit of condescension coming from a girl who was a year younger than herself. "I'm twenty-three years old, Pru. I daresay I've looked grown-up for quite a while now."

"Of course."

A long, awkward pause ensued.

"Do you want something?" Beatrix asked bluntly.

Prudence smiled and drew closer. "Yes. I want to thank you."

"For what?"

"You've been a loyal friend. You could easily have spoiled things for Christopher and me by revealing our secret, but you didn't. You kept your promise, and I didn't believe that you would."

"Why not?"

"I suppose I thought that you might have tried to attract Christopher's attention to yourself. As ludicrous as that would have been."

Beatrix tilted her head slightly. "Ludicrous?"

"Perhaps that's not the right word. I meant unsuitable. Because a man in Christopher's position needs a sophisticated woman. Someone to support his position in society. With his fame and influence, he may enter politics someday. And he could hardly do that with a wife who spent most of her time in the forest . . . or the stables."

That delicate reminder was like an arrow through Beatrix's heart.

"She's more suited to the stables than the drawing room," Christopher had once said.

Beatrix stretched her lips into a careless grin, hoping it didn't resemble a grimace. "Yes, I remember."

"Again, my thanks," Prudence said warmly. "I've never been happier. I'm coming to care for him very much. We'll be betrothed soon." She glanced at Christopher, who was standing near the ballroom entrance with a group of gentlemen. "See how handsome he is," she said with affectionate pride. "I do prefer him in his uniform, with all those lovely medals, but he looks splendid in black, doesn't he?"

Beatrix returned her attention to Prudence, wondering how to get rid of her. "Oh, look! . . . There is Marietta Newbury. Have you told her about your impending betrothal? I'm sure she would be delighted to hear of it."

"Oh, indeed, she would! Will you come with me?"

"Thank you, but I'm terribly thirsty. I'll go to the refreshment tables."

"We'll talk again soon," Prudence promised.

"That would be lovely."

Prudence left her in a swish of white lace.

Beatrix let out an exasperated puff that blew a stray lock of hair away from her forehead. She stole another glance at Christopher, who was involved in conversation. Although his demeanor was calm—stoic, even—there was a gleam of perspiration on his face. Looking away from his companions for a moment, he discreetly passed a shaking hand over his forehead.

Was he feeling ill?

Beatrix watched him closely.

The orchestra was playing a lively composition, obliging the crowd in the ballroom to talk loudly over the music. So much noise and color . . . so many bodies confined in one place. A percussion came from the refreshment room; clinks of glasses, flatware scratching on china. There came a pop of a champagne cork, and Beatrix saw Christopher twitch in response.

At that moment she understood.

It was all too much for him. His nerves were stretched to the breaking point. The effort at self-discipline was requiring everything he had.

Without a second thought, Beatrix made her way to Christopher as quickly as possible.

"Here you are, Captain Phelan," she exclaimed.

The gentlemen's conversation stopped at this untoward interruption.

"There's no use in hiding from me," Beatrix continued brightly. "Recollect, you promised to stroll with me through Lord Westcliff's picture gallery."

Christopher's face was still. His eyes were dilated, the gray irises nearly extinguished by black. "So I did," he said stiffly.

The other gentlemen acceded immediately. It was

the only thing they could do in the face of Beatrix's boldness. "We will certainly not keep you from making good on a promise, Phelan," one of them said.

Another followed suit. "Especially a promise given to a delightful creature such as Miss Hathaway."

Christopher gave an abbreviated nod. "By your leave," he said to his companions, and offered Beatrix his arm. As soon as they were out of the main circuit of rooms, he began to breathe heavily. He was sweating profusely, the muscles of his arm unbelievably hard beneath her fingers. "That did your reputation no good," he muttered, referring to the way she had approached him.

"Bother my reputation."

Being familiar with the arrangement of the manor, Beatrix led him to a small outdoor conservatory. The attached circular roof was supported with slender columns and dimly illuminated with torchlight shed from the surrounding gardens.

Leaning against the side of the house, Christopher closed his eyes and drew in the cool, sweet air. He seemed like a man who had just emerged from a long swim underwater.

Beatrix stood nearby, watching him with concern. "Too much noise in there?"

"Too much of everything," he muttered. After a moment, he slitted his eyes open. "Thank you."

"You're welcome."

"Who was that man?"

"Which one?"

"The one you were dancing with."

"Mr. Chickering?" Her heart felt considerably lighter as she realized that he had noticed. "Oh, he's a delightful gentleman. I'd met him before in London."

She paused. "Did you also happen to see that I spoke to Pru?"

"No."

"Well, I did. She seems convinced that you and she will marry."

There was no change in his expression. "Perhaps we will. It's what she deserves."

Beatrix hardly knew how to reply to that. "Do you care for her?"

Christopher gave her a look of scalding derision. "How could I not?"

Her frown deepened. "If you're going to be sarcastic, I may as well go back inside."

"Go, then." He closed his eyes again, continuing to lean against the wall.

Beatrix was tempted to do just that. However, as she looked at his still, gleaming features, a wave of unaccountable tenderness swept through her.

He looked so large and invulnerable, with no sign of emotion save for that indentation between his brows. But she knew that he was overwrought. No man liked to lose control, especially a man whose very life had depended so often on his ability to govern himself.

Oh, how she wished she could tell him that their secret house was close by. *Come with me,* she would say, *and I'll take you to a lovely quiet place . . .*

Instead she fished a handkerchief from a hidden pocket in her gown, and approached him. "Be still," she said. Standing on her toes, she carefully blotted his face with a handkerchief.

And he let her.

He looked down at her when she was done, his mouth grim. "I have these moments of . . . madness," he said gruffly. "In the middle of a conversation, or doing something perfectly ordinary, a vision appears in my head. And then there's a moment of blankness, and I don't know what I've just said or done."

"What kind of vision?" Beatrix asked. "Things you saw in the war?"

His nod was nearly imperceptible.

"That's not madness," she said.

"Then what is it?"

"I'm not certain."

A humorless laugh escaped him. "You have no damned idea what you're talking about."

"Oh, I don't?" Beatrix stared at him intently, wondering how far she could trust him. The instinct of self-preservation struggled with her desire to help him, share with him. *"Boldness be my friend!"* she thought ruefully, summoning her favorite line from Shakespeare. It was practically the Hathaway family motto.

Very well. She would tell him the shameful secret she had never told anyone outside her family. If it helped him, the risk was worth it.

"I steal things," she said bluntly.

That got his attention. "Pardon?"

"Little things. Snuffboxes, sealing wax, odds and ends. Never intentionally."

"How do you steal things unintentionally?"

"Oh, it's dreadful," Beatrix said earnestly. "I'll be in a shop, or someone's home, and I'll see a little object . . . it could be something as valuable as a jewel, or as insignificant as a piece of string . . . and the most terrible sensation comes over me. A sort of anxious, fidgety feeling . . . Have you ever had an itch so awful that you must scratch it or die? And yet you can't?"

His lips twitched. "Yes. Usually in one's army boot,

while standing in knee-deep water in a trench. While people are shooting. That absolutely guarantees an unreachable itch."

"My goodness. Well, I try to resist, but the feeling gets worse until I finally take the object and slip it into my pocket. And then later when I return home, I'm overcome with shame and embarrassment, and I have to find ways to return the things I took. My family helps me. And it's *so* much more difficult to put something back than it is to steal it." She grimaced. "Sometimes I'm not even fully aware of doing it. That's why I was expelled from finishing school. I had a collection of hair ribbons, pencil stubs, books . . . and I tried to put everything back, but I couldn't remember where it all went." Beatrix glanced at him cautiously, wondering if she would find condemnation in his face.

But his mouth had gentled, and his eyes were warm. "When did it start?"

"After my parents died. My father went to bed one night with pains in his chest, and he never awoke. But it was even worse with my mother . . . she stopped talking, and hardly ate, and withdrew from everyone and everything. She died of grief a few months later. I was very young, and self-centered, I suppose—because I felt abandoned. I wondered why she hadn't loved me enough to stay."

"That doesn't mean you were self-centered." His voice was quiet and kind. "Any child would have reacted that way."

"My brother and sisters took very good care of me," Beatrix said. "But it wasn't long after Mother was gone that my problem appeared. It's much better than it used to be . . . when I feel peaceful and safe, I don't steal anything at all. It's only at difficult times, when I'm uncomfortable or anxious, that I find myself doing it."

She looked up at Christopher compassionately. "I think your problem will fade in time, as mine has. And then it might come back every once in a while, but only briefly. It won't always be this bad."

Torchlight flickered in Christopher's eyes as he stared at her. He reached out and drew her close with slow, stunning tenderness. One of his hands cradled her jaw, his long fingers textured with calluses. To Beatrix's bewilderment, he eased her head against his shoulder. His arms were around her, and nothing had ever felt so wonderful. She leaned against him in a daze of pleasure, feeling the even rise and fall of his chest. He toyed with the tiny wisps at the nape of her neck, the brush of his thumb on her skin sending a rapturous quiver down her spine.

"I have a silver cuff link of yours," Beatrix said unsteadily, her cheek pressed to the smooth fabric of his coat. "And a shaving brush. I went to take back the shaving brush, and stole the cuff link instead. I've been afraid to try and return them, because I'm fairly certain I would only end up stealing something else."

A sound of amusement rustled in his chest. "Why did you take the shaving brush in the first place?"

"I told you, I can't help—"

"No. I meant, what were you feeling anxious about?"

"Oh, that's not important."

"It's important to me."

Beatrix drew back just enough to look up at him. *You. I was anxious about you.* But what she said was, "I don't remember. I have to go back inside."

His arms loosened. "I thought you weren't worried about your reputation."

"Well, it can survive a little damage," Beatrix said reasonably. "But I'd rather not have the whole thing blown to smithereens."

"Go, then." His hands fell away from her, and she began to walk away. "But Beatrix . . ."

She paused and glanced at him uncertainly. "Yes?"

His gaze held hers. "I want my shaving brush back."

A slow grin curved her lips. "I'll return it soon," she promised, and left him alone in the moonlight.

Chapter Sixteen

"Beatrix, see who's here!" Rye came to the paddock with Albert padding beside him.

Beatrix was working with a newly acquired horse, which had been badly trained as a colt and sold by its disgruntled owner. The horse had a potentially fatal habit of rearing, and had once nearly crushed a rider who had been trying to discipline him. The horse started uneasily at the appearance of the boy and dog, but Beatrix soothed him and had him begin a slow circle around the paddock.

She glanced at Rye, who had climbed onto the fence and sat on the top rail. Albert sat and rested his chin on the lowest rail, watching her with alert eyes.

"Did Albert come alone?" Beatrix asked, perplexed.

"Yes. And he wasn't wearing a leash. I think he must have run away from home."

Before Beatrix could reply, the horse stopped and began to rear irritably. Immediately she loosened the reins and leaned forward, sliding her right arm around the horse's neck. As soon as the horse began to come down, Beatrix urged him forward. She doubled the horse in tight half circles, first to the right, then to the left, and began him forward again.

"Why do you double him like that?" Rye asked.

"It's something your father taught me, actually. It's to impress on him that he and I must work together." She patted the horse's neck and kept him at a sedate walk. "One must never pull on the reins when a horse is rearing—it could cause him to fall backward. When I feel him getting light in the front, I urge him forward a little faster. He can't rear as long as he's moving."

"How will you know when he's straightened out?"

"There's never an exact moment when one knows," Beatrix said. "I'll just keep working with him, and he'll improve little by little."

She dismounted and led the horse to the railing, and Rye stroked his satiny neck. "Albert," Beatrix said conversationally, bending to pet the dog. "What are you doing here? Have you run off from your master?"

He wagged his tail enthusiastically.

"I gave him some water," Rye said. "Can we keep him for the afternoon?"

"I'm afraid not. Captain Phelan may be worrying after him. I'm going to take him back now."

The boy heaved a sigh. "I would ask to go with you," he said, "but I have to finish my lessons. I so look forward to the day I know everything. Then I won't have to read any more books or do any more counting."

Beatrix smiled. "I don't wish to be discouraging, Rye, but it's not possible to know *everything*."

"Mama does." Rye paused reflectively. "At least, Papa says we must pretend she does, because it makes her happy."

"Your father," Beatrix informed him with a laugh, "is one of the wisest men I've ever known."

It was only when Beatrix had ridden halfway to

Phelan House, with Albert trotting alongside, that she recalled she was still dressed in boots and breeches. No doubt the outlandish attire would annoy Christopher.

There had been no word from him in the week after the ball at Stony Cross Manor. And although Beatrix had certainly not expected him to pay a call on her, it would have been a cordial gesture on his part. They were neighbors, after all. She had gone out walking every day, hoping to encounter him on a long ramble, but there was no sign of him.

It couldn't have been more obvious that Christopher wasn't interested in her, in any regard. Which led Beatrix to the conclusion that it had been a grave mistake to confide in him. She had been presumptuous in assuming that her problem was comparable to his.

"Recently I realized that I'm no longer in love with him," she told Albert as they neared Phelan House. "It's such a relief. Now I'm not at all nervous about the prospect of seeing him. I suppose this is proof that what I felt for him was infatuation. Because it's completely gone now. I couldn't care less about what he does or whom he marries. Oh, what a feeling of utter freedom." She glanced at the dog, who didn't look at all convinced by her statements. She sighed heavily.

Reaching the entrance of the house, Beatrix dismounted and handed the reins to a footman. She suppressed a sheepish smile as she saw how he was gaping at her. "Keep my horse at the ready, please. I'll be only a moment. Come, Albert."

She was met at the front door by Mrs. Clocker, who was taken aback by her attire. "Why, Miss Hathaway . . ." the housekeeper faltered, "you're wearing . . ."

"Yes, I'm so sorry, I know I'm not presentable, but I came in a dash. Albert appeared at Ramsay House today, and I'm delivering him back to you."

"Thank you," the housekeeper said in a distracted manner. "I hadn't even noticed he was missing. With the master not himself . . ."

"Not himself?" Beatrix was instantly concerned. "In what way, Mrs. Clocker?"

"I shouldn't say."

"Yes you should. I'm the perfect person to confide in. I'm very discreet—I only gossip to animals. Is Captain Phelan ill? Did something happen?"

The housekeeper's voice lowered to a whisper. "Three nights ago, we all smelled smoke coming from the master's bedroom. The master was drunk as David's sow, and he had thrown his uniform onto the fire in the hearth, and all his medals with it! We managed to rescue the medals, although the garments were ruined. After that, the master closed himself in his room and began to drink steadily. He hasn't stopped. We've watered his liquor as much as we dared, but . . ." A helpless shrug. "He will talk to no one. He won't touch the dinner trays I sent up. We sent for the doctor, but he wouldn't see him, and when we brought the pastor yesterday, he threatened to murder him. We've been considering the idea of sending for Mrs. Phelan."

"His mother?"

"Dear me, no. Mrs. Phelan the younger. I do not think his mother would be of any help."

"Yes, Audrey is a good choice. She's levelheaded, and she knows him well."

"The problem," the housekeeper said, "is that it would take at least two days for her to arrive . . . and I fear . . ."

"What?"

"This morning he asked for a razor and hot bath. We were frightened to give it to him, but we daren't refuse. I half wonder if he won't do himself harm."

Two things were immediately clear to Beatrix: first, the housekeeper would never have confided so much in her unless she was desperate, and second, Christopher was in terrible pain.

She felt answering pain, for his sake, piercing beneath her own ribs. Everything she had told herself about her newfound freedom, about the death of her infatuation, was revealed as an absurdity. She was mad for him. She would have done anything for him. Anxiously she wondered what he needed, what words might soothe him. But she was not up to the task. She couldn't think of anything wise or clever. All she knew was that she wanted to be with him.

"Mrs. Clocker," she said carefully, "I wonder if . . . it might be possible for you not to notice if I go upstairs?"

The housekeeper's eyes widened. "I . . . Miss Hathaway . . . I don't think that would be safe. Nor sensible."

"Mrs. Clocker, my family has always believed that when we are faced with large and apparently impossible problems, the best solutions are found by the insane people, not the sensible ones."

Looking confused, the housekeeper opened her mouth to disagree, and closed it. "If you cry out for help," she ventured after a moment, "we will come to your aid."

"Thank you, but I'm certain that won't be necessary."

Beatrix went inside the house and headed to the stairs. As Albert made to follow her, she said, "No, boy. Stay down here."

"Come, Albert," the housekeeper said, "we'll find some scraps for you from the kitchen."

The dog switched directions without pausing, panting happily as he went with Mrs. Clocker.

Beatrix went upstairs, taking her time. How many

times, she reflected ruefully, she had sought to understand a wounded wild creature. But it was another matter
entirely to penetrate the mystery of a human being.

Reaching Christopher's door, she knocked softly.
When there came no response, she let herself inside.

To her surprise, the room brimmed with daylight,
the late August sun illuminating tiny floating dust
motes by the window. The air smelled like liquor and
smoke and bath soap. A portable bath occupied one
corner of the room, sodden footprints tracking across
the carpet.

Christopher reclined on the unmade bed, half propped
on a haphazard stack of pillows, a bottle of brandy
clasped negligently in his fingers. His incurious gaze
moved to Beatrix and held, his eyes becoming alert.

He was clad in a pair of fawn-colored trousers, only
partially fastened, and . . . nothing more. His body was a
long golden arc on the bed, lean and complexly muscled.
Scars marred the sun-browned skin in places . . . there
was a ragged triangular shape where a bayonet had
pierced his shoulder, a liberal scattering of marks from
shrapnel, a small circular depression on his side that
must have been caused by a bullet.

Slowly Christopher levered himself upward and
placed the bottle on the bedside table. Half leaning on
the edge of the mattress, his bare feet braced on the
floor, he regarded Beatrix without expression. The locks
of his hair were still damp, darkened to antique gold.
How broad his shoulders were, their sturdy slopes flowing into the powerful lines of his arms.

"Why are you here?" His voice sounded rusty from
disuse.

Somehow Beatrix managed to drag her mesmerized
gaze away from the glinting fleece on his chest.

"I came to return Albert," she said. "He appeared at

Ramsay House today. He says you've been neglecting him. And that you haven't taken him on any walks lately."

"Has he? I had no idea he was so loose-tongued."

"Perhaps you would like to put . . . more clothes on . . . and come for a walk with me? To clear your head?"

"This brandy is clearing my head. Or it would if my damned servants would stop watering it."

"Come walk with me," she coaxed. "Or I may be forced to use my dog-training voice on you."

Christopher gave her a baleful look. "I've already been trained. By Her Majesty's Royal Army."

Despite the sunlight in the room, Beatrix sensed the nightmares lurking in the corners. Everything in her insisted that he should be outside, in the open air, away from confinement. "What is it?" she asked. "What's caused this?"

He lifted a hand in an annoyed gesture, as if to bat away an insect.

Beatrix moved toward him cautiously.

"Don't," came his sharp rebuke. "Don't come close. Don't say anything. Just leave."

"Why?"

He gave an impatient shake of his head. "Whatever words would make you go, consider them said."

"And if I don't?"

His eyes were devil-bright, his face hard. "Then I'll drag you to this bed and force myself on you."

Beatrix didn't believe that for a second. But it revealed the extremity of his torment, that he would threaten such a thing. Giving him a patently skeptical glance, she said, "You're too drunk to catch me."

She was startled by a burst of movement.

Christopher reached her, fast as a leopard, and slammed his palms on the door on either side of her head. His voice was harsh and low. "I'm not as drunk as I look."

Beatrix had raised her arms reflexively, crossing them over her face. She had to remind herself to start breathing again. The problem was, once she resumed, she couldn't control her lungs, which were working as if she had run miles. Faced with a hard wall of masculine flesh, she could almost feel the heat of his skin.

"Are you afraid of me now?" he asked.

She gave a slight shake of her head, her eyes huge.

"You should be."

Beatrix started as she felt his hand glide from her waist to the side of her ribs in an insolent caress. His breathing deepened as he discovered that she wasn't wearing a corset. His palm moved slowly over her natural shape.

Christopher's lashes half lowered, and his color heightened as he stared at her. His hand came to her breast, lightly shaping the roundness. Beatrix felt her legs threaten to give out beneath her. His thumb and forefinger caught at the rising tip and squeezed gently.

"Last chance," he said in guttural voice. "Get out, or get in my bed."

"Is there a third option?" Beatrix asked weakly, her breast throbbing beneath his touch.

For answer, Christopher picked her up with stunning ease and carried her to the bed. She was tossed to the mattress. Before she could move, he had straddled her, all that sleek golden power poised above her.

"Wait," Beatrix said. "Before you force yourself on me, I would like to have five minutes of rational conversation. Only five. Surely that's not too much to ask."

His eyes were pitiless. "If you wanted rational conversation, you should have gone to another man. Your Mr. Chittering."

"Chickering," Beatrix said, squirming beneath him. "And he's not mine, and—" She swatted his hand away as he touched her breast again. "Stop that. I just want to—" Undeterred, he had gone for the button placket of her shirt. She scowled in exasperation. "All right, then," she snapped, "do as you please! Perhaps afterward we could manage a coherent discussion." Twisting beneath him, she flopped onto her stomach.

Christopher went still. After a long hesitation, she heard him ask in a far more normal voice, "What are you doing?"

"I'm making it easier for you," came her defiant reply. "Go on, start ravishing."

Another silence. Then, "Why are you facing downward?"

"Because that's how it's done." Beatrix twisted to look at him over her shoulder. A twinge of uncertainty caused her to ask, "Isn't it?"

His face was blank. "Has no one ever told you?"

"No, but I've read about it."

Christopher rolled off her, relieving her of his weight. He wore an odd expression as he asked, "From what books?"

"Veterinary manuals. And of course, I've observed the squirrels in springtime, and farm animals and—"

She was interrupted as Christopher cleared his throat loudly, and again. Darting a confused glance at him, she realized that he was trying to choke back amusement.

Beatrix began to feel indignant. Her first time in a bed with a man, and he was *laughing*.

"Look here," she said in a businesslike manner, "I've read about the mating habits of over two dozen species, and with the exception of snails, whose genitalia is on their necks, they all—" She broke off and frowned. "Why are you laughing at me?

Christopher had collapsed, overcome with hilarity. As he lifted his head and saw her affronted expression, he struggled manfully with another outburst. "Beatrix. I'm . . . I'm not laughing at you."

"You are!"

"No I'm not. It's just . . ." He swiped a tear from the corner of his eye, and a few more chuckles escaped. "Squirrels . . ."

"Well, it may be humorous to you, but it's a very serious matter to the squirrels."

That set him off again. In a display of rank insensitivity to the reproductive rights of small mammals, Christopher had buried his face in a pillow, his shoulders shaking.

"What is so amusing about fornicating squirrels?" Beatrix asked irritably.

By this time he had gone into near apoplexy. "No more," he gasped. "Please."

"I gather it's not the same for people," Beatrix said with great dignity, inwardly mortified. "They don't go about it the same way that animals do?"

Fighting to control himself, Christopher rolled to face her. His eyes were brilliant with unspent laughter. "Yes. No. That is, they do, but . . ."

"But you don't prefer it that way?"

Considering how to answer her, Christopher reached out to smooth her disheveled hair, which was falling out of its pins. "I do. I'm quite enthusiastic about it, actually. But it's not right for your first time."

"Why not?"

Christopher looked at her, a slow smile curving his lips. His voice deepened as he asked, "Shall I show you?"

Beatrix was transfixed.

Taking her stillness as assent, he pressed her back

and moved over her slowly. He touched her with care, arranging her limbs, spreading them to receive him. A gasp escaped her as she felt his hips settle on hers. He was aroused, a thick pressure fitting against her intimately. Bracing some of his weight on his arms, he looked down into her reddening face.

"This way," he said, with the slightest nudge, ". . . is usually more pleasing to the lady."

The gentle movement sent a jolt of pleasure through her. Beatrix couldn't speak, her senses filled with him, her hips catching a helpless arch. She looked up at the powerful surface of his chest, covered with a tantalizing fleece of bronze-gold hair.

Christopher lowered further, his mouth hovering just over hers. "Front to front . . . I could kiss you the entire time. And the shape of you would cushion me so sweetly . . . like this . . ." His lips took hers and coaxed them open, wringing heat and delight from her yielding flesh. Beatrix shivered, her arms lifting around his neck. She felt him all along her body, his warmth and weight anchoring her.

He murmured endearments, kissing along her throat, while he tugged at the buttons of her shirt and spread the fabric open. She wore only a short chemise beneath, the kind commonly used as a corset cover. Pulling down the lace-trimmed strap, he exposed a round, pale breast, the peak already tight and rose colored. His head bent, and he caressed her with his mouth and tongue. His teeth grazed lightly over her sensitive nerves. And all the while, that relentless, rhythmic stimulation below . . . he was riding her, owning her, driving the need to an impossible pitch.

His hands cradled her head as he kissed her again, openmouthed and deep, as if he were trying to draw the soul from her body. Beatrix answered eagerly, holding

him with her arms and legs. But then he let go with a
hoarse exclamation, and moved away.

"No," she heard herself moan. "Please—"

His fingers came to her lips, gently stroking her into
silence.

They lay side by side, facing each other, struggling
to regain their breath.

"My God, I want you." Christopher sounded far
from pleased by the fact. His thumb swept over her
kiss-swollen lips.

"Even though I annoy you?"

"You don't annoy me." Carefully he rebuttoned the
placket of her shirt. "I thought you did, at first. But now
I realize it was more like the feeling you get when your
foot's been asleep. And when you start moving, the
blood coming back into it is uncomfortable . . . but also
good. Do you understand what I mean?"

"Yes. I make your feet tingle."

A smile came to his lips. "Among other things."

They continued to lie together, staring at each other.

He had the most remarkable face, Beatrix thought.
Strong, flawless . . . and yet it was saved from cold
perfection by the lines of humor at the corners of his
eyes, and the hint of sensuality edging his mouth. The
subtle weathering made him look . . . experienced. It
was the kind of face that made a woman's heart beat
faster.

Shyly Beatrix reached out to touch the bayonet scar
on his shoulder. His skin was like hot pressed satin,
except for the dark, uneven gouge of that healed-over
wound. "How painful this must have been," she whispered. "Do your wounds still hurt?"

Christopher shook his head slightly.

"Then . . . what is troubling you?"

He was silent, his hand settling on her hip. As he thought, his fingers slipped beneath the untucked hem of her shirt, the backs of his knuckles stroking the skin of her midriff.

"I can't go back to who I was before the war," he eventually said. "And I can't be who I was during the war. And if I'm not either of those men, I'm not sure what I'm left with. Except for the knowledge that I killed more men than I could count." His gaze was distant, as if he were staring into a nightmare. "Always officers first—that sent them into disarray—then I picked off the rest as they scattered. They fell like toys a child had knocked over."

"But those were your orders. They were the enemy."

"I don't give a damn. They were men. They were loved by someone. I could never make myself forget that. You don't know what it looks like, when a man is shot. You've never heard wounded men on the battle-field, begging for water, or for someone to finish what the enemy started—"

Rolling away, he sat up and lowered his head. "I have rages," came his muffled voice. "I tried to attack one of my own footmen yesterday, did they tell you that? Christ, I'm no better than Albert. I can never share a bed with a woman again—I might kill her in her sleep, and not realize what I'm doing until afterward."

Beatrix sat up as well. "You wouldn't do that."

"You don't know that. You're so innocent." Christopher broke off and drew in a shivering breath. "God. I can't crawl out from under this. And I can't live with it."

"With what?" she asked softly, realizing that something in particular was tormenting him, some intolerable memory.

Christopher didn't acknowledge her. His mind was in

another place, watching shadows. When she began to move closer to him, he lifted his arm as if in self-defense, palm turned outward. The broken gesture, made with such a strong hand, cut straight to Beatrix's heart.

She felt an overwhelming need to physically draw him closer, as if to ease him away from a precipice. Instead she kept her hands in her lap, and stared at the place where the ends of his hair rested on his sun-browned neck. The muscles of his back were bunched. If only she could smooth her palm over that hard, rippled surface. If only she could soothe him. But he had to find his own way out.

"A friend of mine died at Inkerman," Christopher finally said, his voice halting and raw. "One of my lieutenants. His name was Mark Bennett. He was the best soldier in the regiment. He was always honest. He joked at the wrong times. If you asked him to do something, no matter how difficult or dangerous, it would be done. He would have risked his life for any of us.

"The Russians had set up rifle pits in caverns and old stone huts built in the side of a hill. They were firing directly into our siege batteries—the general decided the Russian position had to be taken. Three companies of Rifles were chosen.

"A company of Hussars was ordered to ride against the enemy if they tried to flank us. They were led by a man I hated. Lieutenant Colonel Fenwick. Everyone hated him. He commanded the same cavalry regiment I had started in when I bought my first commission."

Christopher fell silent, lost in memory. His half-lowered lashes sent spikes of shadow over his cheeks.

"Why was he so hated?" Beatrix eventually prompted.

"Fenwick was often cruel for no reason. Fond of punishment for its own sake. He ordered floggings and deprivations for the most minor infractions. And when he invented excuses to discipline the men, I intervened. He accused me of insubordination, and I was nearly brought up on charges." Christopher let out a slow, uneven breath. "Fenwick was the main reason I agreed to be transferred to the Rifle Brigade. And then at Inkerman I found out I would have to depend on his cavalry support.

"Before the riflemen got to the trenches, we stopped in a ravine where there was shelter from stray shots. Night was coming. We formed into three groups. We opened fire, the Russians returned it, and we pinpointed the positions we had to take. We advanced with guns . . . took out as many as we could . . . then it turned into hand-to-hand combat. I was separated from Bennett in the fighting. The Russians drove us back when their support came . . . and then shell and grape started raining down. It wouldn't stop. Men around me were falling . . . their bodies opening up, wounds breaking out. My arms and back were burning with shrapnel. I couldn't find Bennett. It was dark, and we had to fall back.

"I'd left Albert waiting in the ravine. I called for him, and he came. Through all that hellfire, against every natural instinct . . . Albert came out with me to find wounded men in the dark. He led me to two men lying at the base of the hill. One of them was Bennett."

Beatrix closed her eyes sickly as she drew an accurate conclusion. "And the other was Colonel Fenwick," she said.

Christopher nodded grimly. "Fenwick had been unseated. His horse was gone. One of his legs was broken . . . a bullet wound in the side . . . there was a good chance he would live. But Bennett . . . his front had been ripped open. He was barely conscious. Dying by degrees. I wanted it to be me, it should have been. I was always taking chances. Bennett was the careful one. He wanted to go back to his family, and to the woman he cared for. I don't know why it wasn't me. That's the hell of battle—it's all chance, you never know if you'll be next. You can try to hide, and a shell will find you. You can run straight at the enemy, and a bullet might jam in a rifle, and you're spared. It's all luck." He clenched his jaw against a tremor of emotion. "I wanted to take them both to safety, but there was no one to help. And I couldn't leave Fenwick there. If he was captured, the enemy would get crucial intelligence from him. He'd had access to all the general's dispatches, knew all about strategies and supplies . . . everything."

Beatrix stared at his partially averted profile. "You had to save Colonel Fenwick first," she whispered, her chest aching with compassion and pity as she finally understood. "Before you could save your friend."

"I told Mark, 'I'll come back for you. I'll come back, I swear it. I'm leaving Albert with you.' There was blood in his mouth. I knew he wanted to say something, but he couldn't. Albert stayed next to him, and I picked up Fenwick, and carried him over my shoulder, and took him back to the ravine.

"When I went back for Bennett, the sky was on fire, the smoke made it difficult to see more than a few feet ahead. The ammunition flashes were like lightning. Bennett was gone. Literally gone. They had taken him. Albert was wounded—someone had jabbed him with a bayonet. One of his ears was half dangling—there's a little ragged place where it wasn't stitched properly afterward. I stayed beside Albert with my rifle, and we held the position until the Rifle companies advanced again. And finally we took the pits, and it was done."

"Lieutenant Bennett was never found?" Beatrix asked faintly.

Christopher shook his head. "He wasn't returned in the prisoner exchange. He couldn't have lived long after he was captured. But I might have saved him. I'll never know. Jesus." Blotting his glittering eyes with his sleeve, he fell silent.

He seemed to be waiting for something . . . sympathy that he would not accept, condemnation that he did not deserve. Beatrix wondered what some person far wiser or more worldly than she might have said. She didn't know. All she could offer was the truth. "You must listen to me," she said. "It was an impossible choice. And Lieutenant Bennett . . . Mark . . . didn't blame you."

"I blame myself." He sounded weary.

How tired of death he must be, she thought compassionately. *How tired of grief and guilt.* But what she said was, "Well, that's not reasonable. I know that it must torment you to think that he died alone, or worse, at the hands of the enemy. But it's not how we die that matters, it's how we live. While Mark lived, he knew that he was loved. He had his family and his friends. That was as much as any man could have."

Christopher shook his head. No good. No words could help him.

Beatrix reached out to him then, unable to hold back any longer. She let her hand glide gently over the warm golden skin of his shoulder. "I don't think you should blame yourself," she said. "But it doesn't matter what I believe. You'll have to come to that conclusion on your own. It wasn't your fault that you were faced with a terrible choice. You must give yourself enough time to get better."

"How much time will that take?" he asked bitterly.

"I don't know," she admitted. "But you have a lifetime."

A caustic laugh broke from him. "That's too damned long."

"I understand that you feel responsible for what happened to Mark. But you've already been forgiven for whatever you think your sins are. You *have*," she insisted as he shook his head. "Love forgives all things. And so many people—" She stopped as she felt his entire body jerk.

"What did you say?" she heard him whisper.

Beatrix realized the mistake she had just made. Her arms fell away from him.

The blood began to roar in her ears, her heart thumping so madly she felt faint. Without thinking, she scrambled away from him, off the bed, to the center of the room.

Breathing in frantic bursts, Beatrix turned to face him.

Christopher was staring at her, his eyes gleaming with a strange, mad light. "I knew it," he whispered.

She wondered if he might try to kill her.

She decided not to wait to find out.

Fear gave her the speed of a terrified hare. She bolted before he could catch her, tearing to the door, flinging it open, and scampering to the grand staircase. Her boots made absurdly loud thuds on the stairs as she leaped downward.

Christopher followed her to the threshold, bellowing her name.

Beatrix didn't pause for a second, knowing he was going to pursue her as soon as he donned his clothes.

Mrs. Clocker stood near the entrance hall, looking worried and astonished. "Miss Hathaway? What—"

"I think he'll come out of his room now," Beatrix said rapidly, jumping down the last of the stairs. "It's time for me to be going."

"Did he . . . are you . . ."

"If he asks for his horse to be saddled," Beatrix said breathlessly, "please have it done *slowly*."

"Yes, but—"

"Good-bye."

And Beatrix raced from the house as if demons were at her heels.

Chapter Seventeen

Beatrix fled to the one place where she knew he wouldn't find her.

The irony was hardly lost on her, that she was hiding from Christopher in the place she had most longed to share with him. And she was well aware that she could not hide from him forever. There would be a reckoning.

But after having seen his face when he realized that she was the one who had deceived him, Beatrix wanted to put off that reckoning for as long as possible.

She rode pell-mell to the secret house on Lord Westcliff's estate, tethered the horse, and went upstairs to the tower room. It was sparsely furnished with a pair of battered chairs, an ancient settee with a low back, a ramshackle table, and a bed frame propped against one wall. Beatrix had kept the room swept clean and dusted, and she had adorned the walls with unframed sketches of landscapes and animals.

A dish of burned-out candle stubs was set at the window.

After admitting fresh air into the room, Beatrix paced back and forth, muttering frantically to herself.

"He'll probably kill me. Good, that's better than

having him hate me. A quick throttling, and it will be over. I wish I could throttle myself and spare him the trouble. Maybe I should toss myself out the window. If only I'd never written those letters. If only I'd been honest. Oh, what if he goes to Ramsay House and waits there for me? What if—"

She stopped abruptly as she heard a noise from outside. *A bark.* Creeping to the window, she looked down and saw Albert's jaunty, furry form trotting around the building. And Christopher, tethering his horse near hers.

He had found her.

"Oh God," Beatrix whispered, blanching. She turned and set her back against the wall, feeling like a prisoner facing execution. This was one of the worst moments of her entire life . . . and in light of some of the Hathaways' past difficulties, that was saying something.

In just a few moments, Albert bounded into the room and came to her.

"You led him here, didn't you?" Beatrix accused in a furious whisper. *"Traitor!"*

Looking apologetic, Albert went to a chair, hopped up, and rested his chin on his paws. His ears twitched at the sound of a measured tread on the stairs.

Christopher entered the room, having to bend his head to pass through the small medieval doorway. Straightening, he surveyed their surroundings briefly before his piercing gaze found Beatrix. He stared at her with the barely suppressed wrath of a man to whom entirely too much had happened.

Beatrix wished she were a swooning sort of female. It seemed the only appropriate response to the situation.

Unfortunately, no matter how she tried to summon a swoon, her mind remained intractably conscious.

"I'm so sorry," she croaked.

No reply.

Christopher approached her slowly, as if he thought she might try to bolt again. Reaching her, he took her upper arms in a hard grip that allowed no chance of escape. "Tell me why you did it," he said, his voice low and vibrant with . . . hatred? Fury? "No, damn you, don't cry. Was it a game? Was it only to help Prudence?"

Beatrix looked away with a wretched sob. "*No,* it wasn't a game . . . Pru showed me your letter, and she said she wasn't going to answer it. And I *had* to. I felt as if it had been written for me. It was only supposed to be once. But then you wrote back, and I let myself answer just once more . . . and then one more time, and another . . ."

"How much of it was the truth?"

"All of it," Beatrix burst out. "Except for signing Pru's name. The rest of it was real. If you believe nothing else, please believe that."

Christopher was quiet for a long moment. He had begun to breathe heavily. "Why did you stop?"

She sensed how difficult it was for him to ask. But God help her, it was infinitely worse to have to answer.

"Because it hurt too much. The words meant too much." She forced herself to go on, even though she was crying. "I fell in love with you, and I knew I could never have you. I couldn't pretend to be Pru any longer. I loved you so much, and I couldn't—"

Her words were abruptly smothered.

He was kissing her, she realized dazedly. What did it mean? What did he want? What . . . but her thoughts dissolved, and she stopped trying to make sense of anything.

His arms had closed around her, one hand gripping the back of her neck. Shaken to her soul, she molded against him. Taking her sobs into his mouth, he licked deep, his kiss strong and savage. It had to be a dream, and yet her senses insisted it was real, the scent and warmth and toughness of him engulfing her. He pulled her even more tightly against him, making it difficult to breathe. She didn't care. The pleasure of the kiss suffused her, drugged her, and when he pulled his head back, she protested with a bewildered moan.

Christopher forced her to look back at him. "Loved?" he asked hoarsely. "Past tense?"

"Present tense," she managed to say.

"You told me to find you."

"I didn't mean to send you that note."

"But you did. You wanted me."

"Yes." More tears escaped her stinging eyes. He bent and pressed his mouth to them, tasting the salt of grief.

Those gray eyes looked into hers, no longer bright as hellfrost, but soft as smoke. "I love you, Beatrix."

Maybe she was capable of swooning after all.

It certainly felt like a swoon, her knees giving way, her head lolling against his shoulder as he lowered them both to the threadbare carpet. Fitting his arm beneath her neck, Christopher covered her mouth with his again. Beatrix answered helplessly, unable to withhold anything. Their legs tangled, and he let his thigh nuzzle between hers.

"I th-thought you would hate me . . ." Her dazed voice seemed to come from far away.

"Never. You could run to the farthest corners of the earth. There's no place you could go where I wouldn't love you. Nothing you could do to stop me."

She shivered at what he was doing, his hands opening her clothes, sliding inside them. Her breasts felt hot, the tips hardening as he touched them. "I thought you were going to murder me," she said with difficulty.

A ghost of a smile came to his lips. "No. That wasn't

what I wanted to do." He brought his mouth to hers, kissing her with rough, hungry ardor. Unfastening her breeches, he found the taut surface of her stomach. His hand insinuated farther into the loosened garment, curving around her bare hip. His fingers explored with a gentle but insistent curiosity that made her squirm, gooseflesh rising.

"Christopher," she said brokenly, fumbling with the front of his trousers, but he caught her wrist and pulled it back.

"It's been too long. I don't trust myself with you."

Pressing her burning face against his neck, where his shirt had been laid open, Beatrix felt the strong ripple of his swallow against her parted lips. "I want to be yours."

"You are, God help you."

"Then love me." Feverishly she kissed his throat. "Love me—"

"Hush," Christopher whispered. "I have little enough self-control as it is. I can't make love to you here. It wouldn't be right for you." He kissed her tumbled hair, while his hand smoothed her hip in an unsteady caress. "Talk to me. Would you really have let me marry Prudence?"

"If you seemed happy with her. If she was the one you wanted."

"I wanted *you*." He kissed her, his mouth strong and punishing. "It nearly drove me mad, looking for the things I loved in her and not finding them. And then beginning to see them in you."

"I'm sorry."

"You should have told me."

"Yes. But I knew you'd be angry. And I thought she was what you wanted. Pretty and vivacious—"

"With all the wit of a toasting iron."

"Why did you write to her in the first place?"

"I was lonely. I didn't know her well. But I needed . . . someone. When I received that reply, about Mawdsley's donkey and the smell of October, and the rest of it . . . I started falling in love right then. I thought it was another side of Pru I hadn't yet seen. It never occurred to me that the letters were written by someone else entirely." He gave her a dark glance.

Beatrix returned his gaze contritely. "I knew you wouldn't want letters from me. I knew I wasn't the kind of woman you wanted."

Rolling Beatrix to her side, Christopher brought her against his aroused form. "Does this feel as if I don't want you?"

The hard pressure of him, the rampant heat of his body, dazzled her senses . . . it was like being drunk . . . like drinking starlight. Closing her eyes, she leaned her face into his shoulder. "You thought I was peculiar," she said in a muffled voice.

His mouth brushed the edge of her ear and settled against her neck. She felt that he was smiling. "Darling love . . . you are."

An answering grin curled her lips. She shivered as Christopher moved over her, pushing her back, using his thigh to part hers. He took her mouth with endless kisses, deep and impatient, turning her blood to fire. He began to caress her with strong, callused hands, a soldier's hands. Her breeches were dragged away from her pale hips.

They both gasped, breath fragmenting, as his palm cupped her intimately. He stroked the humid warmth, parting and spreading her, a fingertip stroking the entrance to her body.

She lay quiet and unresisting, a mad heartbeat resounding everywhere. He touched inside her, his finger pushing gently past the innocent constriction. Lowering his head, he pressed his mouth to the tender curves of her breasts. A moan escaped her as she felt him take a hard bud between his lips. He began to suckle, his tongue lapping between each rhythmic tug. His finger went deeper, the heel of his hand teasing an unspeakably sensitive place.

Beatrix writhed, seeing nothing. Desperate tension folded in upon itself, and again, centering low and tight. A whimper escaped her as a wave of unimaginable pleasure caught her, and he guided her farther into it. She managed to speak through dry lips, her voice stunned and shaken. "Christopher—I can't—"

"Let it happen," he whispered against her flushed skin. "Let it come."

He stroked her in a wicked, sensual cadence, pushing her higher. Her muscles worked against the alarming rush of sensation, and then her body began pulling it all in, her veins dilating, heat surging. Groping for his head, Beatrix sank her hands into his hair and guided his mouth to hers. He complied at once, drinking in her moans and gasps, his beguiling hands soothing the wrenching spasms.

The delight receded in lazy ebbs, leaving her weak and trembling. Beatrix stirred and opened her eyes, discovering that she was on the floor, half undressed, cradled in the arms of the man she loved. It was a strange, delicious, vulnerable moment. Her head turned in the crook of his arm. She saw Albert, who had fallen asleep in the chair, supremely uninterested in their antics.

Christopher caressed her slowly, his knuckles trailing through the valley between her breasts.

Beatrix tilted her head back to look at him. Perspiration had given his skin the sheen of polished metal, strong masculine features worked in bronze. His expression was engrossed, as if her body fascinated him, as if she were made of some precious substance he had never encountered before. She felt the soft, hot shock of his breath as he bent to kiss the inside of her wrist. He let the tip of his tongue rest against a tiny pulse. So new, this intimacy with him, and yet it was as necessary as the beat of her own heart.

She never wanted to be out of his arms again. She wanted to be with him always.

"When are we going to marry?" she asked, her voice languorous.

Christopher brushed his lips against her cheek. He held her a little more tightly.

And he was silent.

Beatrix blinked in surprise. His hesitation affected her like a splash of cold water. "We *are* going to marry, aren't we?"

Christopher looked into her flushed face. "That's a difficult question."

"No it's not. It's a very simple yes-or-no question!"

"I can't marry you," he said quietly, "until I can be certain that it will be good for you."

"Why is there any doubt of that?"

"You know why."

"I do not!"

His mouth twisted. "Fits of rage, nightmares, strange visions, excessive drinking . . . does any of that sound like a man who's fit for marriage?"

"You were going to marry Prudence," Beatrix said indignantly.

"I wasn't. I wouldn't do this to any woman. Least of all to the woman I love more than my own life."

Beatrix rolled away and sat up, pulling her loosened garments around her. "How long do you intend for us to wait? Obviously you're not perfect, but—"

" 'Not perfect' is having a bald spot or pockmarks. My problems are a bit more significant than that."

Beatrix answered in an anxious tumble of words. "I come from a family of flawed people who marry other flawed people. Every one of us has taken a chance on love."

"I love you too much to risk your safety."

"Love me even more, then," she begged. "Enough to marry me no matter what the obstacles are."

Christopher scowled. "Don't you think it would be easier for me to take what I want, regardless of the consequences? I want you with me every moment of the day. I want to hold you every night. I want to make love to you so badly I can't even breathe. But I won't allow any harm to come to you, especially from my hands."

"You wouldn't hurt me. Your instincts wouldn't let you."

"My instincts are those of a madman."

Beatrix wrapped her arms around her bent knees. "You're willing to accept my problems," she said dolefully, "but you won't allow me to accept yours." She buried her face in her arms. "You don't trust me."

"You know that's not the issue. I don't trust myself."

In her volatile state, it was difficult not to cry. The situation was so vastly unfair. Maddening.

"Beatrix." Christopher knelt beside her, drawing her against him. She stiffened. "Let me hold you," he said near her ear.

"If we don't marry, when will I see you?" she asked miserably. "On chaperoned visits? Carriage drives? Stolen moments?"

Christopher smoothed her hair and stared into her swimming eyes. "It's more than we've had until now."

"It's not enough." Beatrix wrapped her arms around him. "I'm not afraid of you." Gripping the back of his shirt, she gave it a little shake for emphasis. "I want you, and you say you want me, and the only thing standing in our way is *you*. Don't tell me that you survived all those battles, and suffered through so much, merely to come home for *this*—"

He laid his fingers against her mouth. "Quiet. Let me think."

"What is there to—"

"Beatrix," he warned.

She fell silent, her gaze locked on his severe features.

Christopher frowned, weighing possibilities, inwardly debating the issue without seeming to come to any satisfactory conclusion.

In the silence, Beatrix rested her head on his shoulder. His body was warm and comforting, the deep-flexing muscles easily accommodating her weight. She wriggled to press closer to him, until she felt the satisfying hardness of his chest against her breasts. And she adjusted her position as she felt the firm pressure of him lower down. Her body ached to gather him in. Furtively she brushed her lips against the salt-scented skin of his neck.

He clamped his hand on her hip. Amusement threaded through his voice. "Stop squirming. There is no possible way a man can think when you're doing that."

"Haven't you finished thinking yet?"

"No." But she felt him smile as he kissed her forehead. "If you and I marry," he said eventually, "I would be put in the position of trying to protect my wife against myself. And your well-being and happiness are everything to me."

If . . . Beatrix's heart leaped into her throat. She began to speak, but Christopher nudged his knuckles beneath her chin, gently closing her mouth. "And regardless of what fascinating ideas your family may have about the marital relationship," he continued, "I have a traditional view. The husband is master of the household."

"Oh, absolutely," Beatrix said, a bit too quickly. "That's what my family believes, too."

His eyes narrowed skeptically.

Perhaps that had been taking it a bit far. Hoping to distract him, Beatrix nuzzled her cheek into his hand. "Could I keep my animals?"

"Of course." His voice softened. "I would never deny something so important to you. Although I can't help but ask . . . is the hedgehog negotiable?"

"Medusa? Oh, no, she couldn't survive on her own. She was abandoned by her mother as kit, and I've taken care of her ever since. I suppose I could try to find a new home for her, but for some reason people don't take readily to the idea of pet hedgehogs."

"How odd of them," Christopher said. "Very well, Medusa stays."

"Are you proposing to me?" Beatrix asked hopefully.

"No." Closing his eyes, Christopher let out a short sigh. "But I'm considering it against all better judgment."

Chapter Eighteen

They rode directly to Ramsay House, with Albert loping happily along. It was nearly time for dinner, which made it likely that both Leo and Cam would have concluded their work for the day. Beatrix wished that she'd had time to prepare her family for the situation. She was fervently glad that Merripen was still in Ireland, because he tended to view all outsiders with suspicion, and he would not have made the situation easier for Christopher. And Leo might have objections. The best option was to approach Cam, who was by far the most reasonable male in the family.

However, when Beatrix tried to make suggestions to Christopher about whom to approach and what to say, he interrupted her with a kiss and told her that he would manage it on his own.

"Very well," Beatrix said reluctantly. "But I warn you, they may be resistant to the match."

"*I'm* resistant to the match," Christopher informed her. "At least we'll have that in common."

They entered the house and went to the family parlor, where Cam and Leo were involved in conversation, and Catherine was sitting at a small writing desk.

"Phelan," Cam said, looking up with an easy smile, "have you come to see the timber yard?"

"Thank you, but I'm here for another reason."

Leo, who was standing near the window, glanced from Christopher's rumpled attire to Beatrix's disheveled condition. "Beatrix, darling, have you taken to going off the estate dressed like that?"

"Only this once," she said apologetically. "I was in a hurry."

"A hurry involving Captain Phelan?" Leo's sharp gaze moved to Christopher. "What do you wish to discuss?"

"It's personal," Christopher said quietly. "And it concerns your sister." He looked from Cam to Leo. Ordinarily there would have been no question concerning which one of them to approach. As lord of the manor, Leo would have been the first choice. However, the Hathaways seemed to have settled on an unconventional sharing of roles.

"Which one of you should I talk to?" Christopher asked.

They pointed to each other and replied at the same time.

"Him."

Cam spoke to Leo. "You're the viscount."

"You're the one who usually deals with that sort of thing," Leo protested.

"Yes. But you won't like my opinion on this one."

"You're not actually considering giving them your approval, are you?"

"Of all the Hathaway sisters," Cam said equably, "Beatrix is the one most suited to choose her own husband. I trust her judgment."

Beatrix gave him a brilliant smile. "Thank you, Cam."

"What are you thinking?" Leo demanded of his brother-in-law. "You can't trust Beatrix's judgment."

"Why not?"

"She's too young," Leo said.

"I'm twenty-three," Beatrix protested. "In dog years I'd be dead."

"And you're female," Leo persisted.

"I beg your pardon?" Catherine interrupted. "Are you implying that women have poor judgment?"

"In these matters, yes." Leo gestured to Christopher. "Just look at the fellow, standing there like a bloody Greek god. Do you think she chose him because of his intellect?"

"I graduated from Cambridge," Christopher said acidly. "Should I have brought my diploma?"

"In this family," Cam interrupted, "there is no requirement of a university degree to prove one's intelligence. Lord Ramsay is a perfect example of how one has nothing to do with the other."

"Phelan," Leo said, "I don't intend to be offensive, however—"

"It's something that comes naturally to him," Catherine interrupted sweetly.

Leo sent his wife a scowl and returned his attention to Christopher. "You and Beatrix haven't known each other long enough to consider matrimony. A matter of weeks, to my knowledge. And what about Prudence Mercer? You're practically betrothed, aren't you?"

"Those are valid points," Christopher said. "And I will answer them. But you should know right away that I'm against the match."

Leo blinked in bemusement. "You mean you're against a match with Miss Mercer?"

"Well . . . yes. But I'm also against a match with Beatrix."

Silence fell over the room.

"This is a trick of some sort," Leo said.

"Unfortunately, it's not," Christopher replied.

Another silence.

"Captain Phelan," Cam asked, choosing his words with care. "Have you come to ask for our consent to marry Beatrix?"

Christopher shook his head. "If I decide to marry Beatrix, I'll do it with or without your consent."

Leo looked at Cam. "Good God," he said in disgust. "This one's worse than Harry."

Cam wore an expression of beleaguered patience. "Perhaps we should both talk to Captain Phelan in the library. With brandy."

"I want my own bottle," Leo said feelingly, leading the way.

Aside from leaving out a few intimate details, Christopher told them everything. He was unsparing when it came to his own flaws, but he was determined to protect Beatrix from criticism, even from her own family.

"It's not like her to play games," Leo said, shaking his head after Christopher told them about the letters. "God knows what possessed her to do such a thing."

"It wasn't a game," Christopher said quietly. "It turned into something more than either of us expected."

Cam regarded him with a speculative gaze. "In the excitement of all these revelations, Phelan, one could easily be swept away. Are you *very sure* of your feelings for Beatrix? Because she is—"

"Unique," Leo supplied.

"I know that." Christopher felt his mouth twitch with a trace of humor. "I know that she steals things unintentionally. She wears breeches, and references Greek philosophers, and has read far too many veterinary manuals. I know that she keeps the kinds of pets that other people pay to have exterminated." Thinking of Beatrix, he felt an ache of yearning. "I know that she could never reside in London, that she could only thrive by living close to nature. I know that she is compassionate, intelligent, and brave, and the only thing she truly fears is being abandoned. And I would never do that, because I happen to love her to distraction. But there is one problem."

"What is that?" Leo asked.

Christopher answered in a bleak syllable. "Me."

Minutes ticked by as Christopher explained the rest of it . . . his inexplicable behavior since the war, the symptoms of a condition that seemed akin to madness. He probably shouldn't have been surprised that they received the information without apparent alarm. But it made him wonder: what kind of family was this?

When Christopher finished, there was a moment of silence.

Leo looked at Cam expectantly. "Well?"

"Well what?"

"Now is the time when you dredge up one of your blasted Romany sayings. Something about roosters laying eggs, or pigs dancing in the orchard. It's what you always do. Let's have it."

Cam gave him a sardonic glance. "I can't think of one right now."

"By God, I've had to listen to hundreds of them. And Phelan doesn't have to hear even *one*?"

Ignoring Leo, Cam turned his attention to Christopher. "I believe the problems you've described will lessen as time passes." He paused. "Our brother Merripen would attest to that, if he were here."

Christopher looked at him alertly.

"He never fought in a war," Cam continued quietly,

"but violence and damage are hardly limited to the battlefield. He had his own demons to fight, and he conquered them. I see no reason why you can't do the same."

"I think Phelan and Beatrix should wait," Leo said. "Nothing will be lost by waiting."

"I don't know about that," Cam said. "As the Rom say, 'Take too much time, and time will take you.'"

Leo looked smug. "I knew there would be a saying."

"With all due respect," Christopher muttered, "this conversation is leading nowhere. At least one of you should point out that Beatrix deserves a better man."

"That's what I said about my wife," Leo remarked. "Which is why I married her before she could find one." He smiled slightly as he contemplated Christopher's glowering face. "So far, I haven't been all that impressed by your flaws. You drink more than you should, you have trouble controlling your impulses, and you have a temper. All of those are practically requirements in the Hathaway family. I suppose you think Beatrix should marry a quiet young gentleman whose idea of excitement is collecting snuffboxes or writing sonnets. Well, we've tried that, and it hasn't worked. She doesn't want that kind of man. Apparently what she wants is you."

"She's too young and idealistic to know better," Christopher said. "I fault her judgment."

"So do I," Leo shot back. "But unfortunately none of my sisters let me pick their husbands for them."

"Easy, the two of you," Cam interceded calmly. "I have a question for you, Phelan . . . if you decide to wait indefinitely before proposing marriage to Beatrix . . . do you intend to continue seeing her in the meantime?"

"Yes," Christopher said honestly. "I don't think anything could keep me away from her. But we'll be circumspect."

"I doubt that," Leo said. "The only thing Beatrix knows about being circumspect is how to spell it."

"Before long there would be gossip," Cam said, "and criticism, which would harm Beatrix's reputation. With the result that you would have to marry her anyway. There's not much point in delaying the inevitable."

"Are you saying you *want* me to marry her?" Christopher asked incredulously.

"No," Cam replied, looking rueful. "But I can't say I'm all that fond of the alternative. Beatrix would be miserable. Besides, which one of us will volunteer to tell her that she's going to have to wait?"

All three were silent.

Beatrix knew that she would get precious little rest that night, her mind too engaged with worries and questions to allow for sleep. Christopher had not stayed for dinner, but had left soon after his talk with Cam and Leo.

Amelia, who had come downstairs after having put Alex to bed, made no attempt to hide her pleasure in the news. "I like him," she said, hugging Beatrix and drawing back to view her with a smile. "He seems to be a good and honorable man."

"And brave," Cam added.

"Yes," Amelia replied soberly, "one can't forget what he did in the war."

"Oh, I didn't mean that," Cam told her. "I was referring to the fact that he's willing to marry a Hathaway sister."

Amelia stuck her tongue out at him, and he grinned.

The relationship between the pair was so comfortable, and yet spiced with playfulness and flirtation.

Beatrix wondered if she and Christopher could ever achieve anything similar, if he would relinquish enough of his defenses to allow her to be close to him.

Frowning, Beatrix sat next to Amelia. "I keep asking about the conversation Cam and Leo had with Christopher, and it seems nothing was decided or resolved. All they did was drink brandy."

"We assured Phelan that we were more than happy to let him have you and your menagerie," Leo retorted. "After that, he said he needed to think."

"About what?" Beatrix demanded. "What is there to think about? Why is it taking him so long to make a decision?"

"He's a man, dear," Amelia explained kindly. "Sustained thinking is very difficult for them."

"As opposed to women," Leo retorted, "who have the remarkable ability to make decisions without doing any thinking at all."

Christopher came to Ramsay House in the morning, looking very . . . well, *soldierly,* despite the fact that he was dressed in informal walking attire. He was quiet and impeccably polite as he asked to accompany Beatrix on a walk. Although Beatrix was thrilled to see him, she was also uneasy. He looked guarded and severe, a man with a possibly unpleasant duty to perform.

This was not at all auspicious.

Still, Beatrix maintained a cheerful façade, leading Christopher to one of her favorite walks in the forest, an outward leg with farmland to the right and woodland to the left. It continued in a loop that cut directly into the forest, crossed over ancient paths, and finished along a creek. Albert crossed back and forth, sniffing industriously as they progressed.

". . . whenever you find a clearing like this," Beatrix said, leading Christopher to a small, sun-dappled meadow, "it's most likely an ancient field enclosure from the Bronze Age. They knew nothing about fertilizing, so when a patch of land became unproductive, they simply cleared a new area. And the old areas became covered with gorse and bracken and heather. And here"—she showed him the cavity of an oak tree near the clearing—"is where I watched a hobby chick hatch in early summer. Hobbies don't build their own nests, they use ones made by other birds. They're so fast when they fly, they look like sickles cutting through the air."

Christopher listened attentively. With the breeze playing lightly in his dark gold hair, and a slight smile on his lips, he was so handsome that it was difficult not to gape at him. "You know all the secrets of this forest, don't you?" he asked gently.

"There's so much to learn, I've only scratched the surface. I've filled books with sketches of animals and plants, and I keep finding new ones to study." A wistful sigh escaped her. "There is talk of a natural history society to be established in London. I wish I could be part of it."

"Why can't you?"

"I'm sure they won't admit ladies," Beatrix said. "None of those groups do. It will be a room full of whiskered old men smoking pipes and sharing entomological notes. Which is a pity, because I daresay I could talk about insects as well as any of them."

A slow smile crossed his face. "I for one am glad you have neither pipe nor whiskers," he said. "However, it seems a pity that anyone who likes animals and insects as well as you shouldn't be allowed to discuss them. Perhaps we could persuade them to make an exception for you."

Beatrix glanced at him in surprise. "You would do that? You wouldn't mind the idea of a woman pursuing such unorthodox interests?"

"Of course I wouldn't. There would be no point in marrying a woman with unorthodox interests and then trying to make her ordinary, would there?"

Her eyes turned round. "Are you going to propose to me now?"

Christopher turned her to face him, his fingers stroking the underside of her chin, coaxing her face upward. "There are some things I want to discuss first."

Beatrix looked at him expectantly.

His expression sobered. Taking her hand in his, he began to walk with her along a grassy path. "First . . . we won't be able to share a bed."

She blinked. Hesitantly she asked, "We're going to be platonic?"

He stumbled a little. "*No.* God, no. What I meant was, we will have relations, but we will not sleep together."

"But . . . I think I would like sleeping with you."

His hand tightened on hers. "My nightmares would keep you awake."

"I wouldn't mind that."

"I might accidently strangle you in my sleep."

"Oh. Well, I would mind that." Beatrix frowned in concentration as they walked slowly. "May I make a request in turn?"

"Yes, what is it?"

"Could you leave off drinking strong liquor, and only have wine from now on? I know that you use spirits as a medicine to treat your other problems, but it's possible that it actually makes them worse, and—"

"There's no need to talk me into it, love. I've already resolved to do that."

"Oh." She smiled at him, pleased.

"There's only one other thing I'll ask of you," Christopher said. "No more dangerous activities, such as climbing trees or training half-wild horses, or removing feral animals from traps, and so forth."

Beatrix glanced at him in mute protest, resisting the prospect of any curtailment on her freedom.

Christopher understood. "I won't be unreasonable," he said quietly. "But I'd rather not have to worry about you being injured."

"People are injured all the time. Women's skirts catch fire, or people are thrown down by vehicles thundering along the road, or they trip and fall—"

"Precisely my point. Life is dangerous enough without your tempting fate."

It occurred to Beatrix that her family had placed far fewer restrictions on her than a husband would. She had to remind herself that marriage would have compensations as well.

". . . I have to go to Riverton soon," Christopher was saying. "I have much to learn about running an estate, not to mention the timber market. According to the estate manager, the production of Riverton timber is inconsistent. And a new railway station is being built in the region, which is to our benefit only if good roads are laid out. I have to take part in the planning, or I'll have no right to complain later." He stopped and turned Beatrix to face him. "I know how close you are to your family. Could you bear to live away from them? We'll keep Phelan House, but our main residence would be at Riverton."

It was a striking thought, living away from her family. They had been her entire world. Especially Amelia,

her one great constant. The idea touched a note of
anxiety in Beatrix, but also excitement. A new home—
new people, new places to explore . . . and Christopher.
Most of all, Christopher.

"I believe I could," Beatrix said. "I would miss
them. But most of the time I'm left to my own devices
here. My siblings are occupied with their families and
their lives, which is as it should be. As long as I could
travel to see them when I wished, I think I would be
happy."

Christopher fondled her cheek, his knuckles sliding
delicately against the side of her throat. There was understanding in his eyes, and sympathy, and something
else that caused her skin to flush.

"Whatever your happiness requires," he said,
"you'll have it." Easing her closer, he kissed her forehead, working down to the tip of her nose. "Beatrix.
Now I have something to ask you." His lips found the
curve of her smiling mouth. "My love . . . I would
choose the small sum of hours I've spent with you
over a lifetime spent with another woman. You never
needed to write that note, asking me to find you. I've
wanted to find you my entire life. I don't think there's
a man alive who could be all the things you deserve
in a husband . . . but I beg you to let me try. Will you
marry me?"

Beatrix pulled his head down to hers, and brought
her lips close to his ear. "Yes, yes, yes," she whispered,
and for no reason at all other than she wanted to, she
caught the edge of his ear lightly with her teeth.

Startled by the love nip, Christopher looked down at
her. Beatrix's breath quickened as she saw the promises of retribution and pleasure in his eyes. He pressed
a hard kiss against her lips.

"What kind of wedding would you like?" he asked, and stole another kiss before she could reply.

"The kind that turns you into my husband." She touched the firm line of his mouth with her fingers. "What kind would you like?"

He smiled ruefully. "A fast one."

Chapter Nineteen

Christopher supposed he should take it as a bad sign that within a fortnight he had become entirely comfortable around his future in-laws. Whereas he had once avoided them for their peculiarities, he now sought out their company, spending nearly every evening at Ramsay House.

The Hathaways squabbled, laughed, and genuinely seemed to like each other, which made them different from any other family of Christopher's experience. They were interested in everything, new ideas, inventions, and discoveries. No doubt the family's intellectual bent was a result of the influence of their late father, Edward.

Christopher sensed that the happy, often chaotic household was doing him good, whereas the clamor of London had not. Somehow the Hathaways, with all their rough edges, were smoothing the broken places of his soul. He liked all of them, especially Cam, who acted as the leader of the family, or the tribe, as he referred to them. Cam was a soothing presence, calm and tolerant, occasionally herding the Hathaways along when necessary.

Leo wasn't quite so approachable. Although he was charming and irreverent, the sharp edges of his humor reminded Christopher uncomfortably of his own past, when he had often made quips at other people's expense. For example, that remark he had once made about Beatrix belonging in the stables. Which he still didn't remember saying, except that unfortunately it sounded exactly like something he would have said. He hadn't fully understood the power of words then.

The past two years had taught him differently.

In the case of Leo, however, Beatrix assured Christopher that in spite of his sharp tongue, Leo was a caring and loyal brother. "You'll come to like him very well," she said. "But it's no surprise that you feel more comfortable around Cam—you're both foxes."

"Foxes?" Christopher had repeated, amused.

"Yes. I can always tell what kind of animal a person would be. Foxes are hunters, but they don't rely on brute strength. They're subtle and clever. Fond of outwitting others. And although they sometimes travel far, they always like to come back to a snug, safe home."

"I suppose Leo is a lion," Christopher said dryly.

"Oh, yes. Dramatic, demonstrative, and he hates being ignored. And sometimes he'll take a swipe at you. But beneath the sharp claws and the growls, he's still a cat."

"What animal are you?"

"A ferret. We can't help collecting things. When we're awake, we're very busy, but we also like to be still for long periods." She grinned at him. "And ferrets are very affectionate."

Christopher had always imagined that his household would be run with order and precision by a proper wife who would oversee every detail. Instead it seemed there was going to be a wife who strode about in breeches while animals roamed, waddled, crept, or hopped through every room.

He was fascinated by Beatrix's competence at things women were not usually competent at. She knew how to use a hammer or a plane tool. She rode better than any woman he had ever seen, and possibly better than any man. She had an original mind, an intelligence woven of recall and intuition. But the more Christopher learned about Beatrix, the more he perceived the vein of insecurity that ran deep in her. A sense of otherness that often inclined her toward solitude. He thought that perhaps it had something to do with her parents' untimely deaths, especially her mother's, which Beatrix had felt as an abandonment. And perhaps it was partly a result of the Hathaways' having been pushed into a social position they had never been prepared for. Being in the upper classes wasn't merely following a set of rules, it was a way of thinking, of carrying oneself and interacting with the world, that had to be instilled since birth. Beatrix would never acquire the sophistication of the young women who had been raised in the aristocracy.

That was one of the things he loved most about her.

The day after he had proposed to Beatrix, Christopher had reluctantly gone to talk to Prudence. He was prepared to apologize, knowing that he had not been fair in his dealings with her. However, any trace of remorse he might have felt for having deceived Prudence vanished as soon as he saw that Prudence felt no remorse for having deceived him.

It had not been a pleasant scene, to say the least. A plum-colored flush of rage had swept across her face, and she had stormed and shrieked as if she were unhinged.

"You *can't* throw me over for that dark-haired gargoyle and her freakish family! You'll be a laughing-stock. Half of them are Gypsies, and the other half are lunatics—they have few connections and no manners, they're filthy peasants and you'll regret this *to the end of your days*. Beatrix is a rude, uncivilized girl who will probably give birth to a litter."

As she had paused to take a breath, Christopher had replied quietly, "Unfortunately, not everyone can be as refined as the Mercers."

The shot had gone completely over Prudence's head, of course, and she had continued to scream like a fish-wife.

And an image had appeared in Christopher's head . . . not the usual ones of the war, but a peaceful one . . . Beatrix's face, calm and intent, as she had tended a wounded bird the previous day. She had wrapped the broken wing of a small sparrow against its body, and then showed Rye how to feed the bird. As Christopher had watched the proceedings, he had been struck by the mixture of delicacy and strength in Beatrix's hands.

Bringing his attention back to the ranting woman before him, Christopher pitied the man who eventually became Prudence's husband.

Prudence's mother had come into the parlor then, alarmed by the uproar, and she had tried to soothe her. Christopher had taken his leave soon after, regretting every minute he had ever wasted in Prudence Mercer's company.

A week and a half later, all of Stony Cross had been startled by the news that Prudence had eloped with one of her longtime suitors, a member of the local gentry.

The morning of the elopement, a letter had been delivered to Ramsay House, addressed to Beatrix. It was from Prudence. The letter was blotched and angrily scrawled, filled with accusations and dire predictions, and more than a few misspellings. Troubled and guilt-ridden, Beatrix had shown it to Christopher.

His mouth twisted as he tore it in half and gave it back to Beatrix. "Well," he said conversationally, "she's finally written a letter to someone."

Beatrix tried to look reproving, but a reluctant laugh escaped her. "Don't make jest of the situation. I feel so awfully guilty."

"Why? Prudence doesn't."

"She blames me for taking you away from her."

"I was never hers in the first place. And this isn't some game of pass-the-parcel."

That made her grin. "If you're the parcel," she said, giving him a suggestive glance, "I would like to un-wrap you."

Christopher shook his head as she leaned forward to kiss him. "Don't start that, or we'll never get this done." Putting a board in place, he looked at her expectantly. "Start hammering."

They were in the hayloft, where she had taken him to help repair a nest box that she had constructed her-self. Christopher watched, entertained, while Beatrix sank a neat row of nails into the end of the board. He had never expected that a woman's proficiency with tools would be so charming. And he couldn't help but enjoy the way her breeches tightened over her bottom every time she leaned over.

With an effort, he tried to discipline his body, push back the urgent rise of desire, as he'd had to do so often lately. Beatrix offered more temptation than he could bear. Whenever he kissed her, she responded with an innocent sensuality that drove him to the limits of his self-control.

Before he had been called to war, Christopher had never had any difficulty in finding lovers. Sex had been a casual pleasure, something he had enjoyed without guilt or inhibitions. But after prolonged abstinence, he was concerned about the first time he made love to Beatrix. He did not want to hurt or frighten her.

Self-control of any kind was still a struggle.

That was readily apparent on occasions such as the night when one of the twins had accidently stumbled over Beatrix's cat Lucky, who had let out the particular earsplitting screech of an irritated feline. And then both the twins started squalling, while Catherine had rushed to soothe them.

Christopher had nearly jumped out of his skin. The uproar had sent a shock through him, leaving him tense and trembling, and he had lowered his head and squeezed his eyes shut as he was transported in an instant to a battlefield beneath an exploding sky. A few deep breaths, and then he had become aware of Beatrix sitting beside him. She didn't question him, only stayed quiet and near.

And then Albert had come and put his chin on his knee, regarding him with somber brown eyes.

"He understands," Beatrix had said softly.

Christopher reached out to pet the rough head, and Albert nuzzled into his hand, a tongue curling against his wrist. Yes, Albert understood. He had suffered beneath the same rain of shells and cannonfire, knew the feeling of a bullet tearing through his flesh. "We're a pair, aren't we, old fellow?" Christopher had murmured.

His thoughts were wrenched back to the present as Beatrix finished her task, set the hammer aside, and dusted her hands together. "There," she said in satisfaction. "All ready for the next occupant."

She crawled over to where Christopher was half reclining, and stretched out beside him like a cat. His lashes half lowered as he surveyed her. His senses wanted to draw her in, to indulge in the feel of her soft skin, the supple firmness of her beneath him. But he resisted as she tried to pull him closer.

"Your family will suspect we've been doing something other than woodworking," he said. "You'll be covered with hay."

"I'm always covered with hay."

Her slightly crooked grin and lively blue eyes undid him. Relenting, he lowered to her, his mouth covering hers in a warm, lightly probing kiss. Her arms went around his neck. He explored her slowly, taking his time, playing with her until he felt the shy stroke of her tongue against his. The sensation went down to his groin, fueling a fresh wave of erotic heat.

She cradled him, her hips adjusting instinctively beneath his. He couldn't stop himself from pushing against the feminine softness, a pulse of movement that beguiled them both. Murmuring his name, Beatrix let her head fall back on his arm, her throat exposed to the damp caress of his lips. He found sensitive places with his tongue, using the tip of it when he felt her squirm. His hand went to one of her breasts, cupping the natural shape of her through the shirt and chemise, rubbing the tight peak with a warm circling of his palm. Small moans rose in her throat, abbreviated purrs of pleasure.

She was so exquisite, writhing and arching beneath him, that Christopher felt himself begin to drown in lust, his body taking over and his mind going hazy. It would be so easy to open her clothes, free his tortured flesh . . . let himself enter her, and find wholesale relief—

He groaned and rolled to his back, but she stayed with him, clinging.

"Make love to me," she said breathlessly. "Here. Now. Please, Christopher—"

"No." Managing to pry her away, he sat up. "Not in a hayloft, with someone likely to come into the barn at any moment."

"I don't care." Beatrix dove her hot face against his chest. "I don't care," she repeated feverishly.

"I care. You deserve something far better than a tumble in the hay. And so do I, after more than two years of going without."

Beatrix looked up at him, her eyes widening. "Truly? You've been chaste for that long?"

Christopher gave her a sardonic glance. " 'Chaste' implies a purity of thought that I assure you does not apply. But I have been celibate."

Crawling behind him, Beatrix began to brush at the straw clinging to his back. "There were no opportunities to be with a woman?"

"There were."

"Then why didn't you?"

Christopher twisted to glance at her over his shoulder. "Are you really asking for the details?"

"Yes."

"Beatrix, do you know what happens to girls who ask such naughty questions?"

"They're ravished in haylofts?" she inquired hopefully.

Christopher shook his head.

Beatrix's arms slid around him from behind. He felt the light, stimulating pressure of her breasts against his back. "Tell me," she said near his ear, the moist heat of her breath causing the hairs on his nape to prickle pleasantly.

"There were camp prostitutes," he said, "who were kept busy servicing the soldiers. But they were none too attractive, and they helped to spread any number of diseases through the regiment."

"Poor things," Beatrix said sincerely.

"The prostitutes or the soldiers?"

"All of you."

How like her, he thought, to react with compassion rather than distaste. Taking one of her hands, Christopher pressed a kiss into her palm. "I also had offers from one or two of the officers' wives who had traveled with the brigade. But I didn't think it was a very good idea to sleep with another man's wife. Especially when I might have found myself fighting side by side with him afterward. And then when I was in the hospital, there were a few nurses who were probably persuadable . . . the regular ones, of course, not the ones who came with the Sisters Of Mercy . . . but after the long sieges and rounds of grave digging . . . and then being wounded . . . I wasn't exactly in an amorous mood. So I waited." He grimaced. "And I'm still waiting."

Beatrix kissed and nuzzled the back of his neck, sending a new rush of arousal through him. "I'll take care of you, poor lad," she murmured. "Don't worry, I'll break you in gently."

This was new, this mixture of desire and amusement. Christopher turned and put his arms around her, toppling her into his lap. "Oh, you will take care of me," he assured her, and crushed his mouth over hers.

Later in the day Christopher went with Leo to see the Ramsay estate timber yard. Although the Ramsay timber business wasn't comparable in scope to the Riverton production, it was infinitely more sophisticated. According to Leo, the Hathaways' absent brother-in-law, Merripen, was the most knowledgeable about estate forestry, including correct procedures for identifying profitable timber, thinning mixed woods, and planting for regeneration.

In the timber yard itself, several technological innovations had been made at the suggestion of Harry Rutledge, Poppy's husband. After showing Christopher an advanced system of rollers and run planks that allowed the cut timber to be moved efficiently and safely, Leo walked with him back to the house.

Their talk turned toward the timber market and arrangements with merchants. "Anything to do with the market," Leo said, "and sales by auction or private treaty, are handled by Cam. He has a better grasp of finance than any man you'll ever meet."

"I find it interesting, the way you and your brothers-in-law have divided the areas of the business, each to his strengths."

"It works well for us. Merripen is a man of the soil, Cam likes numbers . . . and my part is to do as little as possible."

Christopher wasn't deceived. "You know far too much about the entire enterprise for me to believe that. You've worked long and hard on this place."

"Yes. But I keep hoping if I feign ignorance, they'll stop asking me to do things."

Christopher smiled and focused on the ground before them as they walked, their booted feet crossing into the long shadows cast by the sun behind them. "I won't have to feign ignorance," he said, sobering. "I know next to nothing about timber. My brother prepared for it his entire life. It never occurred to me—or anyone—that I would have to fill his shoes." He paused and wished he had kept that last comment to himself. It sounded as if he were asking for sympathy.

Leo, however, replied in a friendly and matter-of-fact manner. "I know that feeling. But Merripen will help you. He's a fount of information, and he's never so happy as when he's telling people what to do. A fortnight in his company, and you'll be a bloody expert on timber. Has Beatrix yet told you that Merripen and Win will return from Ireland in time for the wedding?"

Christopher shook his head. The wedding would be held in a month, at the church on the village green. "I'm glad for Beatrix's sake. She wants the entire family to be there." A brief laugh escaped him. "I only hope we won't have a parade of animals marching through the church along with her."

"Count yourself fortunate that we got rid of the elephant," Leo said. "She might have turned it into a bridesmaid."

"Elephant?" Christopher glanced at him sharply. "She had an elephant?"

"Only for a short time. She found a new home for him."

"No." Christopher was shaking his head. "Knowing Beatrix, I could almost believe it. But no."

"She had an elephant," Leo insisted. "God's own truth."

Christopher still wasn't convinced. "I suppose it showed up at the doorstep one day and someone made the mistake of feeding it?"

"Ask Beatrix, and she'll tell you—"

But Leo broke off as they neared the paddock, where some kind of commotion was taking place. The squeal of an angry horse rent the air. A chestnut Thoroughbred was rearing and bucking with someone on its back.

"Damn it," Leo said, quickening his pace. "I told them not to buy that ill-tempered nag—he was ruined from bad handling, and not even Beatrix can fix him."

"Is that Beatrix?" Christopher asked, alarm jolting through him.

"Either Beatrix or Rohan—no one else is foolhardy enough to mount him."

Christopher broke into a run. It wasn't Beatrix. It couldn't be. She had promised him that she wouldn't put herself at physical risk anymore. But as he reached the paddock, he saw her hat fly off and her dark hair come loose, while the infuriated horse bucked with increasing force. Beatrix clung to the animal with astonishing ease, murmuring and trying to soothe him. The horse seemed to subside, responding to Beatrix's efforts. But in a quicksilver instant he reared impossibly high, his massive bulk balanced on two slender hind legs.

And then the horse twisted and began to fall.

Time itself slowed, while the huge crushing mass toppled, with Beatrix's fragile form landing beneath.

As so often had happened in battle, Christopher's instincts took over completely, prompting action at a speed faster than thought. He heard nothing, but he felt his throat vibrate with a hoarse cry, while his body vaulted over the paddock fence.

Beatrix reacted from instinct as well. As the horse began to fall, she yanked her booted feet from the stirrups and pushed away from him in midair. She hit the ground and rolled twice, thrice, while the horse's body crashed beside her . . . missing her by a matter of inches.

As Beatrix lay still and dazed, the maddened horse struggled to its feet, its hooves pounding the ground beside her with skull-splitting force. Christopher snatched her up and carried her to the side of the paddock, while Leo approached the enraged horse and somehow managed to grab the reins.

Lowering Beatrix to the ground, Christopher searched her for injuries, running his hands over her limbs, feeling her skull. She was panting and wheezing, the breath having been knocked out of her.

She blinked up at him in confusion. "What happened?"

"The horse reared and fell." Christopher's voice came out in a rasp. "Tell me your name."

"Why are you asking me that?"

"Your name," he insisted.

"Beatrix Heloise Hathaway." She looked at him with round blue eyes. "Now that we know who I am . . . who are you?"

Chapter Twenty

At Christopher's expression, Beatrix snickered and wrinkled her nose impishly. "I'm teasing. Really. I know who you are. I'm perfectly all right."

Over Christopher's shoulder, Beatrix caught sight of Leo shaking his head in warning, drawing a finger across his throat.

She realized too late that it probably hadn't been an appropriate moment for teasing. What to a Hathaway would have been a good chuckle was positively infuriating to Christopher.

He glared at her with incredulous wrath. It was only then that she realized he was shaking in the aftermath of his terror for her.

Definitely not the time for humor.

"I'm sorry—" she began contritely.

"I asked you not to train that horse," Christopher snapped, "and you agreed."

Beatrix felt instantly defensive. She was accustomed to doing as she pleased. This was certainly not the first time she'd ever fallen from a horse, nor the last.

"You didn't ask that specifically," she said reasonably,

"you asked me not to do anything dangerous. And in my opinion, it wasn't."

Instead of calming Christopher, that seemed to enrage him even further. "In light of the fact that you were nearly flattened like a pikelet just now, I'd say you were wrong."

Beatrix was intent on winning the argument. "Well, it doesn't matter in any case, because the promise I made was for *after* we married. And we're not married yet."

Leo covered his eyes with his hand, shook his head, and retreated from her vision.

Christopher gave her an incinerating glare, opened his mouth to speak, and closed it again. Without another word, he lifted himself away from her and went to the stable in a long, ground-eating stride.

Sitting up, Beatrix stared after him in perplexed annoyance. "He's leaving."

"It would appear so." Leo came to her, extended a hand down, and pulled her up.

"Why did he leave right in the middle of a quarrel?" Beatrix demanded, dusting off her breeches with short, aggravated whacks. "One can't just *leave,* one has to finish it."

"If he had stayed, sweetheart," Leo said, "there's every chance I would have had to pry his hands from around your neck."

Their conversation paused as they saw Christopher riding from the stables, his form straight as a blade as he spurred his horse into a swift graceful canter.

Beatrix sighed. "I was trying to score points rather than consider how he was feeling," she admitted. "He was probably frightened for me, seeing the horse topple over like that."

"Probably?" Leo repeated. "He looked like he had

just seen Death. I believe it may have touched off one of his bad spells, or whatever it is you call them."

"I must go to him."

"Not dressed like that."

"For heaven's sake, Leo, just this one time—"

"No exceptions, darling. I know my sisters. Give any one of you an inch, and you'll take a mile." He reached out and pushed back her tumbling hair. "Also . . . don't go without a chaperone."

"I don't want a chaperone. That's never any fun."

"Yes, Beatrix, that's the purpose of a chaperone."

"Well, in our family, anyone who chaperoned me would probably need a chaperone more than I do."

Leo opened his mouth to argue, then closed it.

Rare was the occasion when her brother was unable to argue a point.

Repressing a grin, Beatrix strode toward the house.

Christopher had forgiven Beatrix before he had even reached Phelan House. He was well aware that Beatrix was accustomed to nearly unqualified freedom, and she had no wish to be reined in any more than that devil of a horse had. It would take time for her to adjust to restrictions. He had already known that.

But he had been too rattled to think clearly. She meant too much to him—she was his life. The thought of her being hurt was more than his soul could bear. The shock of seeing Beatrix nearly killed, the overwhelming mixture of terror and fury, had exploded through him and left him in chaos. No, not chaos, something far worse. Gloom. A gray, heavy fog had enclosed him, suffocating all sound and feeling. He felt as if his soul were barely anchored in his body.

This same numb detachment had happened from

time to time during the war, and in the hospital. There
was no cure for it, except to wait it out.

Telling the housekeeper that he didn't want to be
disturbed, Christopher headed to the dark, quiet sanctuary of the library. After searching through the side-
board, he found a bottle of Armagnac, and poured a
glass.

The liquor was harsh and peppery, searing the inside of his throat. Exactly what he wanted. Hoping it
would burn through the chill in his soul, he tossed it
back and poured a second.

Hearing a scratch at the door, he went to open it.
Albert crossed the threshold, wagging and snorting
happily. "Useless mongrel," Christopher said, bending
to pet him. "You smell like the floor of an East End
tavern." The dog pushed back against his palm de-
mandingly. Christopher lowered to his haunches and
regarded him ruefully. "What would you say if you
could talk?" he asked. "I suppose it's better that you
don't. That's the point of having a dog. No conversation. Just admiring gazes and endless panting."

Someone spoke from the threshold behind him,
startling him. "I hope that's not what you'll expect . . ."

Reacting with explosive instinct, Christopher turned
and fastened his hand around a soft throat.

". . . from a wife," Beatrix finished unsteadily.

Christopher froze. Trying to think above the frenzy,
he took a shivering breath, and blinked hard.

What in God's name was he doing?

He had shoved Beatrix against the doorjamb, pinning her by the throat, his other hand drawn back in a
lethal fist. He was a hairsbreadth away from delivering
a blow that would shatter delicate bones in her face.

It terrified him, how much effort it took to un-
clench his fist and relax his arm. With the hand that

was still at her throat, he felt the fragile throb of her pulse beneath his thumb, and the delicate ripple of a swallow.

Staring into her rich blue eyes, he felt the welter of violence washed away in a flood of despair.

With a muffled curse, he snatched his hand from her and went to get his drink.

"Mrs. Clocker said you'd asked not to be disturbed," Beatrix said. "And of course the first thing I did was disturb you."

"Don't come up behind me," Christopher said roughly. "Ever."

"I of all people should have known that. I won't do it again."

Christopher took a fiery swallow of the liquor. "What do you mean, you of all people?"

"I'm used to wild creatures who don't like to be approached from behind."

He shot her a baleful glance. "How fortunate that your experience with animals has turned out to be such good preparation for marriage to me."

"I didn't mean . . . well, my point was that I should have been more considerate of your nerves."

"I don't have nerves," he snapped.

"I'm sorry. We'll call them something else." Her voice was so soothing and gentle that it would have caused an assortment of cobras, tigers, wolverines, and badgers to all snuggle together and take a group nap.

Christopher gritted his teeth and maintained a stony silence.

Pulling what looked like a biscuit from the pocket of her dress, Beatrix offered it to Albert, who bounded over to her and took the treat eagerly. Leading the dog to the door, she gestured for him to cross the threshold. "Go on to the kitchen," she said in an encouraging tone. "Mrs. Clocker is going to feed you." Albert was gone in a flash.

Closing and locking the door, Beatrix approached Christopher. She looked fresh and feminine in a lavender dress, her hair neatly swept up with combs. One could not fathom a different picture from the outlandish girl in breeches.

"I could have killed you," he said savagely.

"You didn't."

"I could have hurt you."

"You didn't do that, either."

"*God,* Beatrix." Christopher went to sit heavily at a hearthside chair, glass in hand.

She followed him in a rustle of lavender silk. "I'm not Beatrix, actually. I'm her much nicer twin. She said you could have me from now on." Her gaze flickered to the Armagnac. "You promised not to drink spirits."

"We're not married yet." Christopher knew he should have been ashamed of the sneering echo of her own earlier words, but the temptation was too much to resist.

Beatrix didn't flinch. "I'm sorry about that. It's no fun, caring about my welfare. I'm reckless. I overestimate my abilities." She lowered to the floor at his feet, resting her arms on his knees. Her earnest blue eyes, starred with heavy dark lashes, stared contritely into his. "I shouldn't have spoken to you as I did earlier. For my family, arguing is a sport—we forget that some people tend to take it personally." One of her fingertips drew an intricate little pattern on his thigh. "But I have redeeming qualities," she continued. "I never mind dog hair, for example. And I can pick up small objects with my toes, which is a surprisingly useful talent."

Christopher's numbness started melting like spring ice. And it had nothing to do with the Armagnac. It was all Beatrix.

God, he adored her.

But the more he thawed, the more volatile he felt. Need surged beneath the thin veneer of self-control. Too much need.

Setting the unfinished liquor on the carpeted floor, Christopher drew Beatrix between his knees. He bent forward to press his lips to her forehead. He could smell the tantalizing sweetness of her skin. Settling back in the chair, he studied her. She looked angelic and guileless, as if sugar wouldn't melt in her mouth. *Little rogue,* he thought with tender amusement. He stroked one of her slender hands, which was resting on his thigh. Taking a deep breath, he let it out slowly.

"So your middle name is Heloise," he said.

"Yes, after the medieval French nun. My father loved her writings. In fact, it occurs to me . . . Héloïse was renowned for the love letters she exchanged with Abélard." Beatrix's expression brightened. "I've rather lived up to my namesake, haven't I?"

"Since Abélard was eventually castrated by Héloïse's family, I'm not especially fond of the comparison."

Beatrix grinned. "You have nothing to worry about." As she stared at him, her smile faded. "Am I forgiven?" she asked.

"For endangering yourself? . . . Never. You're too precious to me." Christopher took up her hand and kissed it. "Beatrix, you are beautiful in that dress, and I love your company more than anything in the world. But I have to take you home."

Beatrix didn't move. "Not until this is resolved."

"It is."

"No, there's still a wall between us. I can feel it."

Christopher shook his head. "I'm just . . . distracted." He reached for her elbows. "Let me help you up."

She resisted. "Something's not right. You're so far away."

"I'm right here."

There were no words to describe this infernal sense of detachment. He didn't know why it appeared or what would make it go away. He only knew that if he waited long enough, it would disappear of its own accord. At least, it had before. Perhaps one day it would appear and never leave him. *Christ.*

Staring at him, Beatrix clamped her hands lightly on his thighs. Instead of standing, she hitched her body higher against him.

Her mouth came to his, gently inquiring. He felt a little shock, a sudden pitch of his heart as if it had remembered to start beating again. Beatrix's lips were soft and hot, teasing in the way he had taught her. He felt lust come raging up, dangerously fast. Her weight was on him, her breasts, the mass of her skirts compressed between his thighs. He surrendered for a moment, fusing his mouth to hers and kissing her the way he wanted to take her, deep and hard. Beatrix immediately went pliant, submissive, in a way that drove him mad, and she knew it.

He wanted everything of her, wanted to subject her to every craving and impulse, and she was too innocent for any of it. Tearing his mouth from hers, Christopher held her at arms' length.

Her eyes were wide and wondering.

To his relief, she levered away from him and stood.

And then she began to unfasten her bodice.

"What are you doing?" he asked hoarsely.

"Don't worry, the door is locked."

"That isn't what I—*Beatrix*—" By the time he had lurched to his feet, her bodice had listed open. A thick, primitive drumbeat started in his ears. "Beatrix, I'm not in the mood for virginal experimentation."

She gave him a purely ingenuous look. "Neither am I."

"You're not safe with me." He reached for the neckline of her bodice and yanked it together. While he fumbled to fasten it, Beatrix hiked up the side of her dress. A tug and a wriggle, and her petticoat dropped to the floor.

"I can undress faster than you can dress me," she informed him.

Christopher clenched his teeth as he saw her push her dress below her hips. "Damn you, I can't do this. Not now." He was perspiring, every muscle hard. His voice shook with the force of suppressed need. "I'm going to lose control." He wouldn't be able to stop himself from hurting her. For their first time, he would have to approach her with absolute restraint, give himself release beforehand to take the edge from his lust . . . but at the moment, he would fall on her like a ravening animal.

"I understand." Beatrix pulled the combs from her hair, tossed them into the pile of discarded lavender silk, and shook out the gleaming sable locks. And she gave him a look that caused every hair on his body to lift. "I know you think that I don't understand, but I do. And I need this as much as you do." Slowly she unhooked her corset and dropped it to the floor.

Dear God. How long it had been since a woman had undressed for him. Christopher couldn't move or speak, just stood there aroused and starving and mindless, his eyes eating up the sight of her.

As she saw the way he watched her, she disrobed even more deliberately, drawing the chemise over her head. Her breasts were high and gently curved, the tips rose colored. They bounced delicately as she bent to remove her drawers.

She stood to face him.

Despite her audacity, Beatrix was nervous, an uneven blush covering her from head to toe. But she watched him closely, taking in his reactions.

She was the most beautiful thing he had ever seen, slim and lithe, her legs sheathed in pale pink stockings and white garters. She devastated him. The sable locks of her hair draped over her body, hanging down to her waist. The little triangle between her thighs looked like rich fur, an erotic contrast to her porcelain skin.

He felt weak and brutal at the same time, desire pumping through him. Nothing mattered except getting inside her . . . he had to have her or die. He didn't understand why she had deliberately pushed him over the edge, why she wasn't frightened. A rough sound was torn from his throat. Although he made no conscious decision to move, somehow he had crossed the space between them and seized her. He let his splayed fingers travel over her back, down to the curve of her bottom. Pulling her high and tight against him, he found her mouth, kissing her, almost savaging her.

She yielded completely, offering her body, her mouth, in any way he chose. As his mouth possessed hers, he reached farther between her thighs, forcing them to part. He found the tender pleats of her sex. Parting the softness, he massaged until he found wetness, and slid two fingers into the supple heat of her. Gasping against his mouth, she strained higher on her toes. He held her like that, tightly impaled on his fingers as he kissed her.

"Let me feel you," she said breathlessly, her hands working at his clothes. "Please . . . yes . . ."

Christopher fought with his waistcoat and shirt, sending buttons scattering in his haste. When his upper half was bared, he enfolded her in his arms. They both groaned and went still, absorbing the feel of it, their skin pressed together, her breasts softly abraded by the hair on his chest.

Half dragging, half carrying her to the settee, he lowered her to the cushioned upholstery. She landed in a slow sprawl, her head and shoulders propped against one corner, one foot coming to the floor. He was there before she could close her legs.

Running his hands along the stockings, he discovered they were made of silk. He had never seen pink stockings before, only black or white. He *loved* them. He stroked along her legs, kissed her knees through the silk, untied the garters and licked the red marks they had left against her skin. Beatrix was quiet. Trembling. As he let his lips stray near the inside of her thigh, she squirmed helplessly. That wanton little movement of her hips maddened him, made him frantic.

He unrolled her stockings and stripped them away. Drugged with arousal, he glanced along her body up to her passion-drowsed face, her half-closed eyes, her dark cascading hair. He pushed her thighs open with his hands. Breathing in the erotic perfume of her body, he ran his tongue through the soft triangle.

"Christopher," he heard her beg, and her hands pressed urgently against his head. She was shocked, her face deeply flushed as she realized what he was going to do.

"You started this," he said thickly. "Now I'm going to finish it."

Without giving her a chance to protest, he bent over her again. He kissed his way into the soft, secret hollow, spreading her with his tongue. She moaned and drew up tightly, her knees bending and her spine curving as if she wanted to gather her entire body around

him. He pushed her back, pressed her wide, and took
what he wanted.

The entire world was nothing but delicate shivering
flesh, the taste of a woman, *his* woman, her intimate
elixir more powerful than wine, opium, exotic spices.
She moaned at the tender traction of his tongue. Her
responses became his, her every sound tugging at his
groin, her desperate quivers sinking into him with darts
of fire. He focused on the most sensitive part of her,
tracing slowly, bewitched by the wet silk. He began to
flick steadily, taunting her, driving her without mercy.
She went still, tensing as the feeling came rolling up to
her, and he knew that nothing existed for her except the
pleasure he was giving her. He made her take it, and
take it, until her sharp breathing turned into repeated
cries. The climax was stronger, deeper, than anything
he had given her before . . . he heard it, felt it, tasted it.

When the last spasm had left her, he pulled her farther beneath him, his mouth going to her breasts. She
slid her arms around his neck. Her body was sated and
ready for him, her legs spreading easily as he settled
between them. Reaching for the fastenings of his trousers, he fumbled and tore at them, freeing himself.

He had no control left, his entire body an ache of
need. He had no words, no way to beg *please don't try
to stop me, I can't, I have to have you*. He had no
strength to resist any longer. Looking down at her, he
said her name, his voice hoarse and questioning.

Beatrix made little crooning sounds and caressed
his back. "Don't stop," she whispered. "I want you, I
love you . . ." She pulled him closer, arching in welcome as he took her with blunt, insistent pressure.

He'd never had a virgin before, had always assumed
it would be a quick, easy breaching. But she was tight
everywhere, untried muscles clenching to keep him

out. He pushed into the innocent resistance, forcing his way deeper, and she gasped and clung to him. He worked inside her, shaking with the effort to be gentle when every instinct screamed to thrust hard into the luscious heat. And then somehow her muscles accepted the futility of trying to close against him, and she relaxed. Her head rested on his supportive arm, her face turning against the hard curve of his bicep. He began to thrust with a groan of relief, knowing nothing except the blinding pleasure of being inside her, being caressed by her. The rapture was severe, absolute as death, delivering him.

He made no effort to prolong it. The peak came fast, slamming into him with a power that took his breath, and then he tumbled into a violent, shuddering release, the spasms piercing. He came endlessly, cradling her in his arms, hunching over her as if he could protect her, even as he lunged into her with ravenous strokes.

She was shaking in the aftermath, thrills of reaction running through her from head to toe. He held her, trying to comfort her, pulling her head against his chest. His eyes were blurred and hot, and he blotted them against a velvet cushion.

It took a while for him to realize that the trembling came not from her, but him.

Chapter Twenty-one

Minutes passed in sated calmness. Beatrix rested quietly in Christopher's embrace, offering no protest even though his grip was too tight. Gradually she was able to divide the sensation into its parts . . . the heat and weight of his body, the scent of perspiration, the slick of rich moisture where they were still joined. She was sore, but at the same time it was a pleasant feeling, that sense of low, warm fullness.

Slowly Christopher's urgent hold began to loosen. One hand came up to play with her hair. His mouth turned to the tender skin of her neck while his free hand traversed her back and side. A tremor passed through his frame, a slow ripple of relief. He slid an arm behind her back, arched her upward, and his lips went to her breast. She drew in an unsteady breath at the wet pull of his mouth.

He moved, turning them both so she lay atop him. His invasion had slid free, and she felt it against her stomach, an intimate brand. Lifting her head, she looked down into his face, into those silvery eyes, slightly dilated. She relished the feel of him, a great warm creature beneath her. She had the sense of having tamed him, although it was a valid question as to whether it had really been the other way around.

She pressed her lips to his shoulder. His skin was even smoother than hers, tightly stretched satin over the hard swell of muscle. Finding the bayonet scar, she touched her tongue to the unevenly mended skin.

"You didn't lose control," she whispered.

"I did, during parts of it." His voice was that of a man who had just awakened after a long sleep. He began to gather the disparate streams of her hair into a single river. "Did you plan this?"

"You're asking if I deliberately set out to seduce you? No, it was entirely spontaneous." At his silence, Beatrix lifted her head and grinned down at him. "You probably think I'm a hussy."

His thumb edged the swollen curve of her lower lip. "Actually, I was thinking about how to get you upstairs to the bedroom. But now that you mention it . . . you are a hussy."

Her grin lingered as she nipped playfully at the tip of his thumb. "I'm sorry for having set you off earlier. Cam is going to work with the horse from now on. I've never had to answer to anyone before—I'll have to get accustomed to it."

"Yes," he said. "Starting now."

Beatrix might have protested his autocratic tone, except there was still a dangerous glint in his eyes, and she understood that he was chafing just as she was. He wasn't comfortable with any woman having such power over him.

Very well. She would certainly not be submissive to him in all things, but she could yield to him on a few points. "I promise to be more careful from now on," she said.

Christopher didn't smile, precisely, but his lips took

on a wry curve. Carefully he deposited her on the settee, went to his discarded clothes, and managed to find a handkerchief.

Beatrix lay half curled on her side and watched him, puzzling over his mood. He seemed as if he were back to himself, for the most part, but there was still a sense of distance between them, of something withheld. Thoughts he wouldn't share, words he wouldn't speak. Even now, after they had engaged in the most intimate act possible.

The distance wasn't new, she realized. It had been there since the beginning. It was only that she was more aware of it now, attuned to the subtleties of his nature.

Returning, Christopher gave her the handkerchief. Although Beatrix would have thought herself to be far beyond blushing after what she had just experienced, she felt a tide of scarlet cover her as she blotted the sore wet place between her thighs. The sight of blood was not unexpected, but it brought home the awareness that she was irrevocably changed. No longer a virgin. A new and vulnerable feeling came over her.

Christopher dressed her in his shirt, surrounding her in soft white linen that retained the scent of his body.

"I should put on my own clothes and go home," Beatrix said. "My family knows I'm here with you unchaperoned. And even they have their limits."

"You'll stay the rest of the afternoon," Christopher said evenly. "You're not going to invade my house, have your way with me, and dash off as if I were some errand you had to take care of."

"I've had a busy day," she protested. "I've fallen from a horse, and seduced you, and now I'm bruised and sore all over."

"I'll take care of you." Christopher looked down at her, his expression stern. "Are you going to argue with me?"

Beatrix tried to sound meek. "No, sir."

A slow smile crossed his face. "That was the worst attempt at obedience I've ever seen."

"Let's practice," she said, wrapping her arms around his neck. "Give me an order and see if I don't follow it."

"Kiss me."

She pressed her mouth to his, and there was silence for a long time afterward. His hands slipped beneath the shirt, tormenting gently until she pressed herself against him. Her insides felt molten, and she weakened all over, wanting him.

"Upstairs," he said against her lips, and picked her up, carrying her as if she weighed nothing.

Beatrix blanched as they approached the door. "You can't take me upstairs like this."

"Why not?"

"I'm only wearing your shirt."

"That doesn't matter. Turn the doorknob."

"What if one of the servants should see?"

Amusement flickered in his eyes. "*Now* you're worried about propriety? Open the damned door, Beatrix."

She complied and kept her eyes tightly closed as he carried her upstairs. If any of the servants saw them, no one said a word.

After bringing Beatrix to his room, Christopher sent for cans of hot water and a hip bath, and a bottle of champagne. And he insisted on washing her, despite her cringing and protesting.

"I can't just sit here," she protested, straddling the metal tub and lowering herself carefully, "and let you do something I'm perfectly capable of doing myself."

Christopher went to the dresser, where a silver tray bearing champagne and two fluted crystal glasses had been set. He poured a glass for her, and brought it to Beatrix. "This will keep you occupied."

Taking a sip of the cool, bubbly vintage, Beatrix leaned back to look at him. "I've never had champagne in the afternoon," she said. "And certainly never while bathing. You won't let me drown, will you?"

"You can't drown in a hip bath, love." Christopher knelt beside the tub, bare-chested and sleek. "And no, I won't let anything happen to you. I have plans for you." He applied soap to a sponge, and more to his hands, and began to bathe her.

She hadn't been washed by anyone since she had been a young child. It gave her a curious sense of safety, of being nurtured. Leaning back, she idly touched one of his forearms, trailing her fingertips through a froth of soap. The sponge drew over her slowly, her shoulders and breasts, her legs and the creases behind her knees. He began to cleanse her more intimately, and all sense of safety vanished as she felt his fingers slipping inside her. She gasped and floundered a little, reaching for his wrist.

"Don't drop the glass," Christopher murmured, his hand still between her thighs.

Beatrix nearly choked on her next swallow of champagne. "That's wicked," she said, her eyes half closing as his exploring finger found a sensitive place deep inside her.

"Drink your champagne," he said gently.

Another head-spinning sip, while his invading touch moved in subtle swirls. Beatrix lost her breath. "I can't swallow when you do that," she said helplessly, her hand gripping the glass.

His gaze was caressing. "Share it with me."

With effort, she guided the glass to his lips and gave him a swallow, while he continued to stroke and tease her beneath the water. His mouth came to hers, the kiss carrying the crisp, sweet flavor of champagne. His tongue played in ways that made her heart thunder.

"Now drink the rest," he whispered. She gave him a dazed look, her hips beginning to rise and fall of their own volition, churning the hot soap-clouded water. She was so hot, inside and out, her body aching for the pleasure he withheld. "Finish," he prompted.

One last convulsive gulp, and then the glass was removed from her nerveless grip and set aside.

Christopher kissed her again, his free arm sliding beneath her neck.

Gripping his bare shoulder, Beatrix tried to bite back a moan. "Please. Christopher, I need more, I need—"

"Patience," he whispered. "I know what you need."

A frustrated gasp escaped her as his touch withdrew, and he helped her from the bath. She was so enervated that she could barely stand, her knees threatening to fold. He dried her efficiently, and kept a supportive arm behind her back as he led her to the bed.

He stretched out beside her, cradled her in his arms, and began to kiss and caress her. Beatrix writhed like a cat, trying to absorb the lessons he was intent on teaching her. A new language of skin and hands and lips, more primal than words . . . every touch promise and provocation.

"Don't struggle for it," he whispered, his hand stealing between her straining thighs once more. "Let me give it to you . . ." His hand cupped her and pressed. His fingers entered, teased, played. But he withheld what she wanted, murmuring for her to relax, give in, let go. There was both fear and relief in giving it to him, yielding every part of herself without reserve. But she did. She let her head fall back on his arm, her body turning pliant, legs spreading. Instantly the climax welled, her flesh contracting, all awareness distilled to that secret inner place he stroked.

When Beatrix finally recovered, emerging from the opulent haze, she saw a glow of concern in his eyes. He was looking at her naked side, his hand passing lightly over the large purple bruise from her fall earlier in the day.

"It's nothing," she said. "I nearly always have something bruised or scratched."

The information didn't seem to reassure him. His mouth twisted, and he shook his head. "Stay here," he said. "I'll be back in a moment."

The instruction was entirely unnecessary. Beatrix had no intention of moving. She crawled farther up to the pillows, letting her cheek press into the down-stuffed linen casing. She sighed and drowsed until she felt Christopher join her on the bed.

His hand settled on her hip, his palm slick with some kind of unguent. She stirred as a strong herbal odor drifted to her nostrils. "Oh, that smells nice. What is it?"

"Clove oil liniment." Carefully he rubbed the balm into her bruise. "My brother and I were covered in the stuff for most of our childhood."

"I know about some of your adventures," Beatrix said. "John told them to Audrey and me. The time the two of you stole the plum tart before dinner . . . and the time when he dared you to jump from the tree limb and you broke your arm . . . John said you were incapable of refusing a dare. He said it was easy to make you do anything, simply by telling you that you couldn't."

"I was an idiot," Christopher said ruefully.

" 'Hellion' was the word he used."

"I took after my father."

"You didn't, actually. At least, not according to John. He said it was unfair that you were always cast as your father's son, when you weren't really like him." Beatrix rolled easily as Christopher nudged her onto her front. His strong, gentle hands rubbed the balm into her strained muscles, the hint of clove oil imparting a mild cooling sensation to her skin.

"John always tried to see the good in everyone," Christopher murmured. "Sometimes he saw what he wanted to believe rather than what was truly there."

Beatrix frowned as he worked her shoulder muscles, easing the tension into softness. "I see the good in you."

"Don't harbor illusions about me. In marrying me, you're going to have to make the best of a bad bargain. You don't understand the situation you're in."

"You're right." Beatrix arched in bliss as he massaged the muscles on either side of her spine. "Any woman would pity me, being in this situation."

"It's one thing to spend an afternoon in bed with me," Christopher said darkly. "It's another to experience day-to-day life with a lunatic."

"I know all about living with lunatics. I'm a Hathaway." Beatrix sighed in pleasure as his hands worked the tender places low on her back. Her body felt relaxed and tingly all over, her bruises and aches forgotten. Twisting to glance at him over her shoulder, she saw the austere lines of his face. She had an overwhelming urge to tease him, to make him play. "You missed a place," she told him.

"Where?"

Levering herself upward, Beatrix turned and crawled

to where Christopher knelt on the mattress. He had donned a velvet dressing robe, the front parting to reveal a tantalizing hint of sun-browned flesh. Linking her arms around his neck, she kissed him. "Inside," she whispered. "That's where I need soothing."

A reluctant smile lurked at the corners of his lips. "This balm is too strong for that."

"No it's not. It feels lovely. Here, I'll show you—" She pounced for the tin of balm and coated her fingertips with the stuff. The rich scent of clove oil spiced the air. "Just hold still—"

"The devil I will." His voice had thickened with amusement, and he reached for her wrist.

Fleet as a ferret, Beatrix twisted to evade him. Rolling once, twice, she dove for the belt of his robe. "You put it all over me," she accused, giggling. "Coward. Now it's your turn."

"Not a chance." He grabbed her, grappled with her, and she thrilled to the sound of his husky laugh.

Somehow managing to clamber over him, she gasped at the feel of his aroused flesh. She wrestled with him until he flipped her over with ease, pinning her wrists. The robe had become loosened during their tussle, their naked flesh rubbing together.

Sparkling silver eyes stared into blue. Already breathless with laughter, Beatrix became positively lightheaded as she saw the way he was looking at her. Lowering his head, he kissed and licked at her smile as if he could taste it.

Christopher let go of her wrists and rolled to his side, exposing his front to her.

Beatrix gave him a questioning glance. Her fingers waggled slightly. "You want me to . . . to touch you with this?"

He was silent, his gaze daring her.

Shy but curious, she reached down and grasped him cautiously. They both jumped a little at the feel of it, coolness and heat, the frictionless glide of oil and silk and intimidating hardness. "Like this?" she whispered, stroking gently.

An indrawn breath hissed through his teeth, and his lashes half lowered. He made no move to stop her.

She drew the pad of her thumb over the smooth, dark head in a sleek circle. Curling her fingers around the heavy, stiffening shaft, she slid them down, marveling at the feel of him. He let her fondle and explore him at will, while his skin turned fever colored, and his chest rose and fell ever more rapidly. Mesmerized by the power of him barely contained beneath her hands, she spread her fingertips and trailed them down his hips and the front of his thighs. She stroked the rock-hard muscles of his legs, scratched lightly through the scattering of glinting hairs, then glided back to his groin. Delicately she cupped the weight of him below, played with him, gripping both hands around the rigid length.

A guttural sound came from his chest. He shoved the sleeves of the robe off his arms, pushed the garment aside, and clutched her hips. Her heart pounded as she saw the tautness of his features, the primitive intent of his gaze. She was brought over his lap, his shaft opening her, pressing into the stinging softness. A whimper broke from her lips as he pushed her fully down, compelling her to straddle him, to take all of him. He reached a new place inside her, and it felt sore but at the same time so unaccountably good that her flesh throbbed tightly in response.

Christopher went still, his searing gaze fixed on her. In a matter of seconds the balm had done its work, the cooling spices relieving her heated flesh while simultaneously awakening intimate nerves. She moved restlessly. Grasping her hips, Christopher pushed her back down and thrust upward.

"Christopher . . ." She was unable to stop herself from squirming and lifting again. With every helpless movement she made, he pulled her hips back to his. His thighs braced behind her, and one of his hands went to the place where they were joined. He watched her, played with her, his fingers sliding across her with flirting strokes while his body never relented its deep, provocative grinding.

"Truce," she managed to say. "I can't bear any more."

"But you will." Reaching up to her, he drew her down and kissed her.

"Please. Finish it."

"Not yet." He trailed his hands down her back. "You're so beautiful," he whispered. "So sensitive. I could make love to you forever."

"Christopher—"

"Let me bring you to pleasure one more time."

"No, I'm exhausted." She took his lower lip between her teeth in a gentle nip. "Finish it now," she said.

"Not yet."

"I'll make you."

"How?"

Beatrix considered him, the arrogantly handsome features, the glitter of challenge in his eyes. Lowering herself over him, her body gently rocked by his ceaseless thrusts, she put her mouth near his ear.

"I love you," she whispered, catching his rhythm, riding it. "I love you."

Nothing more was needed. His breath stopped on a groan, and he drove into her and held, his powerful body trembling with the force of his release. Sliding his arms around her, he poured the years of anguished longing into her. And she continued to murmur to him, promising love, safety, new dreams to replace the broken ones.

Promising forever.

Chapter Twenty-two

After the London season had ended, the peerage continued their social amusements in the country. Invitations were sent for balls, dinners, and dances; gamekeepers prepared grouse to be released for shooting; guns were freshly oiled and cleaned for wildfowling; riding courses were trimmed and repaired; and wine and delicacies were brought from the ports of Bristol and London.

The most sought-after invitation in Hampshire was the mid-September soiree to be held at Ramsay House, to announce Beatrix's betrothal to Christopher Phelan. Usually any event the Hathaways hosted was well attended, but this was different. Everyone they had invited had accepted immediately, followed by a flood of letters and inquiries from people asking for invitations. Demanding them, in some instances.

The Hathaways could only attribute their newfound popularity to the fact that Christopher, England's most admired war hero, would be attending. And Christopher, with his unconcealed loathing of crowds, was glum about the entire matter.

"You must admit," Leo remarked, "it's rather amusing

that the one of us least inclined to mingle in society is the one all of society wants to mingle with."

"Sod off, Ramsay," Christopher muttered, and Leo grinned.

But the phrase "one of us," used so casually, warmed Christopher's heart. Their relationship had acquired an easy, friendly feeling that reminded Christopher of how it used to be with John. Although no one would ever take John's place, Christopher found a great deal of enjoyment in the company of his future brothers-in-law. At least, he found enjoyment in the company of Leo and Cam. Whether the same liking would extend to Merripen remained to be seen.

Merripen and his wife Winnifred, or Win, as the family called her, returned from Ireland with their young son on the first of September. The Hathaways, hardly a subdued lot to begin with, had erupted in a frenzy of joy. Christopher had stayed at the side of the family parlor during the chaotic reunion, watching as the family merged into a tangle of hugs and laughter. Cam and Merripen embraced and thumped each other's backs enthusiastically, speaking in a rapid volley of Romany.

Christopher had met Merripen on one or two occasions before the war. However, Christopher remembered little of him other than as a large and brooding presence, a man of few words. Certainly Christopher had never expected they would belong to the same family someday.

Win was a slim and graceful woman with large blue eyes and light blond hair. She had a fragile quality, almost ethereal, that set her apart from the other Hathaway sisters. Separating from the group in the middle of the room, Win came to Christopher and gave him her hand. "Captain Phelan. How lucky we are to be gaining you as a brother. The men in the family have been quite outmatched—four to five. Now you'll make our total an even ten."

"I still feel outmatched," Leo said.

Merripen approached Christopher, shook his hand with a strong grip, and gave him an appraising glance. "Rohan says you're not bad, for a *gadjo*," he said. "And Beatrix says she loves you, which inclines me to let you marry her. But I'm still considering it."

"If it makes any difference," Christopher said, "I'm willing to take all of her animals."

Merripen considered that. "You can have her."

The discussion at the dinner table was fast-paced and ebullient at first. Eventually, however, the talk turned to Ireland, and the estate Merripen would soon inherit, and the mood became somber.

Approximately ten years earlier Ireland had suffered a prolonged potato blight, leading to a magnitude of disaster the country had still not recovered from. England had offered only minimal assistance in the form of temporary relief measures, assuming that the problem would somehow solve itself through natural means.

Ireland, already impoverished, had fallen into nationwide starvation, followed by a plague of diseases, with the result that entire families had died by the roadside or in their mud huts. And landlords such as Cavan had evicted their penniless tenants, and fought with the ones who remained, resulting in lawsuits and bitterness that would last for generations.

"The Cavan lands and tenants have been neglected for years," Merripen said. "Grandfather was too preoccupied with his properties in England to make improvements or repairs. The land has no drainage, and no machinery for ploughing. The tenants themselves know only the most primitive methods of farming. They live in cottages made of mud and stone. And most of their animals have been sold off to pay the rents." Merripen paused, his face grim. "I met with Cavan before we returned to Stony Cross. He refuses to part with a shilling of his fortune to benefit the people who depend on him."

"How long does he have to live?" Amelia asked.

"Less than a year," Merripen replied. "I would be surprised if he survives past Christmas."

"When he does go," Win interceded, "we'll be free to invest his fortune back into the Cavan lands."

"But it will take far more than money," Merripen said. "We'll have to replace the mud dwellings with sound cottages. We'll have to teach the tenants an entirely new way of farming. They need everything. Machinery, fuel, cattle, seed . . ." His voice trailed away, and he gave Cam an unfathomable glance. "*Phral,* it makes what we accomplished with the Ramsay estates look like child's play."

Cam reached up and absently tugged a forelock of his hair. "We'll have to start preparing now," he said. "I'll need all the information we can obtain on Cavan's finances and holdings. We may sell some of his—your—English properties for capital. You'll have to make estimates for what is needed, and set the priorities. We won't be able to do everything at once."

"It's overwhelming," Merripen said flatly.

From the stunned silence at the table, Christopher gathered that Merripen seldom, if ever, declared that something was overwhelming.

"I'll help, *phral*," Cam said, his gaze steady.

"I'm beginning to have the unpleasant feeling," Leo said, "that I'm going to be handling the Ramsay estates by myself, while the two of you devote yourselves to saving Ireland."

Beatrix was staring at Christopher, a slight smile on her lips. "It puts our situation in perspective, doesn't it?" she murmured.

Which was exactly what he had been thinking.

Merripen's alert gaze went to Christopher's face. "You're to inherit Riverton, now that your brother is dead."

"Yes." Christopher's lips twisted in a self-mocking smile. "And while John was thoroughly prepared for the responsibility, the inverse is true for me. I know little more than how to shoot someone or dig trenches."

"You know how to organize men," Merripen pointed out. "How to form a plan and carry it out. How to assess risk, and adapt when necessary." He threw a swift grin in Cam's direction. "When we started to restore the Ramsay estates, we told ourselves the best thing we could do was make a mistake. It meant we would learn something."

It was then that Christopher fully grasped how much he had in common with the men in this family, even though they couldn't have come from more different environments and upbringings. They were all grappling with a rapidly changing world, facing challenges that none of them had been prepared for. All of society was being tumbled and sifted, the old hierarchy crumbling, power shifting to unfamiliar hands. A man could either let himself sink into irrelevance, or step forward to shape the new age that was upon them. The possibilities were both intriguing and exhausting—he saw that in Merripen's face, and in the faces of the others as well. But none of them would shrink from what had to be done.

Christopher contemplated Beatrix, who was sitting a few places away from him. Those eyes . . . midnight-blue, innocent and wise, alarmingly perceptive. What a curious mixture of qualities she possessed. She was capable of extraordinary composure and yet she was willing to play like a child. She was intellectual, instinctive, droll. Talking with her was like opening a treasure box to sort through unexpected delights.

As a man not yet thirty, Christopher was only six years older than Beatrix, and yet he felt the difference between them as a hundred. He wanted, needed, to be close to her, while at the same time he had to close away the worst of what he had seen and done, so that it would never touch her.

He had not made love to her since that afternoon two weeks earlier, having resolved not to take advantage of her until after they were married. But the erotic memory tantalized him constantly. Beatrix was an experience for which he had no reference point or comparison. The women he had known from the prior time in his life had offered easy and sophisticated pleasures. Nothing remotely similar to Beatrix's headlong passion.

She was too innocent, too fine, to be what fate had intended for him. But he wanted her too badly to care. He would take her, and whatever calamity fate might choose to inflict in return, he would keep Beatrix safe from it.

Or from himself, if necessary.

A shriek came from the drawing room, disrupting all conversation at the Ramsay House soiree.

"What the devil was that?" Christopher's grandfather, Lord Annandale, asked with a scowl. He was holding court in the family parlor, occupying a settee while various guests came to offer their homage. The long journey to Hampshire had made him querulous and exhausted. As a result, Annandale had demanded that Audrey, who had accompanied him from London, stay at his side.

Christopher suppressed a grin as he saw his sister-in-law staring at the doorway of the drawing room with patent longing. Although she had always gotten on fairly well with Annandale, she had spent the entire previous day shut away with the old codger in a private carriage.

"Why would someone scream at a soiree?" Annandale persisted, scowling.

Christopher maintained a bland expression. Since it most likely involved one of the Hathaways, it could have been anything.

"Shall I go and find out?" Audrey asked, clearly desperate to escape her grandfather-in-law.

"No, you may stay here, in case I need something."

Audrey suppressed a sigh. "Yes, my lord."

Beatrix entered the parlor and made her way through the clustered guests. Reaching Christopher, she said in a low tone, "Your mother just met Medusa."

"My mother was the one who screamed?" Christopher asked.

"What was that?" Annandale demanded, remaining seated on the settee. "*My* daughter screamed?"

"I'm afraid so, my lord," Beatrix said apologetically. "She encountered my pet hedgehog, who had escaped from her pen." She glanced at Christopher, adding brightly, "Medusa's always been too plump to climb the walls of her box before. I think her new exercise must be working!"

"Were any quills involved, love?" Christopher asked, repressing a grin.

"Oh, no, your mother wasn't stuck. But Amelia is

taking her to one of the upstairs rooms to rest. Unfortunately Medusa gave her a headache."

Audrey glanced heavenward. "Her head always aches."

"Why do you keep a hedgehog as a pet?" Annandale demanded of Beatrix.

"She can't fend for herself, my lord. My brother rescued her from a fencepost hole when she was still a hoglet, and we couldn't find her mother. So I've taken care of her ever since. Hedgehogs make delightful pets, as long as they're handled properly." She paused and regarded Annandale with frank interest. "My goodness, you are an eagle, aren't you?"

"A what?" the elderly man asked, his eyes narrowing.

"An eagle." Beatrix stared at him closely. "You have such striking features, and you exude power even while sitting still. And you like to watch people. You can assess them instantly, can't you? No doubt you're always right."

Christopher began to intervene, certain that his grandfather would incinerate her with his response. To his astonishment, Annandale practically preened under Beatrix's admiring regard.

"I can," the earl allowed. "And indeed, I am seldom mistaken in my judgments."

Audrey rolled her eyes again.

"You look a bit chilled, my lord," Beatrix observed. "You must be sitting in a draft. One moment—" She bustled off to fetch a lap blanket, and returned to drape the soft blue wool over him.

It wasn't the least bit cool in the room, and there couldn't possibly have been a draft. However, Annandale received the blanket with obvious pleasure. Recalling the overheated rooms in his grandfather's house, Christopher reflected that he probably had been chilled. How Beatrix could have guessed it was a mystery.

"Audrey," Beatrix implored, "do let me sit next to Lord Annandale." As if it were some coveted privilege.

"If you insist." Audrey leaped from the settee as if she had been launched by a spring mechanism.

Before Beatrix took her place, she bent to rummage beneath the settee. Dragging out a drowsing gray cat, she settled it on Annandale's lap. "Here you are. Nothing warms you faster than a cat in your lap. Her name is Lucky. She'll purr if you pet her."

The old man regarded it without expression.

And to Christopher's astonishment, the old man began to stroke the sleek gray fur.

"This cat is missing a leg," he remarked to Beatrix.

"Yes, I would have named her Nelson, after the one-armed admiral, but she's female. She belonged to the cheesemaker until her foot was caught in a trap."

"Why did you name her Lucky?" Annandale asked.

"I hoped it would change her fortunes."

"And did it?"

"Well, she's sitting in the lap of an earl, isn't she?" Beatrix pointed out, and Annandale laughed outright.

He touched the cat's remaining paw. "She is fortunate to have been to able to adapt."

"She was determined," Beatrix said. "You should have seen the poor thing, not long after the amputation. She kept trying to walk on the missing leg, or jump down from a chair, and she would stumble and lose her balance. But one day, she woke up and seemed to have accepted the fact that the leg was gone for good. And she became nearly as agile as before." She added significantly, "The trick was forgetting about what she had lost . . . and learning to go on with what she had left."

Annandale gave her a fascinated stare, his lips curving. "What a clever young woman you are."

Christopher and Audrey glanced at each other in shared amazement, while Beatrix and Annandale launched into a rapt conversation.

"Men have always adored Beatrix," Audrey said in an undertone, turning toward Christopher. Her eyes sparkled with laughter. "Did you think your grandfather would be proof against her?"

"Yes. He doesn't like anyone."

"Apparently he makes exceptions for young women who flatter his vanity and appear to hang on to his every word."

Christopher stole a glance at Beatrix's glowing face. Of course the earl couldn't resist her. Beatrix had a way of looking at someone with undivided attention, making him feel as if he were the most interesting person in the room.

"I'll never understand why she hasn't married before now," Christopher said.

Audrey kept her voice low as she replied. "Most of the peerage view the Hathaway family as a detraction. And although most gentlemen are delighted by Beatrix, they don't want to marry an unconventional girl. As you well know."

Christopher frowned at the gibe. "As soon as I came to know her, I admitted I was in the wrong."

"That is to your credit," Audrey said. "I didn't think you could ever view her without prejudice. In the past, there have been more than a few men who were quite taken with Beatrix, but they did not pursue her. Mr. Chickering, for example. He absolutely begged his father to be allowed to court her, but his father threatened to cut him off. And so he has had to content himself with adoring Beatrix from afar, and flirting madly with her at every opportunity, knowing it will come to naught."

"Those days are over," Christopher said. "If he ever comes near her again . . ."

Audrey grinned. "Careful. Jealousy is quite unfashionable these days. One must have the sophistication to be amused by the attentions paid to one's wife."

"I'll take great amusement in tossing him through the window." Christopher paused as Audrey laughed. Clearly she thought he was jesting. Deciding to change the subject, he said, "I'm glad to see you're out in society again." He meant it. Audrey had spent nearly her entire marriage taking care of John, who had been diagnosed with consumption soon after their wedding. That, combined with the mourning period, had made it a lengthy and lonely ordeal for her. She deserved to find some enjoyment in life, and most definitely some companionship. "Are there any gentlemen you've taken a liking to?"

Audrey made a face. "You mean the ones my brothers haven't managed to frighten off? No, there's no one who appeals to me in *that* way. I'm sure I could have my choice of nearly any fortune hunter in London, in light of my generous jointure. But it counts against me that I'm barren."

Christopher looked at her alertly. "Are you? How do you know?"

"Three years of marriage to John, and no children. Not even a miscarriage. And it's always said that women are to blame in these matters."

"That's a belief I don't happen to share. Women are not always at fault for infertility—that's been proven. And John was ill for most of your marriage. There's every reason to hope that you'll be able to have children with another man."

Audrey smiled wryly. "We'll see what fate has in store for me. But I don't aspire to marry again. I'm weary to the bone. I feel like a woman of five-and-ninety, instead of five-and-twenty."

"You need more time," Christopher murmured. "You'll feel differently someday, Audrey."

"Perhaps," she said, sounding unconvinced.

Their attention was caught by the increasingly animated conversation between Beatrix and Annandale. ". . . I can climb a tree as well as any of the Ramsay estate woodsmen," Beatrix was telling him.

"I don't believe you," the earl declared, tremendously entertained.

"Oh, yes. Off with the skirts, off with the corset, I put on a pair of breeches, and—"

"Beatrix," Audrey interrupted, before this scandalous discussion of intimate apparel progressed any further. "I just caught a glimpse of Poppy in the next room. It's been ages since I've seen her. And I've never been introduced to her husband."

"Oh." Reluctantly Beatrix turned her attention away from Annandale. "Shall I take you to them?"

"*Yes.*" Audrey seized her arm.

Annandale looked disgruntled, his black brows lowering as Audrey propelled Beatrix away.

Christopher bit back a grin. "What do you think of her?" he asked.

Annandale replied without hesitation. "I would marry her myself, were I five years younger."

"Five?" Christopher repeated skeptically.

"Ten, damn you." But a slight smile had appeared on the earl's time-weathered face. "I commend you on your choice. She's a spirited girl. Fearless. Lovely in her own way, and with her charm she has no need of true beauty. You'll need to keep a firm hand on the reins, but the trouble will be worth it." He paused, looking wistful. "Once you've had a woman like that, you can never be content with the ordinary kind."

Christopher had been about to argue over the question of Beatrix's beauty, which in his opinion was unequaled. But that last sentence caught his attention. "You're referring to Grandmother?" he asked.

"No. Your grandmother was the kind of woman I thought I should marry. I was in love with someone else—a far less suitable girl. And I let her go, to my everlasting regret." He sighed, pondering some distant memory. "A lifetime without her . . ."

Fascinated, Christopher wanted to ask more . . . but this was hardly the time or place for such a conversation. However, it gave him an unexpected insight into his grandfather. What would it do to a man, to marry a Prudence when one might have had a Beatrix? It would be enough to turn anyone bitter.

Later in the evening, trays of champagne were brought out, and the assembled guests waited expectantly for the betrothal announcement to be made.

Unfortunately, the man designated to do it was temporarily missing.

After a brief search, Leo was found and urged into the drawing room, where he launched into a charming toast and listed any number of amusing reasons for marriage. Although most of the guests listened with close attention and chuckled throughout, Christopher heard a pair of women gossiping nearby, whispering in disapproving undertones.

". . . Ramsay was found flirting in the corner with a woman. They had to drag him away from her."

"Who was it?"

"His *own wife*."

"Oh, dear."

"Yes. How unseemly for a married couple to carry on so."

"I suppose the Hathaways know no better."

Christopher suppressed a grin and fought the temptation to turn and inform the two old hens that the Hathaways actually did know better. They just didn't give a damn. He glanced down at Beatrix, wondering if she had heard, but she was oblivious to the gossip, her attention fixed on her brother.

Leo concluded the toast with heartfelt wishes for the betrothed couple's future happiness and prosperity. The guests raised their glasses and cheered in agreement.

Taking Beatrix's gloved hand in his, Christopher lifted it and pressed a kiss to the back of her wrist. He wanted to carry her away from the crowded drawing room and have her all to himself.

"Soon," Beatrix whispered, as if she had read his thoughts, and he let his gaze caress her. "And don't look at me like that," she added. "It makes my knees wobbly."

"Then I won't tell you what I'd like to do with you right now. Because you'd topple over like a ninepin."

The private, pleasurable moment ended all too soon.

Lord Annandale, who was standing near Leo, pushed his way to the fore, holding up his champagne glass. "My friends," he said, "I hope to contribute to the happiness of this occasion by sharing some news from London."

The crowd quieted respectfully.

A cold feeling slithered down Christopher's spine. He glanced at Leo, who looked bemused and shrugged.

"What is it?" Beatrix whispered.

Christopher shook his head, staring at his grandfather. "God help me, I don't know."

"Before departing for Hampshire," Annandale continued, "I was informed by His Grace the Duke of Cambridge that my grandson is to be invested with the Victoria Cross. The medal, created this January past, is the highest possible military decoration for valor in the face of the enemy. The queen herself will present the medal to Captain Phelan at an investiture ceremony in London next June."

Everyone in the room exclaimed and cheered. Christopher felt all the warmth in his body drain away. This was nothing that he wanted, another bloody piece of metal to pin to his chest, another fucking ceremony to honor events he didn't want to remember. And for *that* to intrude on one of the sweetest moments of his life was revolting. Damn his grandfather for doing this to him without giving him one word of advance warning.

"What will the Victoria Cross be awarded for, my lord?" someone asked.

Annandale sent a smile to Christopher. "Perhaps my grandson can hazard a guess."

Christopher shook his head, regarding him without expression.

Annoyance crossed the earl's face at Christopher's demonstrable lack of enthusiasm. "Captain Phelan was recommended for this honor by a regimental officer who gave an account of seeing him carry a wounded officer to safety under heavy gunfire. Our men had been driven back in an attempt to overtake Russian rifle pits. After rescuing the officer, Captain Phelan held the position until relief arrived. The Russian positions were captured, and the wounded officer, Lieutenant Fenwick, was saved."

Christopher didn't trust himself to speak as a volley of cheers and congratulations filled the air. He forced himself to finish the champagne, to stand still and appear calm, when he could feel himself sliding toward a dangerous precipice. Somehow he found the traction to stop it, to hold the madness at bay, reaching for the sense of detachment he both needed and feared.

Please, God, he thought. *Not for saving Fenwick.*

Chapter Twenty-three

Sensing the explosive quality in Christopher's stillness, Beatrix waited until he had drained his champagne. "Oh, my," she said in a voice loud enough to carry to the people around them. "I fear all this excitement is bringing on a touch of the vapors. Captain Phelan, if you wouldn't mind escorting me to the parlor . . . ?"

The question was greeted with sympathetic murmurs, as any evidence of a woman's delicate constitution was always encouraged.

Trying to look fragile and wan, Beatrix clung to Christopher's arm as he led her from the drawing room. Instead of proceeding to the parlor, however, they found a place outside, a bench set on a graveled walkway.

They sat together in wordless communication. Christopher slid his arm around her, pressing his mouth against her hair. She listened to the night sounds from the nearby wood; peeps and rustlings, the melodious conversations of frogs, the flappings of birds and bats. Eventually she felt Christopher's chest lift and lower in a long sigh.

"I'm sorry," she said quietly, knowing that he was

thinking about Mark Bennett, the friend he hadn't been able to save. "I know why this medal is so odious to you."

Christopher made no reply. From the near-palpable tension he radiated, she understood that of all the dark memories he harbored, this was one of the worst.

"Is it possible to refuse the medal?" she asked. "To forfeit it?"

"Not voluntarily. I'd have to do something illegal or hideous to invoke the expulsion clause."

"We could plan a crime for you to commit," Beatrix suggested. "I'm sure my family would have some excellent suggestions."

Christopher looked at her then, his eyes like silvered glass in the moonlight. For a moment Beatrix feared the attempt at levity might have annoyed him. But then there was a catch of laughter in his throat, and he folded her into his arms. "Beatrix," he whispered. "I'll never stop needing you."

They lingered outside for a few minutes longer than they should have, kissing and caressing until they were both breathless with frustrated need. A quiet groan escaped him, and he tugged her up from the bench and brought her back into the house.

As Beatrix mingled among the guests, chatting brightly and feigning interest in the advice they offered, she kept stealing glances at Christopher whenever possible. He appeared calm to the point of stoicism, maintaining a soldierly demeanor. Everyone fawned on him, even those whose social rank and aristocratic blood far eclipsed his. Despite Christopher's controlled façade, she sensed his unease, perhaps even antagonism, in trying to readjust to a landscape that had once been so familiar. He felt out of place among old friends, none of whom wanted to dwell on the reality of what he had experienced and done in the war. The medals and gold braid and patriotic music were all that anyone felt comfortable discussing. And therefore he could only allow his feelings to show in brief and cautious increments.

"Beatrix." Audrey was at her side, gently drawing her away before she could become involved in another conversation. "Come with me. I want to give you something."

Beatrix took her to the back of the house, to a set of stairs leading to an oddly shaped room on the second floor. It was one of the many charms of Ramsay House, that rooms and eccentric spaces with no apparent purpose seemed to have grown organically from the main residence.

They sat together companionably on the stairs.

"You've done Christopher so much good already," Audrey said. "I thought when he first returned after the war that he had lost all capacity for happiness. But he seems far easier with himself now . . . not nearly so brooding or tightly strung. Even his mother has remarked on the difference—and she is grateful."

"She has been kind to me," Beatrix said. "Even though it's obvious that I am not what she expected of a daughter-in-law."

"No," Audrey conceded with a grin. "However, she is determined to make the best of things. You are the only chance of keeping Riverton in our branch of the family. If you and Christopher produce no offspring, it will go to her cousins, which she could not abide. I think she would have liked me much better, had I been able to conceive."

"I'm sorry," Beatrix murmured, taking her hand.

Audrey's smile turned bittersweet. "It wasn't meant to be. That is the lesson I've had to learn. Some things aren't meant to be, and one can either rail against it, or accept it. John told me near the end that we had to be grateful for the time we had been given. He said he saw things very clearly, as his life drew to a close. Which leads me to what I wanted to give you."

Beatrix looked at her expectantly.

Carefully Audrey removed a neatly folded bit of parchment from her sleeve. It was an unsealed letter.

"Before you read it," Audrey said. "I must explain. John wrote it the week before he died—he insisted on doing it himself—and he told me to give it to Christopher when—or if—he returned. But after reading it, I wasn't certain what to do with it. When Christopher came back from the Crimea, he was so volatile and troubled . . . I thought it better to wait. Because no matter what John had asked of me, I knew above all that I must do no further harm to Christopher, after all he's been through."

Beatrix's eyes widened. "You think this letter might harm him?"

"I'm not sure. In spite of our kinship, I don't understand Christopher well enough to judge." Audrey shrugged helplessly. "You'll know what I mean when you read it. I don't want to give it to Christopher unless I can be sure it will do him good, and not create some unintended torment. I leave it in your hands, Beatrix, and trust in your wisdom."

Chapter Twenty-four

A month later, on a sunny and dry October day, the wedding took place at the parish church on the village green. To the general pleasure of Stony Cross, the ceremony adhered to long-standing village traditions. The wedding party emerged from their carriages a few streets away from the church, and walked the rest of the way along a path heavily strewn with flowers and fertility herbs. More and more people joined them as they passed, until it was less of a wedding procession than a jovial mob.

Additional flowers had been piled into a pair of massive baskets that were strapped across the back of Beatrix's mule, Hector. The little mule led the crowd at a dignified pace, while the women walking beside him reached into the baskets and tossed fresh handfuls of petals and blossoms to the ground. A straw hat festooned with flowers had been tied to Hector's head, his ears sticking out at crooked angles through the holes at the sides.

"Good God, Albert," Christopher said ruefully to the dog beside him. "Between you and the mule, I think you got the best of the bargain." Albert had been freshly washed and trimmed, a collar of white roses fastened around his neck. The dog looked wary, clearly not liking the close-packed crowd around them any more than Christopher did.

As the women occupied one half of the street, and the men the other, Christopher caught only occasional glimpses of Beatrix. She was surrounded by village girls dressed in white, ostensibly to confuse evil spirits that might have had designs on the bride. Christopher, for his part, was surrounded by an honor guard comprised of friends from the Rifle Brigade, and a few men from his original cavalry unit.

Finally they reached the church, which was already filled. Violin music filled the air in buoyant strains.

While Christopher went to the front of the church to wait at the altar, Beatrix remained at the back with Leo.

"Beatrix," her brother asked, "what did you do to Hector?"

"He's a flower mule," she said reasonably.

"I hope it won't distress you to learn that he's eating his hat."

Beatrix stifled a giggle.

Bending his head over hers, Leo murmured, "When I give you away at the altar, Bea, I want you to remember something. I'm not really giving you away. I'm merely allowing him the chance to love you as much as the rest of us do."

Beatrix's eyes watered, and she leaned against him. "He does," she whispered.

"I think so, too," her brother whispered back. "I wouldn't let you marry him otherwise."

The rest of the morning and afternoon passed in a daze of happiness. After they exchanged vows, they left the church beneath an arch of swords held up by the honor guard. The front gate was closed—another Stony Cross tradition—and would not be opened until the

groom paid the toll. Christopher reached into a velvet
bag, pulled out a fistful of gold coins, and tossed them
to the crowd. The shower of coins elicited squeals of
glee. Three more handfuls were sent into the air, most
of the glittering pieces caught before they ever reached
the ground.

When every last coin had been retrieved, the assem-
blage swarmed to the village green, where long tables
had been piled high with cakes brought by everyone
in Stony Cross. Beatrix and Christopher fed each other
bites of cake, while villagers showered them with crumbs
to ensure the couple's fertility.

The crowd continued their celebration on the green
as the wedding party departed for Ramsay House. A
massive wedding breakfast ensued, with endless rounds
of toasting and merriment.

When the lengthy affair was finished, Beatrix was
relieved to be able to go upstairs and remove her wedding dress. As Amelia and a housemaid helped to remove the voluminous dress, the three of them started
laughing as a shower of cake crumbs fell to the floor.

"That is my least favorite Stony Cross wedding custom," Beatrix said ruefully, brushing at the remaining
few crumbs that clung to her arms. "On the other hand,
it's probably made more than a few birds happy."

"Speaking of birds, dear . . ." Amelia waited until the
maid had gone to draw a bath. "That brings to mind
the line from Samuel Coleridge's poem about spring,
'The bees are stirring—birds are on the wing—'"

Beatrix gave her a quizzical glance. "Why do you
mention that? It's autumn, not spring."

"Yes, but that particular poem mentions birds *pair-
ing*. I thought you might have some questions for me on
that topic."

"About birds? Thank you, but I know far more about birds than you."

Amelia sighed, giving up the attempt to be delicate. "Forget the blasted birds. It's your wedding night—do you want to ask me anything?"

"*Oh.* Thank you, but Christopher has already, er . . . provided the information."

Amelia's brows lifted. "Has he?"

"Yes. Although he used a different euphemism than birds or bees."

"Did he? What did he reference, then?"

"Squirrels," Beatrix said. And she turned aside to hide a grin at her sister's expression.

Although they would be leaving on the morrow for a fortnight in the Cotswolds, Beatrix had assumed that they would spend their wedding night at Phelan House. She had sent a trunk containing some clothes, toiletries, and a nightgown to Christopher's home. She was surprised, therefore, when Christopher informed her that he had different plans in mind.

After bidding her family good-bye, Beatrix went out to the front drive with Christopher. He had changed from his uniform, with its gleaming jangle of medals, and wore simple tweed and broadcloth, with a simple white cravat tied at his neck. She much preferred him this way, in rougher, simpler clothing—the splendor of Christopher in military dress was nearly too dazzling to bear. The sun was a rich autumn gold, lowering into the black nest of treetops.

Instead of the carriage Beatrix had expected, there was a single horse on the drive, Christopher's large bay gelding.

Beatrix turned to give him a questioning look. "Don't

I get a horse? A pony cart? Or am I to trot along behind you?"

His lips twitched. "We'll ride together, if you're willing. I have a surprise for you."

"How unconventional of you."

"Yes, I thought that would please you." He helped her to mount the horse, and swung up easily behind her.

No matter what the surprise was, Beatrix thought as she leaned back into his cradling arms, this moment was bliss. She savored the feel of him, all his strength around her, his body adjusting easily to every movement of the horse. He bade her to close her eyes as they went into the forest. Beatrix relaxed against his chest. The forest air turned sweeter as it cooled, infused with scents of resin and dark earth.

"Where are we going?" she asked against his coat.

"We're almost there. Don't look."

Soon Christopher reined in the horse and dismounted, helping her down.

Viewing their surroundings, Beatrix smiled in perplexity. It was the secret house on Lord Westcliff's estate. Light glowed through the open windows. "Why are we here?"

"Go upstairs and see," Christopher said, and went to tether the horse.

Picking up the skirts of her blue dress, Beatrix ascended the circular staircase, which had been lit with strategically placed lamps in the wall brackets where ancient torches had once hung. Reaching the circular room upstairs, Beatrix crossed the threshold.

The room had been transformed.

A small fire glowed in the formerly dark hearth, and golden lamplight filled the air. The scarred wooden floors had been scrubbed clean and covered with rich, thick Turkish carpets. Floral tapestries softened the old stone walls. The ancient bedframe had been replaced by a large chestnut bed with carved panels and spiral columns. The bed had been made up with a deep mattress and luxurious quilts and linens, and plump white pillows piled three deep. The table in the corner was draped in mauve damask and laden with covered silver trays and baskets spilling over with food. Condensation glittered on the sides of a silver bucket of iced champagne. And there was her trunk, set beside a painted dressing screen.

Stunned, Beatrix wandered farther into the room, trying to take it all in.

Christopher came up behind her. As Beatrix turned to face him, he searched her face with a gently quizzical gaze. "If you like, we can spend our first night together here," he said. "But if this doesn't suit you, we'll go to Phelan House."

Beatrix could hardly speak. "You did this for me?"

He nodded. "I asked Lord Westcliff if we might stay the night here. And he had no objections to a little redecorating. Do you—"

He was interrupted as Beatrix flung herself at him and wrapped her arms tightly around his neck.

Christopher held her, his hands coursing slowly over her back and hips. His lips found the tender skin of her cheeks, her chin, the yielding softness of her mouth. Through the descending diaphanous layers of pleasure, Beatrix answered him blindly, taking a shivering breath as his long fingers curved beneath her jaw. He shaped her lips with his own, his tongue questing gently. The taste of him was smooth and subtle and masculine. Intoxicating. Needing more of him, she struggled to draw him deeper, to kiss him harder, and he resisted with a quiet laugh.

"Wait. Easy . . . love, there's another part of the surprise that I don't want you to miss."

"Where?" Beatrix asked drowsily, her hand searching over his front.

Christopher gave a muffled laugh, taking her by the shoulders and easing her away. He stared down at her, his gray eyes glowing.

"Listen," he whispered.

As the thrumming of her own heart quieted, Beatrix heard music. Not instruments, but human voices joined in harmony. Bemused, she went to the window and looked out. A smile lit her face.

A small group of officers from Christopher's regiment, still in uniform, were standing in a row and singing a slow, haunting ballad.

> *Were I laid on Greenland's coast,*
> *And in my arms embrac'd my lass;*
> *Warm amidst eternal frost,*
> *Too soon the half year's night would pass.*
> *And I would love you all the day.*
> *Ev'ry night would kiss and play,*
> *If with me you'd fondly stray.*
> *Over the hills and far away . . .*

"Our song," Beatrix whispered, as the sweet strains floated up to them.

"Yes."

Beatrix lowered to the floor and braced her folded arms on the windowsill . . . the same place where she had lit so many candles for a soldier fighting in a far-away land.

Christopher joined her at the window, kneeling with his arms braced around her. At the conclusion of the song, Beatrix blew the officers a kiss. "Thank you, gentlemen," she called down to them. "I will treasure this memory always."

One of them volunteered, "Perhaps you're not aware of it, Mrs. Phelan, but according to Rifle Brigade wedding tradition, every man on the groom's honor guard gets to kiss the bride on her wedding night."

"What rot," Christopher retorted amiably. "The only Rifles wedding tradition I know of is to avoid getting married in the first place."

"Well, you bungled that one, old fellow." The group chortled.

"Can't say as I blame him," one of them added. "You are a vision, Mrs. Phelan."

"As fair as moonlight," another said.

"Thank you," Christopher said. "Now stop wooing my wife, and take your leave."

"We started the job," one of the officers said. "It's left to you to finish it, Phelan."

And with cheerful catcalls and well wishes, the Rifles departed.

"They're taking the horse with them," Christopher said, a smile in his voice. "You're well and truly stranded with me now." He turned toward Beatrix and slid his fingers beneath her chin, nudging her to look at him. "What's this?" His voice gentled. "What's the matter?"

"Nothing," Beatrix said, seeing him through a shimmer of tears. "Absolutely nothing. It's just . . . I spent so many hours in this place, dreaming of being with you someday. But I never dared to believe it could really happen."

"You had to believe, just a little," Christopher whispered. "Otherwise it wouldn't have come true." Pulling her between his spread thighs, he wrapped her in a comforting hug. After a long time, he spoke quietly into her hair. "Beatrix. One of the reasons I haven't made love to you since that afternoon is that I didn't want to take advantage of you again."

"You didn't," she protested. "I gave myself to you freely."

"Yes, I know." Christopher kissed her head. "You were generous, and beautiful, and so passionate that you've ruined me for any other woman. But it wasn't what I had intended for your first time. Tonight I'm going to make amends."

Beatrix shivered at the sensual promise of his tone. "There's no need. But if you insist . . ."

"I do insist." He smoothed his hand over her back and continued to hold her, making her feel safe. And then he began to kiss his way along the side of her neck, his mouth hot and deliberate, and she began to feel not entirely safe. She drew in a quick breath as he lingered at a sensitive place.

Feeling the ripple of her convulsive swallow, he lifted his head and smiled down at her. "Shall we have supper first?" Standing in an easy movement, he pulled her up with him.

"After that enormous wedding breakfast," Beatrix replied, "I'll never be hungry again. However . . ."— she gave him a brilliant grin—"I wouldn't mind a glass of champagne."

Taking her face in his hands, Christopher kissed her swiftly. "For that smile, you can have the entire bottle."

She pressed her cheek into his palm. "Would you unfasten my dress first?"

Turning her away from him, he began on the row of concealed hooks that held the back of her dress together.

It felt like a husbandly act, this unfastening of her dress, both comforting and pleasant. As he bared her nape, he pressed his lips to the delicate skin, and strung more lingering kisses to the top of her spine.

"Shall I do the corset as well?" he asked, his voice close to her ear.

Beatrix was privately amazed that her legs were still supporting her. "No, thank you, I can manage that by myself." She fled to the privacy of the dressing screen, and tugged her trunk behind it. Opening the lid, Beatrix found her neatly folded clothes and a drawstring muslin bag containing a brush and a rack of hairpins, and other small necessities. There was also a package wrapped in pale blue paper and tied with a matching ribbon. Picking up a small folded note that had been tucked under the ribbon, Beatrix read:

A gift for your wedding night, darling Bea. This gown was made by the most fashionable modiste in London. It is rather different from the ones you usually wear, but it will be very pleasing to a bridegroom. Trust me about this.
—Poppy

Holding the nightgown up, Beatrix saw that it was made of black gossamer and fastened with tiny jet buttons. Since the only nightgowns she had ever worn had been of modest white cambric or muslin, this was rather shocking. However, if it was what husbands liked . . .

After removing her corset and her other underpinnings, Beatrix drew the gown over her head and let it slither over her body in a cool, silky drift. The thin fabric draped closely over her shoulders and torso and buttoned at the waist before flowing to the ground in transparent panels. A side slit went up to her hip, exposing her leg when she moved. And her back was shockingly exposed, the gown dipping low against her spine. Pulling the pins and combs from her hair, she dropped them into the muslin bag in the trunk.

Tentatively she emerged from behind the screen.

Christopher had just finished pouring two glasses of champagne. He turned toward her and froze, except for his gaze, which traveled over her in a burning sweep. "My God," he muttered, and drained his champagne. Setting the empty glass aside, he gripped the other as if he were afraid it might slip through his fingers.

"Do you like my nightgown?" Beatrix asked.

Christopher nodded, not taking his gaze from her. "Where's the rest of it?"

"This was all I could find." Unable to resist teasing him, Beatrix twisted and tried to see the back view. "I wonder if I put it on backward . . ."

"Let me see." As she turned to reveal the naked line of her back, Christopher drew in a harsh breath.

Although Beatrix heard him mumble a curse, she didn't take offense, deducing that Poppy had been right about the nightgown. And when he drained the second glass of champagne, forgetting that it was hers, Beatrix sternly repressed a grin. She went to the bed and climbed onto the mattress, relishing the billowy softness of the quilts and linens. Reclining on her side, she made no attempt to cover her exposed leg as the gossamer fabric fell open to her hip.

Christopher came to her, stripping off his shirt along the way. The sight of him, all that flexing muscle and sun-glazed skin, was breathtaking. He was a beautiful man, a scarred Apollo, a dream lover. And he was hers.

She reached for him, a breath catching in her throat as her hand flattened on his chest. She let her fingertips trail through the crisp, glinting fur. He bent over her, his eyes heavy lidded, his mouth firming in the way it did when he was aroused.

Overwhelmed by a mingling of love and desire, she said breathlessly, "Christopher—"

He touched her lips with a single finger, stroking the

tremulous curves, using the tip of his thumb to part them. He kissed her, fitting his mouth to hers at varying angles. Each kiss delivered a deep, sweet shock to her nerves, spreading fire inside her, making it impossible to think clearly. His hands swept over her with a sensitive lightness that promised rather than satisfied. She was being seduced, quite skillfully.

She felt herself being pressed to her back, one of his legs pushing between hers. His fingers smoothed over her breast, finding the aching point of a nipple veiled in silk. His thumb prodded the bud, swirled lightly, stroked with a softness that made her writhe in agitation. Taking the tip of her breast in his thumb and forefinger, he squeezed gently through the gossamer, sending a bolt of desire through her. She moaned against his lips and broke their kiss as she struggled to draw in more air.

Christopher bent to her chest, the mist of his breath penetrating the shimmering fabric and heating the skin beneath. His tongue touched the taut peak, flickered wetly over the silk, the gauzy stimulation affording both frustration and pleasure. Beatrix reached with shaking hands to push the nightgown out of the way.

"Slowly," he whispered, trailing his tongue across her skin, not quite reaching the place where she most wanted it.

Her fingers went to his cheeks and jaw, the abrasion of his shaven bristle like raw velvet against her palms. She tried to guide his mouth, and he laughed quietly, resisting. "Slowly," he repeated, brushing kisses in the soft space between her breasts.

"Why?" she asked between agitated breaths.

"It's better for both of us." He cupped beneath her breast and shaped it in gentle fingers. "Especially you. It makes the pleasure deeper . . . sweeter . . . let me show you, love . . ."

Her head tossed restlessly as his tongue played on her flesh. "Christopher . . ." Her voice was trembling. "I wish . . ."

"Yes?"

It was so terribly selfish, and yet she couldn't help from blurting out, "I wish there had been no other women before me."

He looked down at her in a way that made her feel as if she were dissolving in honey. His mouth descended, caressing hers with tender, urgent warmth. "My heart belongs only to you," he whispered. "It was never love-making before. This is a first for me, too."

She puzzled over that, staring into his bright, lambent eyes. "Then it's different, when one is in love?"

"Beatrix, dearest love, it's beyond anything I've ever known. Beyond dreams." His hand glided over her hip, fingers gently tugging the black gossamer aside to reach her skin. Her stomach tightened at the temptation and knowledge in his touch. "You're the reason I live. If it weren't for you, I never would have come back."

"Don't say that." It was unbearable, the thought of anything happening to him.

"'It's all come down to the hope of being with you,' . . . Do you remember when I wrote that?"

Beatrix nodded and bit her lip as his hand slid farther beneath the transparent silk panels.

"I meant every word," he murmured. "I would have written much more, but I didn't want to frighten you."

"I wanted to write more, too," she said shakily. "I wanted to share every thought with you, every—" She broke off with a gasp as he found the vulnerable place between her thighs.

"You're so warm here," he whispered, stroking her intimately. "So soft. Oh, Beatrix . . . I fell in love with you by words alone . . . but I have to admit . . . I prefer this way of communicating."

She could barely speak, her mind dazzled by sensation. "It's still a love letter," she said, sliding her hand over the golden slope of his shoulder. "Only in bed."

He smiled. "Then I'll try to use proper punctuation."

"And no dangling participles," she added, making him laugh.

But she lost all reason for amusement as he stroked and cradled and tormented her. Too many sensations, coming from different directions. She twisted in the gathering heat. Christopher tried to ease her as the rapture rose too high, too fast, his hands gentle on her quivering limbs.

"Please," she said, perspiration gathering on her skin and at the roots of her hair. "I need you now."

"No, love. Wait just a little longer." He caressed her thighs, his thumbs stroking up to the humid folds of her sex.

She discovered that the most impossible thing in the world was to hold climax at bay, that the more he told her not to, the more powerfully it surged toward her. And he knew it, the devil, a teasing light in his eyes as he whispered to her . . . "Not yet. It's too soon." And all the while, his fingers stroked idly between her thighs, and his mouth grazed over her breast. Every part of her body was filled with desperate craving. "Don't give in to it," he said against her twitching skin. "Wait . . ."

Beatrix panted and stiffened, trying to hold back the rush of sensation. But his lips opened over her nipple, and he began to tug gently, and she was lost. Crying out, she hitched upward against his mouth and hands, and let the wrenching delight overtake her. She jerked and moaned as the voluptuous spasms went through her, while tears of chagrin filled her eyes.

Looking down at her, Christopher murmured sympathetically. His hands moved over her body in soothing strokes, and he kissed away an escaping tear. "Don't be upset," he whispered.

"I couldn't stop it from happening," she said in a plaintive voice.

"You weren't supposed to," he said tenderly. "I was playing with you. Teasing you."

"But I wanted it to last longer. It's our wedding night, and it's already over." Pausing, Beatrix added glumly, "At least my part of it is."

Christopher averted his face, but she could see that he was struggling to contain a laugh. When he had mastered himself, he looked down at her with a slight smile and smoothed her hair back from her face. "I can make you ready again."

Beatrix was quiet for a moment as she evaluated her spent nerves and limp body. "I don't think so," she said. "I feel like a wrung-out kitchen mop."

"I *promise* to make you ready again," he said, his voice threaded with amusement.

"It will take a long time," Beatrix said, still frowning.

Gathering her into his arms, Christopher crushed his mouth over hers. "I can only hope so."

After undressing them both, Christopher kissed her sated body everywhere, tasting her leisurely. She stretched and arched, her breath quickening. He followed the subtle signs of her response, coaxing out heat as if he were nurturing a flame set to kindling. Compulsively her hands wandered over the masculine textures of him, the rough hair and hard satiny muscles, the scars that were slowly becoming familiar.

Turning Beatrix to her side, he pulled her top knee

upward. She felt him enter her from behind, the pressure of him opening her, stretching her impossibly tight. Too much, and yet she wanted more. She dropped her head to his supportive arm, and sobbed as he bent to kiss her neck. He surrounded her, filled her . . . she felt her flesh swelling with heat and sensation, her body adjusting instinctively to his.

He whispered in her ear, words of lust and praise and adoration, telling her all the ways he wanted to pleasure her. Very gently he pushed her onto her stomach, and kneed her thighs wider. She groaned as she felt one of his hands slide beneath her hips. He cupped her sex, stroking in counterpoint as he began a deep, insistent rhythm. Faster than before, deliberate . . . ruthless. She moaned and gripped the quilt in handfuls as the sensation blazed.

When she was at the verge of another peak, he stopped and turned her over. She couldn't look away from the molten silver of his eyes, storms stirred by lightning.

"I love you," he whispered, and she jolted as he entered her again. Wrapping her arms and legs around him, she kissed and bit the thick, enticing muscle of his shoulder. He made a low sound, almost a growl, and cupped her bottom to lift her more tightly into his thrusts. Every time he lunged forward, his body rubbed intimately against hers, stroking her sex over and over, sending her into a climax that shimmered through every cell and nerve.

Christopher buried himself and held, letting the convulsions of her body pull at him wetly, severely, the mutual release exacting groans from them both. And yet the need didn't stop. The physical release opened into a craving for even more intimacy. Rolling them both to their sides, Christopher cradled her with their bodies locked together. Even now, he wasn't close enough to her, he wanted more of her.

They emerged from the bed some time later to feast on the delectable cold supper that had been left for them, slices of game pie, salads, ripe black plums, cake soaked in elderflower cordial. They washed it all down with champagne, and took the last two glasses to bed, where Christopher made any number of lascivious toasts. And Beatrix made a project of applying her champagne-chilled mouth to various parts of his body. They played, and made each other laugh, and then they were silent for a while, watching the candles burn down.

"I don't want to fall asleep," Beatrix mumbled. "I want tonight to last forever."

She felt Christopher smile against her cheek. "It doesn't have to last. I'm personally quite optimistic about tomorrow night."

"In that case, I'm going to sleep. I can't keep my eyes open any longer."

He kissed her gently. "Good night, Mrs. Phelan."

"Good night." A drowsy smile curved her lips as she watched him leave the bed to extinguish the last of the candles.

But first he took a pillow from the bed, and dropped it to the carpet along with a spare quilt.

"What are you doing?"

Christopher glanced at her over his shoulder, one brow arching. "You'll recollect that I told you we can't sleep together."

"Not even on our wedding night?" she protested.

"I'll be within arm's reach, love."

"But you won't be comfortable on the floor."

He went to snuff out the light. "Beatrix, compared to some of the places I've slept in the past, this is a palace. Believe me, I'll be comfortable."

Disgruntled, Beatrix drew the covers around herself and lay on her side. The room went dark, and she heard the sounds of Christopher settling, and the measured sound of his breathing. Soon she felt herself slipping into the welcoming blackness . . . leaving him to contend with the demons of his sleep.

Chapter Twenty-five

Although Beatrix considered Hampshire to be the most beautiful place in England, the Cotswolds very nearly eclipsed it. The Cotswolds, often referred to as the heart of England, were formed by a chain of escarpments and hills that crossed Gloucestershire and Oxfordshire. Beatrix was delighted by the storybook villages with their small, neat cottages, and by the green hills covered with plump sheep. Since wool had been the most profitable industry of the Cotswolds, with profits being used to improve the landscape and build churches, more than one plaque proclaimed, THE SHEEP HATH PAID FOR ALL.

To Beatrix's delight, the sheepdog had a similarly elevated status. The villagers' attitude toward dogs reminded Beatrix of a Romany saying she had once heard from Cam . . . "To make a visitor feel welcome, you must also make his dog feel welcome." Here in this Cotswold village, people took their dogs everywhere, even to churches in which the pews were worn with grooves where leashes had been tied.

Christopher took Beatrix to a thatched-roof cottage on the estate of Lord Brackley. The viscount, an elderly friend and connection of Annandale's, had offered to make the place available to them indefinitely. The cottage was just out of sight of Brackley Manor, built on the other side of an ancient tithe barn. With its low arched doors, sloping thatched roof, and twice-flowering pink clematis climbing the outside walls, the cottage was enchanting.

The main room featured a stone fireplace, beamed ceilings and comfortable furnishings, and mullioned windows overlooking a back garden. Albert went to investigate the upstairs rooms, while a pair of footmen carried in trunks and valises.

"Does it please you?" Christopher asked, smiling as he saw Beatrix's excitement.

"How could it not?" she asked, turning a slow circle to view everything.

"It's a rather humble place for a honeymoon," Christopher said, smiling as she bounded to him and threw her arms around his neck. "I could take you anywhere—Paris, Florence—"

"As I told you before, I want a quiet, snug place." Beatrix pressed impulsive kisses on his face. "Books . . . wine . . . long walks . . . and *you*. It's the most wonderful place in the world. I'm already sorry to leave."

He chuckled, endeavoring to catch her mouth with his own. "We don't have to leave for two weeks." After he captured her lips in a long, searing kiss, Beatrix melted against him and sighed.

"How could ordinary life possibly compare to this?"

"Ordinary life will be just as wonderful," he whispered. "As long as you're there."

At Christopher's insistence, Beatrix slept in one of two adjoining upstairs bedrooms, separated only by a thin wall of lath and plaster. He knew it bothered her not to share a room with him, but his sleep was too restless, his nightmares too unpredictable, for him to take any chances.

Even here, in this place of unfolding happiness, there were difficult nights. He woke and sat bolt upright from dreams of blood and bullets, of faces contorted with agony, and he found himself reaching for a gun, a sword, some means of defending himself. Whenever the nightmares were especially bad, Albert always crept onto the foot of the bed and kept him company. Just as he had during the war, Albert guarded Christopher while he slept, ready to alert him if an enemy approached.

No matter how troubled the nights were, however, the days were extraordinary . . . pleasure filled, serene, imparting a sense of well-being that Christopher hadn't felt in years. There was something about the light in the Cotswolds, a smooth opalesence that covered the hills and farmland in a soft binding. The morning usually began with sun, the sky gradually thickening to clouds in the afternoon. Later in the day, rain fell on the brilliant autumn leaves and gave them a boiled-sugar glaze, and drew out a dark, fresh scent from the loam and clay.

They quickly fell into a pattern of things, a simple breakfast followed by a long ramble with Albert, and then they ventured out to visit the nearby market town with its shops and bakeries, or to explore old ruins and monuments. One could not employ a purposeful stride with Beatrix. She stopped frequently to look at spiderwebs, insects, moss, nests. She listened to out-of-doors sounds with the same appreciation that other people showed while listening to Mozart. It was all a symphony to her . . . sky, water, land. She approached the world anew each day, living fully in the present, keeping pace with everything around her.

One evening they accepted an invitation from Lord and Lady Brackley to have dinner at the manor. Most of the time, however, they secluded themselves, their privacy disrupted only when servants came from the nearby manor to bring food and fresh linens. Many an afternoon was spent making love before the hearth or in bed. The more Christopher had of Beatrix, the more he wanted.

But Christopher was determined to shelter her from the darker side of himself, the memories that he couldn't escape. She was patient when they came to stumbling blocks in their conversations, when one of her questions had veered close to dangerous territory. She was equally forbearing when a shadow crossed his mood. And Christopher was ashamed that she had to accommodate such complexities in his nature.

There were moments when her gentle prying spurred a flare of irritation, and rather than snap at her, he withdrew into a cool silence. And their sleeping arrangements were a frequent source of tension. Beatrix could not seem to accept the fact that he wanted no one near him while he slept. It wasn't merely his nightmares—he was literally incapable of falling asleep if there was someone else next to him. Every touch or sound would jolt him awake. Every night was a struggle.

"At least take a nap with me," Beatrix had coaxed one afternoon. "One little nap. It will be lovely. You'll see. Just lie with me, and—"

"Beatrix," he had said in barely contained exasperation, "don't badger. You won't accomplish anything except to drive me mad."

"I'm sorry," she had replied, chastened. "It's only that I want to be close to you."

Christopher understood. But the uncompromised closeness she desired would always be impossible for him. The only thing left was to make it up to her in every other way he could think of.

His need for her ran so deep that it seemed to be part of his blood, woven into his bones. He didn't understand all the reasons for such mysterious alchemy. But did reasons really matter? One could pick apart love, examine every filament of attraction, and still it would never be fully explained.

It simply was.

Upon their return to Stony Cross, Christopher and Beatrix found Phelan House in disorder. The servants were still accustoming themselves to the new residents of the stables and the house, including the cat, hedgehog, goat, birds and rabbits, the mule, and so forth. The main reason for the disarray, however, was that most of the rooms at Phelan House were being closed and their contents stored in preparation for the household to be moved to Riverton.

Neither Audrey nor Christopher's mother intended to take up residence at Phelan House. Audrey preferred to live in town with her family, who surrounded her with affection and attention. Mrs. Phelan had elected to remain in Hertfordshire with her brother and his family. The servants who were either unable or unwilling to move away from Stony Cross would remain behind to care for Phelan House and its grounds.

Mrs. Clocker gave Christopher a detailed report of what had occurred in his absence. "More wedding gifts have arrived, including some lovely crystal and silver, which I have placed on the long table in the library along with the cards that accompanied them. There is a stack of correspondence and calling cards as well. And sir . . . there was a call paid by an army officer. Not one of those who attended your wedding, but another. He left his card and said he would return soon."

Christopher's face was expressionless. "His name?" he asked quietly.

"Colonel Fenwick."

He gave no response. However, as Beatrix stood beside him, she saw the twitch of the fingers at his side, and the nearly imperceptible double blink of his lashes. Looking grim and distant, Christopher gave the housekeeper a short nod. "Thank you, Mrs. Clocker."

"Yes, sir."

Without a word to Beatrix, Christopher left the parlor and strode to the library. She was at his heels immediately.

"Christopher—"

"Not now."

"What could Colonel Fenwick want?"

"How should I know?" he asked curtly.

"Do you think it has something to do with the Victoria Cross?"

Christopher stopped and turned to face Beatrix with an aggressive swiftness that caused to her fall back on her heels. His eyes were hard, bladelike. She realized that he was overwhelmed with one of the rages that happened when his nerves had been stretched to the breaking point. The mere mention of Colonel Fenwick had overset him completely. To his credit, Christopher took a few deep breaths and managed to control his raging emotions. "I can't talk now," he muttered. "I need a reprieve, Beatrix." And he turned and strode away.

"From *me*?" Beatrix asked, frowning after him.

The coolness between them persisted for the rest of the day. Christopher was monosyllabic at dinner, which made Beatrix miserable and resentful. In the Hathaway family, whenever there was conflict, there was always someone else in the house to talk to. When one was married and childless, however, quarreling with one's husband meant one was, for all purposes, friendless. Should she apologize to him? No, something in her balked at the idea. She had done nothing wrong, she had only asked a question.

Just before bedtime, Beatrix recalled something Amelia had advised: never go to bed angry with your husband. Dressed in nightgown and robe, she went through the house until she found him in the library, sitting by the hearth.

"This isn't fair," she said, standing at the threshold.

Christopher looked at her. Firelight slid over his face in washes of yellow and red, gleaming in the amber layers of his hair. His hands were joined together neatly, like a folding knife. Albert was stretched on the floor beside the chair, resting his chin between his paws.

"What have I done?" Beatrix continued. "Why won't you talk to me?"

Her husband's face was expressionless. "I have been talking to you."

"Yes, as a stranger would. Completely without affection."

"Beatrix," he said, looking weary, "I'm sorry. Go to bed. Everything will be back to rights tomorrow, after I go to see Fenwick."

"But what have I—"

"It's nothing you've done. Let me deal with this on my own."

"Why must I be shut out? Why can't you trust me?"

Christopher's expression altered, softening. He regarded her with a hint of something like compassion. Standing, he came to her slowly, his form large and dark against the glow of the hearth. Beatrix set her spine against the doorjamb, her heartbeat quickening as he reached her.

"It was a selfish act to marry you," he said. "I knew you wouldn't find it easy to settle for what I could give you, and not push for more. But I did warn you." His opaque gaze slid over her. Bracing one hand on the jamb above her head, he brought the other to the front of her robe, where a hint of her white lace nightgown spilled over the neckline. He toyed with the bit of lace, and bent his head over hers. "Shall I make love to you?" he asked softly. "Would that suffice?"

Beatrix knew when she was being placated. She was being offered sexual pleasure in lieu of real communication. As far as palliatives went, it was a very good substitute. But even as her body responded to his nearness, kindling at the warm scent of him and the sensual promise of his touch, her mind objected. She did not want him to make love to her merely as ploy to distract her. She wanted to be a *wife*, not an object to toy with.

"Would you share my bed afterward?" she asked stubbornly. "And stay with me until morning?"

His fingers stilled. "No."

Beatrix scowled and stepped away from him. "Then I'll go to bed alone." Giving in to momentary frustration, she added as she strode away from him, "As I do every night."

Chapter Twenty-six

"I am cross with Christopher," Beatrix told Amelia in the afternoon, as they strolled arm in arm along the graveled paths behind Ramsay House. "And before I tell you about it, I want to make it clear that there is only one reasonable side of the issue. Mine."

"Oh, bother," Amelia said sympathetically. "Husbands do make one cross at times. Tell me your side, and I will agree completely."

Beatrix began by explaining about the calling card left by the Colonel Fenwick, and Christopher's subsequent behavior.

Amelia sent Beatrix a wry sideways smile. "I believe these are the problems that Christopher took pains to warn you about."

"That's true," Beatrix admitted. "But that doesn't make it any easier to contend with. I love him madly. But I see how he struggles against certain thoughts that jump into his head, or reflexes that he tries to suppress. And he won't discuss any of it with me. I've won his heart, but it's like owning a house in which most of the doors are permanently locked. He wants to shield me from all unpleasantness. And it's not really marriage—not like the marriage you have with Cam—until he's willing to share the worst of himself as well as the best of himself."

"Men don't like to put themselves at risk in that way," Amelia said. "One has to be patient." Her tone became gently arid, her smile rueful. "But I can assure you, dear . . . no one is ever able to share only the best of himself."

Beatrix gave her a brooding glance. "No doubt I'll provoke him into some desperate act before long. I push and pry, and he resists, and I'm afraid that will be the pattern of our marriage for the rest of my life."

Amelia smiled at her fondly. "No marriage stays in the same pattern forever. It is both the best feature of marriage and the worst, that it inevitably changes. Wait for your chance, dear. I promise it will come."

After Beatrix had left to visit her sister, Christopher reluctantly contemplated the prospect of visiting Lieutenant Colonel William Fenwick. He hadn't seen the bastard since Fenwick had been sent back to England to recover from the wounds he'd received at Inkerman. To say the least, they hadn't parted on good terms.

Fenwick had made no secret of his resentment toward Christopher, for having gained all the attention and homage that he felt he had deserved. As universally loathed as Fenwick had been, one thing had been acknowledged by all: he had been destined for military glory. He was an unequaled horseman, unquestionably brave, and aggressive in combat. His ambition had been to distinguish himself on the battlefield, and gain a place in Britain's pantheon of legendary war heroes.

The fact that Christopher had been the one to save his

life had been especially galling for Fenwick. One would not have been far off the mark to guess that Fenwick would rather have perished on the battlefield than see Christopher receive a medal for it.

Christopher couldn't fathom what Fenwick might want of him now. Most likely he had learned about the Victoria Cross investiture, and had come to air his grievances. Very well. Christopher would let him speak his piece, and then he would make certain that Fenwick left Hampshire. There was a scrawled address on the calling card Fenwick had left. It seemed he was staying at a local inn. Christopher had no choice but to meet with him there. He'd be damned if he would let Fenwick into his house or anywhere near Beatrix.

The afternoon sky was gray and wind whipped, the woodland paths choked with dried brown leaves and fallen branches. Clouds had veiled the sun, imparting a dull blue cast. A damp chill had settled over Hampshire as winter shouldered autumn aside. Christopher took the main road beside the forest, his bay Thoroughbred invigorated by the weather and eager to stretch his legs. The wind blew through the lattice of branches in the woodland, eliciting whispery movements like restless ghosts flitting among the trees.

Christopher felt as if he were being followed. He actually glanced over his shoulder, half expecting to see death or the devil. It was the kind of morbid thought that had plagued him so mercilessly after the war. But far less often lately.

All because of Beatrix.

He felt a sudden pull in his chest, a yearning to go wherever she was, find her and draw her tightly against him. Last night it had seemed impossible to talk to her. Today he thought it might be easier. He would do anything to try and be the husband she needed. It would not be done in one fell swoop. But she was patient, and forgiving, and dear Lord, he loved her for it. Thoughts of his wife helped to steady his nerves as he arrived at the inn. The village was quiet, shop doors closed against the November bluster and damp.

The Stony Cross Inn was well-worn and comfortable, smelling of ale and food, the plastered walls aged the color of dark honey. The innkeeper, Mr. Palfreyman, had known Christopher since his boyhood. He welcomed him warmly, asked a few jovial questions about the honeymoon, and readily supplied the location of the room that Fenwick occupied. A few minutes later, Christopher knocked on the door and waited tensely.

The door opened, one corner scraping against the uneven hallway flooring.

It was jarring to see Lieutenant Colonel William Fenwick wearing civilian attire, when all Christopher had ever seen him in was the scarlet and gold cavalry uniform. The face was the same, except for a complexion faded to an indoors pallor that seemed utterly wrong for a man who had been so obsessed with horsemanship.

Christopher was instinctively reluctant to go near him. "Colonel Fenwick," he said, and he had to check himself from saluting. Instead he reached out to shake hands. The feel of the other man's hand, moist and cool, gave him a creeping sensation.

"Phelan." Fenwick moved awkwardly to the side. "Will you come in?"

Christopher hesitated. "There are two parlors downstairs, and a taproom."

Fenwick smiled slightly. "Unfortunately, I'm troubled by old wounds. Stairs are an inconvenience. I beg your indulgence in remaining up here." He looked rueful, even apologetic.

Relaxing marginally, Christopher entered the room.

Like the other sleeping rooms in the inn, the private space was commodious, clean, and sparely furnished. He noticed as Fenwick took one of the chairs that he didn't move well, one leg noticeably stiff.

"Please be seated," Fenwick said. "Thank you for coming to the inn. I would have called at your residence again, but I'm glad to have been spared the effort." He indicated his leg. "The pain has worsened of late. I was told it was miraculous to have kept the leg, but I've wondered if I wouldn't have been better served by amputation."

Christopher waited for Fenwick to explain why he was in Hampshire. When it became clear that the colonel was in no hurry to address the subject, he said abruptly, "You're here because you want something."

"You're not nearly as patient as you used to be," the colonel observed, looking amused. "What happened to the sharpshooter renowned for his ability to wait?"

"The war is over. And I have better things to do now."

"No doubt involving your new bride. It seems congratulations are in order. Tell me, what kind of woman managed to land the most decorated soldier in England?"

"The kind who cares nothing for medals or laurels."

Giving him a frankly disbelieving glance, Fenwick said, "How can that be true? Of course she cares about such things. She is now the wife of an immortal."

Christopher stared at him blankly. "Pardon?"

"You'll be remembered for decades," Fenwick said. "Perhaps centuries. Don't tell me that it means nothing to you."

Christopher shook his head slightly, his gaze locked on the other man's face.

"There is an ancient tradition of military honor in my family," Fenwick said. "I knew that I would achieve the most, and be remembered the longest. No one ever thinks about the ancestors who led small lives, who were known principally as husbands and fathers, benevolent masters, loyal friends. No one cares about those nameless ciphers. But warriors are revered. They are never forgotten." Bitterness creased his face, leaving it puckered and uneven like the skin of an overripe orange. "A medal like the Victoria Cross—that is all I've ever wanted."

"A half ounce of die-stamped gunmetal?" Christopher asked skeptically.

"Don't use that supercilious tone with me, you arrogant ass." Oddly, despite the venom of the words, Fenwick was calm and controlled. "From the beginning, I knew you were nothing more than an empty-headed fop. Handsome stuffing for a uniform. But you turned out to have one useful gift—you could shoot. And then you went to the Rifles, where somehow you became a soldier. When I first read the dispatches, I thought there had to be some other Phelan. Because the Phelan of the reports was a warrior, and I knew you hadn't the makings of one."

"I proved you wrong at Inkerman," Christopher said quietly.

The jab brought a smile to Fenwick's face, the smile of a man standing at a distance from life and seeing unimaginable irony. "Yes. You saved me, and now you're to get the nation's highest honor for it."

"I don't want it."

"That makes it even worse. I was sent home while you became the lauded hero, and took everything that should have been mine. Your name will be remembered, and you don't even care. Had I died on the battlefield, that would have at least been something. But you took even that away. And you betrayed your closest friend in the process. A friend who trusted you. You left Lieutenant Bennett to die alone." He watched Christopher keenly, hunting for any sign of emotion.

"If I had it to do again, I would make the same choice," Christopher said flatly.

An incredulous look came over Fenwick's face.

"Do you think I dragged you off the battlefield for either of our sakes?" Christopher demanded. "Do you think I gave a damn about you, or about winning some godforsaken medal?"

"Why did you do it, then?"

"Because Mark Bennett was dying," Christopher said savagely. "And there was enough life left in you to save. In all that death, something had to survive. If it was you, so be it."

A long silence passed, while Fenwick digested the statement. He gave Christopher a shrewd look that raised the hairs on his neck. "Bennett's wound wasn't as bad as it must have appeared," he said. "It wasn't mortal."

Christopher stared at him without comprehension. He shook himself a little and refocused on Fenwick, who had continued to speak.

". . . a pair of Russian Hussars found Bennett and took him prisoner," Fenwick was saying. "He was treated by one of their surgeons, and sent to a prison camp far inland. He was subjected to hardships, lacking proper food or shelter, and later he was put to work. After a few unsuccessful escape attempts, Lieutenant Bennett finally managed to free himself. He made his way to friendly territory, and was brought back to London approximately a fortnight ago."

Christopher was afraid to believe his ears. Could it be true? Steady . . . steady . . . his mind was buzzing. His muscles had gone tense against the threat of deep tremors. He couldn't let the shaking start, or it wouldn't stop.

"Why wasn't Bennett released in the prisoner exchange at the war's end?" he heard himself ask.

"It seems his captors were trying to negotiate his exchange for a stipulated sum of money, along with provisions and weapons. I suspect Bennett admitted under questioning that he was the heir to the Bennett shipping fortune. In any event, negotiations were problematic, and it was kept secret from all but the highest levels at the War Office."

"Damn those bastards," Christopher said in anguished fury. "I would have rescued him, had I known . . ."

"No doubt you would have," Fenwick said dryly. "However, difficult as it is to believe, the matter was resolved without your heroic efforts."

"Where is Bennett now? What is his condition?"

"That is why I've come to see you. To warn you. And after this, I am no longer in your debt, do you understand?"

Christopher stood, his fists clenched. "Warn me about what?"

"Lieutenant Bennett is not in his right mind. The doctor accompanying him on the ship back to England recommended a stay in a lunatic asylum. That is why Bennett's return has not been reported in the gazettes or newspapers. His family desires to maintain absolute privacy. Bennett was sent to his family in Buckinghamshire, but subsequently disappeared without a word to anyone. His whereabouts are unknown. The reason I'm warning you is that according to his relations, Bennett blames you for his ordeal. They believe he wants to kill you." A cold, thin smile split his face, like a crack in a sheet of ice. "How ironic, that you're being given a medal for saving a man who despises you, and you'll probably be murdered by the one you should have saved. You had better find him, Phelan, before he finds you."

Christopher stumbled from the room and went along the hallway in swift strides. Was it true? Was this some obscene manipulation by Fenwick, or was Mark Bennett truly unhinged? And if so, what had he endured? He tried to reconcile his memories of the dashing, good-humored Bennett with what Fenwick had just told him. It was impossible.

Holy hell . . . if Bennett was looking for him, it would be an easy matter to find Phelan House.

A new kind of fear came over him, more piercing than anything he had ever felt. He had to make certain Beatrix was safe. Nothing in the world mattered beyond protecting her. He went down the stairs, his heart thundering, the pounding of his feet seeming to echo the syllables of her name.

Mr. Palfreyman was standing near the inn's entrance. "A tankard of ale before you leave?" he suggested. "Always free for England's greatest hero."

"No. I'm going home."

Palfreyman reached out to stop him, looking concerned. "Captain Phelan, there's a table in the taproom— come sit for a moment, there's a good lad. You're a bit gray around the gills. I'll bring out a good brandy or rum. One for the stirrups, eh?"

Christopher shook his head. "No time." No time for anything. He ran outside. It was darker, colder than it had been before. The late afternoon sky was nightmare colored, swallowing up the world.

He rode for Phelan House, his ears filled with the ghostly cries of men on the battlefield, sounds of distress and pleading and pain. Bennett, alive . . . how was it possible? Christopher had seen the wound in his chest, had seen enough similar injuries to know that death had been inevitable. But what if by some miracle . . .

As he neared the house, he saw Albert bounding out of the woods, followed by Beatrix's slender form. She was returning from Ramsay House. A strong gust of wind blew against her wine-colored cloak, causing it to flap wildly, and her hat flew from her head. She laughed as the dog went to chase it. Seeing Christopher approach on the road, she waved at him.

He was nearly overcome with relief. The panic eased. The darkness began to recede. *Thank you, God.* Beatrix was there, and safe. She belonged to him, she was beautiful and vibrant, and he would spend his life taking care of her. Whatever she desired of him, whatever words or memories she asked for, he would give. It almost seemed easy now—the force of his love would make anything easy.

Christopher slowed the horse to a walk. "Beatrix." His voice was carried away in the wind.

She was still laughing, her hair having come free, and she waited for him to come to her.

He was startled by a streak of bright pain in his head. A fraction of a second later, he heard the crack of a rifle shot. A familiar sound . . . an indelible tattoo on his memory. Shots and the whistling of shells, explosions, men shouting, the screams of panicked horses . . .

He'd been unseated. He was tumbling slowly, the world a confusion of sight and sound. The sky and ground had been reversed. Was he falling up, or down? He slammed against a hard surface, the breath knocked from him, and he felt the hot trickle of blood sliding along his face into his ear.

Another nightmare. He had to wake up, get his bearings. But oddly, Beatrix was in the nightmare with him, crying out and running toward him. Albert reached him in a fury of barking.

His lungs strained to take in a breath, his heart leaping like a fish freshly pulled from water. Beatrix dropped to her knees beside him, her skirts a billow of blue, and she tugged his head to her lap.

"Christopher—let me—oh, God—"

Albert bayed and snarled as someone approached. A momentary pause, and then the dog's ferocious barks were mingled with high-pitched whines.

Christopher levered upward to a sitting position, using his coat sleeve to blot the rivulet of blood that rolled from his temple. Blinking hard, he saw the rawboned, disheveled figure of a man coming to stand a few yards away from them. The man held a revolver.

Instantly Christopher's brain made an assessment of the weapon—a cap-and-ball revolver, five-shot percussion. British military issue.

Before he glanced up at the man's haggard face, Christopher knew who he was.

"Bennett."

Chapter Twenty-seven

Beatrix's first instinct was to interpose herself between her husband and the stranger, but Christopher shoved her behind him. Breathing hard from fear and shock, she looked over his shoulder.

The man was dressed in civilian clothes that hung on his near-skeletal limbs. He was tall and large framed, looking as if he hadn't slept or eaten well in months. The shaggy layers of his dark hair badly needed cutting. He regarded them with the wild, unnerving stare of a madman. Despite all that, it wasn't difficult to see that he had once been handsome. Now he was a barely salvaged wreck. A young man, with an old face and haunted eyes.

"Back from the dead," Bennett said hoarsely. "You didn't think I'd make it, did you?"

"Bennett . . . Mark." As Christopher spoke, Beatrix felt the fine, nearly undetectable tremors running through his body. "I never knew what happened to you."

"No." The revolver shook in Bennett's grip. "You were too busy rescuing Fenwick."

"Bennett, put that damn thing down. I—*quiet*, Albert—it nearly killed me to leave you there."

"But you did. And I've gone through hell ever since. I rotted and starved, while you became England's great hero. Traitor. Bastard—" He aimed the pistol at Christopher's chest. Beatrix gasped and huddled against his back.

"I had to save Fenwick first," Christopher said coolly, his pulse racing. "I had no choice."

"Like hell. You wanted the glory for saving a superior officer."

"I thought you were done for. And if Fenwick had been captured, they would have dragged all kinds of damaging intelligence out of him."

"Then you should have shot him, and taken me out of there."

"You're out of your bloody mind," Christopher snapped. Which probably wasn't the wisest thing to say to a man in Bennett's condition, but Beatrix could hardly blame him. "Murder a defenseless soldier in cold blood? Not for any reason. Not even Fenwick. If you want to shoot me for that, go ahead, and the devil take you. But if you harm one hair on my wife's head, I'll drag you down to hell with me. And the same goes for Albert—he was wounded while defending you."

"Albert wasn't there."

"I left him with you. When I came back for you, he was bleeding from a bayonet wound, and one of his ears was nearly cut off. And you were gone."

Bennett blinked and stared at him with a flicker of uncertainty. His gaze moved to Albert. He surprised Beatrix by lowering to his haunches and gesturing to the dog. "Come here, boy."

Albert didn't move.

"He knows what a gun is," Beatrix heard Christopher say curtly. "He won't go to you unless you set it aside."

Bennett hesitated. Slowly he set the revolver on the ground. "Come," he said to the dog, who whimpered in confusion.

"Go on, boy," Christopher said in a low tone.

Albert approached Bennett warily, his tail wagging. Bennett rubbed the shaggy head and scratched the dog's neck. Panting, Albert licked his hand.

Leaning against Christopher's back, Beatrix felt some of the tension leave him.

"Albert was there," Bennett said in a different voice. "I remember him licking my face."

"Do you think I would have left him with you, if I hadn't meant to come back?" Christopher demanded.

"Doesn't matter. If the situation were reversed, I would have shot Fenwick, and saved you."

"No you wouldn't have."

"I would," Bennett insisted unsteadily. "I'm not like you, you fucking honorable sod." He sat full on the ground, and buried his face in Albert's shaggy coat. His voice was muffled as he said, "You should have at least finished me off before you let them capture me."

"But I didn't. And you survived."

"The price of surviving wasn't worth it. You don't know what I went through. I can't bloody live with it." Bennett let go of Albert, his tortured gaze alighting on the revolver beside him.

Before Bennett could reach for the weapon, Beatrix said, "*Fetch,* Albert." Instantly the dog took up the revolver and brought it to her. "Good boy." She took careful possession of the gun and patted him on the head.

Bracing his arms on his knees, Bennett buried his face on them, a broken posture that Beatrix recognized all too well. He let out a few incoherent words.

Christopher went to kneel beside him, laying a strong arm across his back. "Listen to me. You're not alone.

You're with friends. Damn you, Bennett ... come to
the house with us. Tell me what you went through. I'll
listen. And then we'll find some way for you to live with
it. I couldn't help you then. But let me try to help you
now."

They brought Bennett to the house, where he collapsed
from exhaustion, hunger, and nervous distress. Before
Christopher could begin to tell Mrs. Clocker what needed
to be done, she had taken stock of the situation and mar-
shaled the servants to action. This was a household well
accustomed to illness and the needs of an invalid. A bath
was drawn, a bedroom was prepared, and a tray of bland
and nourishing food was brought up. After Bennett was
taken care of, Mrs. Clocker dosed him with tonic and
laudanum.

Going to Bennett's bedside, Christopher stared down
at the nearly unrecognizable features of his old friend.
Suffering had altered him, within and without. But he
would recover. Christopher would see to that.

And with that hope and sense of purpose, Christopher was aware of a new and fragile feeling of absolu-
tion. Bennett wasn't dead. With all the sins on his
conscience, at least that one had been taken from him.

Bennett looked up at him drowsily, his once-vibrant
dark eyes now dim and dull.

"You're going to stay with us until you're better,"
Christopher said. "You won't try to leave, will you?"

"Nowhere else to go," Bennett mumbled, and went
to sleep.

Christopher left the room, closed the door with care,
and walked slowly toward the other wing of the house.

Medusa the hedgehog was wandering casually along
the hallway. She paused as Christopher approached. A
faint smile touched his lips. He bent to pick her up as

Beatrix had showed him, inserting his hands beneath her. The hedgehog's quills flattened naturally as he turned her up to look at him. Relaxed and curious, she viewed him with her perpetual hedgehog smile.

"Medusa," he said softly, "I wouldn't advise climbing out of your pen at night. One of the maids might find you, and then what? You might find yourself taken to the scullery and used to scrub a pot." Taking her to the private upstairs receiving room, he lowered her into her pen.

Continuing on to Beatrix's room, he reflected that his wife viewed poor Bennett as yet another wounded creature. She had shown no hesitation in welcoming him into their home. One would expect no less of Beatrix.

Entering the room quietly, he saw his wife at her dressing table, carefully filing the claws of Lucky's remaining paw. The cat regarded her with a bored expression, tail flicking lazily. ". . . you must stay away from the settee cushions," Beatrix was lecturing, "or Mrs. Clocker will have both our heads."

Christopher's gaze traveled over the long, elegant lines of her figure, her silhouette revealed in the lampglow that shone through her muslin nightgown.

Becoming aware of Christopher's presence, Beatrix stood and came to him with natural, unselfconscious grace. "Does your head pain you?" she asked in concern, reaching up to touch the small plaster at his temple. In all the commotion of bringing Bennett to their home, there had been no opportunity for private conversation.

He bent to brush a soft kiss on her lips. "No. With a head as hard as mine, bullets merely bounce off."

She let her hand linger at the side of his face. "What happened when you spoke to Colonel Fenwick? Did he try to shoot you, too?"

Christopher shook his head. "Only my friends do that."

Beatrix smiled slightly, then sobered. "Lieutenant Bennett isn't mad, you know. He'll be well again, with time and rest."

"I hope so."

Her blue eyes searched his. "You blame yourself, don't you?"

He nodded. "I made the best decision I could at the time. But knowing that doesn't make the consequences any easier to bear."

Beatrix was momentarily still, appearing to consider something. Pulling away from him, she went to the dressing table. "I have something for you." Busily she rummaged through the small drawer in the front of the table, and extracted a folded piece of paper. "It's a letter."

He gave her a warm, quizzical glance. "From you?"

Beatrix shook her head. "From John." She brought it to him. "He wrote it before he died. Audrey was reluctant to give it to you. But I think it's time that you read it."

Christopher made no move to take it, only reached out and pulled her close. Picking up a handful of her flowing brown hair, he rubbed it gently against his cheek. "Read it to me."

Together they went to the bed and sat on the mattress. Christopher kept his gaze on Beatrix's profile as she unfolded the letter and began to read.

Dear Christopher,

It seems I have less time than I had hoped for. I confess I find myself surprised by how short this life has been. As I draw back to view it, I see that I

spent too much time dwelling on the
wrong things, and not enough on what
mattered. But I also see that I have been
blessed far beyond other men. I needn't
ask you to look after Audrey and
Mother. I know that you will do so to
the extent that they will allow.

If you are reading this, it means you
have returned from the war and are
facing responsibilities that you have
never been prepared for. Let me offer a
few words of counsel. I have watched
you for your entire life . . . your restless
nature, your lack of satisfaction in
anything. You put the people you love
on pedestals, and are inevitably disap-
pointed by them. And you do the same
to yourself. My dear brother, you are
your own worst enemy. If you can learn
to stop expecting impossible perfection,
in yourself and others, you may find the
happiness that has always eluded you.

Forgive me for not being able to
survive . . . and forgive yourself for
surviving.

This is the life you were meant to have.
Not a single day should be squandered.

John

Christopher was silent for a long time, his chest
tight. It sounded like his brother . . . that loving, slightly

lecturing tone. "How I miss him," he whispered. "He knew me well."

"He knew you as you were," Beatrix said. "But I think you've changed. You don't expect perfection now. How else could you explain your attraction to me?"

Christopher gently took her face in his hands. "You are my idea of perfection, Beatrix Heloise."

She leaned forward until their noses touched. "Have you forgiven yourself?" she asked softly. "For surviving?"

"I'm trying to." The proximity of her warm, scantily clad body was too much for him to resist. He slid his hand behind her neck, and kissed her throat. A little shiver chased over her skin. He undressed her carefully, fighting to contain a need that threatened to rage out of control. He kept every movement gentle, light, while his body ached with the violent desire to possess her. His hands swept over her, mapping the physical contours of what words had already expressed. Making love, creating it, letting sensation flow over both of them. Emotion became movement. Movement became pleasure.

He let his tongue explore her mouth at the same time he entered her, his hands clutched in the pouring dark silk of her hair. She tried to move, but he held her still, feeding more pleasure into her, and more, until her every breath was a moan, and she trembled without stopping.

Beatrix dug her heels into the bedclothes, her fingertips digging into his back. He relished the little crescents of pain, loving the dazed, lost look on her face. The rhythms of her body gathered in one impetus, a delicate watercolor flush spreading across her fine skin. But he didn't want it to end yet, despite his own ravening hunger. With agonized effort, he forced himself to hold still inside her.

She cried out, her hips lifting against his weight. "Christopher, please—"

"Shhh . . ." He pressed her down, kissed her neck, worked slowly to her breasts. He pulled her nipple into his mouth, caressing her with his teeth and tongue, leaving a residue of damp heat. Small hungering sounds came from her throat, and her inner muscles clasped him in a helpless rhythm. He began to follow the tender pattern, pressing forward, letting her clasp him on each withdrawal stroke. "Look at me," he whispered, and her lashes lifted to reveal the depths of her soul.

Cupping a hand beneath her head, he fused his lips to hers, while he entered her more deeply than ever before. She took him, wrapping her arms and legs around him, holding him with her entire body. He let the rhythm roughen, quicken, his lovemaking turning wild and unrestrained as he rode the fast, relentless rhythm of her hips. Arching upward, she convulsed violently, her flesh gripping him in tight, wet ripples that drew out a wrenching release.

They were both too love dazed to move for a while. Saturated in the feeling of being open, unguarded, Christopher let his hand wander over her, not with sexual intent, but reverence. She stretched and moved to trap his legs beneath a slender thigh, her arm slung across his chest. Climbing farther atop him, she rubbed her mouth and nose lightly through the hair on his chest. He lay still beneath the warm scaffolding of her body, letting her play and explore as she would.

When they finally left the bed, they were giddy. Christopher made a project of bathing her, drying her, even brushing her hair. She brought his robe and sat beside the bathtub as he washed. Occasionally she leaned downward to steal a kiss. They invented endearments for each other. Small marital intimacies that meant nothing and everything. They were collecting them, just as they were collecting words and memories, all of it containing special resonance for the two of them.

Beatrix turned down all the lamps except the one on the night table. "Time for bed," she murmured.

Christopher stood at the threshold, watching his wife slip beneath the covers, her hair falling in a loose braid over one shoulder. She gave him the look that by now had become familiar . . . patiently encouraging. A Beatrix look.

A lifetime with such a woman was not nearly enough.

Taking a deep breath, Christopher made a decision.

"I want the left side," he said, and turned down the last lamp.

He got into bed with his wife, taking her into his arms. And together they slept until morning.

Epilogue

26 June 1857
Hyde Park, London

Christopher waited with the Rifle Brigade in a large space on the northern side of Hyde Park, a half mile broad and three quarters of a mile long, reserved for nine thousand men of all arms. There were Marines, Dragoons, Rifles, Hussars, Life Guards, Highlanders, and more, all glittering in the abundant sun. The morning was hot and breezeless, promising to roast the hundred thousand people in attendance at the very first Victoria Cross ceremony.

The soldiers in their full dress uniforms were already miserable, some from the heat, others from envy. "We've got the bloody ugliest uniforms in the Empire," one of the Rifles muttered, casting a glance at the infinitely more splendid dress of the nearby Hussars. "I hate this gloomy dark green."

"Pretty target you'd make, crawling forward of the front lines in bright red and gold," another Rifle replied in a scornful undertone. "You'd have your arse shot off."

"I don't care. Women like red coats."

"You'd choose a woman over not having your arse shot off?"

"Wouldn't you?"

The other man's silence conceded the point.

A faint smile curved Christopher's mouth. He glanced at the enclosure near the Grosvenor Gate galleries, where seven thousand ticket holders had been seated. Beatrix and the rest of the Hathaways were there, as well as his grandfather, and Audrey, and several cousins. After this elaborate and unwanted presentation was over, Christopher and the entire mass of his family and in-laws would return to the Rutledge Hotel. There would be a private dinner with feasting and merriment, and Harry Rutledge had hinted at some special entertainment. Knowing Rutledge, it could be anything from a trio of opera singers to a troop of performing monkeys. Only two things were certain—the Hathaways were in London, and it would be a wild, mad romp.

Another guest would attend the family dinner at the Rutledge—Mark Bennett, who had sold his army commission and was preparing to take the reins of his family shipping business. It had taken months for Bennett to recover from the trauma of his wartime experiences, and the process was far from complete. However, a long stay in the Phelan household had done him a world of good. Piece by piece, Bennett had put his psyche back together in a necessary but painful process. With the support of understanding friends, he had gradually come back to himself.

Now more and more, Bennett resembled the dashing and quick-witted rogue he had once been. During long vigorous rides through the countryside, he had acquired healthy color and vitality, and had regained lost muscle. Even after returning to his family estate in Gloucestershire, Bennett often visited Christopher and Beatrix at Riverton. It so happened that during one of these visits, he had met Audrey, who had come to stay a fortnight.

Audrey's reaction to the tall, dark-haired ex-soldier had been more than a little perplexing. Christopher hadn't understood why his normally sanguine sister-in-law became so shy and clumsy whenever Bennett was near.

"It's because he's a tiger," Beatrix had explained in private, "and Audrey is a swan, and tigers always make swans nervous. She finds him very attractive, but she doesn't think he's the kind of gentleman she should keep company with."

Bennett, for his part, seemed quite taken with Audrey, but every time he had made a careful advance to her, she had retreated.

And then with startling quickness, the two of them seemed to have become fast friends. They went on rides and walks together and corresponded frequently when they were apart. When they were both in London, they were always seen in each other's company.

Mystified by the change in their formerly awkward relationship, Christopher asked Bennett what had happened to alter it.

"I told her I was impotent from old war wounds," Bennett said. "That calmed her nerves considerably."

Taken aback, Christopher had brought himself to ask gingerly, "Are you?"

"Hell no," came Bennett's indignant reply. "I only said it because she was so skittish around me. And it worked."

Christopher had given him a sardonic glance. "Are you ever going to tell Audrey the truth?"

A mischievous smile had played at the corners of Bennett's lips. "I may let her cure me soon," he admitted. Seeing Christopher's expression, he had added hastily that his intentions were entirely honorable.

It was a good match. And in Christopher's opinion, his brother would have approved.

The Royal Salute was sounded, the heavy artillery guns booming. The national anthem played as the inspection of the ranks commenced, the entire force lowering colors and presenting arms. Slowly the royal party rode along the lines. At the conclusion of the inspection, the queen, her escorts, and a detachment of Royal Horse Guards proceeded to the center of the galleries between the Legislature and the *Corps Diplomatique*.

A minor commotion occurred when the queen did not dismount at the center dais as planned, but instead remained on her charger. It appeared she intended to award the Victoria Crosses from her seat on horseback, with the prince consort on her left.

The medal recipients, sixty-two in all, were summoned to the dais. Like many of the other men, Christopher was dressed in private clothes, having left the ranks at the conclusion of the war. Unlike the other men, Christopher was holding a leash. Attached to a dog. For reasons that had not been explained, he had been told to bring Albert to the presentation. The other Rifles whispered encouragements as Albert walked obediently beside Christopher.

"There's a good boy!"

"Look smart, fellow!"

"No accidents in front of the queen!"

"And all that goes for you too, Albert," someone added, causing the lot of them to snicker.

Giving his friends a damning glance, which only amused them further, Christopher took Albert to meet the queen.

Her Majesty was even shorter and stouter than he had expected, her nose hawklike, her chin nonexistent, her eyes penetrating. She was dressed in a scarlet riding coat, a general's sash over one shoulder, and a general's plume of red and white feathers on her open riding hat. A band of black mourning crepe, a customary token of military mourning, had been tied around one plump arm. On horseback beside the dais, she was at the same level as the medal recipients.

Christopher was gratified by the businesslike manner with which she conducted the ceremony. The men filed past her, each stopping to be presented and have the queen pin a bronze cross with a red ribbon to his chest, and then he was efficiently ushered away. At this rate, the entire process wouldn't take more than a quarter hour.

As soon as Christopher and Albert stepped up to the dais, he was disconcerted to hear a cheer rising from the crowd, spreading and growing until the noise was deafening. It wasn't right for him to receive more acclamation than the other soldiers—they deserved just as much recognition for their courage and gallantry. And yet the ranks were cheering as well, humbling him utterly. Albert looked up at him uneasily, staying close to his side. "Easy, boy," he murmured.

The queen regarded the pair of them curiously as they stopped before her.

"Captain Phelan," she said. "Our subjects' enthusiasm does you honor."

Christopher replied carefully. "The honor belongs to all the soldiers who have fought in Your Majesty's service—and to the families who waited for them to return."

"Well and modestly said, Captain." There was a slight deepening of the creases at the corners of her eyes. "Come forward."

As he complied, the queen leaned from the horse to pin the bronze cross with its crimson ribbon to his coat. Christopher made to withdraw, but she stopped him with a gesture and a word. "Remain." Her attention switched to Albert, who sat on the dais and cocked his head as he regarded her curiously. "What is your companion's name?"

"His name is Albert, Your Majesty."

Her lips quirked as if she were tempted to smile. She slid a brief glance to her left, at the prince consort. "We are informed that he campaigned with you at Inkerman and Sebastopol."

"Yes, Your Majesty. He performed many difficult and dangerous duties to keep the men safe. This cross belongs partly to him—he assisted in recovering a wounded officer under enemy fire."

The general charged with handing the orders to the queen approached and gave her a curious object. It looked like . . . a dog collar?

"Come forward, Albert," she said.

Albert obeyed promptly, sitting at the edge of the dais. The queen reached over and fastened the collar around his neck with a deft efficiency that revealed some experience with the procedure. Christopher recalled having heard that she owned several dogs and was partial to collies. "This collar," she said to Albert, as if he could understand her, "has been engraved with regimental distinctions and battle honors. We have added a silver clasp to commend the valor and devotion you have displayed in our service."

Albert waited patiently until the collar was fastened, and then licked her wrist.

"Impertinent," she scolded in a whisper, and patted his head. And she sent a brief, discreet smile to Christopher as they left to make way for the next recipient.

"Albert, friend to royalty," Beatrix said later at the Rutledge Hotel, laughing as she sat on the floor of their suite and examined the new collar. "I hope you don't get above yourself, and put on airs."

"Not around your family, he won't," Christopher said, stripping off his coat and waistcoat, and removing his cravat. He lowered himself to the settee, relishing the coolness of the room. Albert went to drink from his bowl of water, lapping noisily.

Beatrix went to Christopher, stretched full length atop him, and braced her arms on his chest. "I was so proud of you today," she said, smiling down at him. "And perhaps a tiny bit smug that with all the women swooning and sighing over you, I'm the one you went home with."

Arching a brow, Christopher asked, "Only a tiny bit smug?"

"Oh, very well. *Enormously* smug." She began to play with his hair. "Now that all this medal business is done with, I have something to discuss with you."

Closing his eyes, Christopher enjoyed the sensation of her fingers stroking his scalp. "What is it?"

"What would you say to adding a new member to the family?"

This was not an unusual question. Since they had established a household at Riverton, Beatrix had increased the size of her menagerie, and was constantly occupied with animal-related charities and concerns. She had also compiled a report for the newly established natural history society in London. For some reason it had not been at all difficult to convince the group of elderly entomologists, ornithologists, and other naturalists to include a pretty young woman in their midst. Especially when it became clear that Beatrix could talk for hours about migration patterns, plant cycles, and other matters relating to animal habitats and behavior. There was even discussion of Beatrix's joining a board to form a new natural history museum, to provide a lady's perspective on various aspects of the project.

Keeping his eyes closed, Christopher smiled lazily. "Fur, feathers, or scales?" he asked in response to her earlier question.

"None of those."

"God. Something exotic. Very well, where will this creature come from? Will we have to go to Australia to collect it? Iceland? Brazil?"

A tremor of laughter went through her. "It's already here, actually. But you won't be able to view it for, say . . . eight more months."

Christopher's eyes flew open. Beatrix was smiling down at him, looking shy and eager and more than a little pleased with herself.

"Beatrix." He turned carefully so that she was underneath him. His hand came to cradle the side of her face. "You're sure?"

She nodded.

Overwhelmed, Christopher covered her mouth with his, kissing her fiercely. "My love . . . precious girl . . ."

"It's what you wanted, then?" she asked between kisses, already knowing the answer.

Christopher looked down at her through a bright sheen of joy that made everything blurred and radiant. "More than I ever dreamed. And certainly more than I deserve."

Beatrix's arms slid around his neck. "I'll show you what you deserve," she informed him, and pulled his head down to hers again.

CHRISTMAS EVE AT FRIDAY HARBOR

Coming in hardcover this Christmas, 2010, from
St. Martin's Press

Three weeks before Christmas, Mark found the letter.

It had been left in a pile on the table in Halle's playroom, tucked into an envelope made with Scotch tape, construction paper, and glittery star stickers.

Dear Santa,

I think I am on the nice list. I don't want any presents this year except for one thing. I need a new mom. I may not get one because I heard nowadays its hard to find a good woman. But if you know one, please drop her off at Friday Harbor.

Love,
Halle

P.S. I was going to talk to you when you were here last week but my uncle Mark said the line was too long.

"Damn it," Mark whispered. He read the letter again, an eight-year-old girl's Christmas wish for something that every child deserved. A mother.

He wasn't ready for the bolt of pain that shot through his chest. That was the strange thing about grieving— even when you thought you'd gotten over the worst of it, it could still hit you just as hard as it did the first moment you heard the words *she's gone*.

He'd gotten that call six months ago.

"I'm so sorry . . . I'm a friend of Virginia and Phil's, I'm watching over Halle and the police just called and . . ." The babysitter had started crying, forcing out words between sobs, and it took a minute or two for Mark to understand that his sister and her husband had been in a car wreck in Seattle. Their sedan had hydro-planed and crossed into oncoming traffic, where they'd been broadsided. They had both died instantly.

There had been a feeling of unreality about the situa-tion, a layer of numbness covering a reservoir of pain that Mark had had no idea how to deal with. Nolans didn't do well with loss, any more than they knew what to do with happiness. In a family that had not exactly been equipped for emotional closeness, Virginia had been the only one who had managed to draw them all together on occasion. Mark had been fine with seeing Virginia and his younger brother Sam during the oblig-atory once-a-year get-together at Christmas. Other than that, he sent e-mails or texted once in a blue moon. He had seen no point in sharing their lives with each other.

Victoria's death had changed everything.

His sister had neglected to mention to Mark that she and Phil had named him as Halle's guardian if anything ever happened to them. As a man who hated to be tied down, who enjoyed his fast-paced and disposable life-style, Mark was the last man on the planet who should have been named as anyone's guardian. It was Halle's rotten luck, however, that he was her best option, the other potential guardian being Sam.

"You're not actually going to keep her, are you?" Sam had asked at the reception after the funeral.

Mark had scowled at him. "Of course I'm going to keep her. What the hell else am I supposed to do?"

"Give her to someone else."

"Like who? Phil's parents are too old to look after a kid."

"Maybe one of the cousins could take her. There's Carla and her husband . . . what's his name . . ."

"Divorced."

"Damn." Sam's mouth was grim. "No offense, bro, but you're not exactly the dad type. You could screw up what's left of her childhood."

"Since both her parents are dead, I'd say her chances of having a great childhood are pretty well screwed by now."

They talked in undertones that cut beneath the subdued conversation of the mourners. Guests filled their plates at the buffet table, serving spoons clinking against chafing dishes, drinks being poured. From time to time someone laughed quietly at some shared memory. Tissues were pressed gently against eyes and noses. The rituals of mourning were being observed, and while it seemed to bring comfort to the people around him, it did nothing for Mark.

He had slid covert glances at Halle, who was sitting at a table on the other side of the room with a book. Her soft brown hair, usually neatly braided, was drawn back in an off-center ponytail. Already the loss of a mother was showing. Mark had gone through her closet that morning and had found nothing that looked appropriate for a funeral. Half her wardrobe consisted of sparkly

ballgowns, and the other half was bright T-shirts and
embroidered jeans.

Halle had been surrounded by women who fussed
over her and brought her little plates of food as she sat
at a table with a book. Countless slips of paper with
phone numbers had been pressed into Mark's hand,
with offers of "help with Halle." One had insisted on
entering her number into his iPhone. "You're not alone,
Mark," she had told him meaningfully.

More than a few female gazes were drawn to the pair
of Nolan brothers standing in the corner. Neither of the
brothers was precisely handsome, but both had looks
that carried. They were big-framed and dark-haired,
rough-natured but soft-spoken in the way of native-born
islanders. Mark was the only one who'd ever moved
away from San Juan Island, staying in Seattle after he'd
graduated from U-Dub.

The city was only a ferry ride or a half-hour flight
from Friday Harbor, but it was a world away. Mark
loved Seattle, the gray winter downpours and lemon-
colored summers, the culture of books and coffee, the
restaurants that always told you where and when the
fish was caught. And he loved the spectacular variety
of women, stylish, smart, sexy, funny. He had no desire
to commit to any particular woman. He wasn't just
afraid of commitment, he was allergic to it.

Now, apparently, he was settling down with someone
whether he was ready or not.

And she was eight.

It had been enough to make Mark panic. Except that
when he looked across the room at his niece, the enormity of her loss, her aloneness, had hit him like a ton of
bricks. Halle had no choice about what was happening
to her. But Mark did have a choice, and for once in his
life he was going to try to do the right thing. It was

obvious that he was going to be a rotten parent, but maybe that was still better for Halle than being shoved off on strangers.

And then Mark had looked at Sam, and it had occurred to him that Sam owed her just as much as he did. "We're a family," he had heard himself saying.

Sam had looked at him blankly.

"You, me, and Halle," Mark had said. "There's only the three of us. We should do this together."

"Do what together? You mean . . . you want me to help you raise Halle? Jesus, Mark. *No.* Not happening."

"Why not?"

"I don't know anything about kids."

"Neither do I."

"We're not really a family," Sam had said. "I'm pretty sure I don't even like you."

"Tough luck," Mark said, gaining confidence in the idea. "If I'm doing this, you're helping me. Halle and I are moving in with you at Rainshadow. There's plenty of room."

Sam lived on San Juan Island in a big Victorian country house, running the vineyard and winery their father had started more than thirty years earlier. The place was named after the rain shadow cast by the Olympic Mountains, which spared the island much of the drizzle and grayness that surged over the rest of the Pacific Northwest.

Of the group of islands that formed an archipelago belonging to Washington State, San Juan was the farthest from the mainland. The air was dry and weighted with ocean salt, sweetened by the lavender harvests in summer. It was an easygoing, bare-limbed, full-flowered island, a place where bald eagles looped from tree to tree, and resident pods of orcas swam and fed and sometimes drifted lazily with the tide.

"There may be room in the house," Sam had said, "but not in my life. You're not bringing her there, Mark." Seeing the intractable look on his brother's face, he had cursed softly and said, "You're going to do it anyway, aren't you?"

"Yeah, I'm going to do it. Just for a while." He had sighed shortly at Sam's expression. "Damn it, Sam, help me get through this beginning part. Halle and I don't even know each other."

"And you think Friday Harbor's a better place to raise her than Seattle?" Sam had asked skeptically.

"Yes," Mark had replied without hesitation. "I've got to slow things down. Living on island time is better for both of us."

"What about your business?"

"Seattle's only a half-hour flight from Friday Harbor. I can go back and forth."

They were both quiet for a minute. Sam looked around Mark, at Halle's downbent head. She was methodically picking raisins out of a cookie and making a little pile on her plate. "Poor kid," Sam whispered. "How do you think we're going to pull this off, Mark?"

"Like the saying goes . . . fake it so real you're beyond fake."

Usually when your life went in a new direction, you had some kind of warning. You got to think it over, try it on for size, back out if it wasn't working. With a child . . . with Halle . . . there was no backing out. Which meant the only thing left to do was give it their best shot. They had made it through six months of painful holidays . . . Halle's first birthday without parents, the first Halloween, the first Thanksgiving without every place at the family table filled. Mark thought they were doing okay.

Until the letter.

... I don't want any presents this year except for one thing. I need a new mom.

"You realize what this means," Mark told Sam after Halle had gone to bed that night.

"That we stink as parents," Sam said, staring morosely at the glittering envelope in his hand. "She needs a woman in her life. Maybe we should find her a nanny."

"It means," Mark said quietly, "one of us needs to get married."

Don't miss

A WALLFLOWER
CHRISTMAS

ISBN: 978-0-312-36073-3

from *New York Times* bestselling author

LISA KLEYPAS

Available in November 2010 from
St. Martin's Paperbacks